THROWAWAYS™

IMAGE COMICS, INC.

Robert Kirkman — Chief Operating Officer
Erik Larsen — Chief Financial Officer
Todd McFarlane — President
Marc Silvestri — Chief Executive Officer
Jim Valentino — Vice President

Eric Stephenson — Publisher
Corey Murphy — Director of Sales
Jeff Boison — Director of Publishing Planning & Book Trade Sales
Chris Ross — Director of Digital Sales
Jeff Stang — Director of Specialty Sales
Kat Salazar — Director of PR & Marketing
Branwyn Bigglestone — Controller
Kali Dugan — Senior Accounting Manager
Sue Korpela — Accounting & HR Manager
Drew Gill — Art Director
Heather Doornink — Production Director
Leigh Thomas — Print Manager
Tricia Ramos — Traffic Manager
Briah Skelly — Publicist
Aly Hoffman — Events & Conventions Coordinator
Sasha Head — Sales & Marketing Production Designer
David Brothers — Branding Manager
Melissa Gifford — Content Manager
Drew Fitzgerald — Publicity Assistant
Vincent Kukua — Production Artist
Erika Schnatz — Production Artist
Ryan Brewer — Production Artist
Shanna Matuszak — Production Artist
Carey Hall — Production Artist
Esther Kim — Direct Market Sales Representative
Emilio Bautista — Digital Sales Representative
Leanna Caunter — Accounting Analyst
Chloe Ramos-Peterson — Library Market Sales Representative
Marla Eizik — Administrative Assistant

IMAGECOMICS.COM

CAITLIN KITTREDGE
Writer

STEVEN SANDERS
Artist

STEVE WANDS
Letterer

CLARK HOLLIDAY
Color Assistance

CHAPTER FIVE

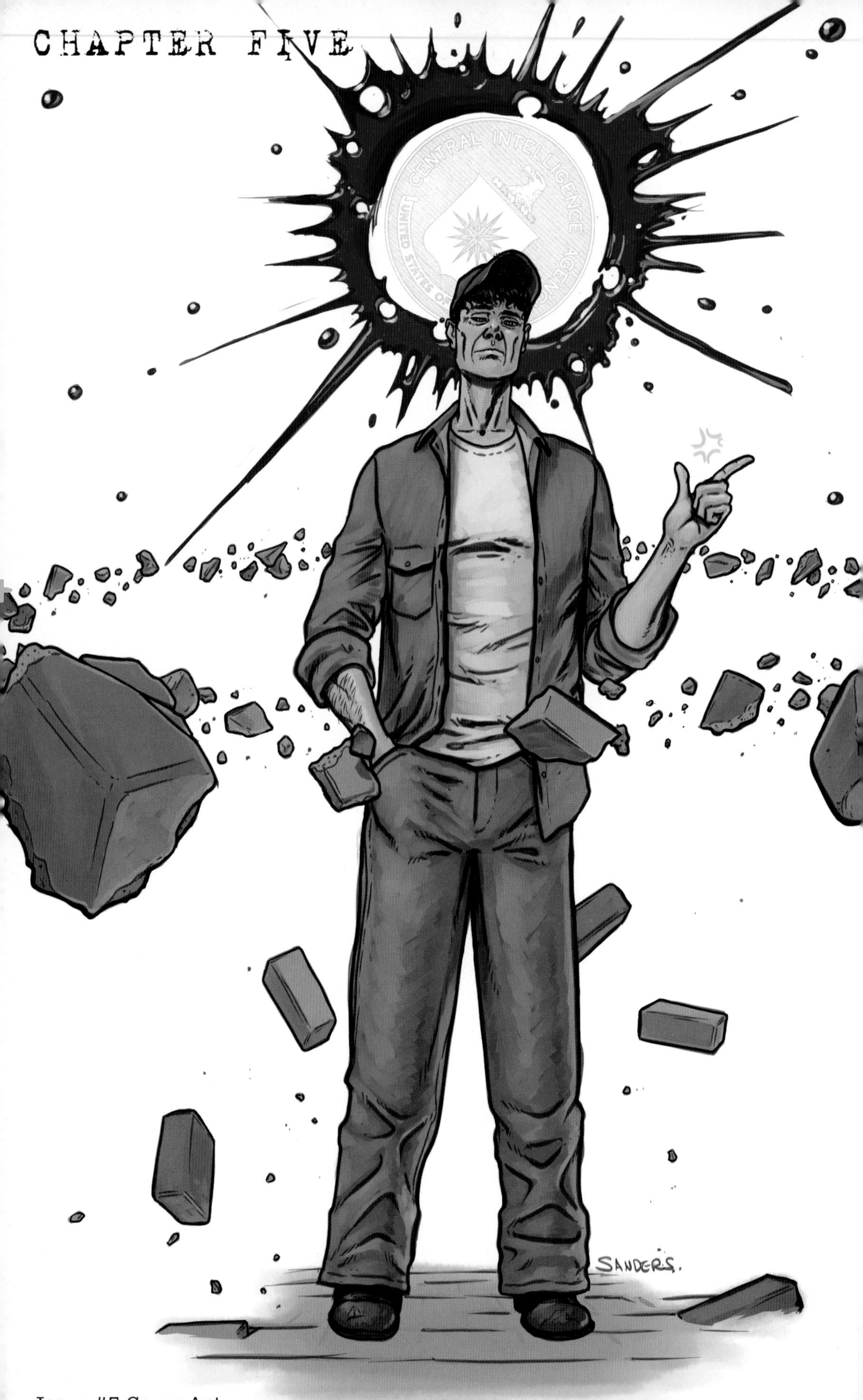
CENTRAL INTELLIGENCE AGENCY
UNITED STATES OF
SANDERS.

Issue #5 Cover Art

tHROwaWAy (n.)

Espionage slang. Used by intelligence handlers.

1. A disposable asset, used for a single mission. 2. A disavowed assassin, meant to die alongside their target.

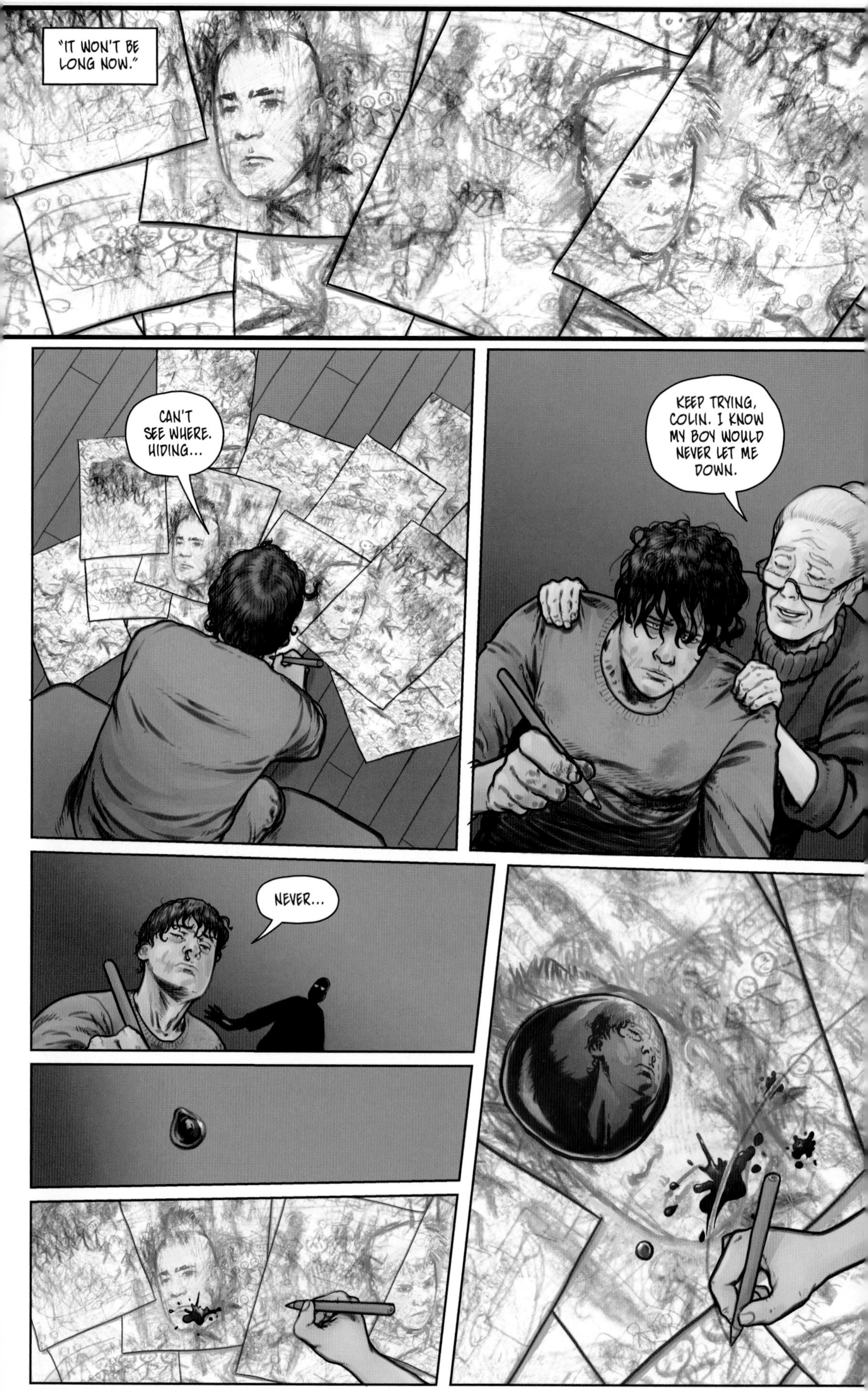
"IT WON'T BE LONG NOW."
CAN'T SEE WHERE. HIDING...
KEEP TRYING, COLIN. I KNOW MY BOY WOULD NEVER LET ME DOWN.
NEVER...

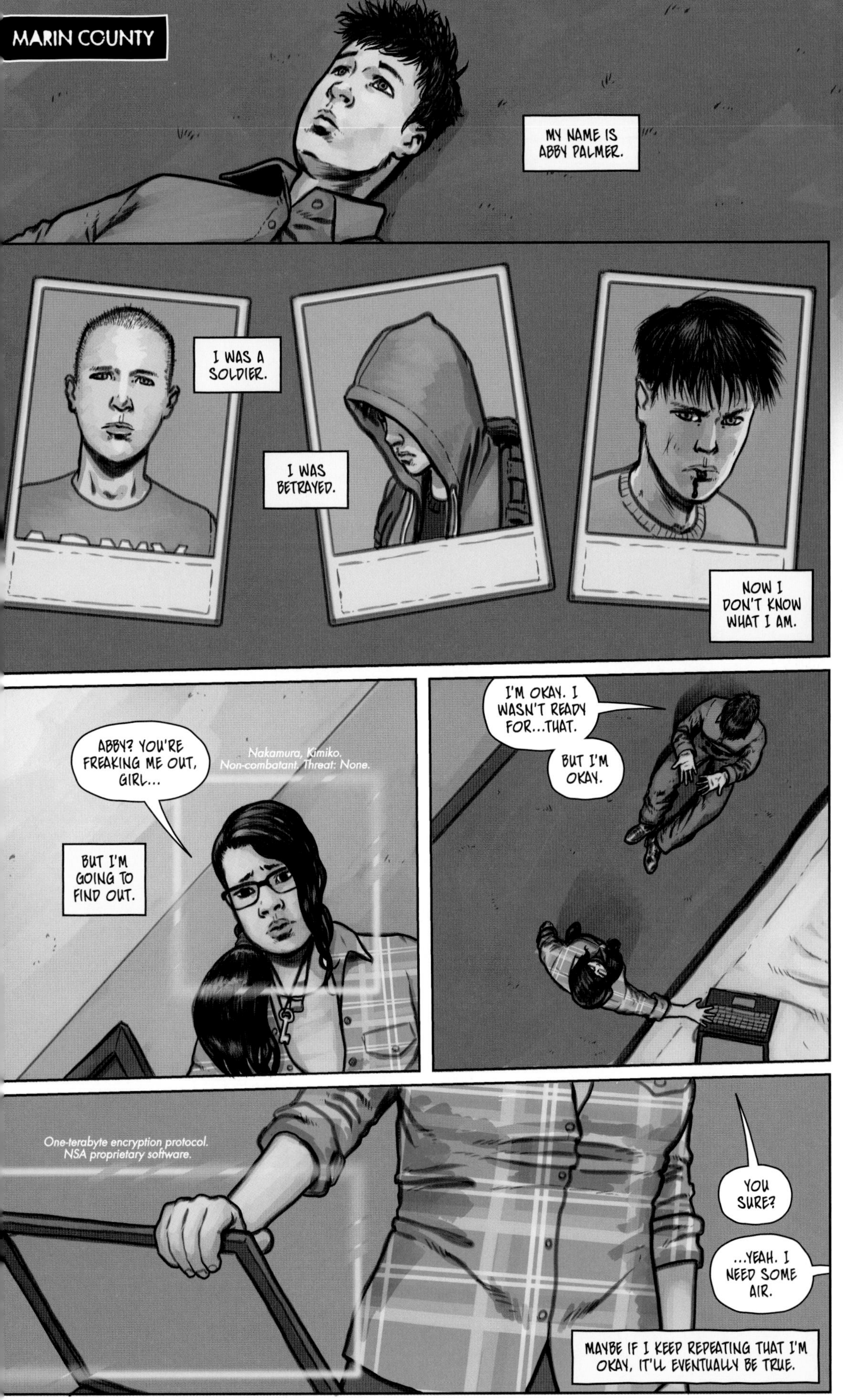
MARIN COUNTY
MY NAME IS ABBY PALMER.
I WAS A SOLDIER.
I WAS BETRAYED.
NOW I DON'T KNOW WHAT I AM.
ABBY? YOU'RE FREAKING ME OUT, GIRL...
Nakamura, Kimiko. Non-combatant. Threat: None.
BUT I'M GOING TO FIND OUT.
I'M OKAY. I WASN'T READY FOR...THAT.
BUT I'M OKAY.
One-terabyte encryption protocol. NSA proprietary software.
YOU SURE?
...YEAH. I NEED SOME AIR.
MAYBE IF I KEEP REPEATING THAT I'M OKAY, IT'LL EVENTUALLY BE TRUE.

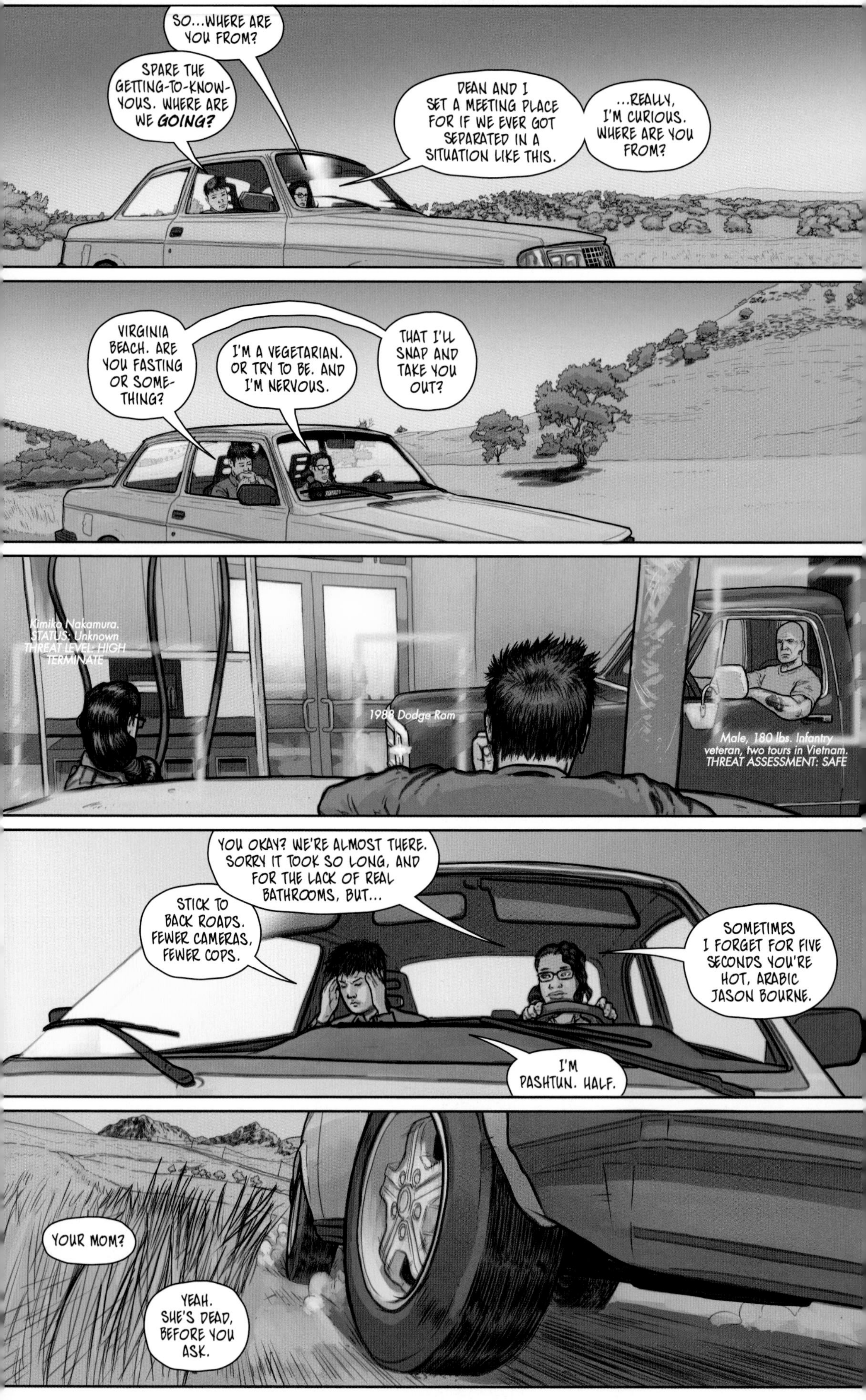
SO...WHERE ARE YOU FROM?
SPARE THE GETTING-TO-KNOW-YOUS. WHERE ARE WE **GOING?**
DEAN AND I SET A MEETING PLACE FOR IF WE EVER GOT SEPARATED IN A SITUATION LIKE THIS.
...REALLY, I'M CURIOUS. WHERE ARE YOU FROM?
VIRGINIA BEACH. ARE YOU FASTING OR SOMETHING?
I'M A VEGETARIAN. OR TRY TO BE. AND I'M NERVOUS.
THAT I'LL SNAP AND TAKE YOU OUT?
Kimiko Nakamura.
STATUS: Unknown
THREAT LEVEL: HIGH
TERMINATE
1988 Dodge Ram
Male, 180 lbs. Infantry veteran, two tours in Vietnam.
THREAT ASSESSMENT: SAFE
YOU OKAY? WE'RE ALMOST THERE. SORRY IT TOOK SO LONG, AND FOR THE LACK OF REAL BATHROOMS, BUT...
STICK TO BACK ROADS. FEWER CAMERAS, FEWER COPS.
SOMETIMES I FORGET FOR FIVE SECONDS YOU'RE HOT, ARABIC JASON BOURNE.
I'M PASHTUN. HALF.
YOUR MOM?
YEAH. SHE'S DEAD, BEFORE YOU ASK.

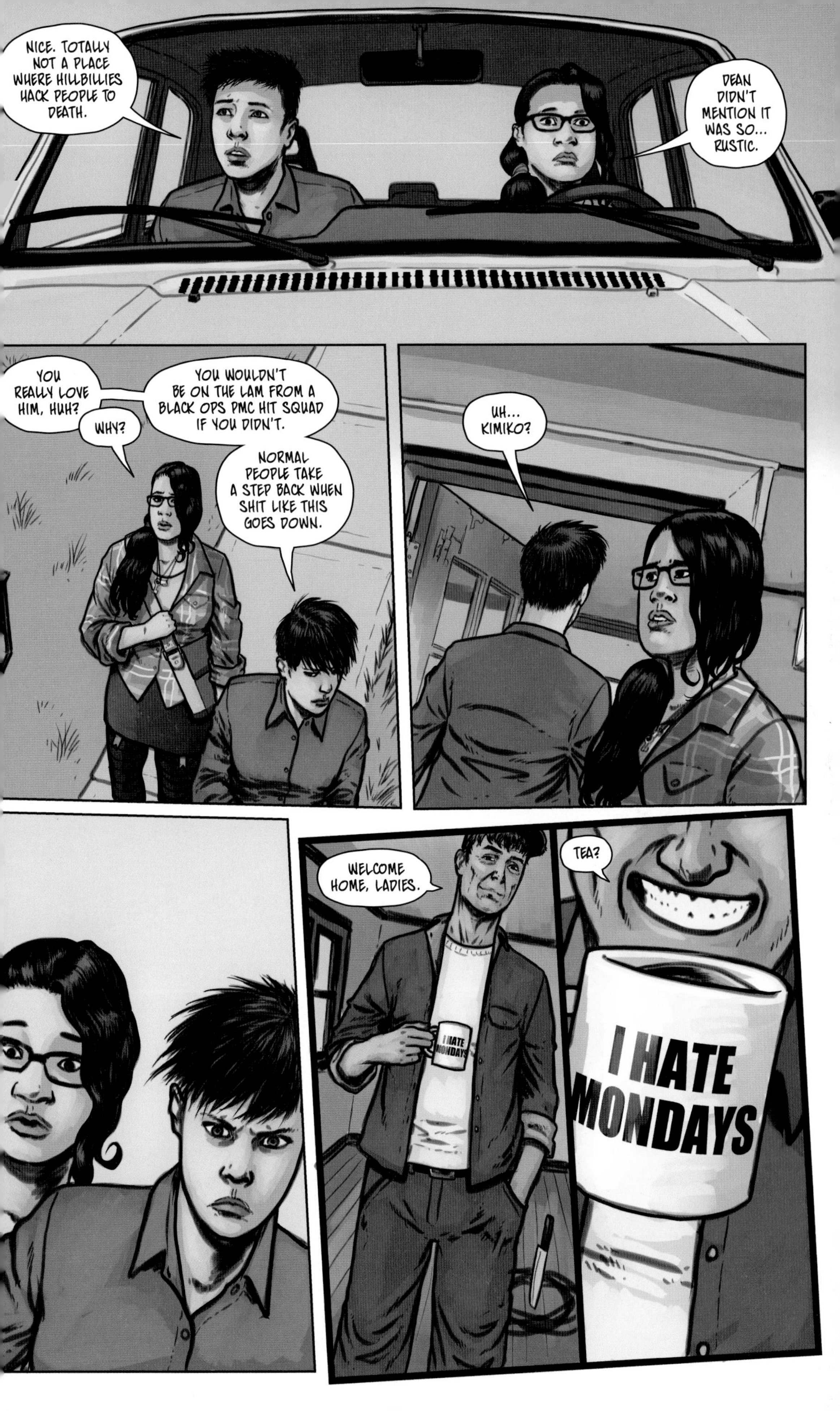
NICE. TOTALLY NOT A PLACE WHERE HILLBILLIES HACK PEOPLE TO DEATH.
DEAN DIDN'T MENTION IT WAS SO... RUSTIC.
YOU REALLY LOVE HIM, HUH?
WHY?
YOU WOULDN'T BE ON THE LAM FROM A BLACK OPS PMC HIT SQUAD IF YOU DIDN'T.
NORMAL PEOPLE TAKE A STEP BACK WHEN SHIT LIKE THIS GOES DOWN.
UH... KIMIKO?
WELCOME HOME, LADIES.
I HATE MONDAYS
TEA?
I HATE MONDAYS

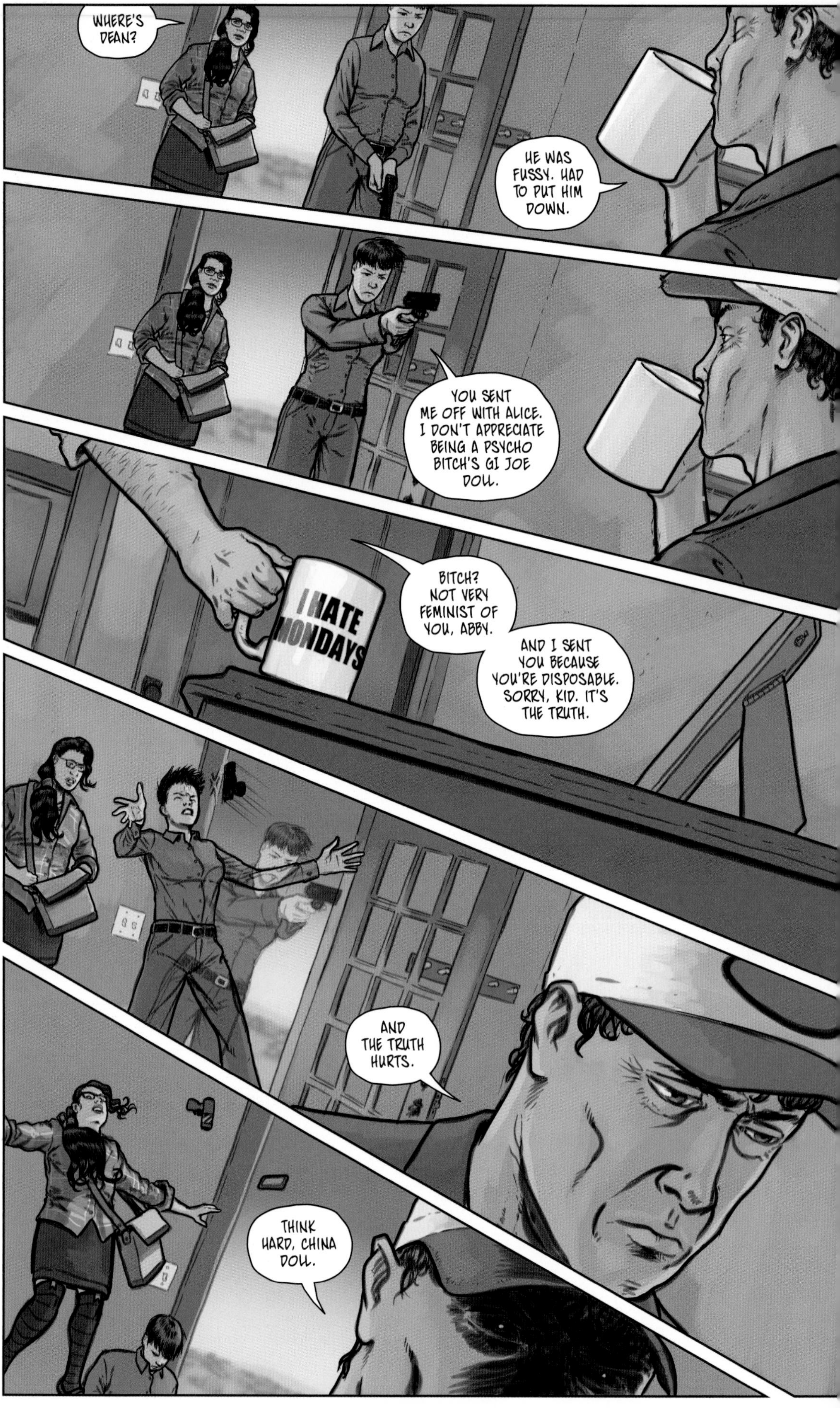
WHERE'S DEAN?
HE WAS FUSSY. HAD TO PUT HIM DOWN.
YOU SENT ME OFF WITH ALICE. I DON'T APPRECIATE BEING A PSYCHO BITCH'S GI JOE DOLL.
I HATE MONDAYS
BITCH? NOT VERY FEMINIST OF YOU, ABBY.
AND I SENT YOU BECAUSE YOU'RE DISPOSABLE. SORRY, KID. IT'S THE TRUTH.
AND THE TRUTH HURTS.
THINK HARD, CHINA DOLL.

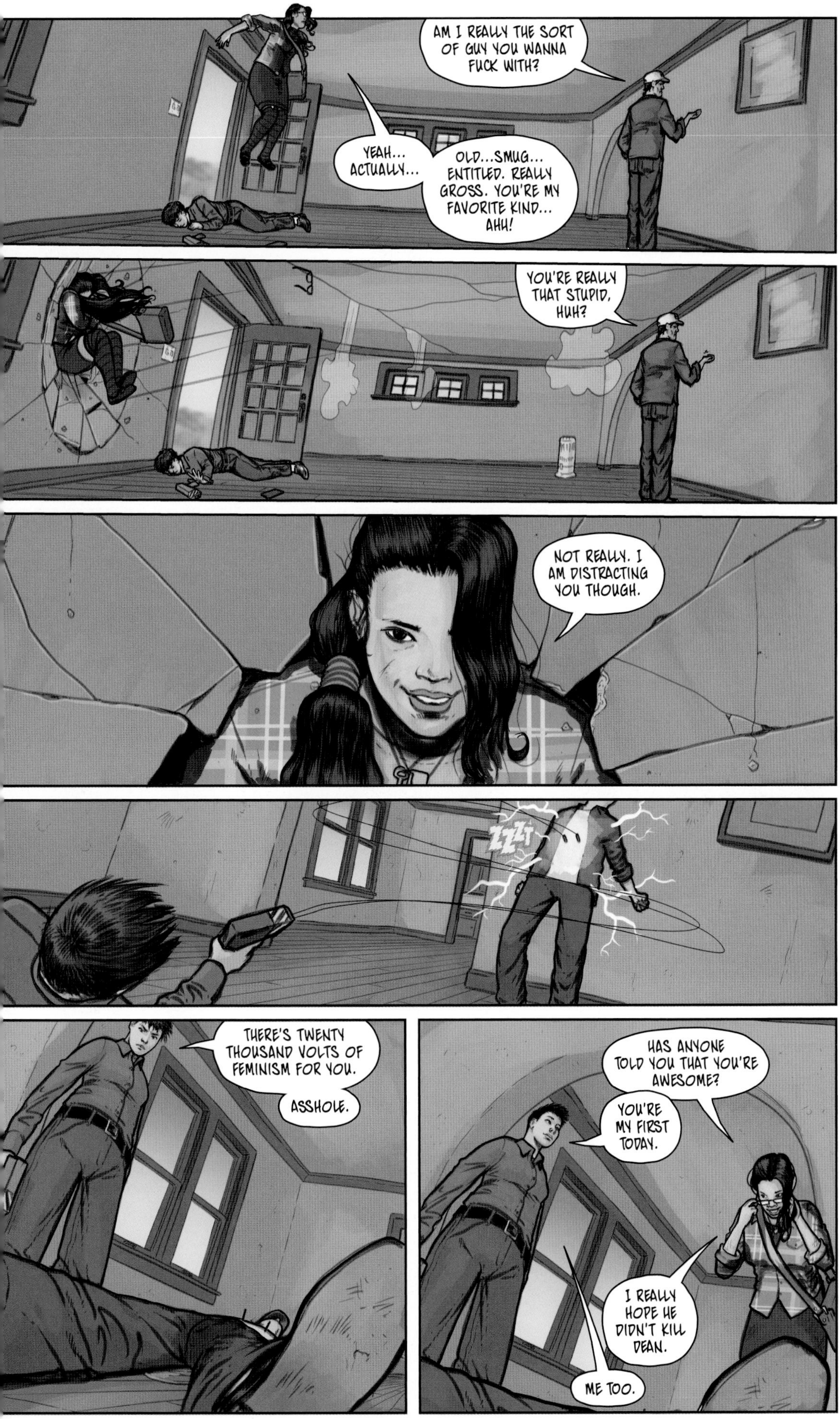

AM I REALLY THE SORT OF GUY YOU WANNA FUCK WITH?
YEAH... ACTUALLY...
OLD...SMUG... ENTITLED. REALLY GROSS. YOU'RE MY FAVORITE KIND... AHH!
YOU'RE REALLY THAT STUPID, HUH?
NOT REALLY. I AM DISTRACTING YOU THOUGH.
ZZZT
THERE'S TWENTY THOUSAND VOLTS OF FEMINISM FOR YOU.
ASSHOLE.
HAS ANYONE TOLD YOU THAT YOU'RE AWESOME?
YOU'RE MY FIRST TODAY.
I REALLY HOPE HE DIDN'T KILL DEAN.
ME TOO.

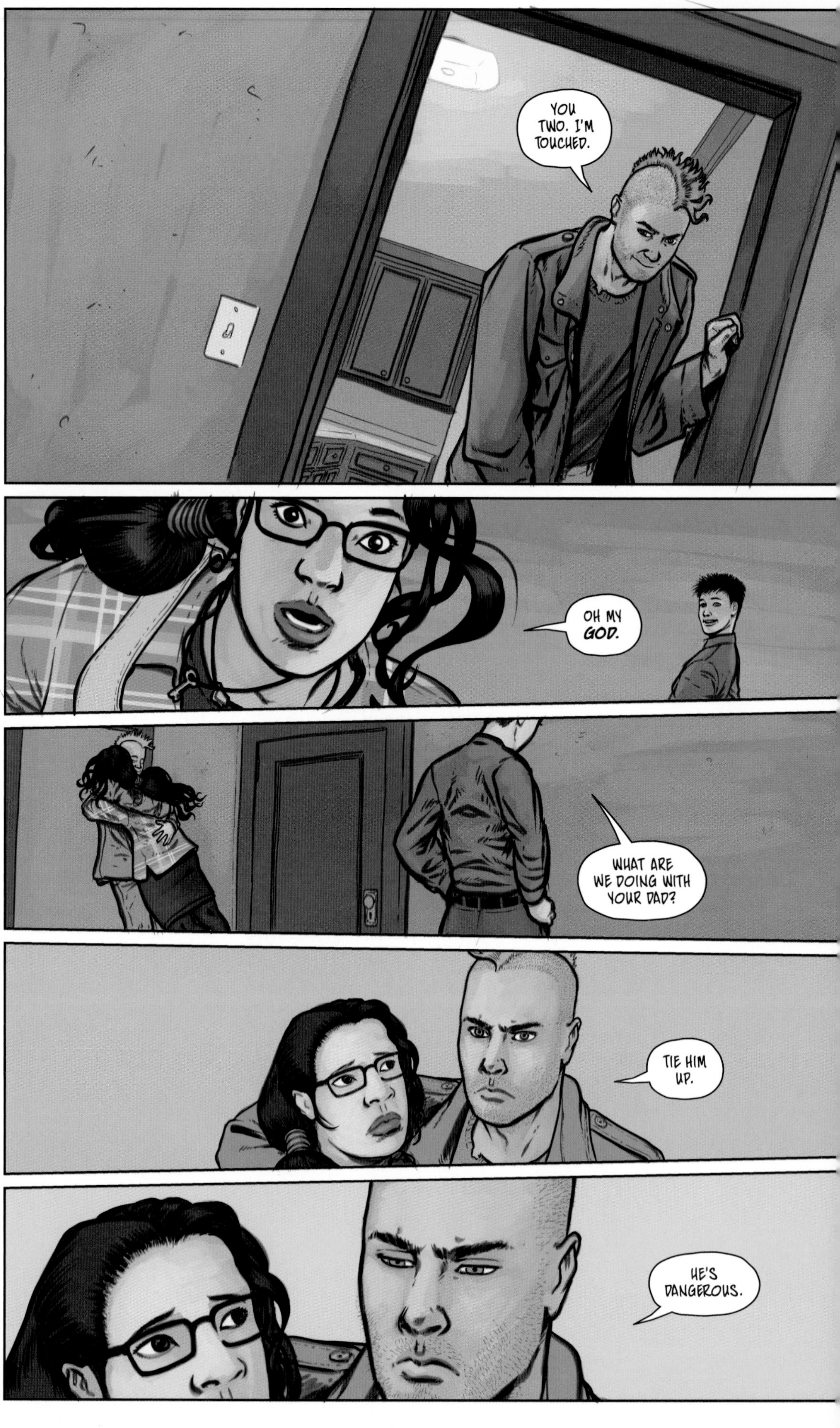
YOU TWO. I'M TOUCHED.
OH MY **GOD.**
WHAT ARE WE DOING WITH YOUR DAD?
TIE HIM UP.
HE'S DANGEROUS.

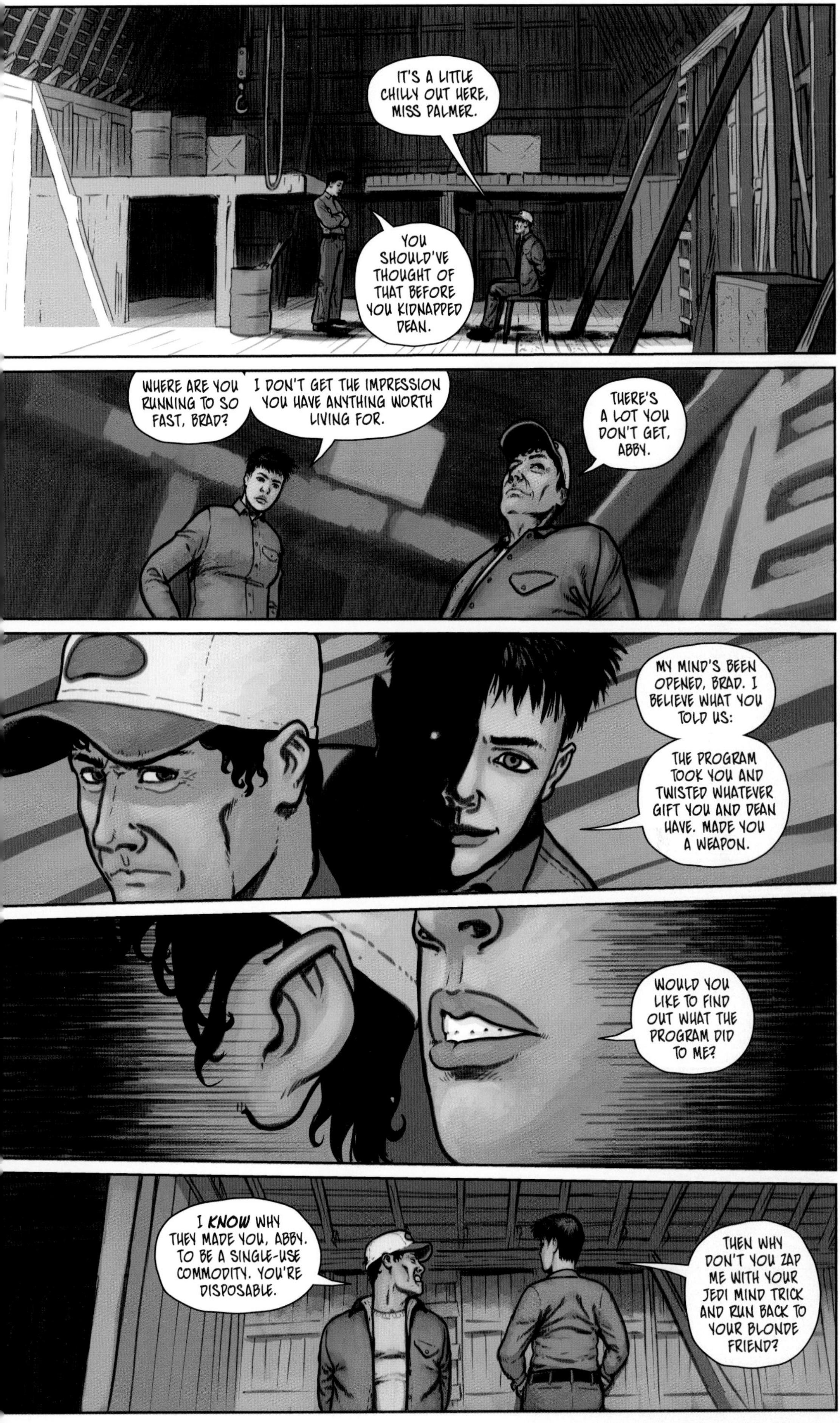
IT'S A LITTLE CHILLY OUT HERE, MISS PALMER.
YOU SHOULD'VE THOUGHT OF THAT BEFORE YOU KIDNAPPED DEAN.
WHERE ARE YOU RUNNING TO SO FAST, BRAD?
I DON'T GET THE IMPRESSION YOU HAVE ANYTHING WORTH LIVING FOR.
THERE'S A LOT YOU DON'T GET, ABBY.
MY MIND'S BEEN OPENED, BRAD. I BELIEVE WHAT YOU TOLD US:
THE PROGRAM TOOK YOU AND TWISTED WHATEVER GIFT YOU AND DEAN HAVE. MADE YOU A WEAPON.
WOULD YOU LIKE TO FIND OUT WHAT THE PROGRAM DID TO ME?
I ***KNOW*** WHY THEY MADE YOU, ABBY. TO BE A SINGLE-USE COMMODITY. YOU'RE DISPOSABLE.
THEN WHY DON'T YOU ZAP ME WITH YOUR JEDI MIND TRICK AND RUN BACK TO YOUR BLONDE FRIEND?

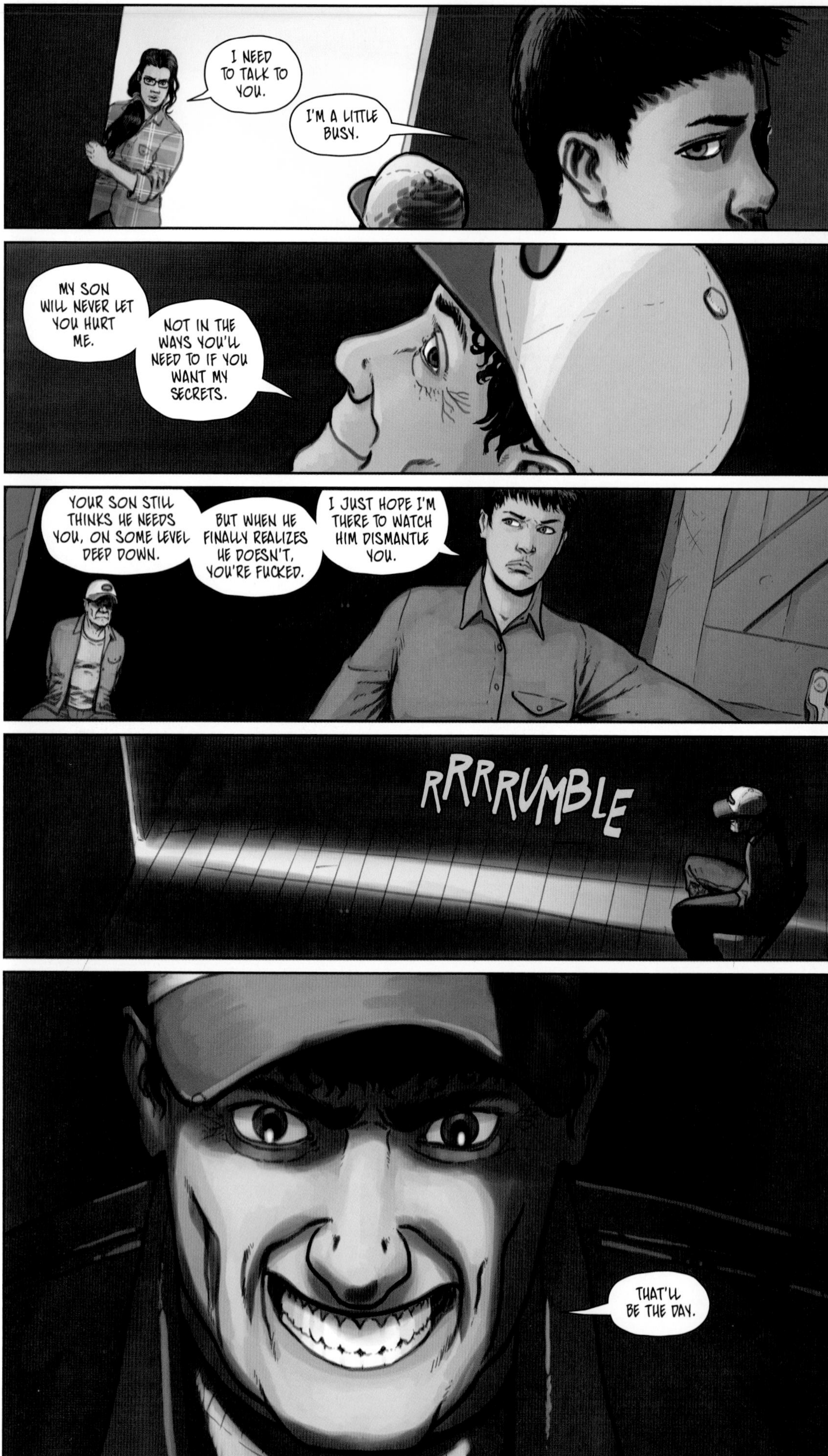
I NEED TO TALK TO YOU.
I'M A LITTLE BUSY.
MY SON WILL NEVER LET YOU HURT ME.
NOT IN THE WAYS YOU'LL NEED TO IF YOU WANT MY SECRETS.
YOUR SON STILL THINKS HE NEEDS YOU, ON SOME LEVEL DEEP DOWN.
BUT WHEN HE FINALLY REALIZES HE DOESN'T, YOU'RE FUCKED.
I JUST HOPE I'M THERE TO WATCH HIM DISMANTLE YOU.
RRRRUMBLE
THAT'LL BE THE DAY.

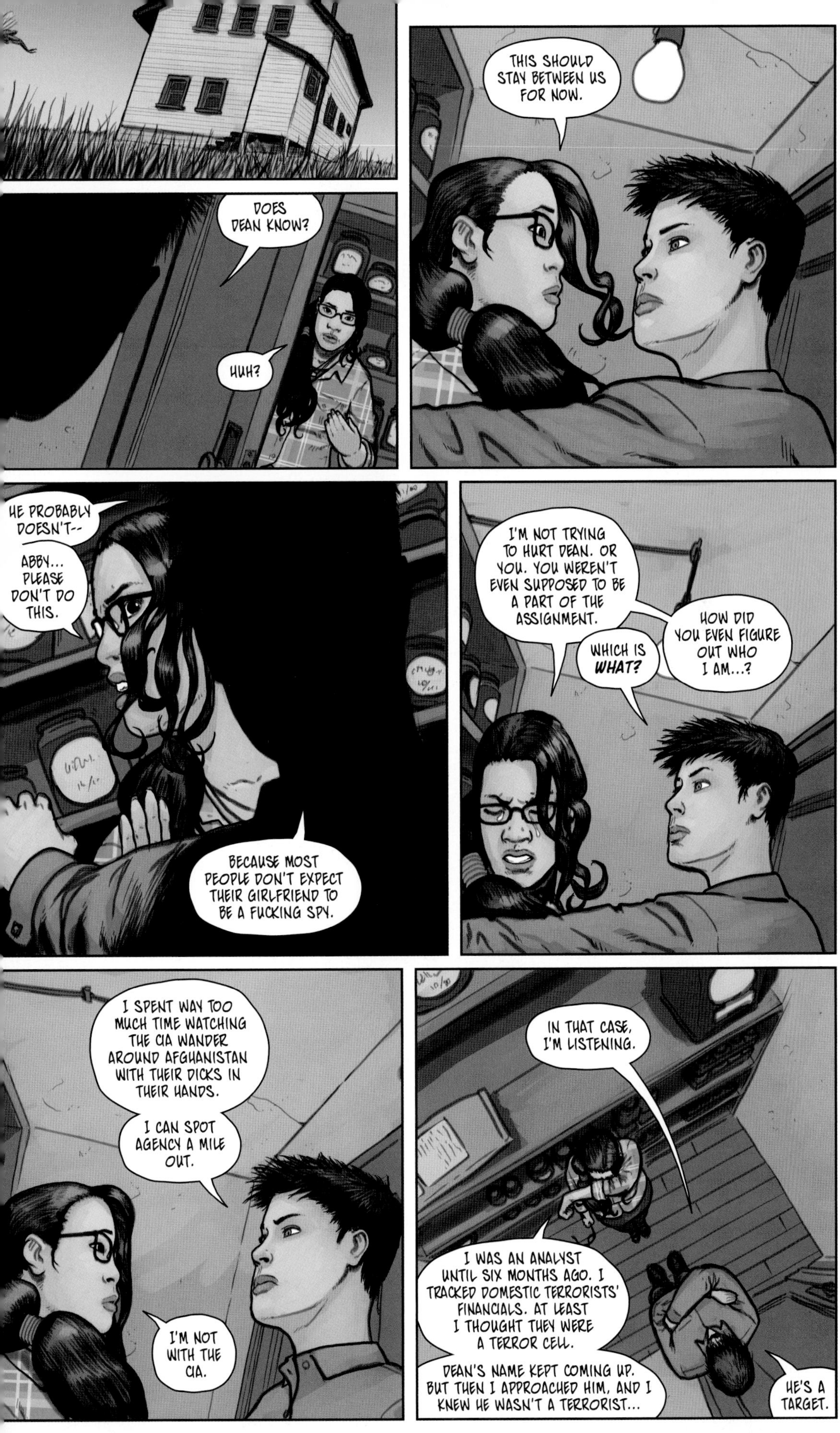
DOES DEAN KNOW?
HUH?
THIS SHOULD STAY BETWEEN US FOR NOW.
HE PROBABLY DOESN'T--
ABBY... PLEASE DON'T DO THIS.
BECAUSE MOST PEOPLE DON'T EXPECT THEIR GIRLFRIEND TO BE A FUCKING SPY.
I'M NOT TRYING TO HURT DEAN. OR YOU. YOU WEREN'T EVEN SUPPOSED TO BE A PART OF THE ASSIGNMENT.
WHICH IS *WHAT?*
HOW DID YOU EVEN FIGURE OUT WHO I AM...?
I SPENT WAY TOO MUCH TIME WATCHING THE CIA WANDER AROUND AFGHANISTAN WITH THEIR DICKS IN THEIR HANDS.
I CAN SPOT AGENCY A MILE OUT.
I'M NOT WITH THE CIA.
IN THAT CASE, I'M LISTENING.
I WAS AN ANALYST UNTIL SIX MONTHS AGO. I TRACKED DOMESTIC TERRORISTS' FINANCIALS. AT LEAST I THOUGHT THEY WERE A TERROR CELL.
DEAN'S NAME KEPT COMING UP. BUT THEN I APPROACHED HIM, AND I KNEW HE WASN'T A TERRORIST...
HE'S A TARGET.

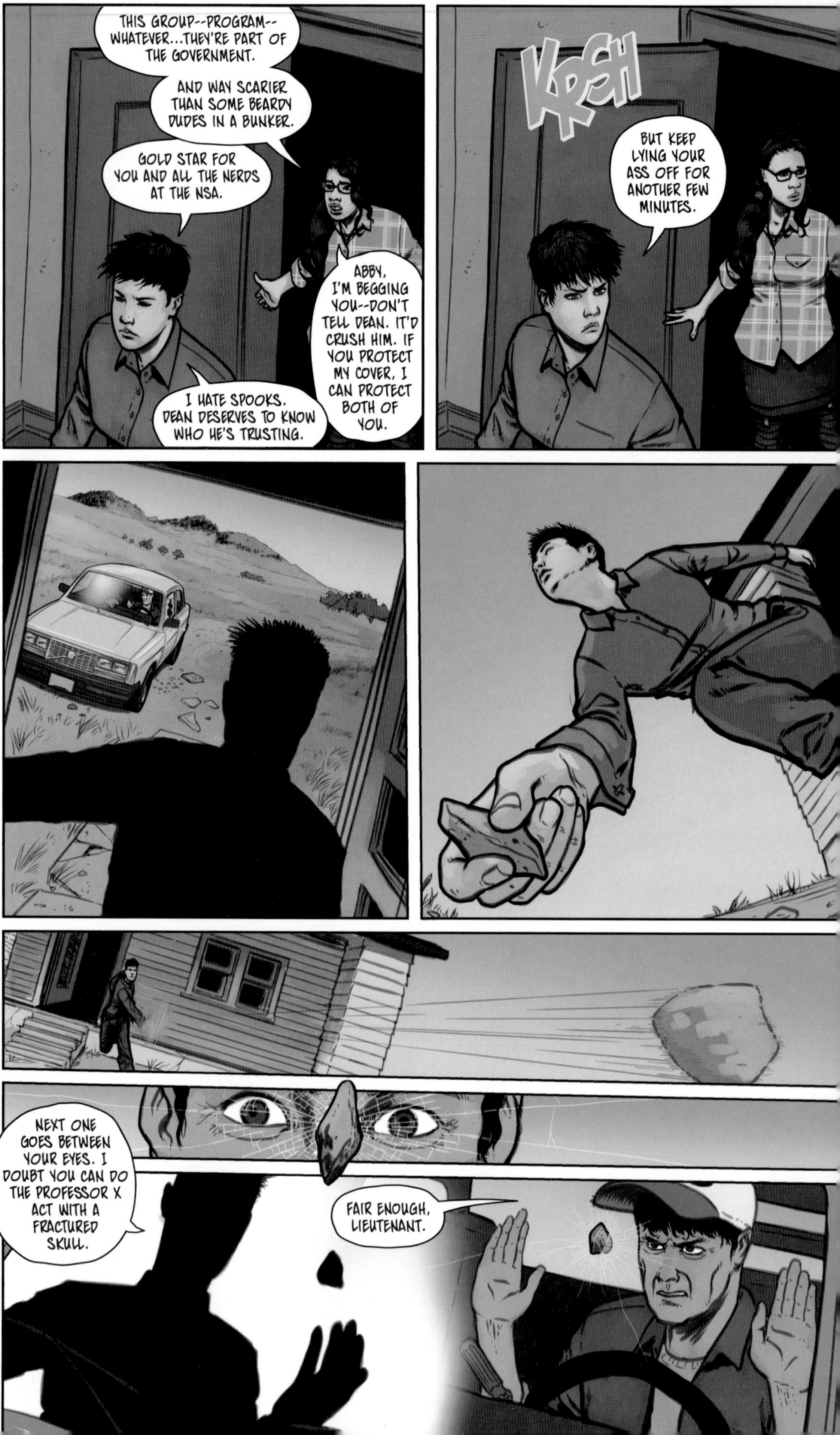
THIS GROUP--PROGRAM--WHATEVER...THEY'RE PART OF THE GOVERNMENT.
AND WAY SCARIER THAN SOME BEARDY DUDES IN A BUNKER.
GOLD STAR FOR YOU AND ALL THE NERDS AT THE NSA.
I HATE SPOOKS. DEAN DESERVES TO KNOW WHO HE'S TRUSTING.
ABBY, I'M BEGGING YOU--DON'T TELL DEAN. IT'D CRUSH HIM. IF YOU PROTECT MY COVER, I CAN PROTECT BOTH OF YOU.
KRSH
BUT KEEP LYING YOUR ASS OFF FOR ANOTHER FEW MINUTES.
NEXT ONE GOES BETWEEN YOUR EYES. I DOUBT YOU CAN DO THE PROFESSOR X ACT WITH A FRACTURED SKULL.
FAIR ENOUGH, LIEUTENANT.

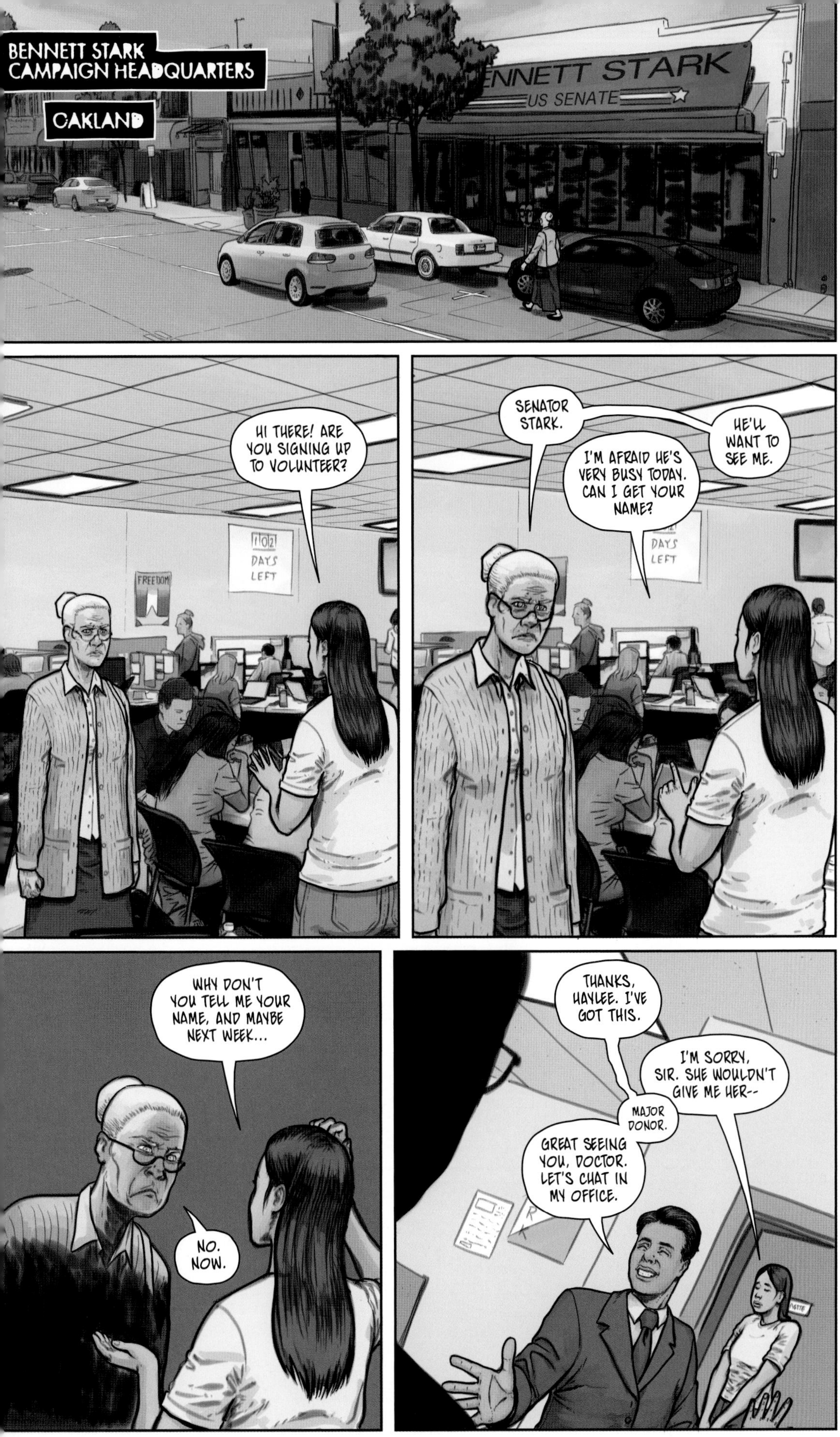

BENNETT STARK CAMPAIGN HEADQUARTERS
OAKLAND
BENNETT STARK
US SENATE
HI THERE! ARE YOU SIGNING UP TO VOLUNTEER?
102 DAYS LEFT
FREEDOM
SENATOR STARK.
I'M AFRAID HE'S VERY BUSY TODAY. CAN I GET YOUR NAME?
HE'LL WANT TO SEE ME.
WHY DON'T YOU TELL ME YOUR NAME, AND MAYBE NEXT WEEK...
NO. NOW.
THANKS, HAYLEE. I'VE GOT THIS.
I'M SORRY, SIR. SHE WOULDN'T GIVE ME HER--
MAJOR DONOR.
GREAT SEEING YOU, DOCTOR. LET'S CHAT IN MY OFFICE.

DO YOU HAVE ANY IDEA WHAT YOU'RE DOING COMING HERE?

I TRUST YOU'VE HEARD.

I HEARD BEFORE THE PRESS DID.

SENATOR KENT CHAMBERS DEAD IN FATAL CAR CRASH

DOESN'T ANSWER ANY OF MY QUESTIONS.

YOU WILL BE THE NEXT HEAD OF THE INTELLIGENCE COMMITTEE, NATURALLY.

...I'M FLYING BACK TONIGHT. HOW DID YOU...?

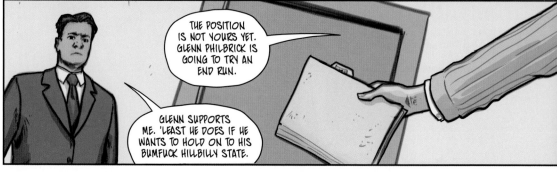

THE POSITION IS NOT YOURS YET. GLENN PHILBRICK IS GOING TO TRY AN END RUN.

GLENN SUPPORTS ME. 'LEAST HE DOES IF HE WANTS TO HOLD ON TO HIS BUMFUCK HILLBILLY STATE.

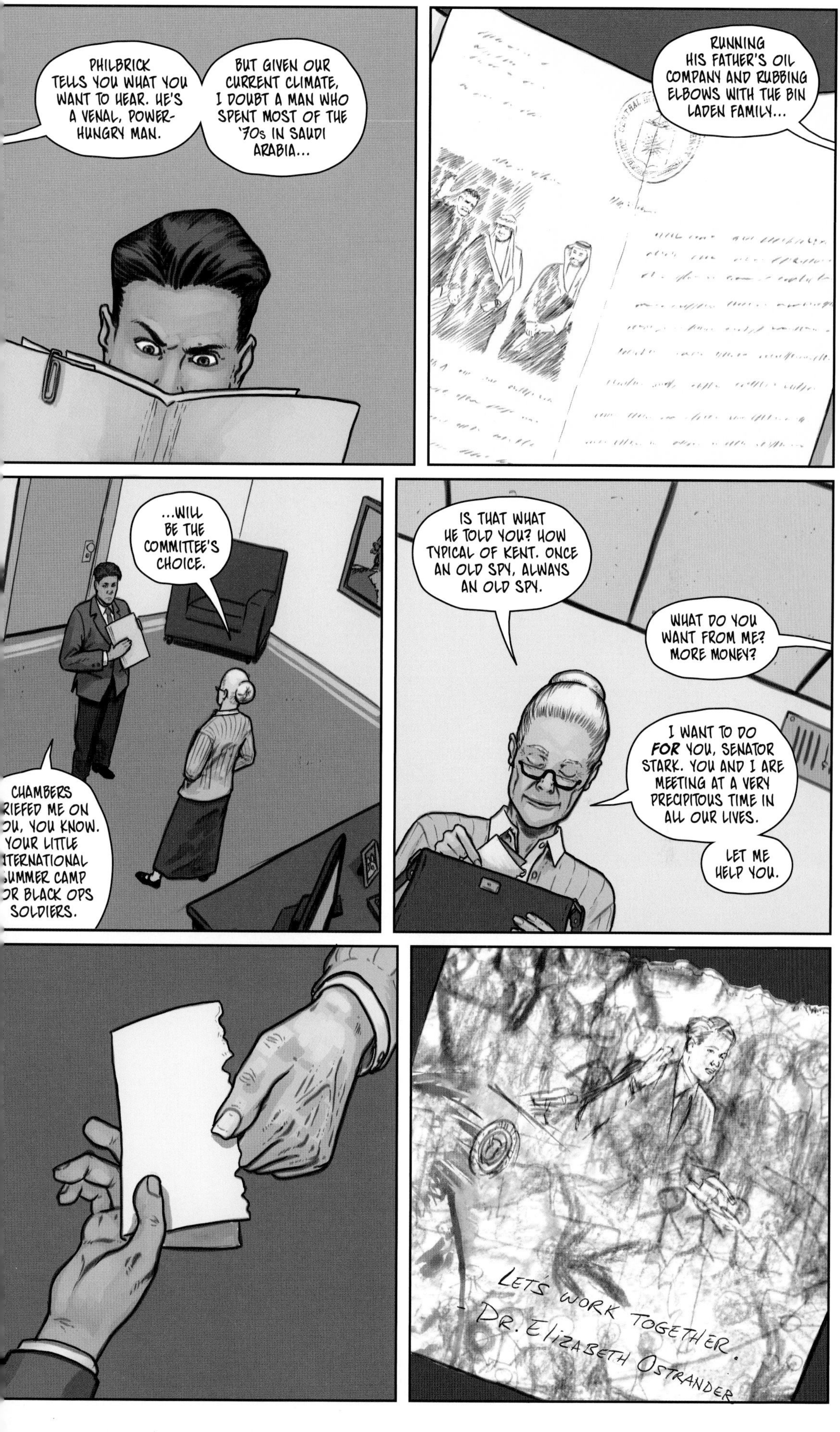

PHILBRICK TELLS YOU WHAT YOU WANT TO HEAR. HE'S A VENAL, POWER-HUNGRY MAN.
BUT GIVEN OUR CURRENT CLIMATE, I DOUBT A MAN WHO SPENT MOST OF THE '70s IN SAUDI ARABIA...
RUNNING HIS FATHER'S OIL COMPANY AND RUBBING ELBOWS WITH THE BIN LADEN FAMILY...
...WILL BE THE COMMITTEE'S CHOICE.
CHAMBERS RIEFED ME ON OU, YOU KNOW. YOUR LITTLE TERNATIONAL UMMER CAMP OR BLACK OPS SOLDIERS.
IS THAT WHAT HE TOLD YOU? HOW TYPICAL OF KENT. ONCE AN OLD SPY, ALWAYS AN OLD SPY.
WHAT DO YOU WANT FROM ME? MORE MONEY?
I WANT TO DO **FOR** YOU, SENATOR STARK. YOU AND I ARE MEETING AT A VERY PRECIPITOUS TIME IN ALL OUR LIVES.
LET ME HELP YOU.
LET'S WORK TOGETHER.
- DR. ELIZABETH OSTRANDER

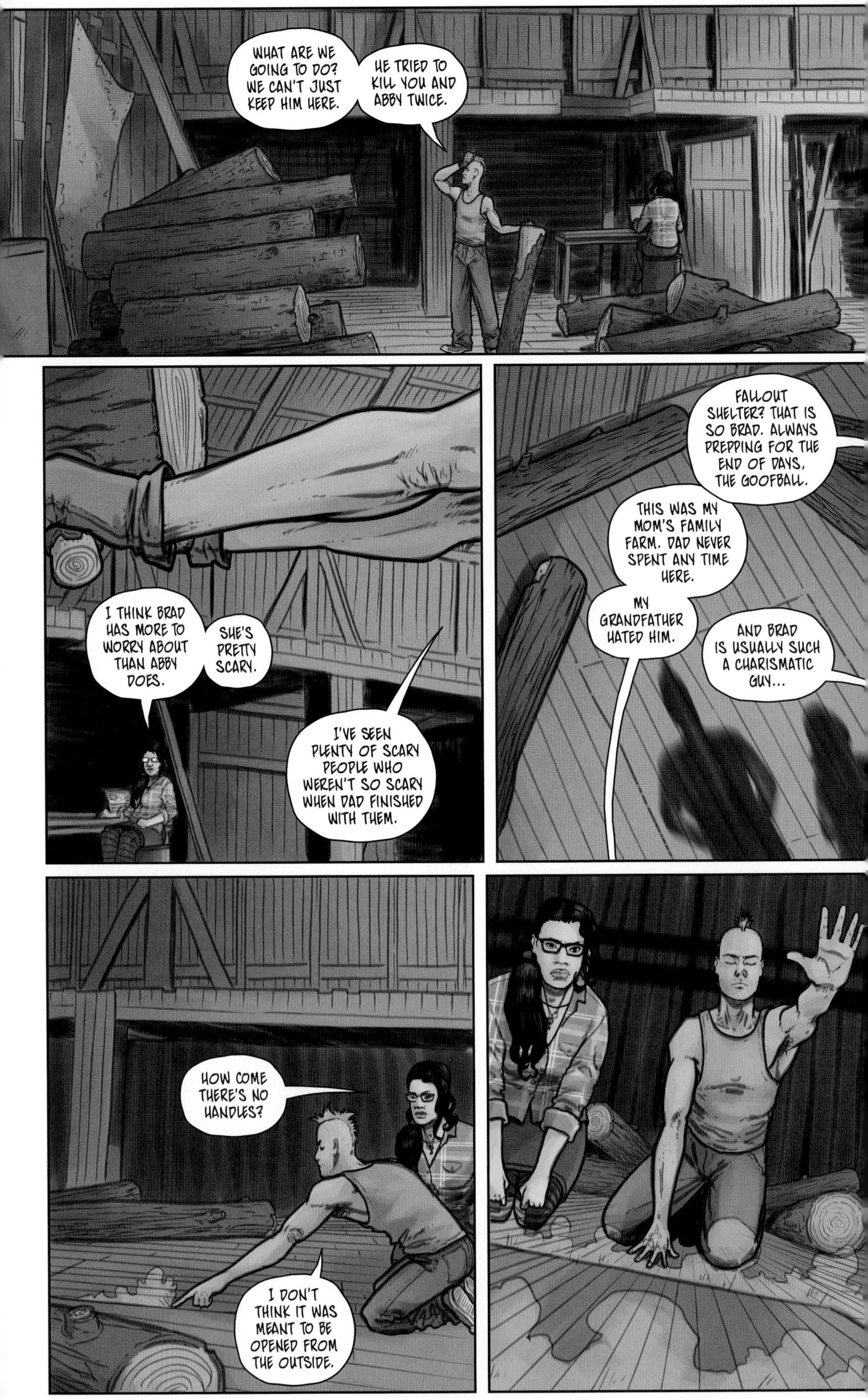

WHAT ARE WE GOING TO DO? WE CAN'T JUST KEEP HIM HERE.
HE TRIED TO KILL YOU AND ABBY TWICE.
I THINK BRAD HAS MORE TO WORRY ABOUT THAN ABBY DOES.
SHE'S PRETTY SCARY.
I'VE SEEN PLENTY OF SCARY PEOPLE WHO WEREN'T SO SCARY WHEN DAD FINISHED WITH THEM.
FALLOUT SHELTER? THAT IS SO BRAD. ALWAYS PREPPING FOR THE END OF DAYS, THE GOOFBALL.
THIS WAS MY MOM'S FAMILY FARM. DAD NEVER SPENT ANY TIME HERE.
MY GRANDFATHER HATED HIM.
AND BRAD IS USUALLY SUCH A CHARISMATIC GUY...
HOW COME THERE'S NO HANDLES?
I DON'T THINK IT WAS MEANT TO BE OPENED FROM THE OUTSIDE.

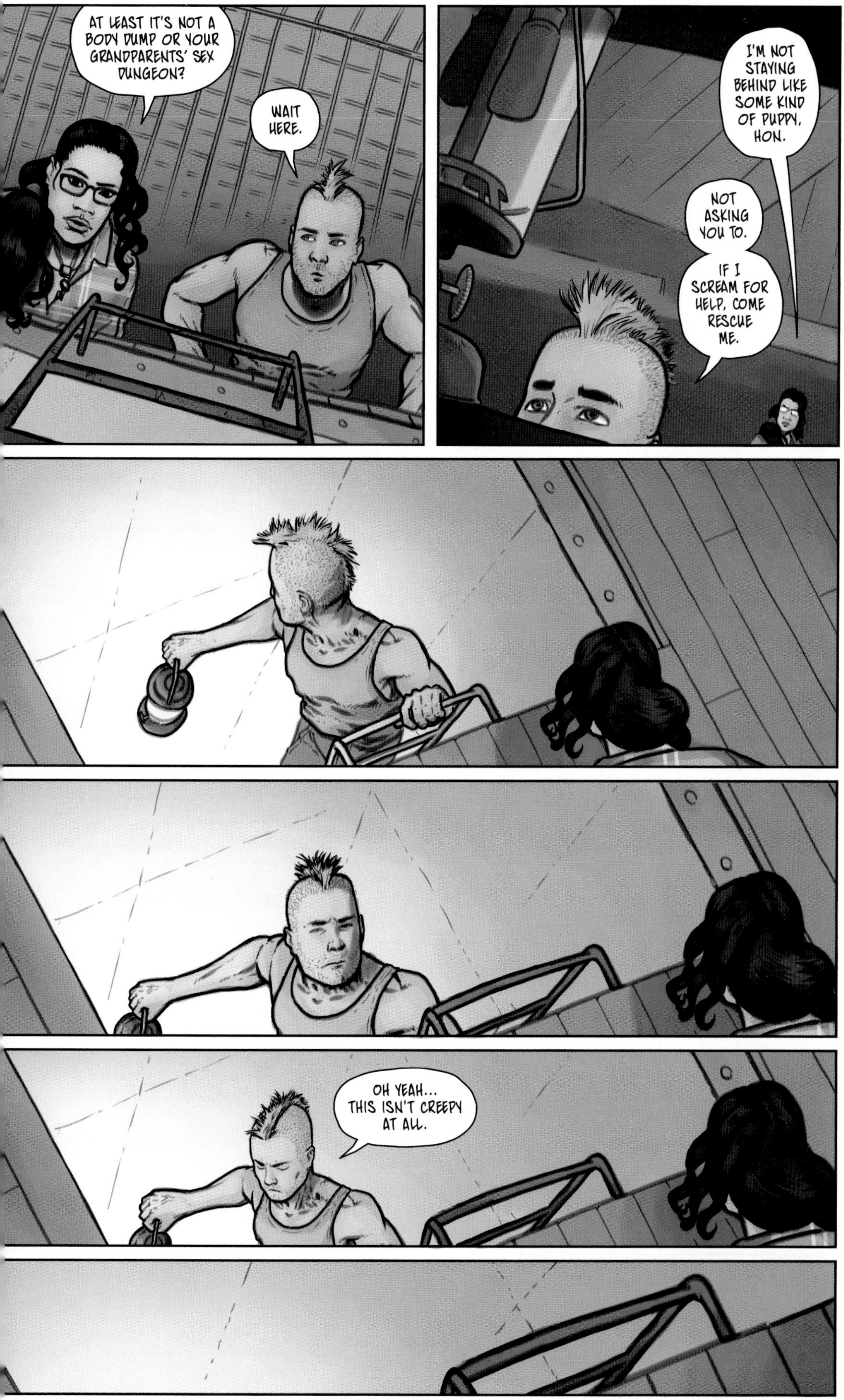
AT LEAST IT'S NOT A BODY DUMP OR YOUR GRANDPARENTS' SEX DUNGEON?
WAIT HERE.
I'M NOT STAYING BEHIND LIKE SOME KIND OF PUPPY, HON.
NOT ASKING YOU TO.
IF I SCREAM FOR HELP, COME RESCUE ME.
OH YEAH... THIS ISN'T CREEPY AT ALL.

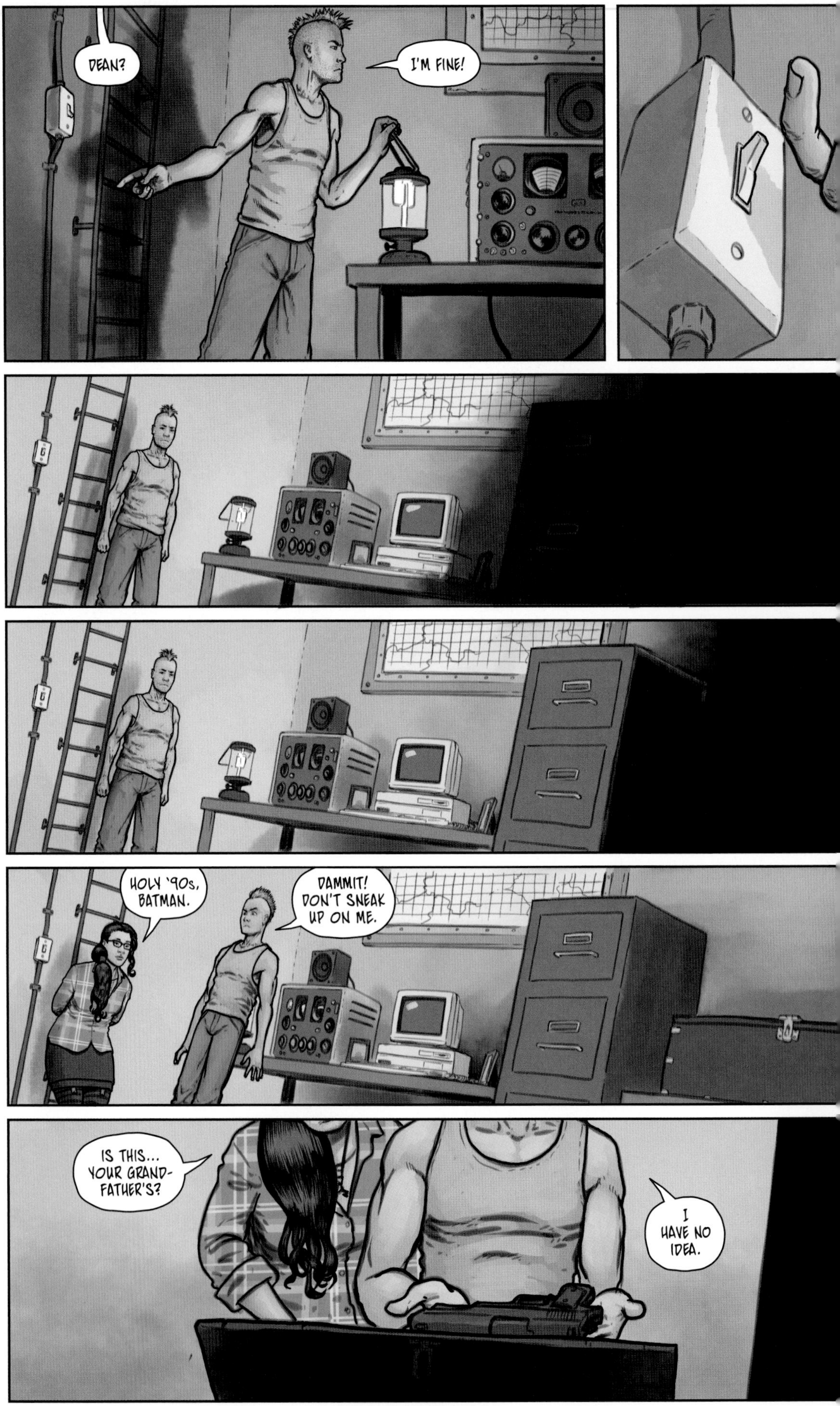
DEAN?
I'M FINE!
HOLY '90s, BATMAN.
DAMMIT! DON'T SNEAK UP ON ME.
IS THIS... YOUR GRAND-FATHER'S?
I HAVE NO IDEA.

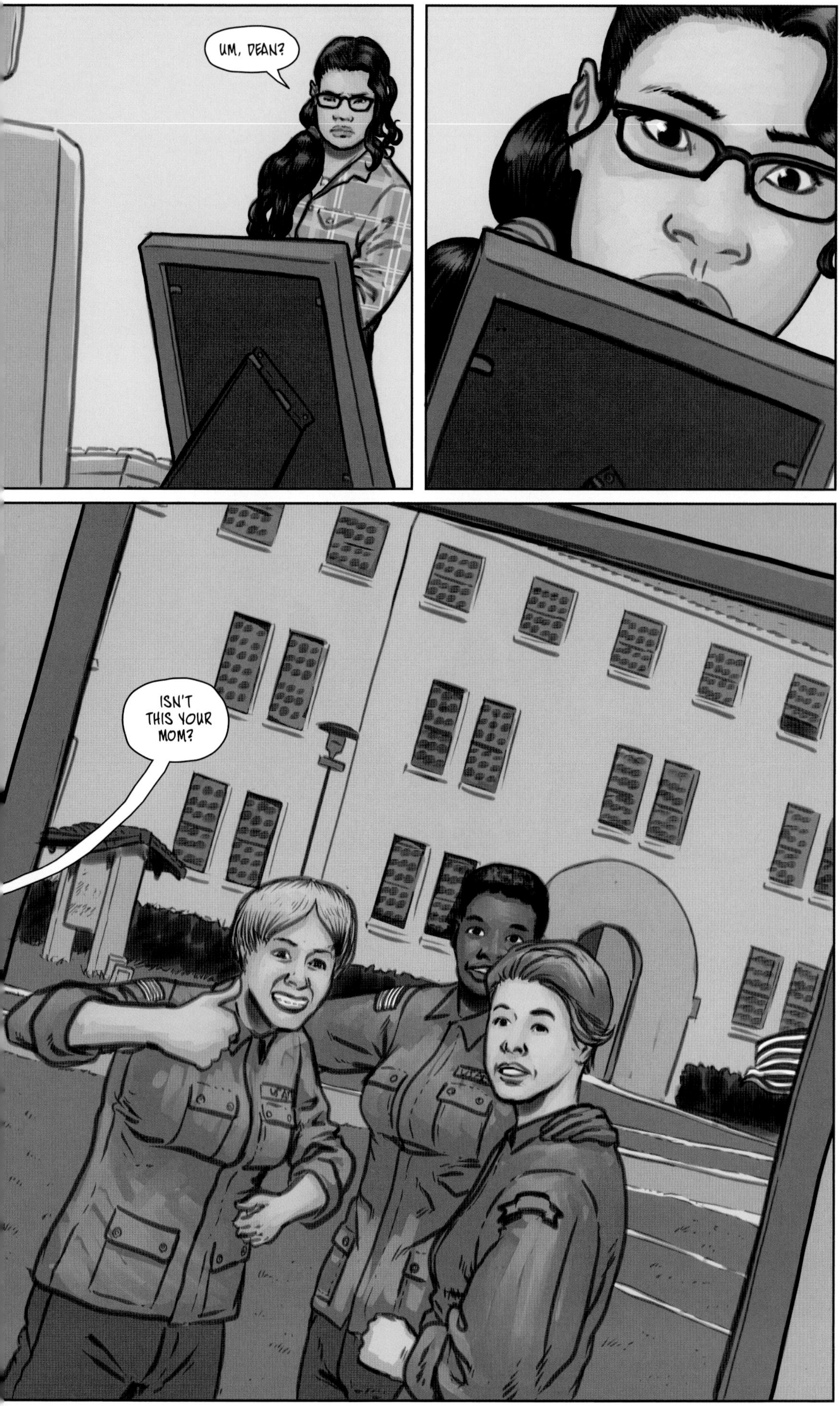
UM, DEAN?
ISN'T THIS YOUR MOM?

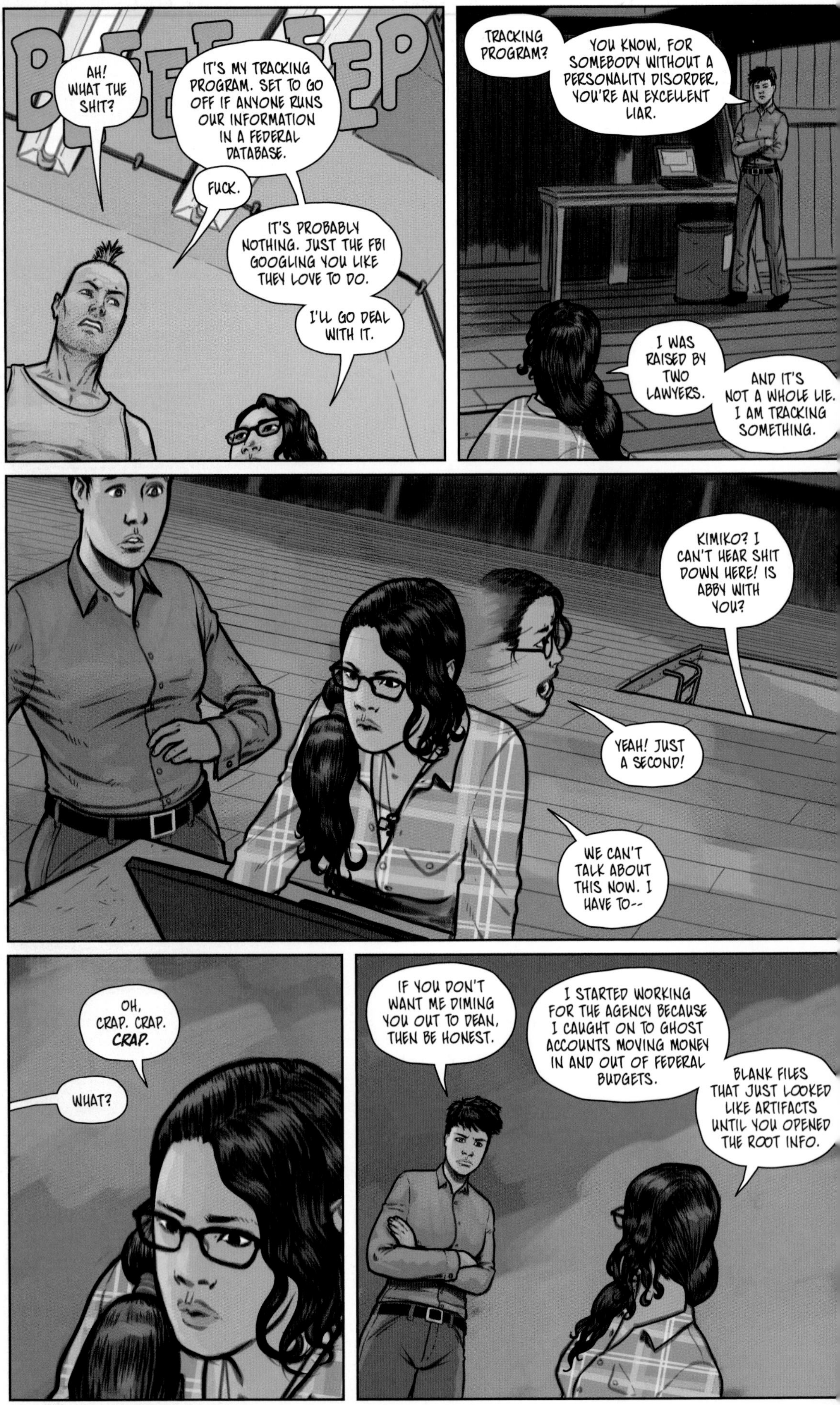
BEEEEEP
AH! WHAT THE SHIT?
IT'S MY TRACKING PROGRAM. SET TO GO OFF IF ANYONE RUNS OUR INFORMATION IN A FEDERAL DATABASE.
FUCK.
IT'S PROBABLY NOTHING. JUST THE FBI GOOGLING YOU LIKE THEY LOVE TO DO.
I'LL GO DEAL WITH IT.
TRACKING PROGRAM?
YOU KNOW, FOR SOMEBODY WITHOUT A PERSONALITY DISORDER, YOU'RE AN EXCELLENT LIAR.
I WAS RAISED BY TWO LAWYERS.
AND IT'S NOT A WHOLE LIE. I AM TRACKING SOMETHING.
KIMIKO? I CAN'T HEAR SHIT DOWN HERE! IS ABBY WITH YOU?
YEAH! JUST A SECOND!
WE CAN'T TALK ABOUT THIS NOW. I HAVE TO--
OH, CRAP. CRAP. CRAP.
WHAT?
IF YOU DON'T WANT ME DIMING YOU OUT TO DEAN, THEN BE HONEST.
I STARTED WORKING FOR THE AGENCY BECAUSE I CAUGHT ON TO GHOST ACCOUNTS MOVING MONEY IN AND OUT OF FEDERAL BUDGETS.
BLANK FILES THAT JUST LOOKED LIKE ARTIFACTS UNTIL YOU OPENED THE ROOT INFO.

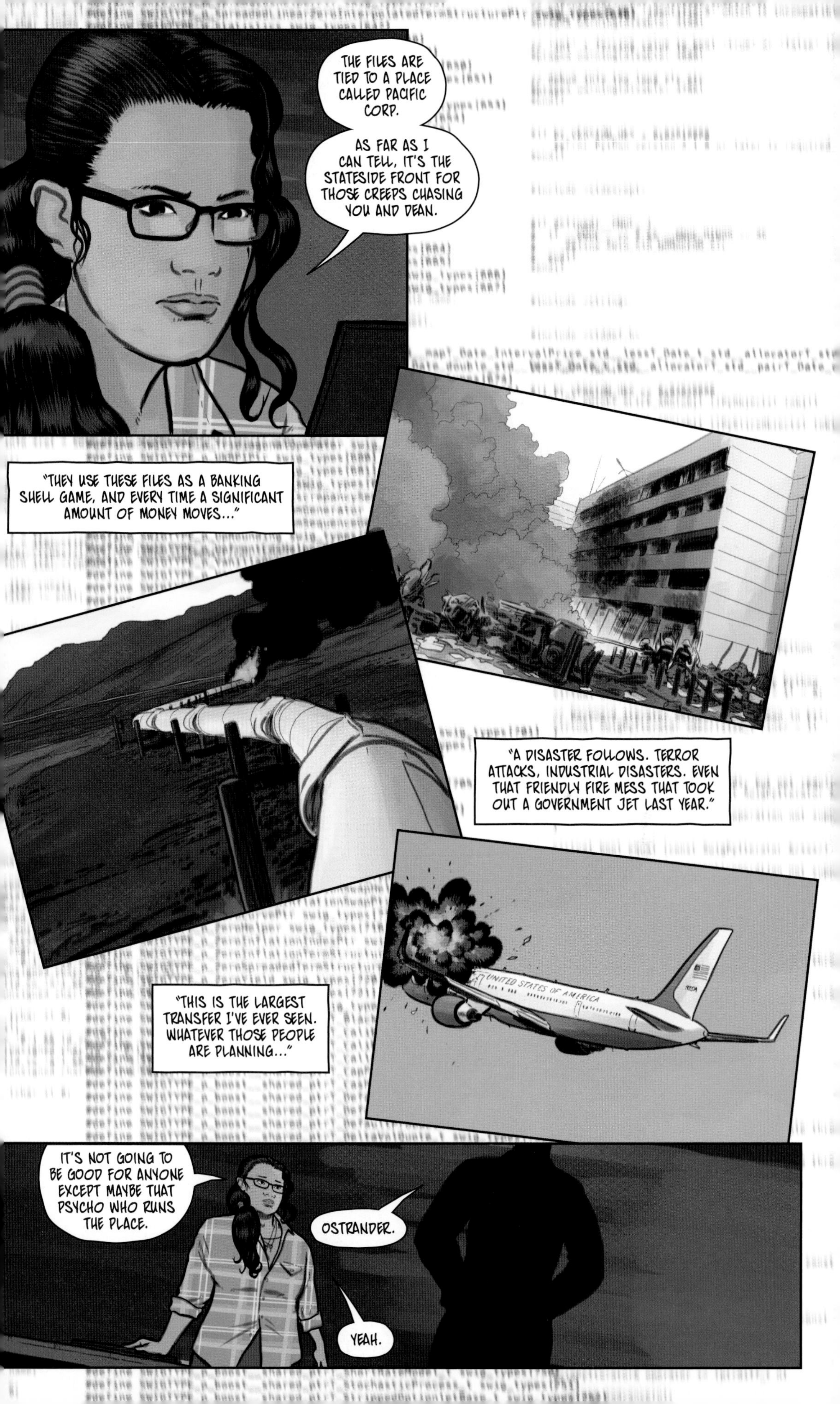
THE FILES ARE TIED TO A PLACE CALLED PACIFIC CORP.
AS FAR AS I CAN TELL, IT'S THE STATESIDE FRONT FOR THOSE CREEPS CHASING YOU AND DEAN.
"THEY USE THESE FILES AS A BANKING SHELL GAME, AND EVERY TIME A SIGNIFICANT AMOUNT OF MONEY MOVES..."
"A DISASTER FOLLOWS. TERROR ATTACKS, INDUSTRIAL DISASTERS. EVEN THAT FRIENDLY FIRE MESS THAT TOOK OUT A GOVERNMENT JET LAST YEAR."
"THIS IS THE LARGEST TRANSFER I'VE EVER SEEN. WHATEVER THOSE PEOPLE ARE PLANNING..."
UNITED STATES OF AMERICA
IT'S NOT GOING TO BE GOOD FOR ANYONE EXCEPT MAYBE THAT PSYCHO WHO RUNS THE PLACE.
OSTRANDER.
YEAH.

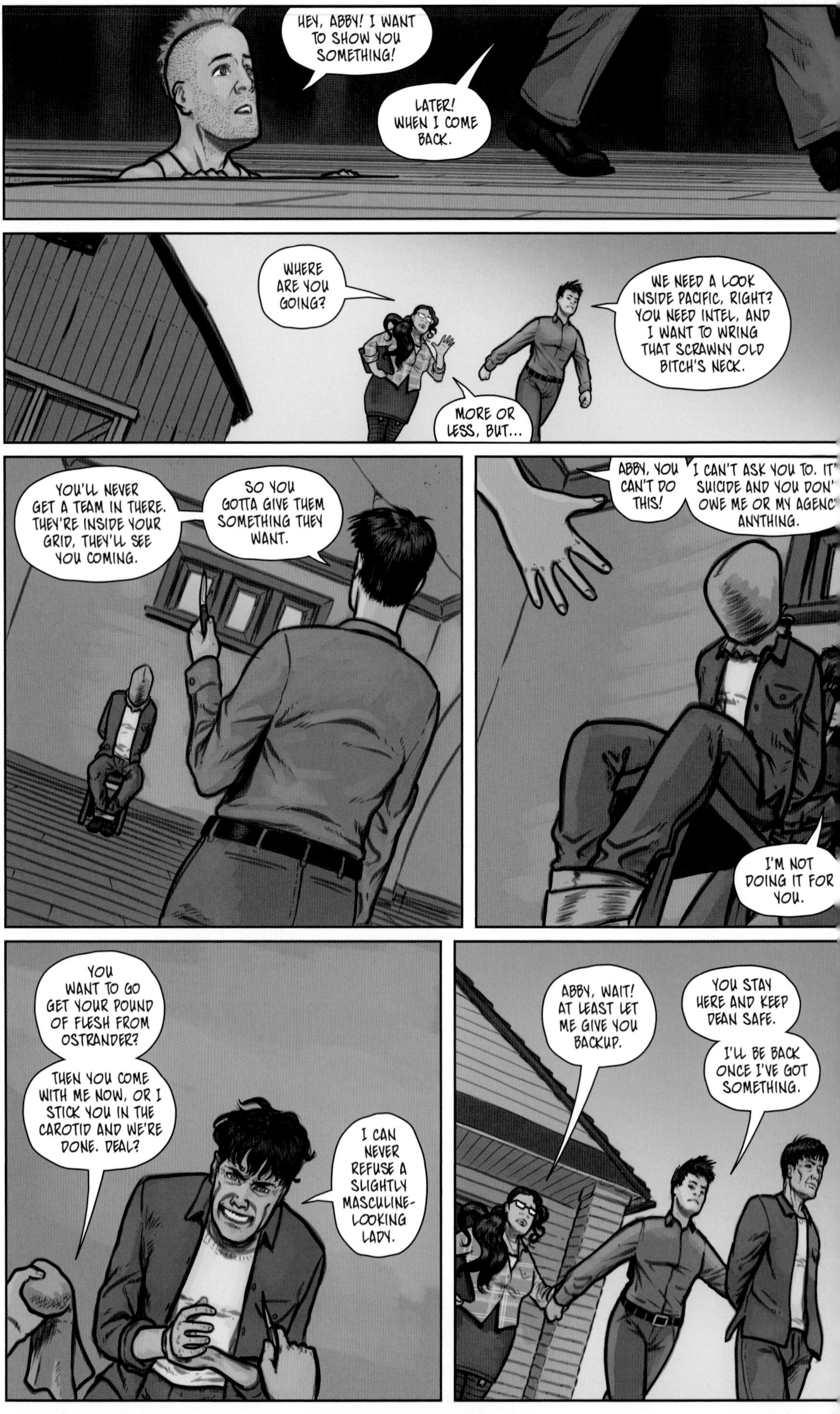
HEY, ABBY! I WANT TO SHOW YOU SOMETHING!
LATER! WHEN I COME BACK.
WHERE ARE YOU GOING?
WE NEED A LOOK INSIDE PACIFIC, RIGHT? YOU NEED INTEL, AND I WANT TO WRING THAT SCRAWNY OLD BITCH'S NECK.
MORE OR LESS, BUT...
YOU'LL NEVER GET A TEAM IN THERE. THEY'RE INSIDE YOUR GRID, THEY'LL SEE YOU COMING.
SO YOU GOTTA GIVE THEM SOMETHING THEY WANT.
ABBY, YOU CAN'T DO THIS!
I CAN'T ASK YOU TO. IT' SUICIDE AND YOU DON' OWE ME OR MY AGENC ANYTHING.
I'M NOT DOING IT FOR YOU.
YOU WANT TO GO GET YOUR POUND OF FLESH FROM OSTRANDER?
THEN YOU COME WITH ME NOW, OR I STICK YOU IN THE CAROTID AND WE'RE DONE. DEAL?
I CAN NEVER REFUSE A SLIGHTLY MASCULINE-LOOKING LADY.
ABBY, WAIT! AT LEAST LET ME GIVE YOU BACKUP.
YOU STAY HERE AND KEEP DEAN SAFE.
I'LL BE BACK ONCE I'VE GOT SOMETHING.

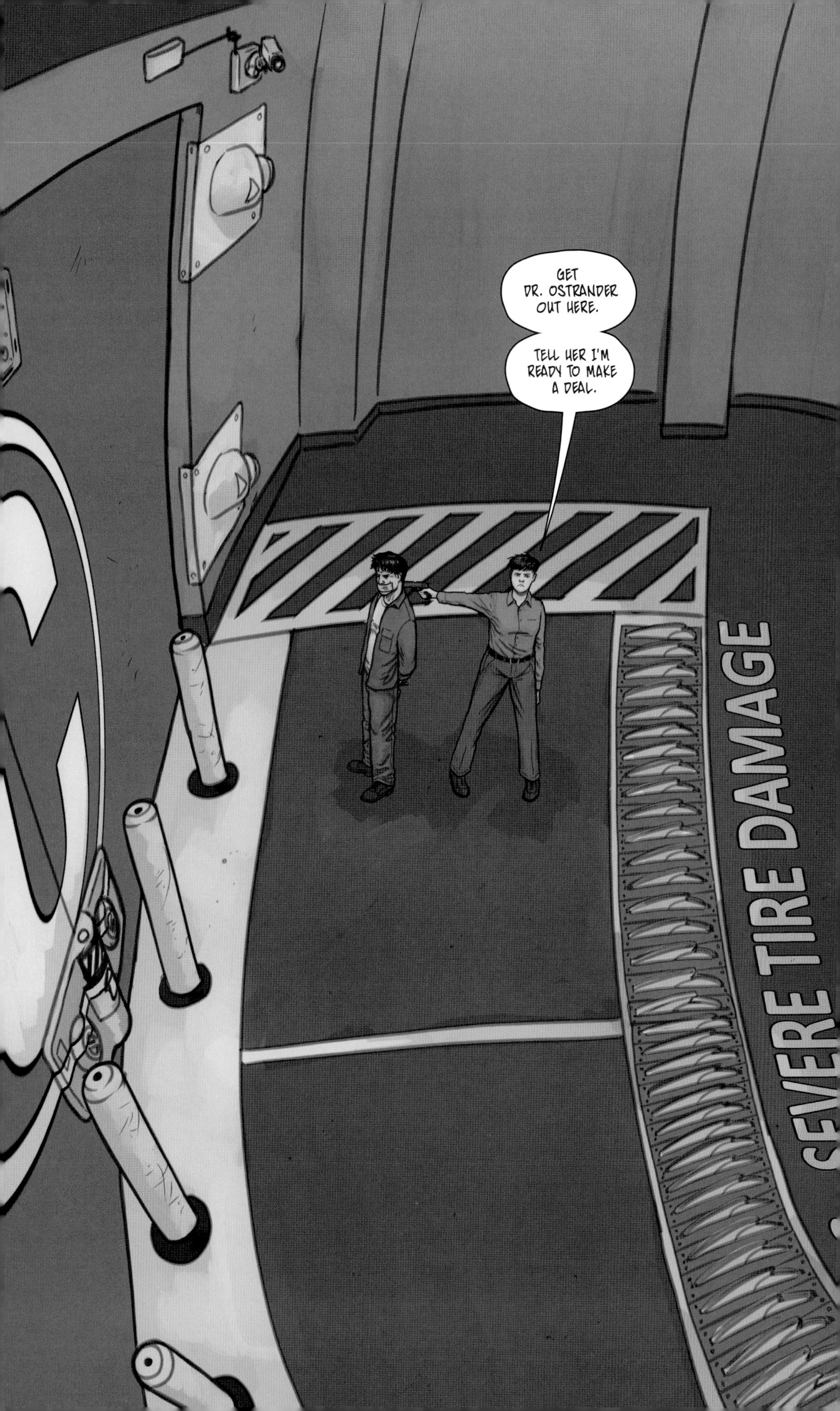
GET DR. OSTRANDER OUT HERE.
TELL HER I'M READY TO MAKE A DEAL.
SEVERE TIRE DAMAGE

CHAPTER SIX

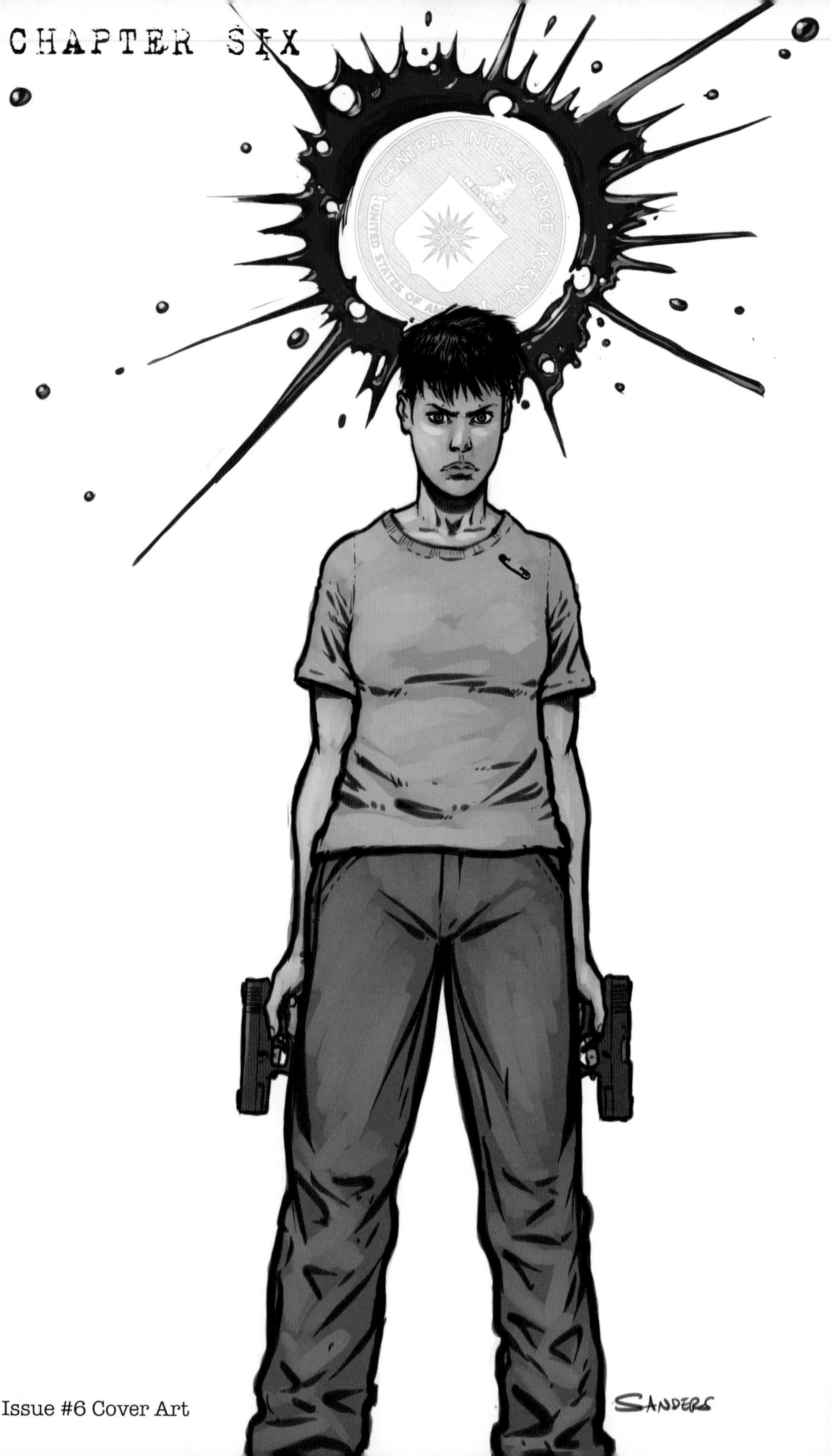
CENTRAL INTELLIGENCE AGENCY
UNITED STATES OF AM
SANDERS

Issue #6 Cover Art

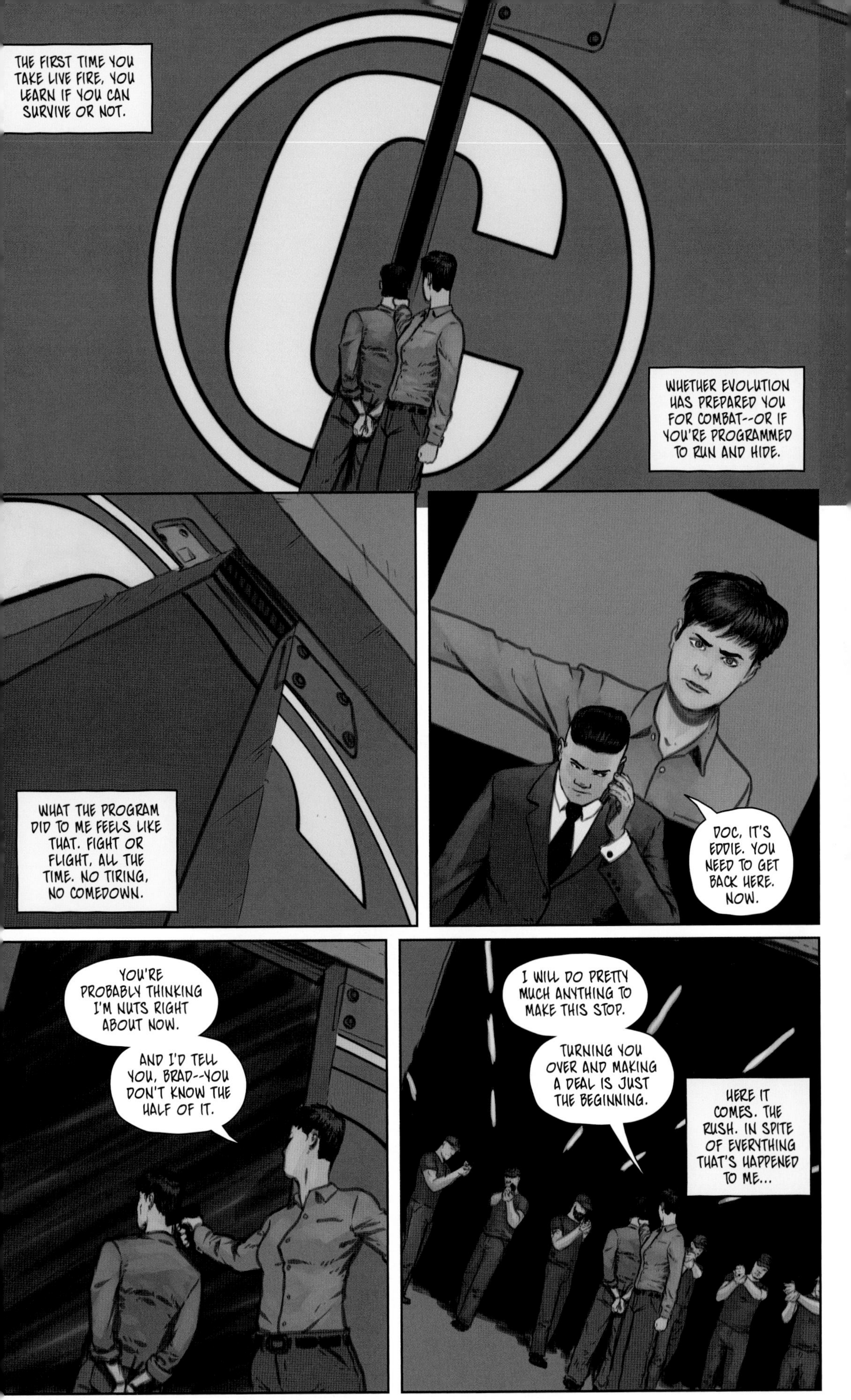
THE FIRST TIME YOU TAKE LIVE FIRE, YOU LEARN IF YOU CAN SURVIVE OR NOT.
WHETHER EVOLUTION HAS PREPARED YOU FOR COMBAT--OR IF YOU'RE PROGRAMMED TO RUN AND HIDE.
WHAT THE PROGRAM DID TO ME FEELS LIKE THAT. FIGHT OR FLIGHT, ALL THE TIME. NO TIRING, NO COMEDOWN.
DOC, IT'S EDDIE. YOU NEED TO GET BACK HERE. NOW.
YOU'RE PROBABLY THINKING I'M NUTS RIGHT ABOUT NOW.
AND I'D TELL YOU, BRAD--YOU DON'T KNOW THE HALF OF IT.
I WILL DO PRETTY MUCH ANYTHING TO MAKE THIS STOP.
TURNING YOU OVER AND MAKING A DEAL IS JUST THE BEGINNING.
HERE IT COMES. THE RUSH. IN SPITE OF EVERYTHING THAT'S HAPPENED TO ME...

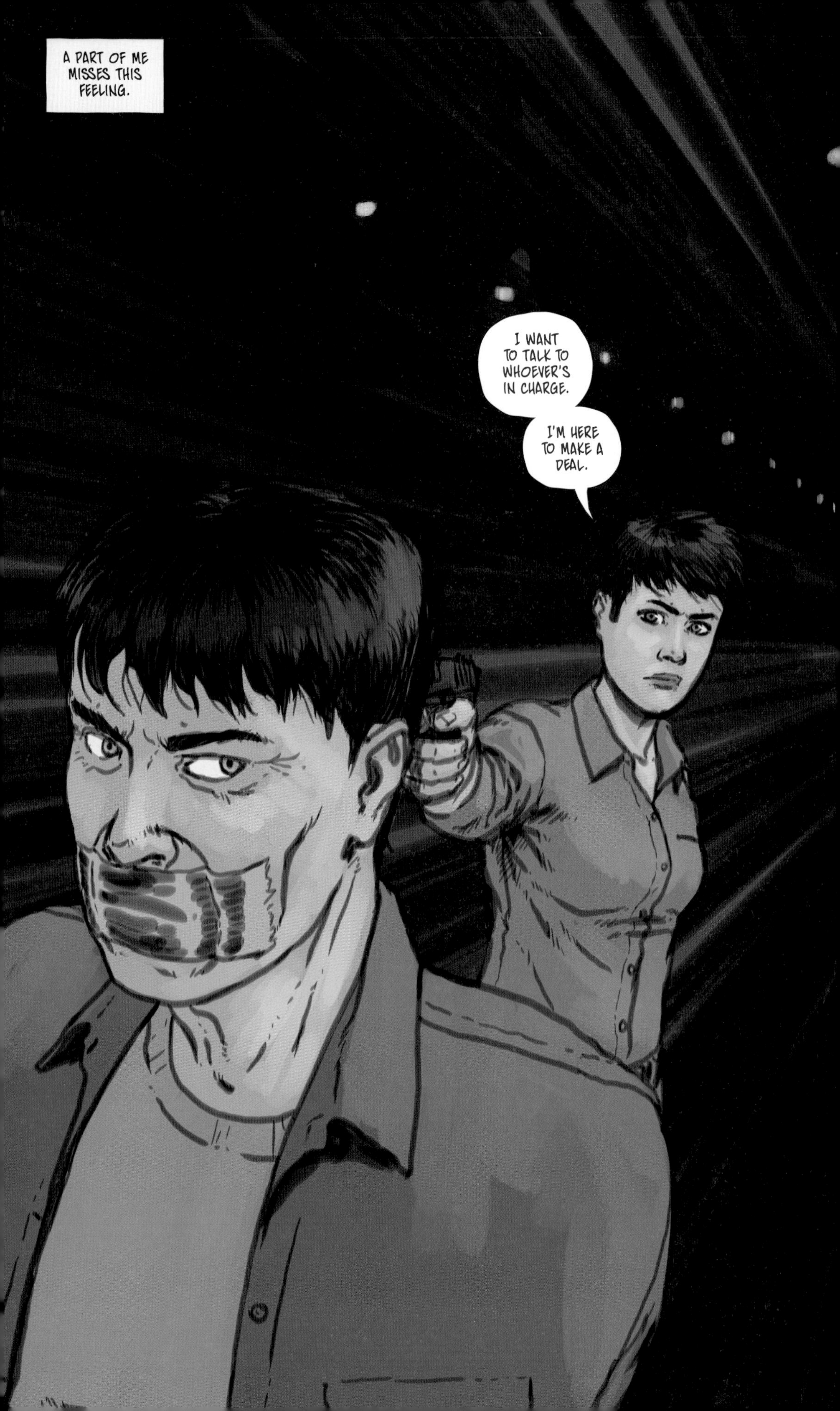
A PART OF ME MISSES THIS FEELING.
I WANT TO TALK TO WHOEVER'S IN CHARGE.
I'M HERE TO MAKE A DEAL.

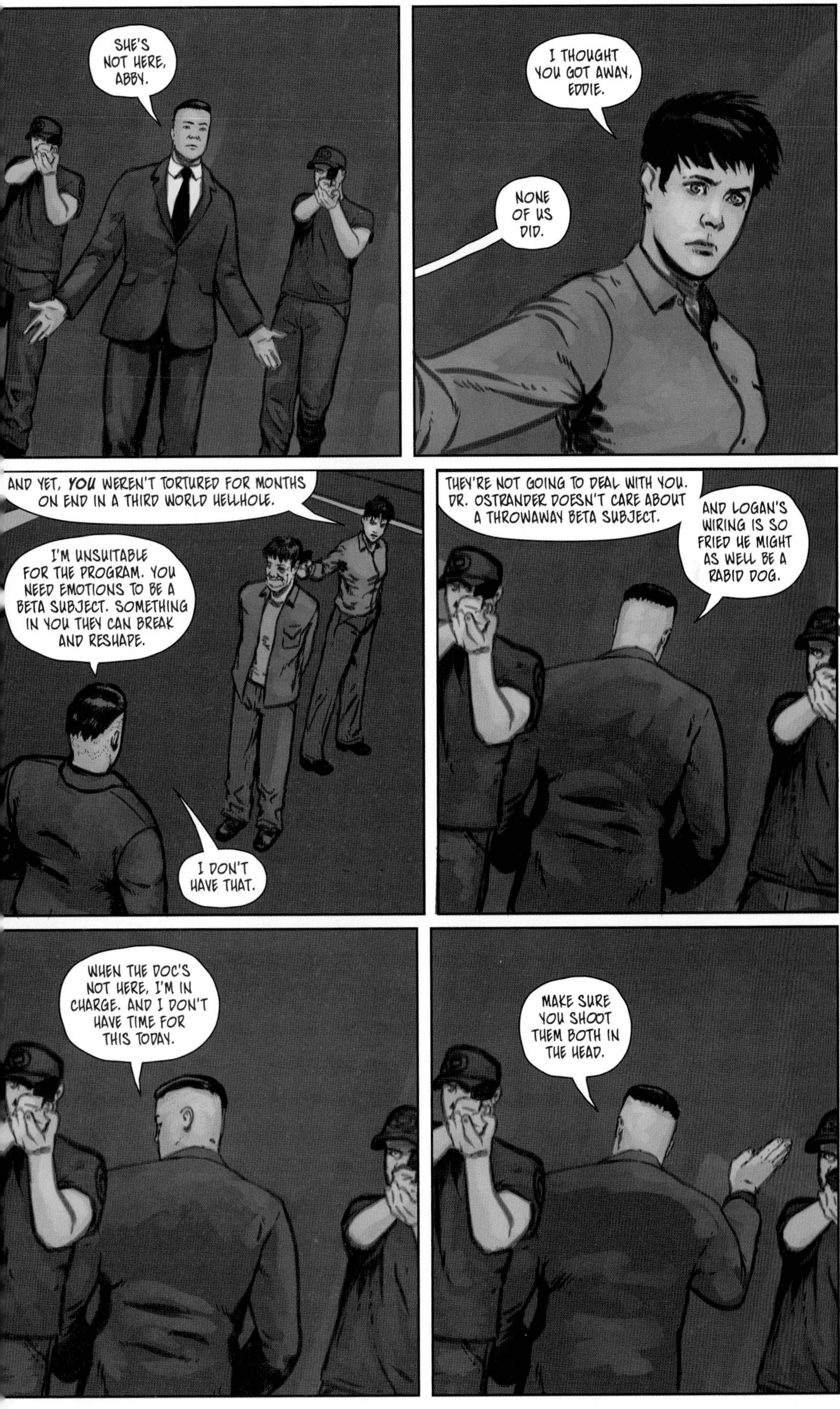

SHE'S NOT HERE, ABBY.
I THOUGHT YOU GOT AWAY, EDDIE.
NONE OF US DID.
AND YET, YOU WEREN'T TORTURED FOR MONTHS ON END IN A THIRD WORLD HELLHOLE.
I'M UNSUITABLE FOR THE PROGRAM. YOU NEED EMOTIONS TO BE A BETA SUBJECT. SOMETHING IN YOU THEY CAN BREAK AND RESHAPE.
I DON'T HAVE THAT.
THEY'RE NOT GOING TO DEAL WITH YOU. DR. OSTRANDER DOESN'T CARE ABOUT A THROWAWAY BETA SUBJECT.
AND LOGAN'S WIRING IS SO FRIED HE MIGHT AS WELL BE A RABID DOG.
WHEN THE DOC'S NOT HERE, I'M IN CHARGE. AND I DON'T HAVE TIME FOR THIS TODAY.
MAKE SURE YOU SHOOT THEM BOTH IN THE HEAD.

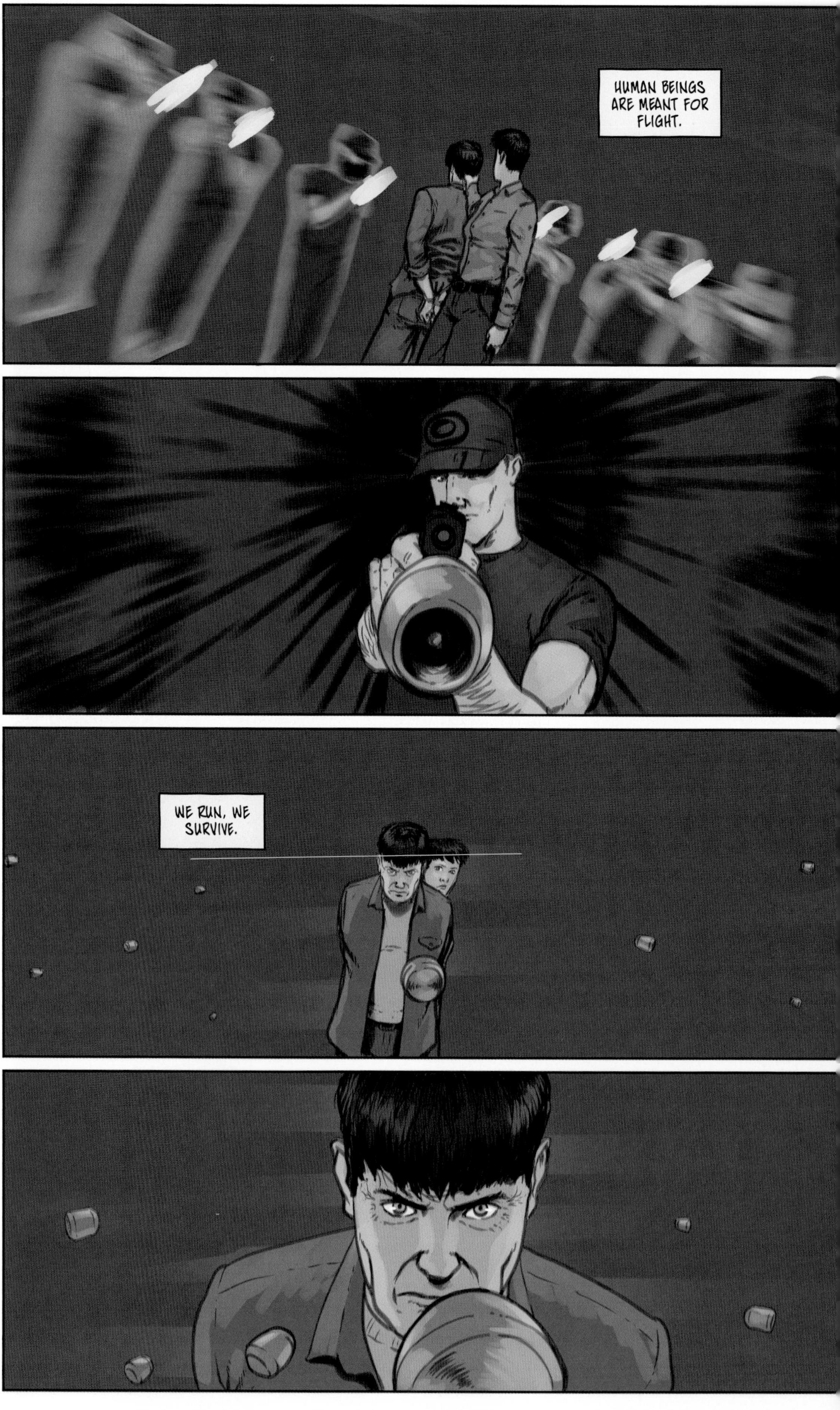
HUMAN BEINGS ARE MEANT FOR FLIGHT.
WE RUN, WE SURVIVE.

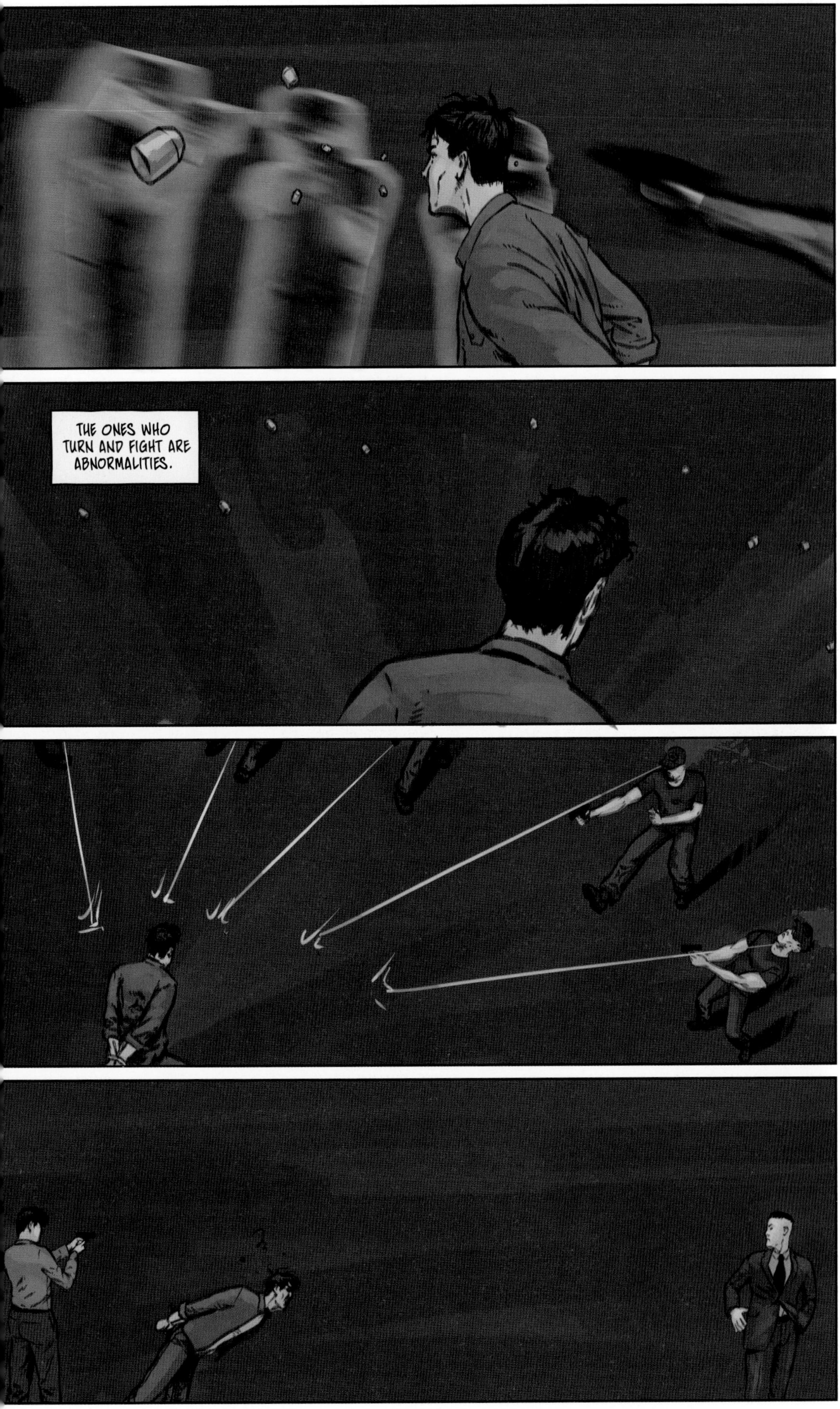
THE ONES WHO TURN AND FIGHT ARE ABNORMALITIES.

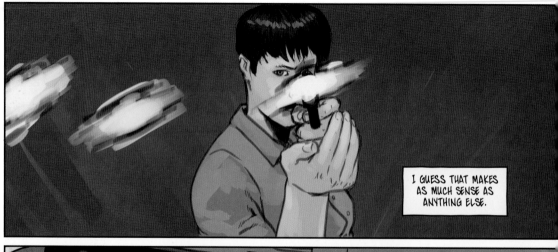

I GUESS THAT MAKES AS MUCH SENSE AS ANYTHING ELSE.

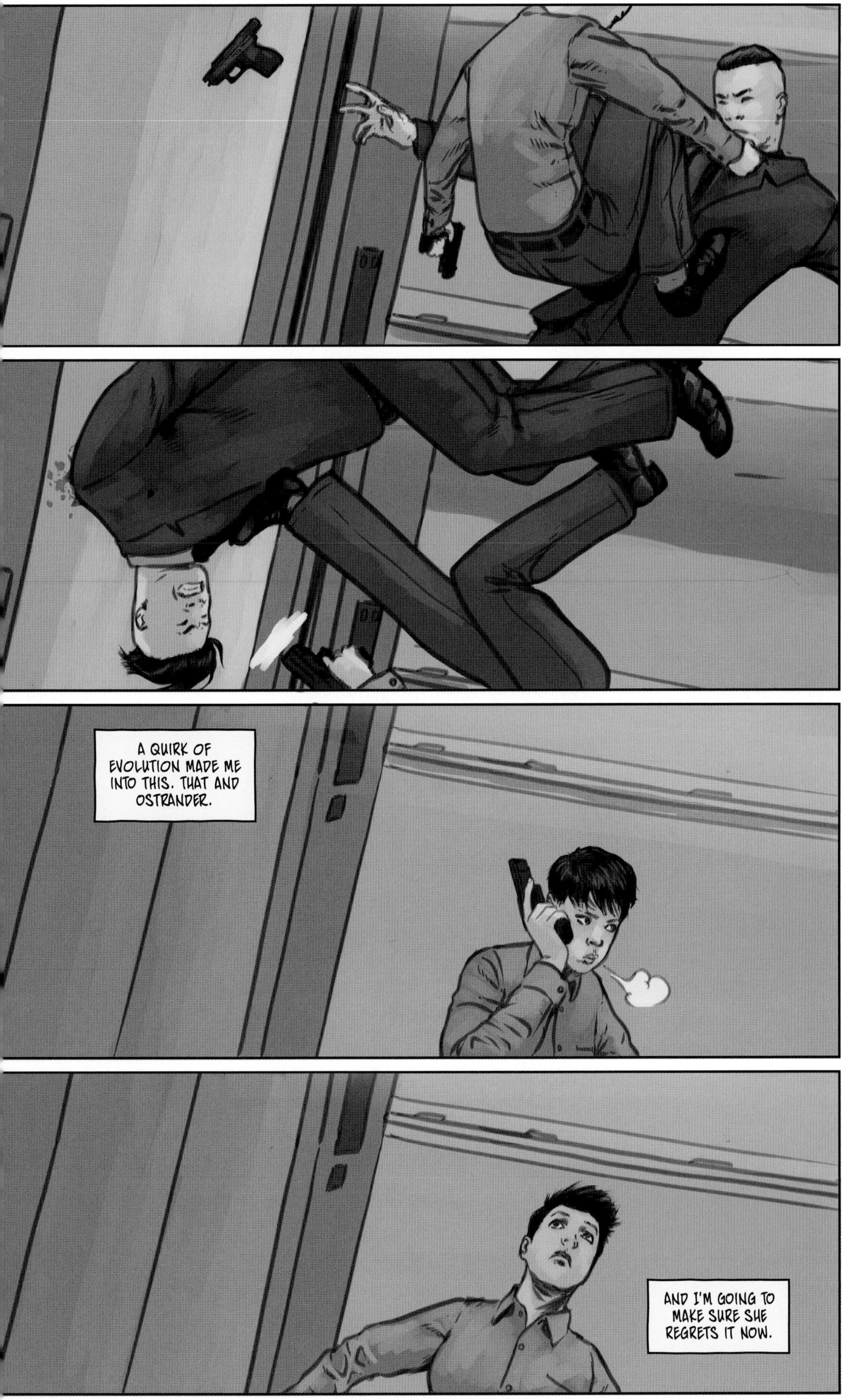
A QUIRK OF EVOLUTION MADE ME INTO THIS. THAT AND OSTRANDER.
AND I'M GOING TO MAKE SURE SHE REGRETS IT NOW.

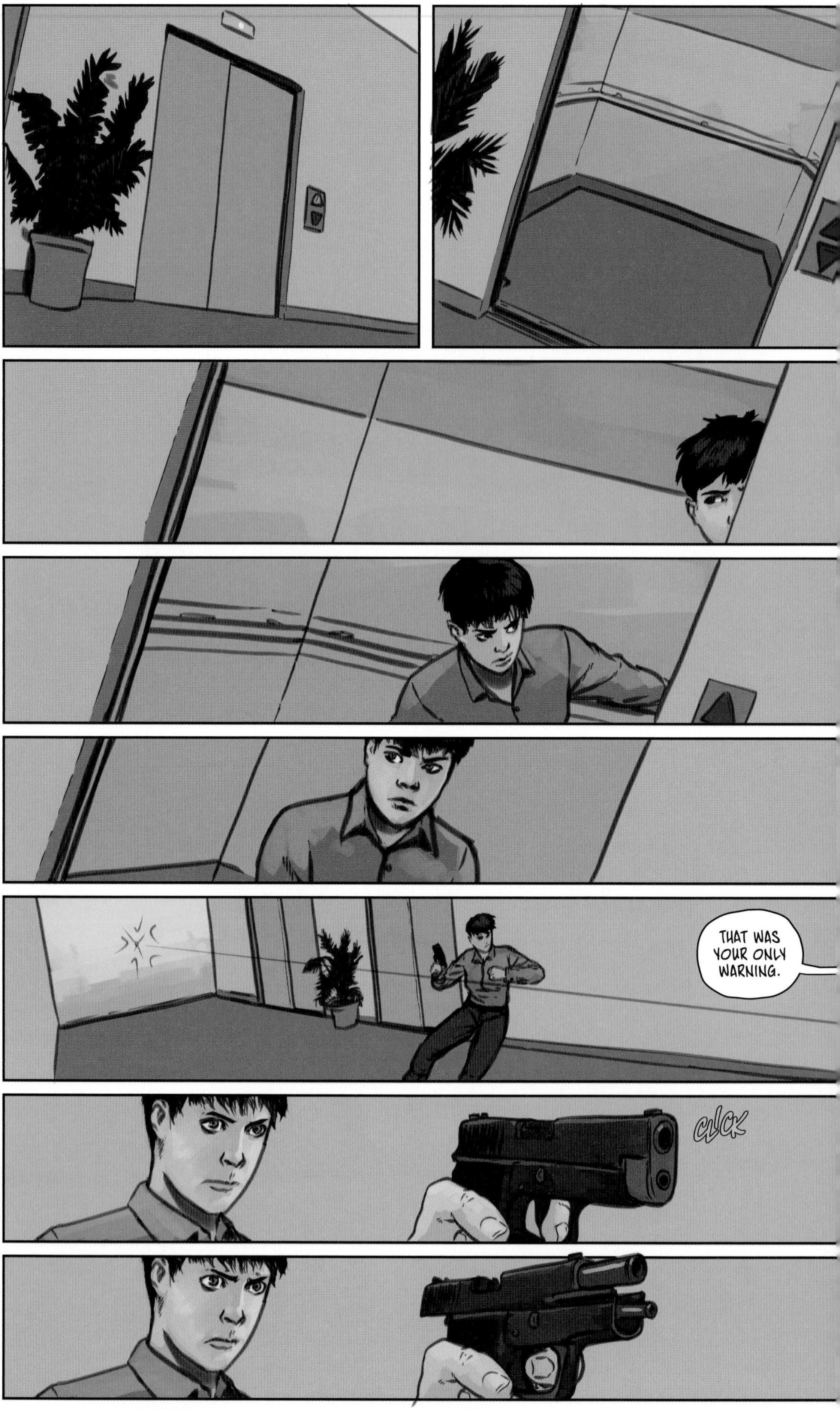
THAT WAS YOUR ONLY WARNING.
CLICK

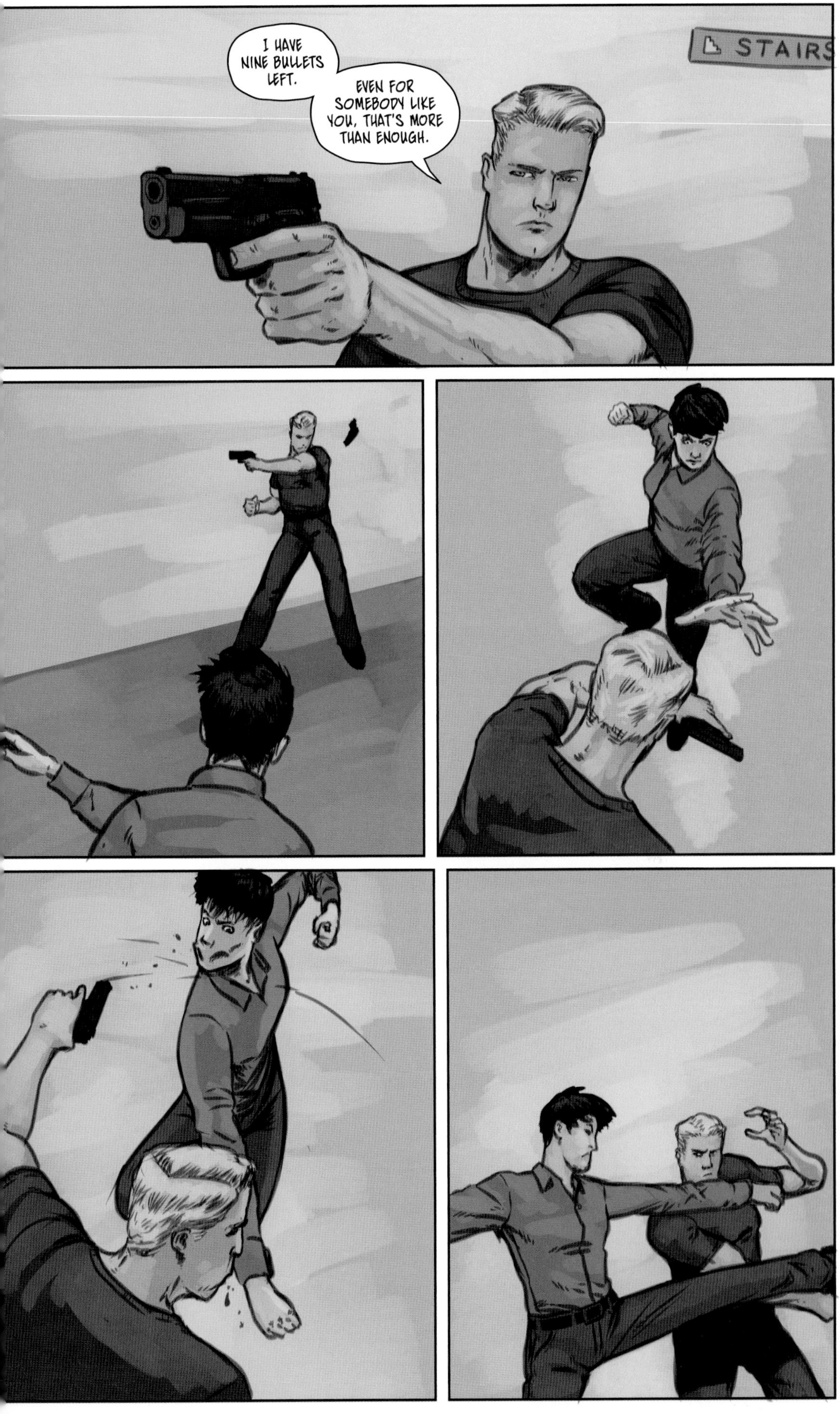

I HAVE NINE BULLETS LEFT.
EVEN FOR SOMEBODY LIKE YOU, THAT'S MORE THAN ENOUGH.
STAIRS

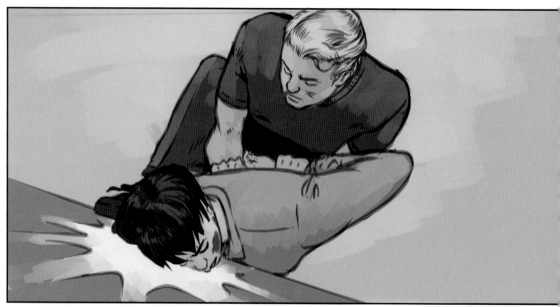

I DON'T KNOW WHAT YOU THOUGHT YOU'D ACCOMPLISH BY COMING HERE, BUT I'M GLAD YOU DID.

SAVED ME THE TROUBLE OF FINDING YOU AND BRINGING YOU IN.

YOU'RE CONFUSED. YOU'VE GOT BAD PROGRAMMING. I DON'T BLAME YOU FOR WHAT YOU'VE DONE.

BUT IT STOPS NOW.

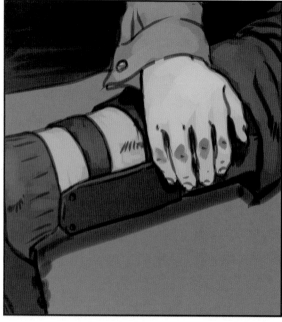

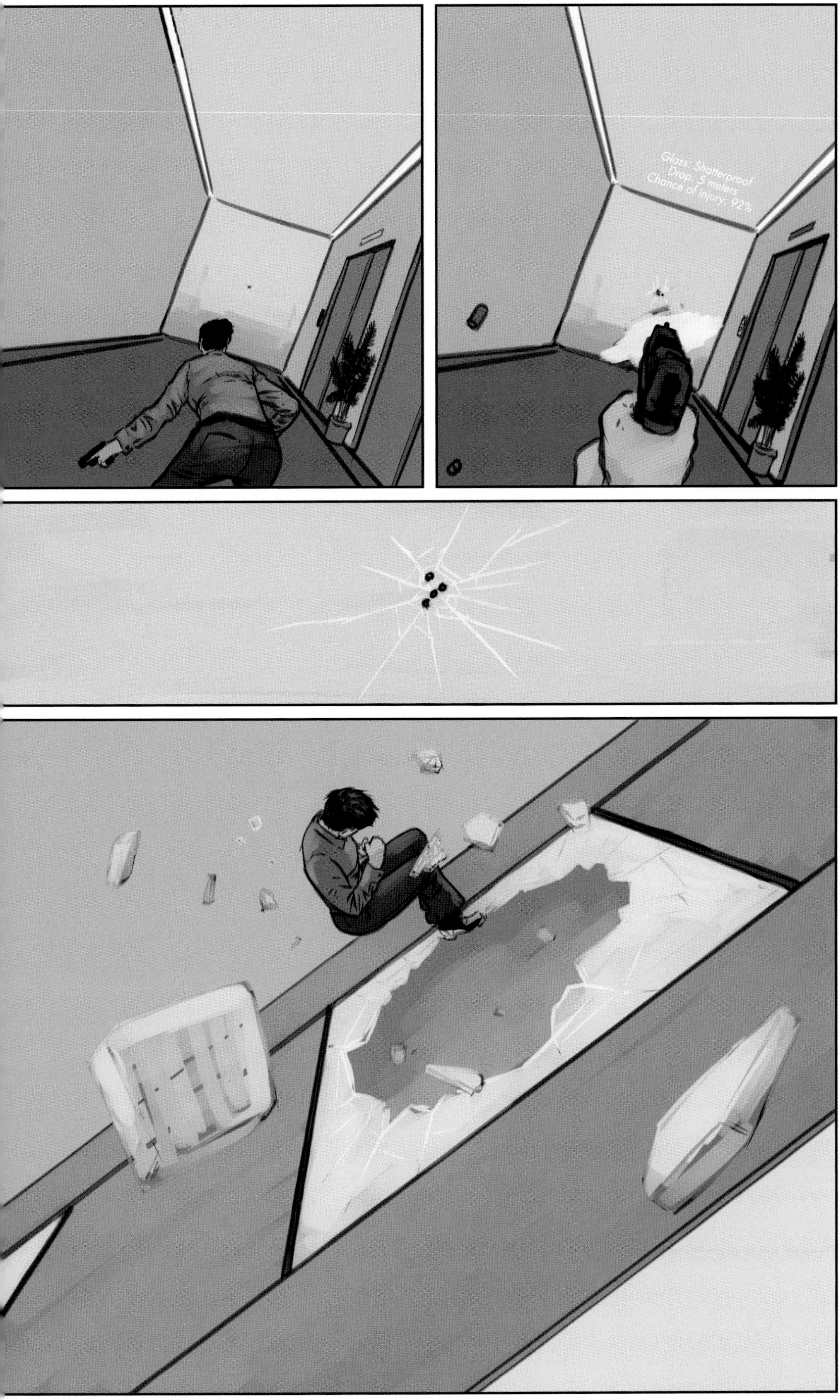
Glass: Shatterproof
Drop: 5 meters
Chance of injury: 92%

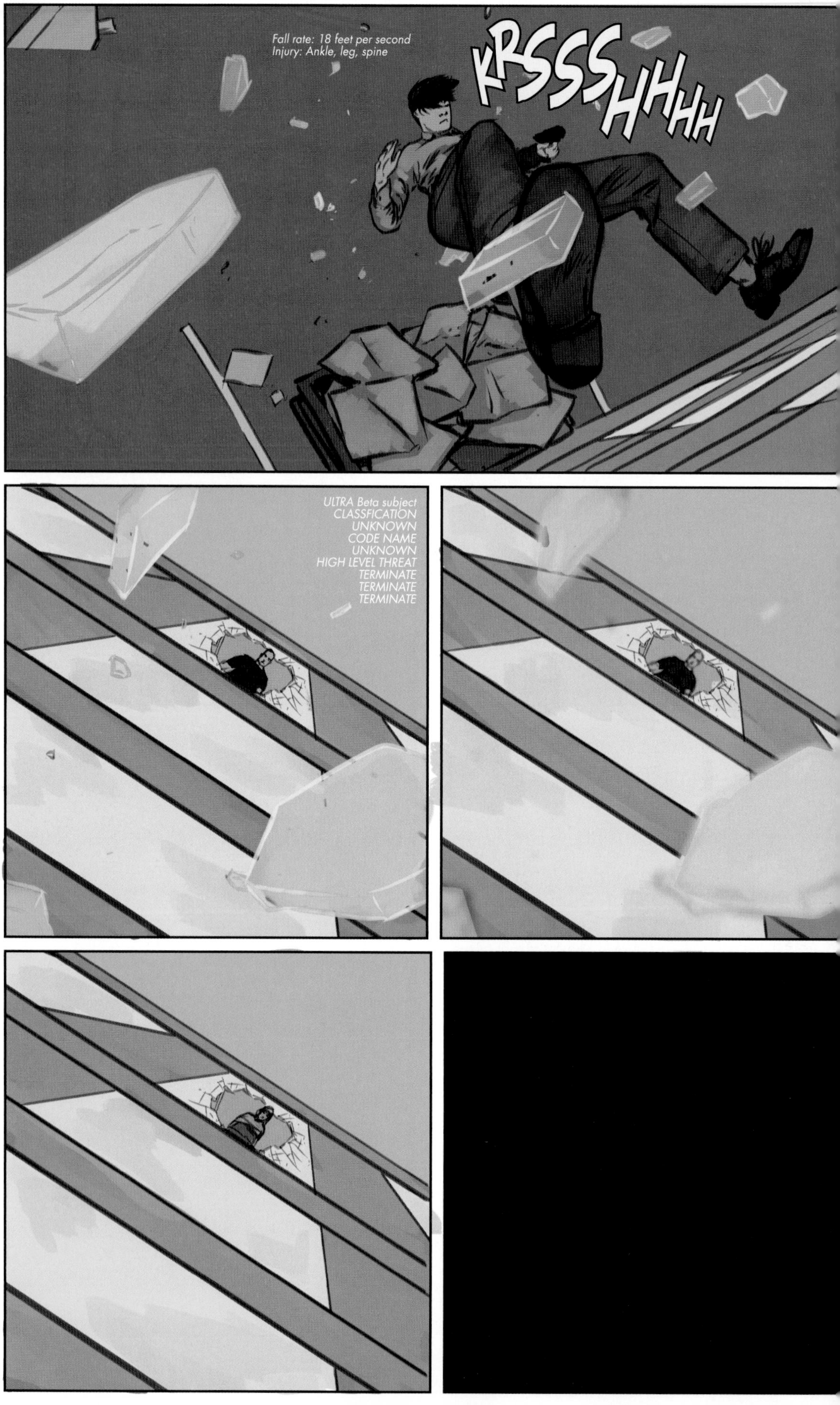

Fall rate: 18 feet per second
Injury: Ankle, leg, spine
KRSSSHHHH
ULTRA Beta subject
CLASSFICATION
UNKNOWN
CODE NAME
UNKNOWN
HIGH LEVEL THREAT
TERMINATE
TERMINATE
TERMINATE

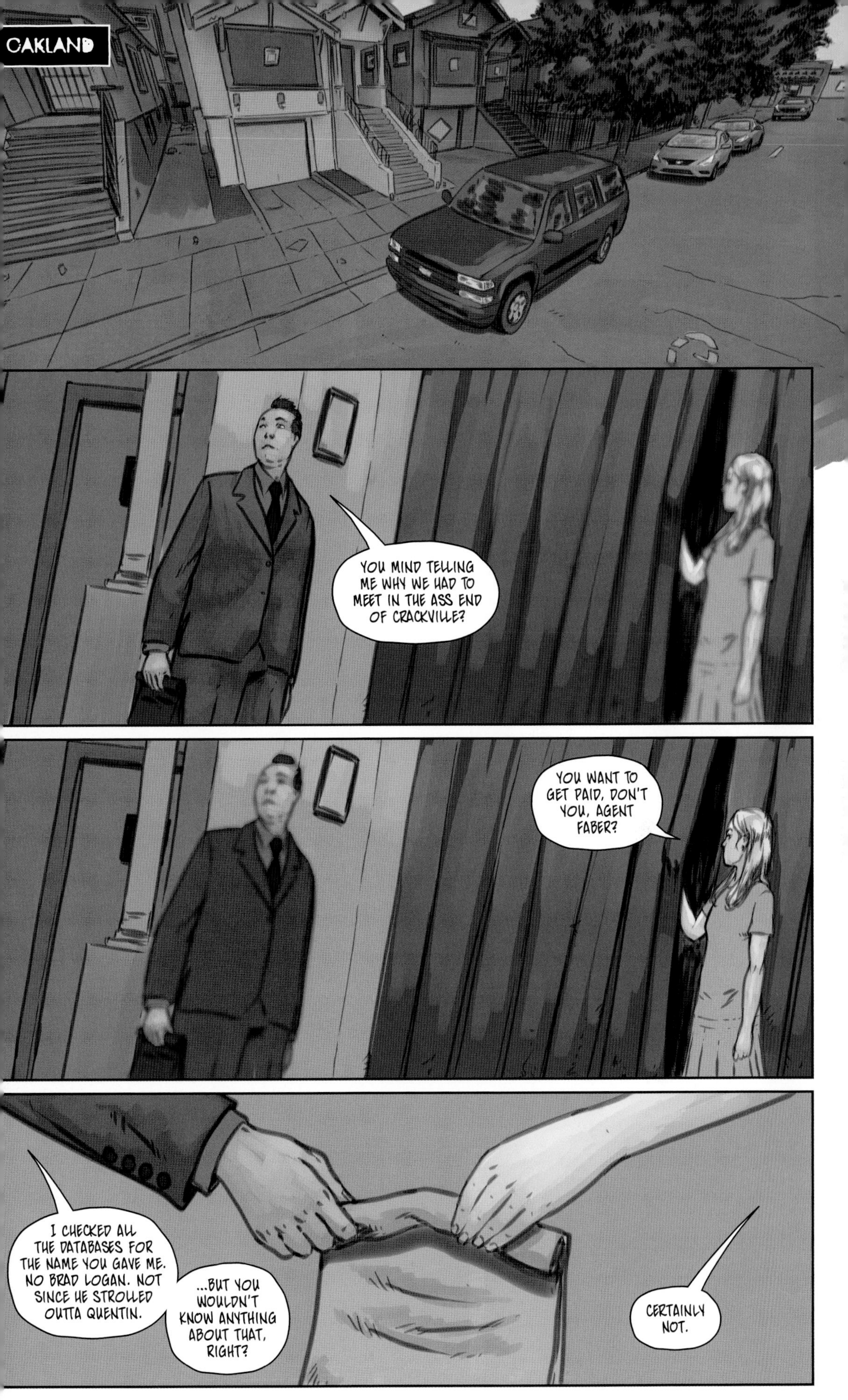
OAKLAND
YOU MIND TELLING ME WHY WE HAD TO MEET IN THE ASS END OF CRACKVILLE?
YOU WANT TO GET PAID, DON'T YOU, AGENT FABER?
I CHECKED ALL THE DATABASES FOR THE NAME YOU GAVE ME. NO BRAD LOGAN. NOT SINCE HE STROLLED OUTTA QUENTIN.
...BUT YOU WOULDN'T KNOW ANYTHING ABOUT THAT, RIGHT?
CERTAINLY NOT.

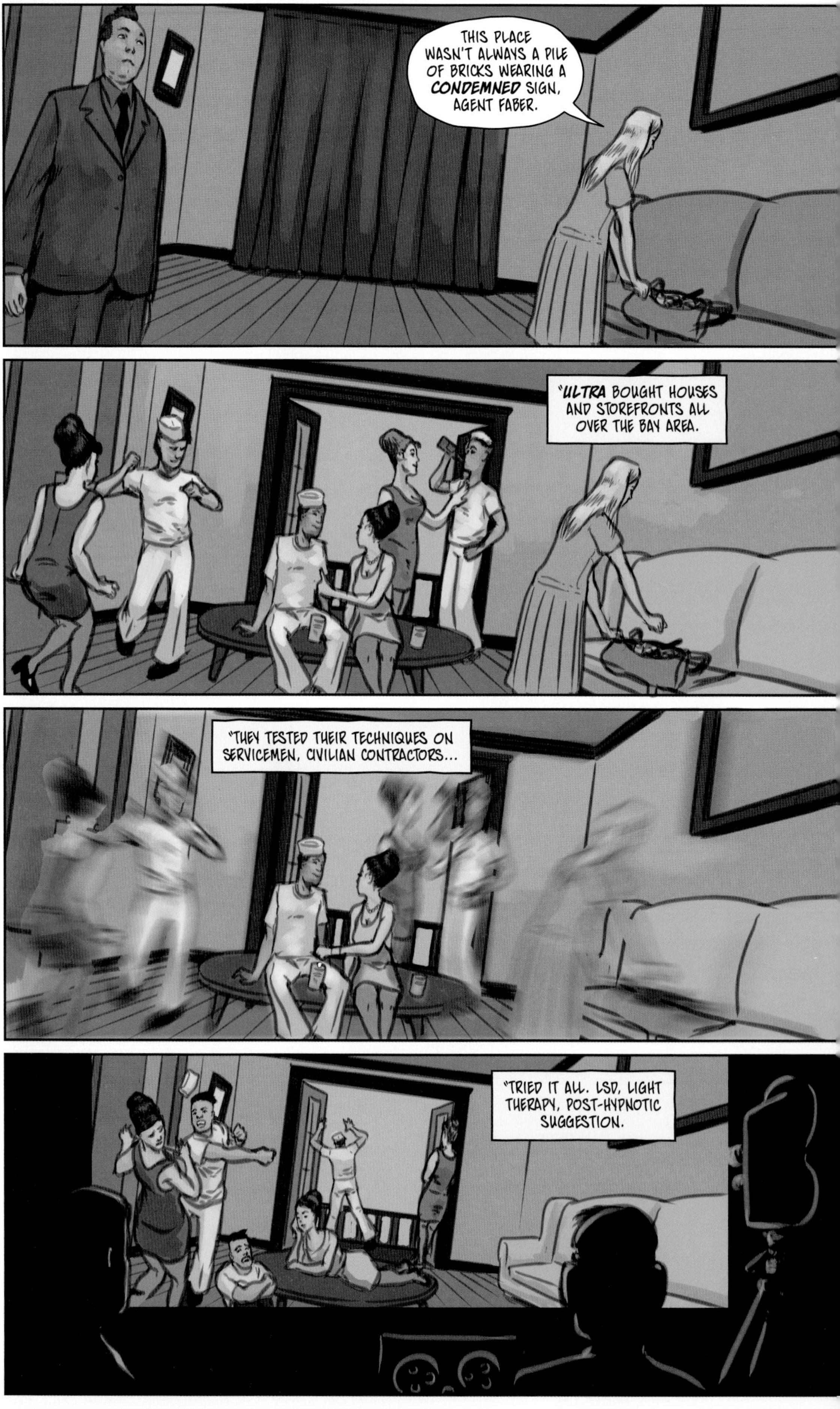
THIS PLACE WASN'T ALWAYS A PILE OF BRICKS WEARING A CONDEMNED SIGN, AGENT FABER.
"ULTRA BOUGHT HOUSES AND STOREFRONTS ALL OVER THE BAY AREA.
"THEY TESTED THEIR TECHNIQUES ON SERVICEMEN, CIVILIAN CONTRACTORS...
"TRIED IT ALL. LSD, LIGHT THERAPY, POST-HYPNOTIC SUGGESTION.

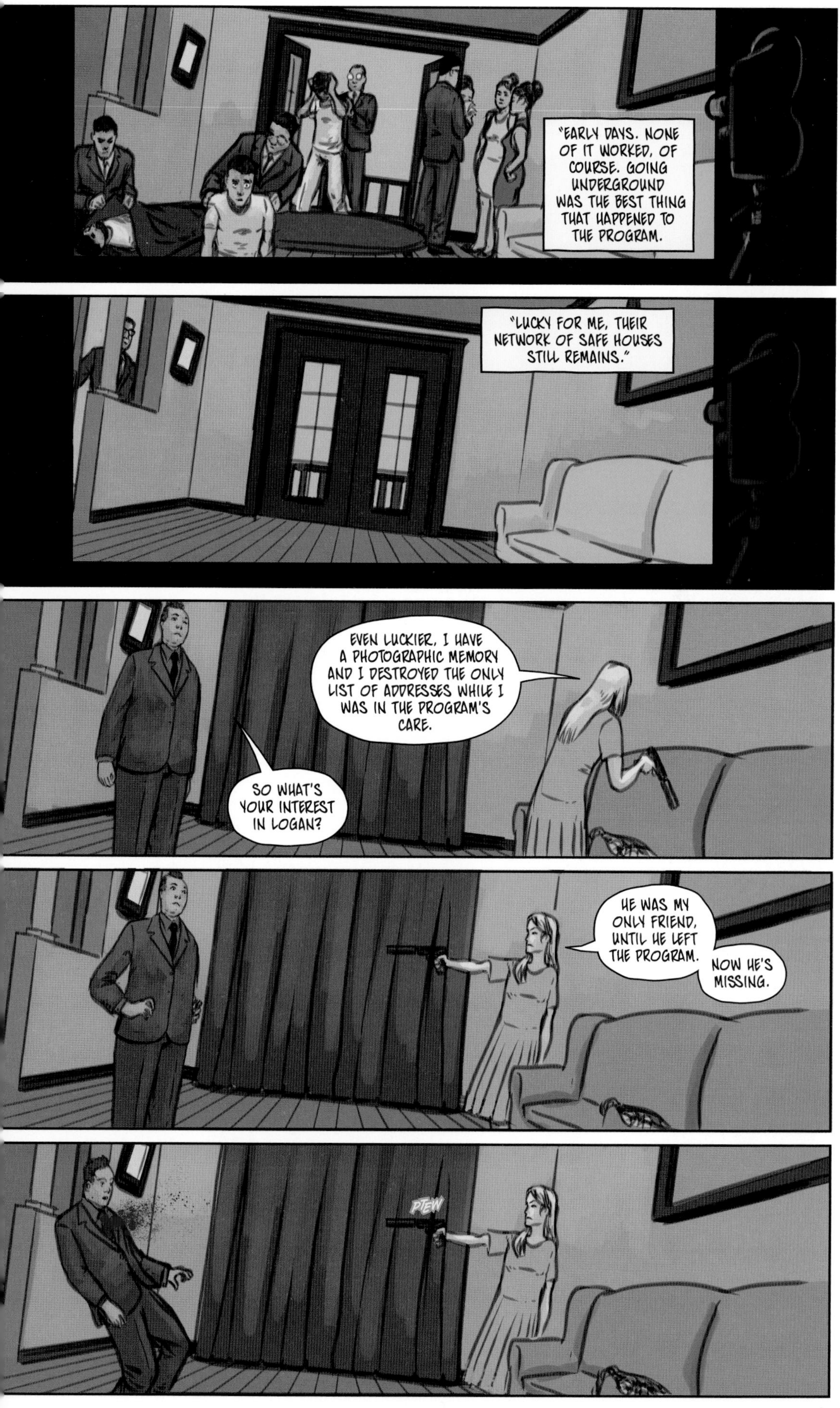
"EARLY DAYS. NONE OF IT WORKED, OF COURSE. GOING UNDERGROUND WAS THE BEST THING THAT HAPPENED TO THE PROGRAM.
"LUCKY FOR ME, THEIR NETWORK OF SAFE HOUSES STILL REMAINS."
EVEN LUCKIER, I HAVE A PHOTOGRAPHIC MEMORY AND I DESTROYED THE ONLY LIST OF ADDRESSES WHILE I WAS IN THE PROGRAM'S CARE.
SO WHAT'S YOUR INTEREST IN LOGAN?
HE WAS MY ONLY FRIEND, UNTIL HE LEFT THE PROGRAM.
NOW HE'S MISSING.
PTEW

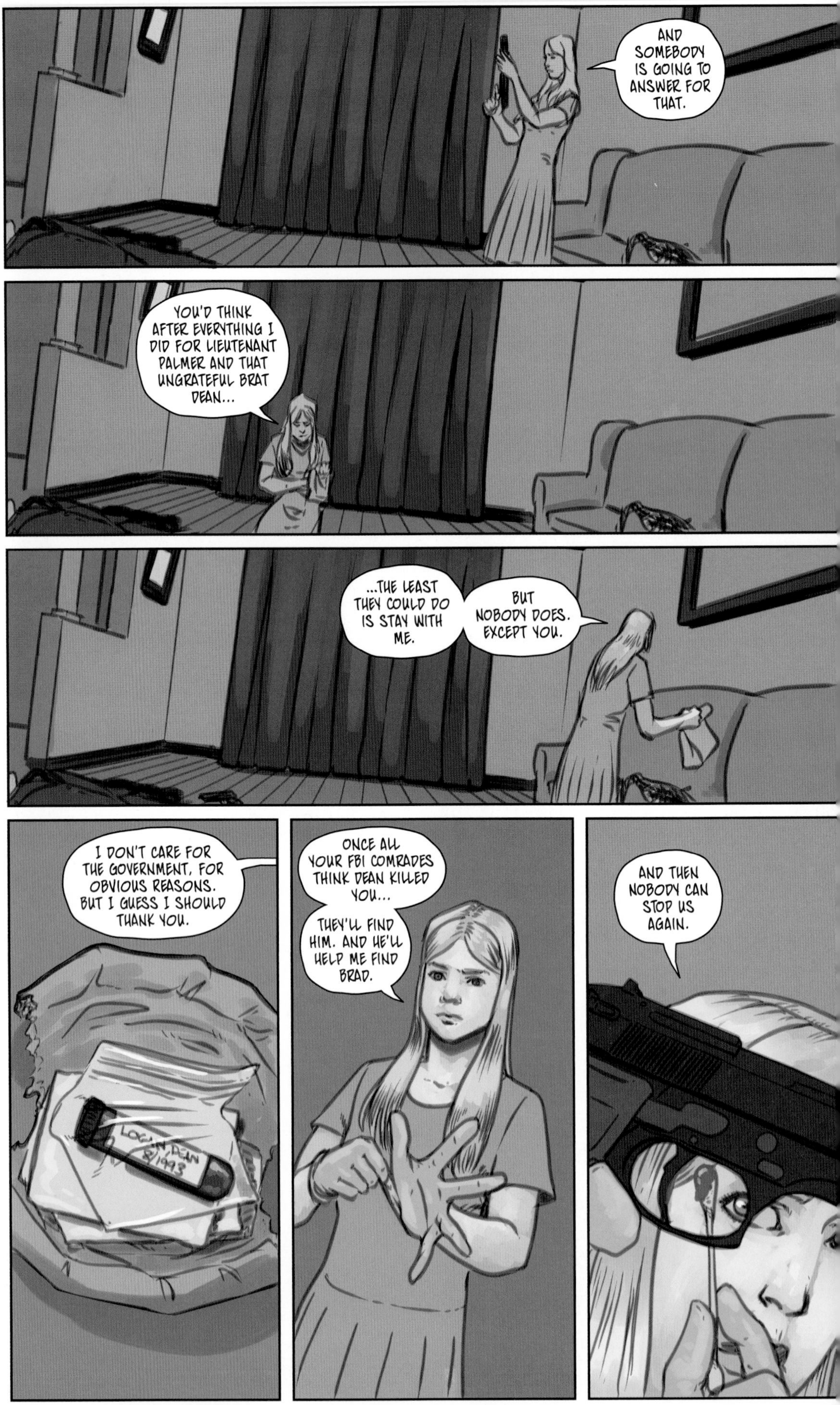
AND SOMEBODY IS GOING TO ANSWER FOR THAT.
YOU'D THINK AFTER EVERYTHING I DID FOR LIEUTENANT PALMER AND THAT UNGRATEFUL BRAT DEAN...
...THE LEAST THEY COULD DO IS STAY WITH ME.
BUT NOBODY DOES. EXCEPT YOU.
I DON'T CARE FOR THE GOVERNMENT, FOR OBVIOUS REASONS. BUT I GUESS I SHOULD THANK YOU.
ONCE ALL YOUR FBI COMRADES THINK DEAN KILLED YOU...
THEY'LL FIND HIM. AND HE'LL HELP ME FIND BRAD.
AND THEN NOBODY CAN STOP US AGAIN.

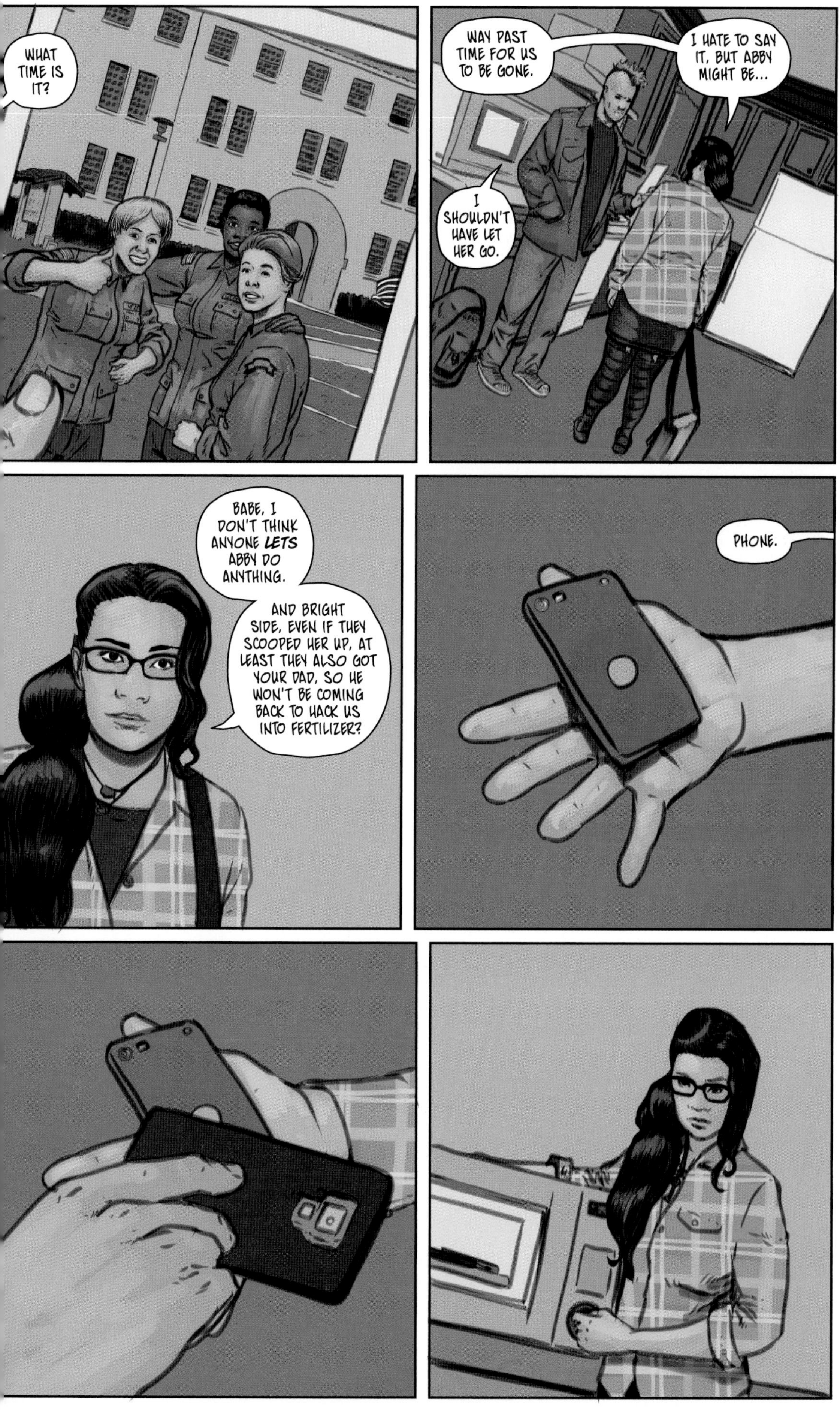

WHAT TIME IS IT?
WAY PAST TIME FOR US TO BE GONE.
I HATE TO SAY IT, BUT ABBY MIGHT BE...
I SHOULDN'T HAVE LET HER GO.
BABE, I DON'T THINK ANYONE LETS ABBY DO ANYTHING.
AND BRIGHT SIDE, EVEN IF THEY SCOOPED HER UP, AT LEAST THEY ALSO GOT YOUR DAD, SO HE WON'T BE COMING BACK TO HACK US INTO FERTILIZER?
PHONE.

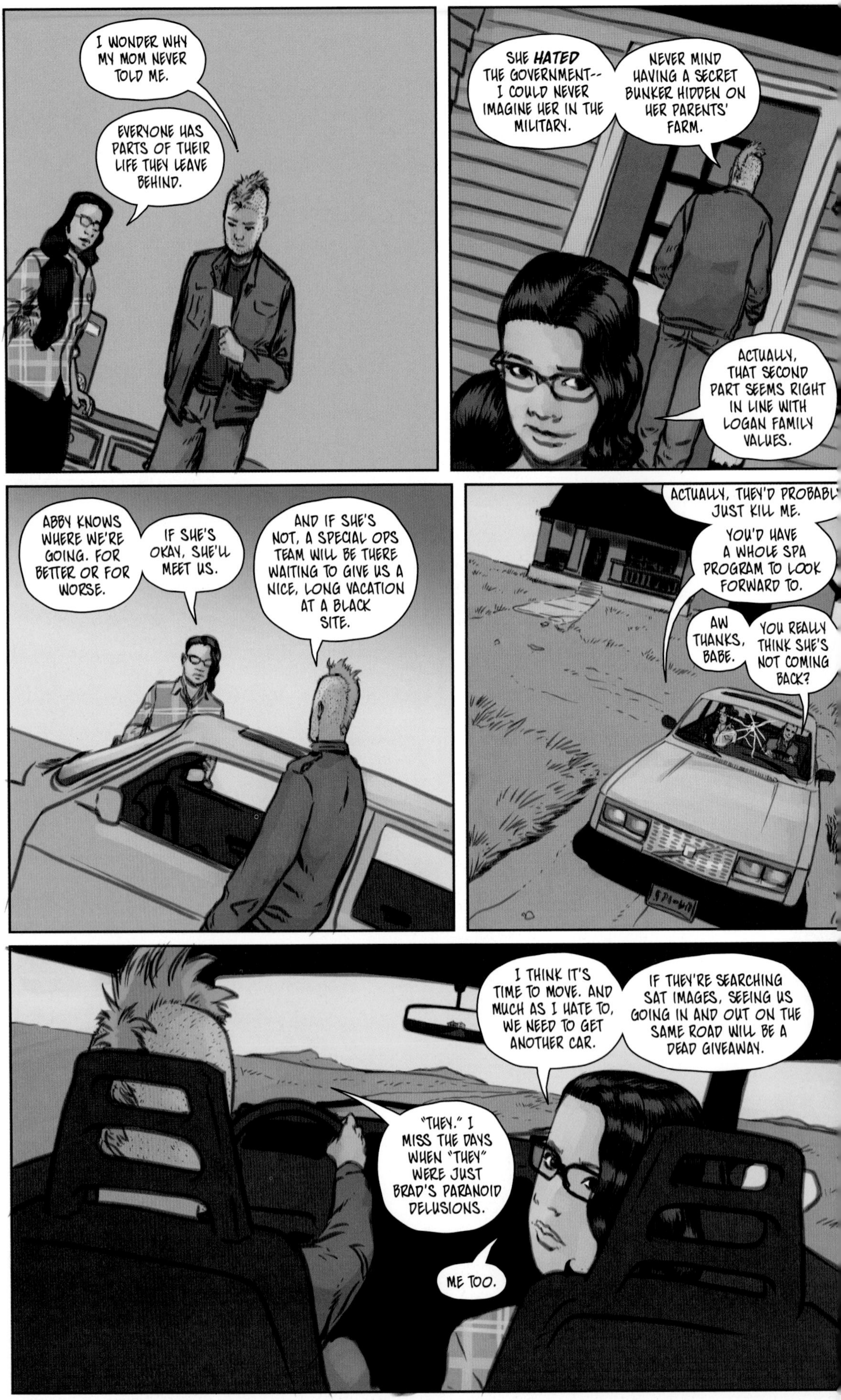
I WONDER WHY MY MOM NEVER TOLD ME.
EVERYONE HAS PARTS OF THEIR LIFE THEY LEAVE BEHIND.
SHE HATED THE GOVERNMENT--I COULD NEVER IMAGINE HER IN THE MILITARY.
NEVER MIND HAVING A SECRET BUNKER HIDDEN ON HER PARENTS' FARM.
ACTUALLY, THAT SECOND PART SEEMS RIGHT IN LINE WITH LOGAN FAMILY VALUES.
ABBY KNOWS WHERE WE'RE GOING. FOR BETTER OR FOR WORSE.
IF SHE'S OKAY, SHE'LL MEET US.
AND IF SHE'S NOT, A SPECIAL OPS TEAM WILL BE THERE WAITING TO GIVE US A NICE, LONG VACATION AT A BLACK SITE.
ACTUALLY, THEY'D PROBABL
JUST KILL ME.
YOU'D HAVE A WHOLE SPA PROGRAM TO LOOK FORWARD TO.
AW THANKS, BABE.
YOU REALLY THINK SHE'S NOT COMING BACK?
I THINK IT'S TIME TO MOVE. AND MUCH AS I HATE TO, WE NEED TO GET ANOTHER CAR.
IF THEY'RE SEARCHING SAT IMAGES, SEEING US GOING IN AND OUT ON THE SAME ROAD WILL BE A DEAD GIVEAWAY.
"THEY." I MISS THE DAYS WHEN "THEY" WERE JUST BRAD'S PARANOID DELUSIONS.
ME TOO.

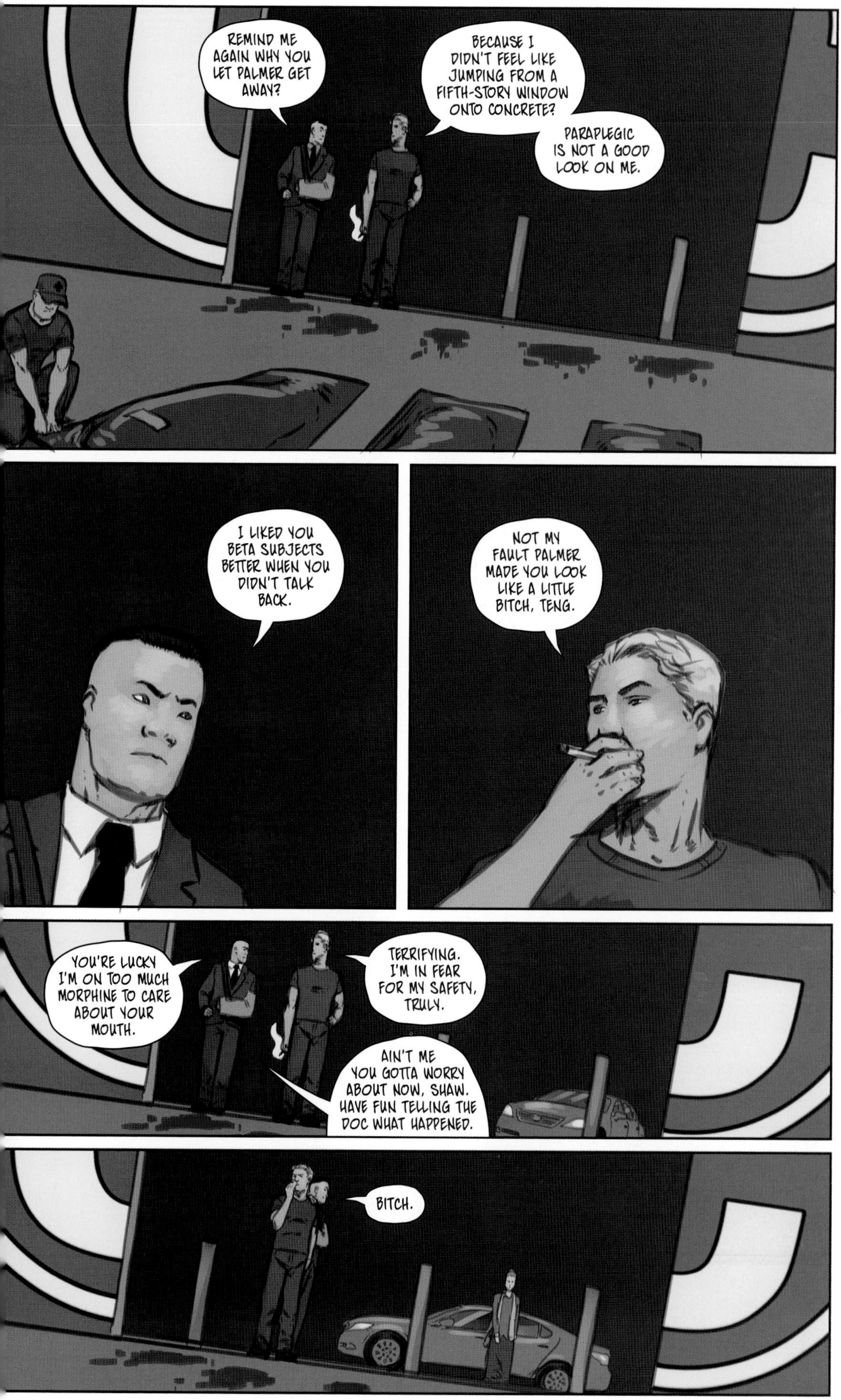
REMIND ME AGAIN WHY YOU LET PALMER GET AWAY?
BECAUSE I DIDN'T FEEL LIKE JUMPING FROM A FIFTH-STORY WINDOW ONTO CONCRETE?
PARAPLEGIC IS NOT A GOOD LOOK ON ME.
I LIKED YOU BETA SUBJECTS BETTER WHEN YOU DIDN'T TALK BACK.
NOT MY FAULT PALMER MADE YOU LOOK LIKE A LITTLE BITCH, TENG.
YOU'RE LUCKY I'M ON TOO MUCH MORPHINE TO CARE ABOUT YOUR MOUTH.
TERRIFYING. I'M IN FEAR FOR MY SAFETY, TRULY.
AIN'T ME YOU GOTTA WORRY ABOUT NOW, SHAW. HAVE FUN TELLING THE DOC WHAT HAPPENED.
BITCH.

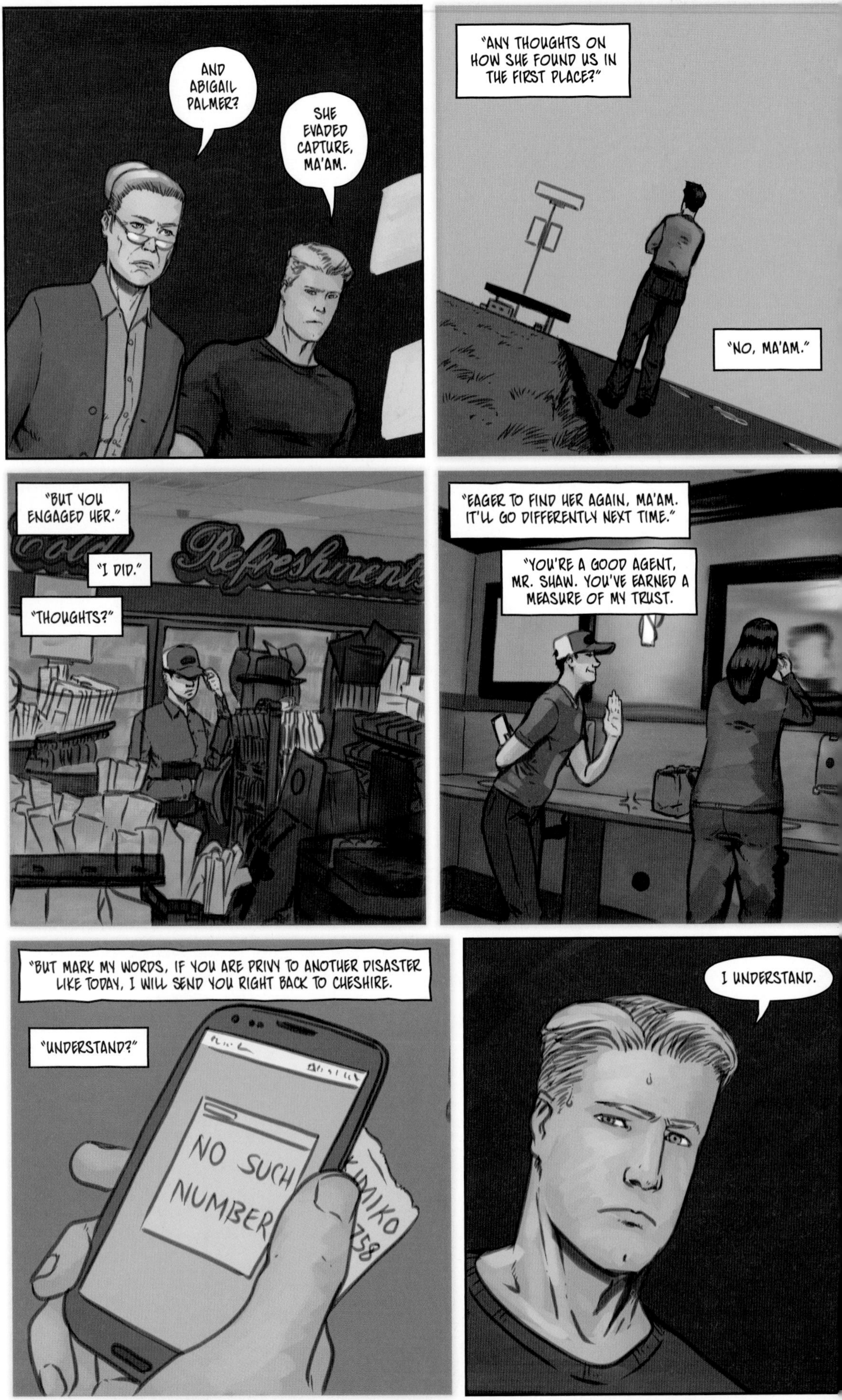
AND ABIGAIL PALMER?
SHE EVADED CAPTURE, MA'AM.
"ANY THOUGHTS ON HOW SHE FOUND US IN THE FIRST PLACE?"
"NO, MA'AM."
"BUT YOU ENGAGED HER."
"I DID."
"THOUGHTS?"
Refreshments
"EAGER TO FIND HER AGAIN, MA'AM. IT'LL GO DIFFERENTLY NEXT TIME."
"YOU'RE A GOOD AGENT, MR. SHAW. YOU'VE EARNED A MEASURE OF MY TRUST.
"BUT MARK MY WORDS, IF YOU ARE PRIVY TO ANOTHER DISASTER LIKE TODAY, I WILL SEND YOU RIGHT BACK TO CHESHIRE.
"UNDERSTAND?"
NO SUCH NUMBER
I UNDERSTAND.

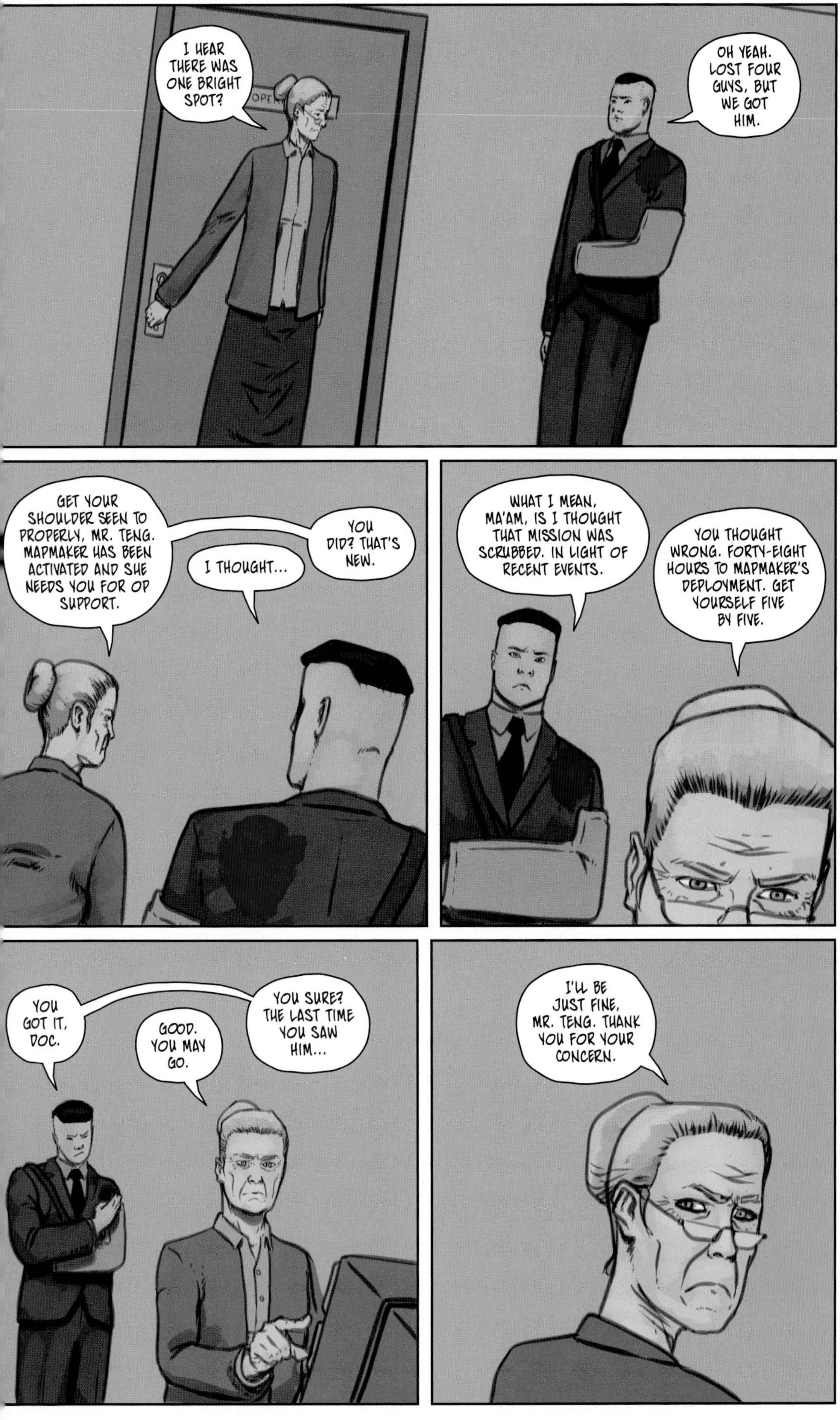
I HEAR THERE WAS ONE BRIGHT SPOT?
OH YEAH. LOST FOUR GUYS, BUT WE GOT HIM.
GET YOUR SHOULDER SEEN TO PROPERLY, MR. TENG. MAPMAKER HAS BEEN ACTIVATED AND SHE NEEDS YOU FOR OP SUPPORT.
YOU DID? THAT'S NEW.
I THOUGHT...
WHAT I MEAN, MA'AM, IS I THOUGHT THAT MISSION WAS SCRUBBED. IN LIGHT OF RECENT EVENTS.
YOU THOUGHT WRONG. FORTY-EIGHT HOURS TO MAPMAKER'S DEPLOYMENT. GET YOURSELF FIVE BY FIVE.
YOU GOT IT, DOC.
YOU SURE? THE LAST TIME YOU SAW HIM...
GOOD. YOU MAY GO.
I'LL BE JUST FINE, MR. TENG. THANK YOU FOR YOUR CONCERN.

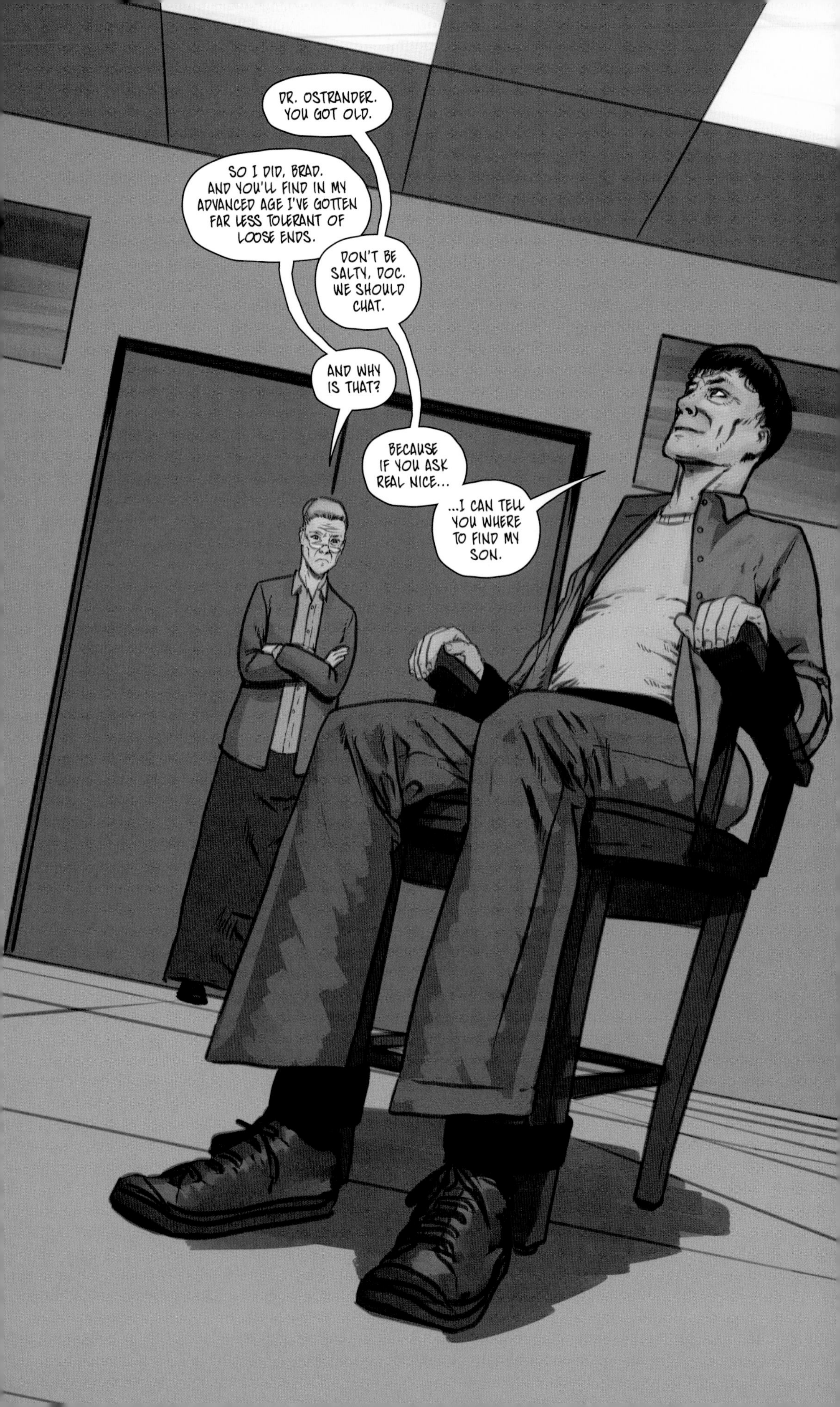
DR. OSTRANDER. YOU GOT OLD.
SO I DID, BRAD. AND YOU'LL FIND IN MY ADVANCED AGE I'VE GOTTEN FAR LESS TOLERANT OF LOOSE ENDS.
DON'T BE SALTY, DOC. WE SHOULD CHAT.
AND WHY IS THAT?
BECAUSE IF YOU ASK REAL NICE...
...I CAN TELL YOU WHERE TO FIND MY SON.

CHAPTER SEVEN

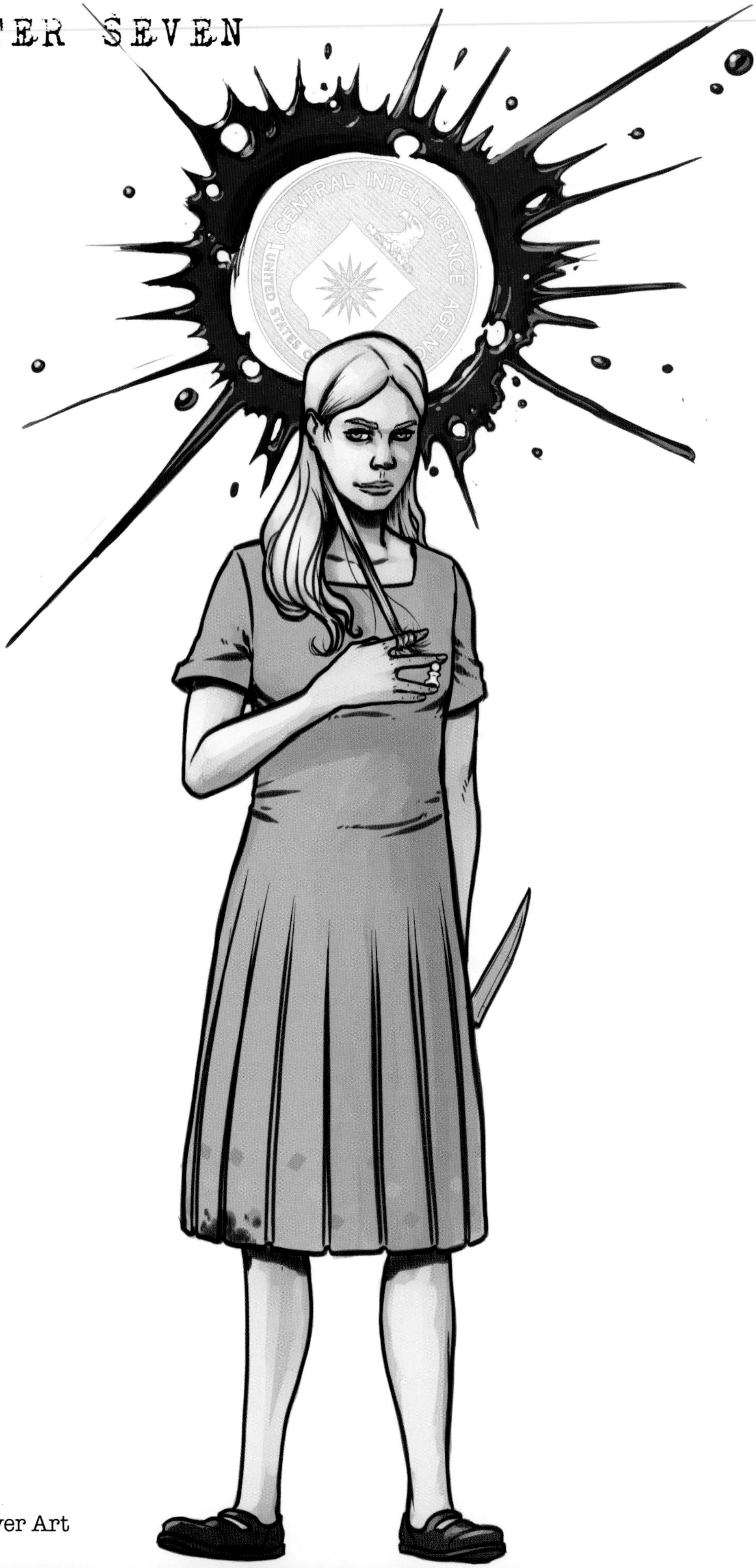
CENTRAL INTELLIGENCE AGENCY
UNITED STATES OF

Issue #7 Cover Art

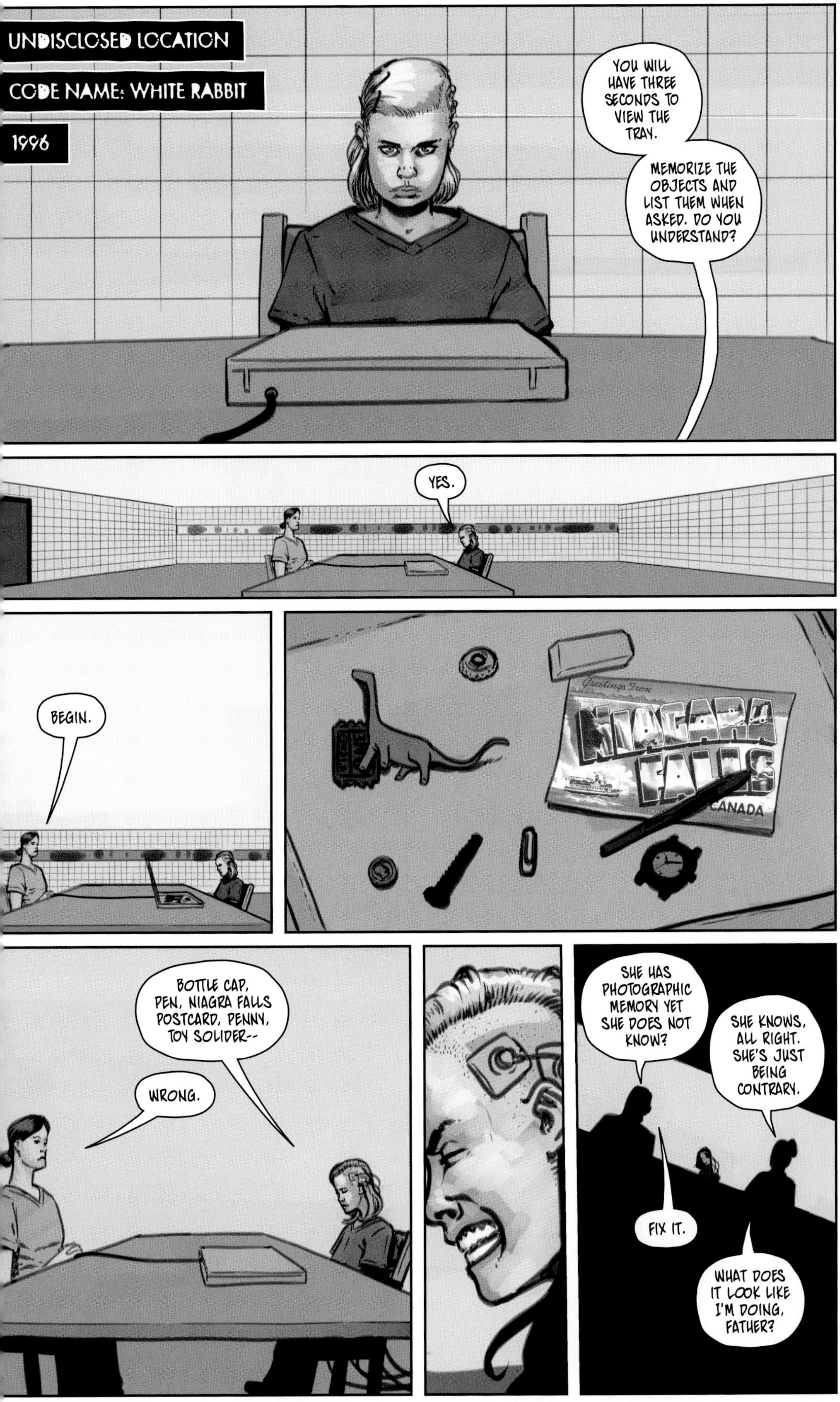

UNDISCLOSED LOCATION
CODE NAME: WHITE RABBIT
1996
YOU WILL HAVE THREE SECONDS TO VIEW THE TRAY.
MEMORIZE THE OBJECTS AND LIST THEM WHEN ASKED. DO YOU UNDERSTAND?
YES.
BEGIN.
Greetings from NIAGARA FALLS CANADA
BOTTLE CAP, PEN, NIAGRA FALLS POSTCARD, PENNY, TOY SOLIDER--
WRONG.
SHE HAS PHOTOGRAPHIC MEMORY YET SHE DOES NOT KNOW?
SHE KNOWS, ALL RIGHT. SHE'S JUST BEING CONTRARY.
FIX IT.
WHAT DOES IT LOOK LIKE I'M DOING, FATHER?

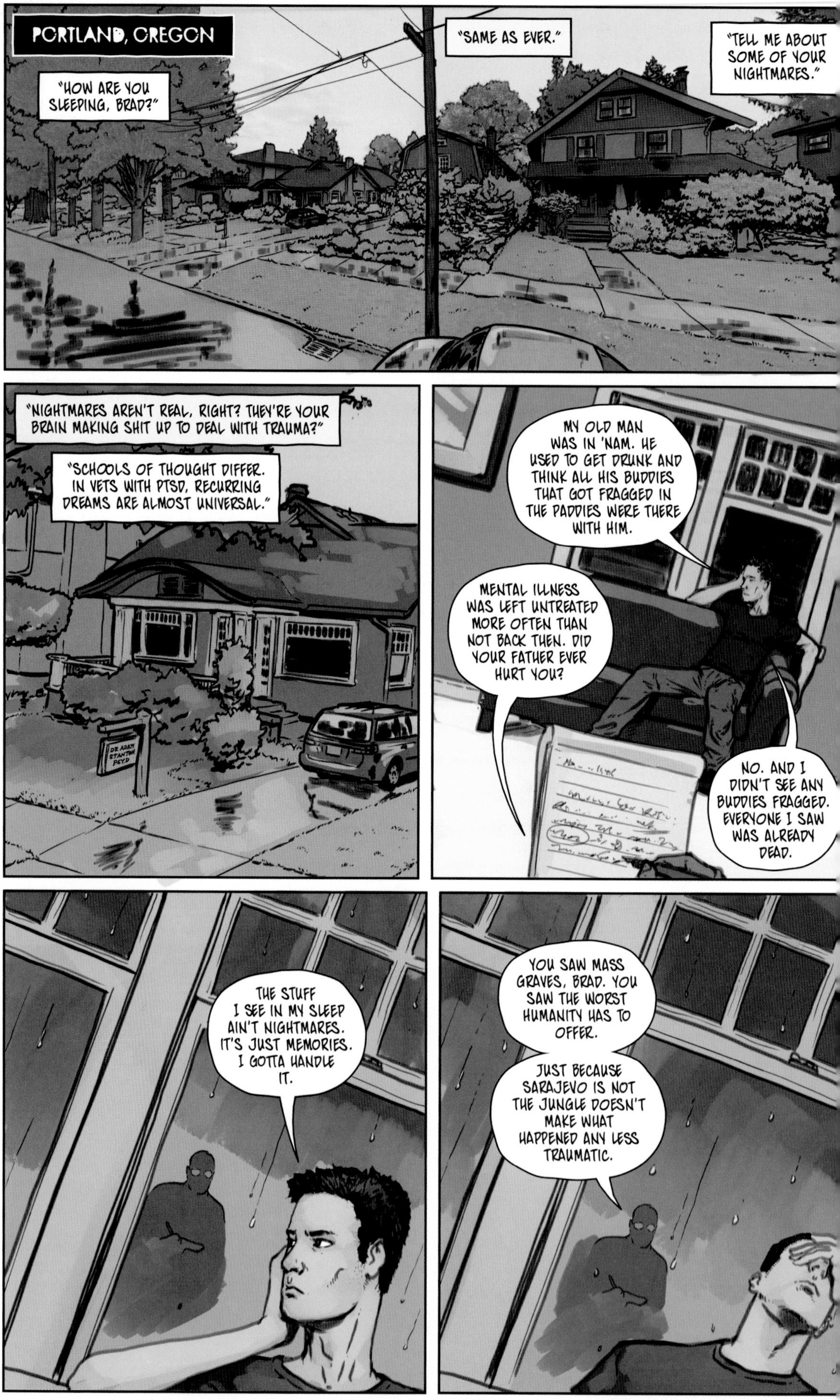
PORTLAND, OREGON
"HOW ARE YOU SLEEPING, BRAD?"
"SAME AS EVER."
"TELL ME ABOUT SOME OF YOUR NIGHTMARES."
"NIGHTMARES AREN'T REAL, RIGHT? THEY'RE YOUR BRAIN MAKING SHIT UP TO DEAL WITH TRAUMA?"
"SCHOOLS OF THOUGHT DIFFER. IN VETS WITH PTSD, RECURRING DREAMS ARE ALMOST UNIVERSAL."
DR ADAM STANTON PSY.D
MY OLD MAN WAS IN 'NAM. HE USED TO GET DRUNK AND THINK ALL HIS BUDDIES THAT GOT FRAGGED IN THE PADDIES WERE THERE WITH HIM.
MENTAL ILLNESS WAS LEFT UNTREATED MORE OFTEN THAN NOT BACK THEN. DID YOUR FATHER EVER HURT YOU?
NO. AND I DIDN'T SEE ANY BUDDIES FRAGGED. EVERYONE I SAW WAS ALREADY DEAD.
THE STUFF I SEE IN MY SLEEP AIN'T NIGHTMARES. IT'S JUST MEMORIES. I GOTTA HANDLE IT.
YOU SAW MASS GRAVES, BRAD. YOU SAW THE WORST HUMANITY HAS TO OFFER.
JUST BECAUSE SARAJEVO IS NOT THE JUNGLE DOESN'T MAKE WHAT HAPPENED ANY LESS TRAUMATIC.

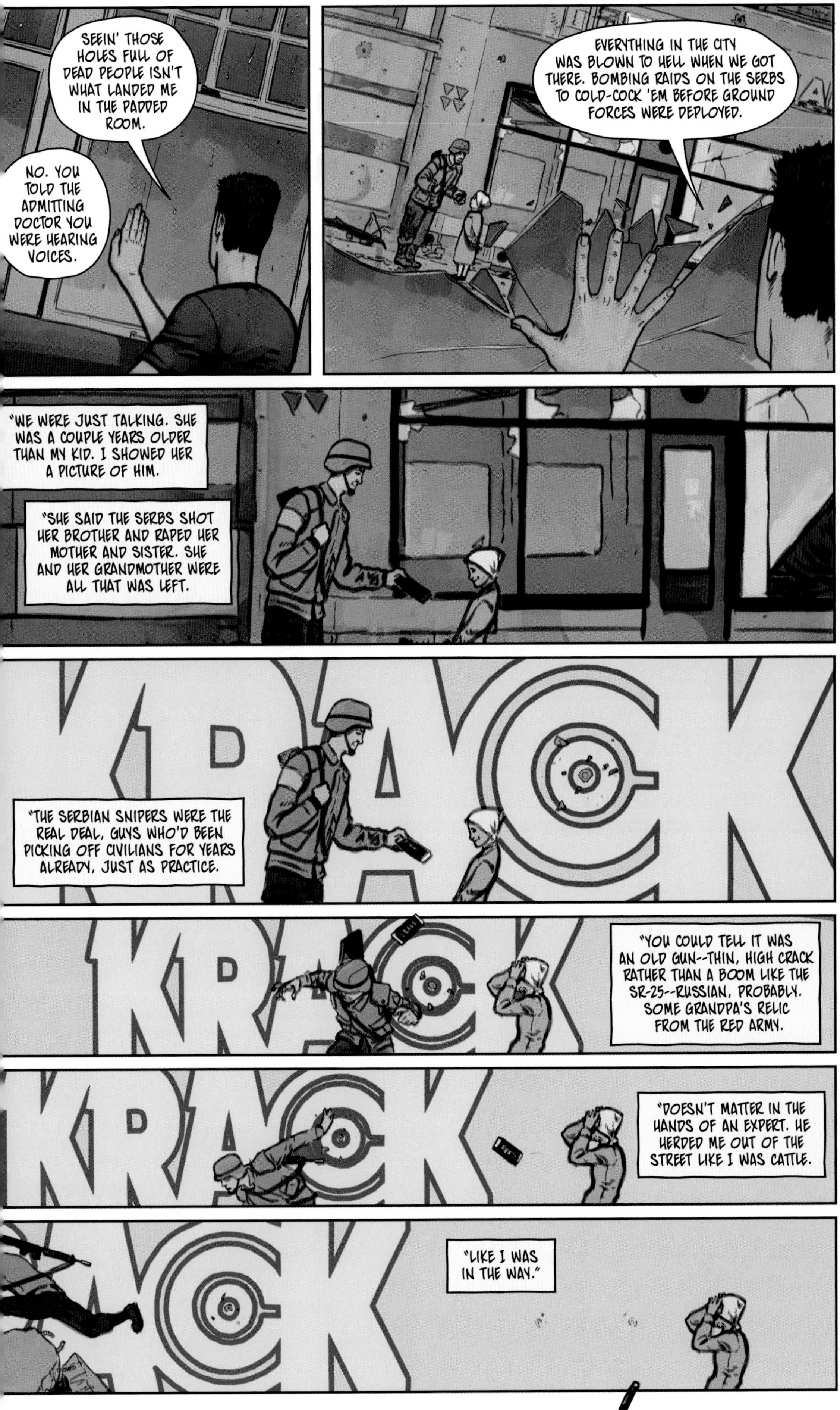
SEEIN' THOSE HOLES FULL OF DEAD PEOPLE ISN'T WHAT LANDED ME IN THE PADDED ROOM.
NO. YOU TOLD THE ADMITTING DOCTOR YOU WERE HEARING VOICES.
EVERYTHING IN THE CITY WAS BLOWN TO HELL WHEN WE GOT THERE. BOMBING RAIDS ON THE SERBS TO COLD-COCK 'EM BEFORE GROUND FORCES WERE DEPLOYED.
"WE WERE JUST TALKING. SHE WAS A COUPLE YEARS OLDER THAN MY KID. I SHOWED HER A PICTURE OF HIM.
"SHE SAID THE SERBS SHOT HER BROTHER AND RAPED HER MOTHER AND SISTER. SHE AND HER GRANDMOTHER WERE ALL THAT WAS LEFT.
KRACK
"THE SERBIAN SNIPERS WERE THE REAL DEAL, GUYS WHO'D BEEN PICKING OFF CIVILIANS FOR YEARS ALREADY, JUST AS PRACTICE.
KRACK
"YOU COULD TELL IT WAS AN OLD GUN--THIN, HIGH CRACK RATHER THAN A BOOM LIKE THE SR-25--RUSSIAN, PROBABLY. SOME GRANDPA'S RELIC FROM THE RED ARMY.
KRACK
"DOESN'T MATTER IN THE HANDS OF AN EXPERT. HE HERDED ME OUT OF THE STREET LIKE I WAS CATTLE.
"LIKE I WAS IN THE WAY."

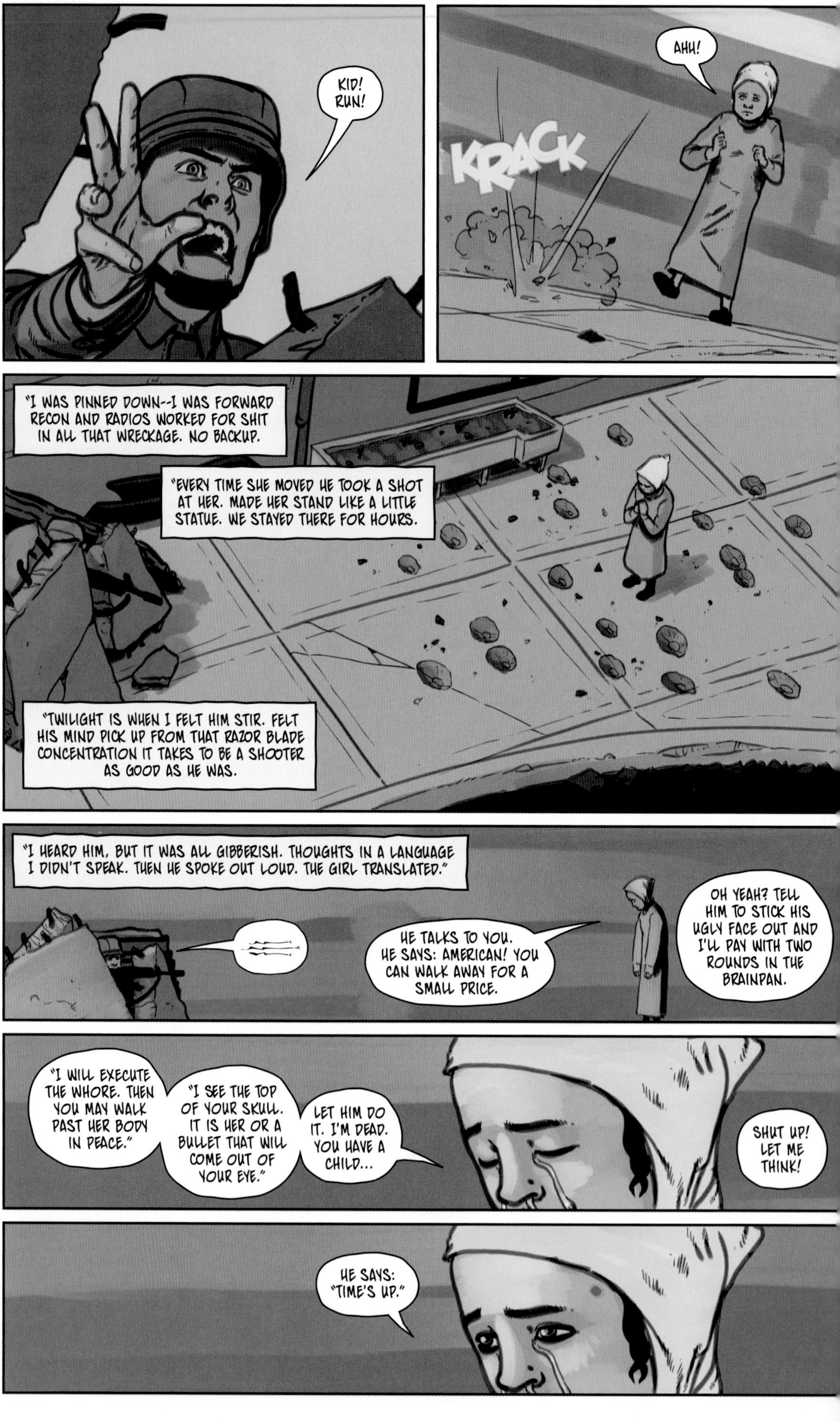
KID! RUN!
KRACK
AHH!
"I WAS PINNED DOWN--I WAS FORWARD RECON AND RADIOS WORKED FOR SHIT IN ALL THAT WRECKAGE. NO BACKUP.
"EVERY TIME SHE MOVED HE TOOK A SHOT AT HER. MADE HER STAND LIKE A LITTLE STATUE. WE STAYED THERE FOR HOURS.
"TWILIGHT IS WHEN I FELT HIM STIR. FELT HIS MIND PICK UP FROM THAT RAZOR BLADE CONCENTRATION IT TAKES TO BE A SHOOTER AS GOOD AS HE WAS.
"I HEARD HIM, BUT IT WAS ALL GIBBERISH. THOUGHTS IN A LANGUAGE I DIDN'T SPEAK. THEN HE SPOKE OUT LOUD. THE GIRL TRANSLATED."
HE TALKS TO YOU. HE SAYS: AMERICAN! YOU CAN WALK AWAY FOR A SMALL PRICE.
OH YEAH? TELL HIM TO STICK HIS UGLY FACE OUT AND I'LL PAY WITH TWO ROUNDS IN THE BRAINPAN.
"I WILL EXECUTE THE WHORE. THEN YOU MAY WALK PAST HER BODY IN PEACE."
"I SEE THE TOP OF YOUR SKULL. IT IS HER OR A BULLET THAT WILL COME OUT OF YOUR EYE."
LET HIM DO IT. I'M DEAD. YOU HAVE A CHILD...
SHUT UP! LET ME THINK!
HE SAYS: "TIME'S UP."

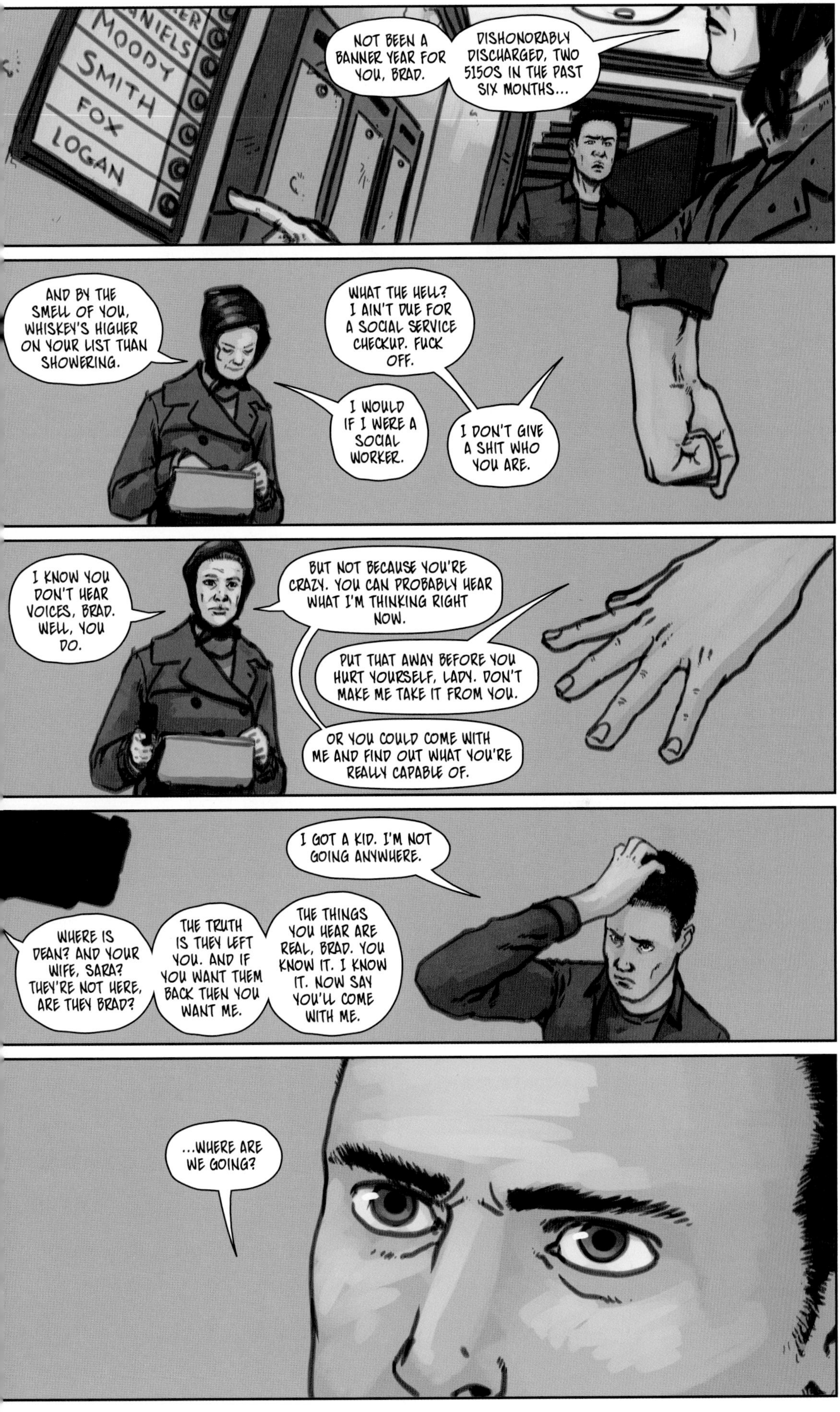
NIELS
MOODY
SMITH
FOX
LOGAN
NOT BEEN A BANNER YEAR FOR YOU, BRAD.
DISHONORABLY DISCHARGED, TWO 5150S IN THE PAST SIX MONTHS...
AND BY THE SMELL OF YOU, WHISKEY'S HIGHER ON YOUR LIST THAN SHOWERING.
WHAT THE HELL? I AIN'T DUE FOR A SOCIAL SERVICE CHECKUP. FUCK OFF.
I WOULD IF I WERE A SOCIAL WORKER.
I DON'T GIVE A SHIT WHO YOU ARE.
I KNOW YOU DON'T HEAR VOICES, BRAD. WELL, YOU DO.
BUT NOT BECAUSE YOU'RE CRAZY. YOU CAN PROBABLY HEAR WHAT I'M THINKING RIGHT NOW.
PUT THAT AWAY BEFORE YOU HURT YOURSELF, LADY. DON'T MAKE ME TAKE IT FROM YOU.
OR YOU COULD COME WITH ME AND FIND OUT WHAT YOU'RE REALLY CAPABLE OF.
I GOT A KID. I'M NOT GOING ANYWHERE.
WHERE IS DEAN? AND YOUR WIFE, SARA? THEY'RE NOT HERE, ARE THEY BRAD?
THE TRUTH IS THEY LEFT YOU. AND IF YOU WANT THEM BACK THEN YOU WANT ME.
THE THINGS YOU HEAR ARE REAL, BRAD. YOU KNOW IT. I KNOW IT. NOW SAY YOU'LL COME WITH ME.
...WHERE ARE WE GOING?

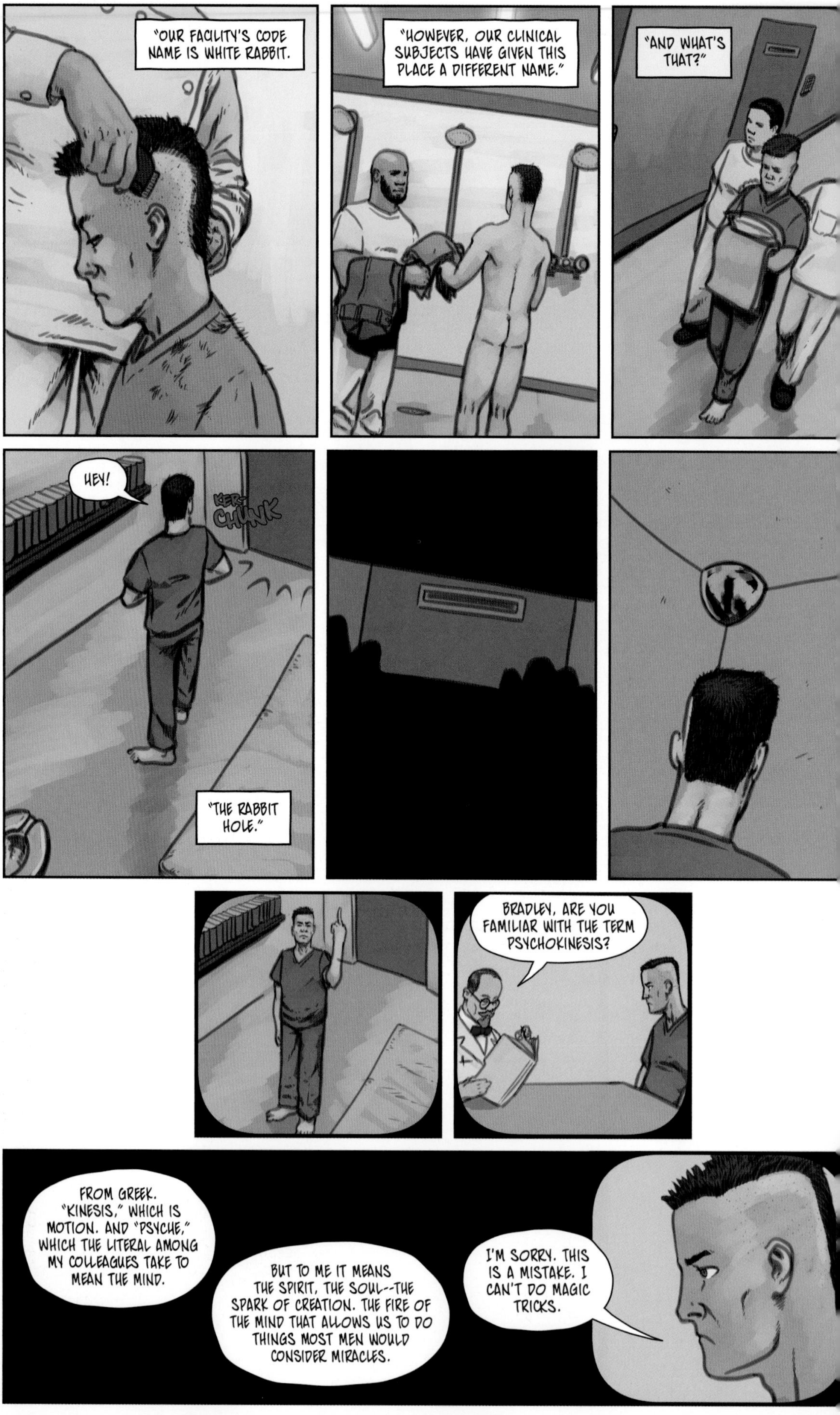
"OUR FACILITY'S CODE NAME IS WHITE RABBIT.
"HOWEVER, OUR CLINICAL SUBJECTS HAVE GIVEN THIS PLACE A DIFFERENT NAME."
"AND WHAT'S THAT?"
HEY!
KER-CHUNK
"THE RABBIT HOLE."
BRADLEY, ARE YOU FAMILIAR WITH THE TERM PSYCHOKINESIS?
FROM GREEK. "KINESIS," WHICH IS MOTION. AND "PSYCHE," WHICH THE LITERAL AMONG MY COLLEAGUES TAKE TO MEAN THE MIND.
BUT TO ME IT MEANS THE SPIRIT, THE SOUL--THE SPARK OF CREATION. THE FIRE OF THE MIND THAT ALLOWS US TO DO THINGS MOST MEN WOULD CONSIDER MIRACLES.
I'M SORRY. THIS IS A MISTAKE. I CAN'T DO MAGIC TRICKS.

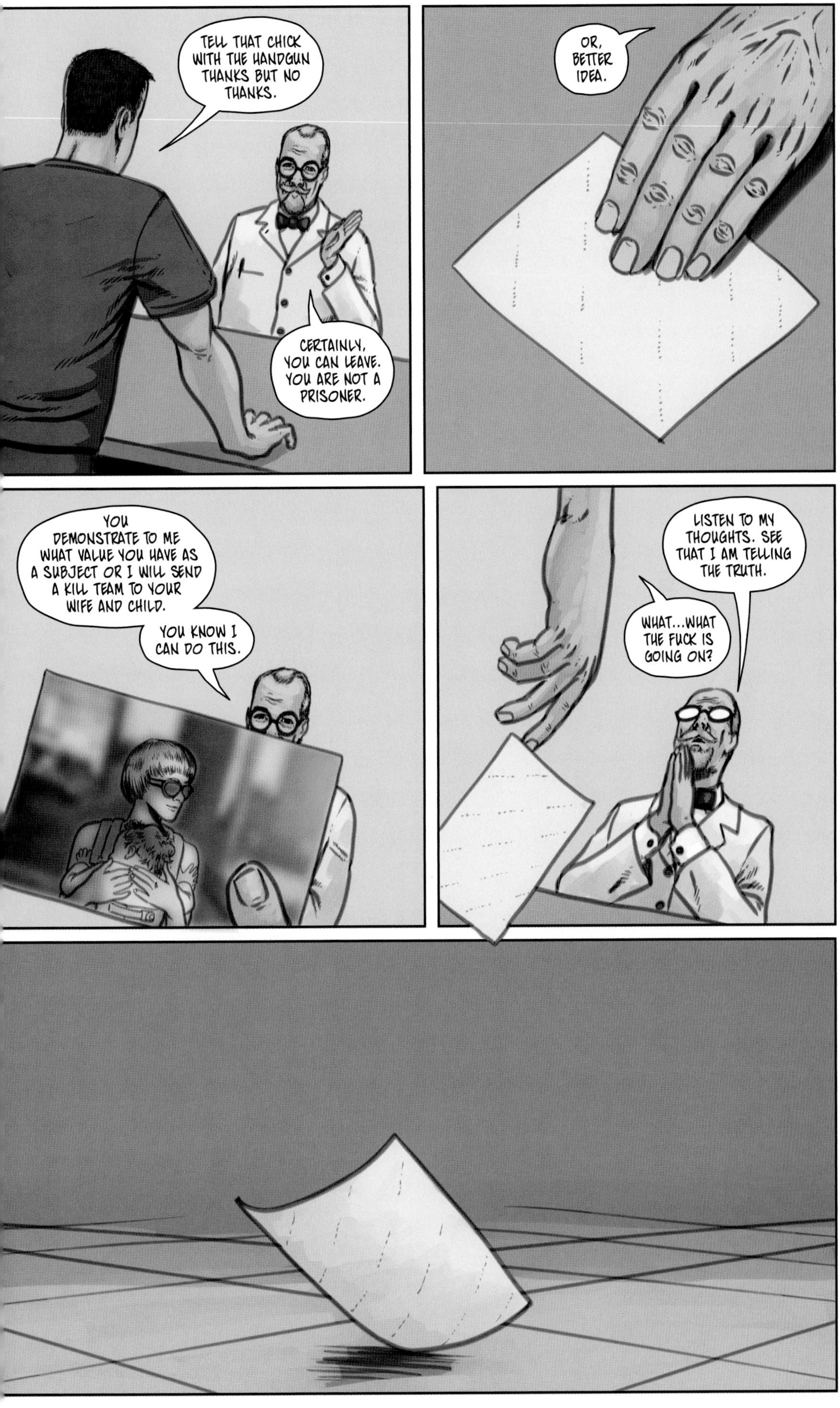

TELL THAT CHICK WITH THE HANDGUN THANKS BUT NO THANKS.
CERTAINLY, YOU CAN LEAVE. YOU ARE NOT A PRISONER.
OR, BETTER IDEA.
YOU DEMONSTRATE TO ME WHAT VALUE YOU HAVE AS A SUBJECT OR I WILL SEND A KILL TEAM TO YOUR WIFE AND CHILD.
YOU KNOW I CAN DO THIS.
LISTEN TO MY THOUGHTS. SEE THAT I AM TELLING THE TRUTH.
WHAT...WHAT THE FUCK IS GOING ON?

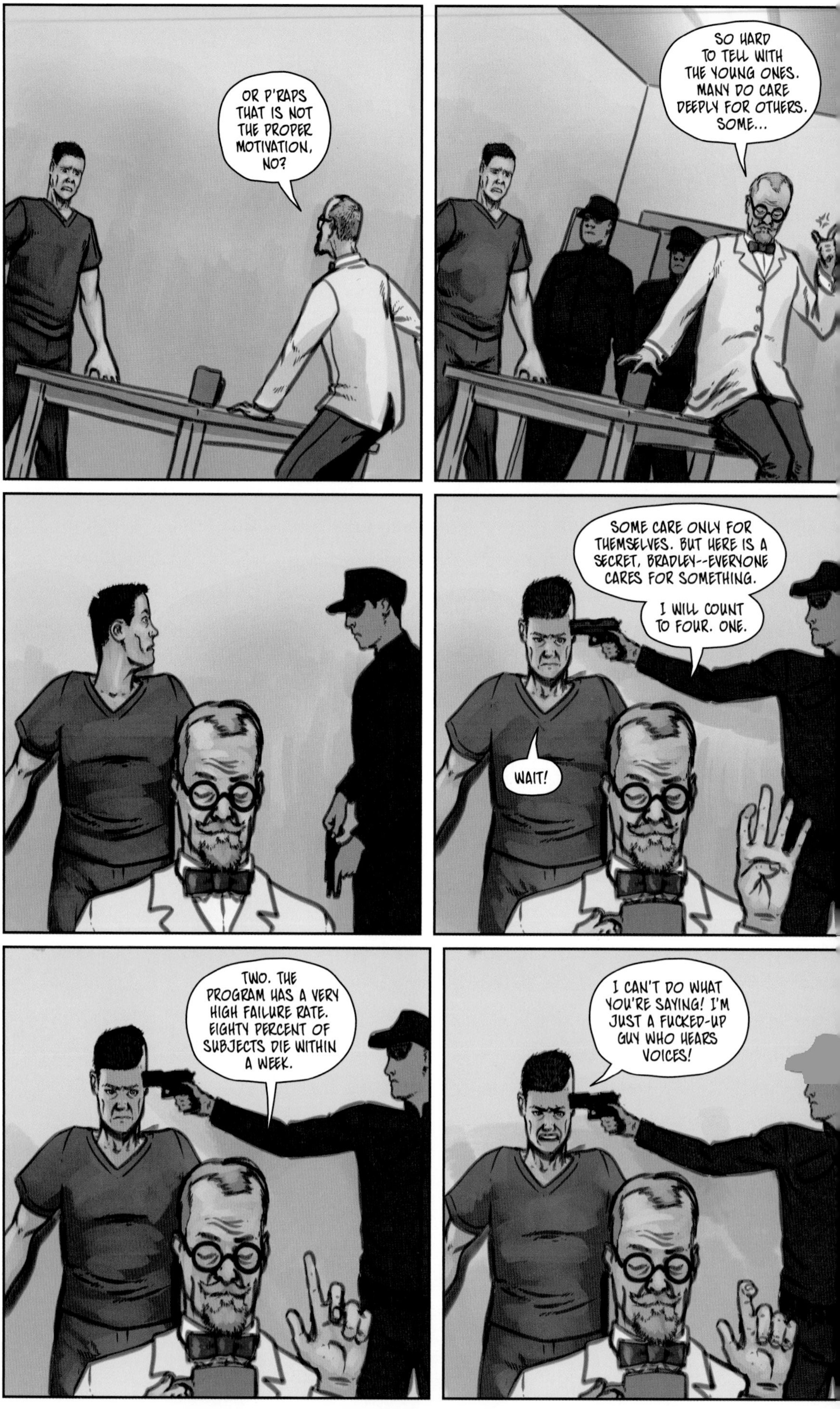
OR P'RAPS THAT IS NOT THE PROPER MOTIVATION, NO?
SO HARD TO TELL WITH THE YOUNG ONES. MANY DO CARE DEEPLY FOR OTHERS. SOME...
SOME CARE ONLY FOR THEMSELVES. BUT HERE IS A SECRET, BRADLEY--EVERYONE CARES FOR SOMETHING.
I WILL COUNT TO FOUR. ONE.
WAIT!
TWO. THE PROGRAM HAS A VERY HIGH FAILURE RATE. EIGHTY PERCENT OF SUBJECTS DIE WITHIN A WEEK.
I CAN'T DO WHAT YOU'RE SAYING! I'M JUST A FUCKED-UP GUY WHO HEARS VOICES!

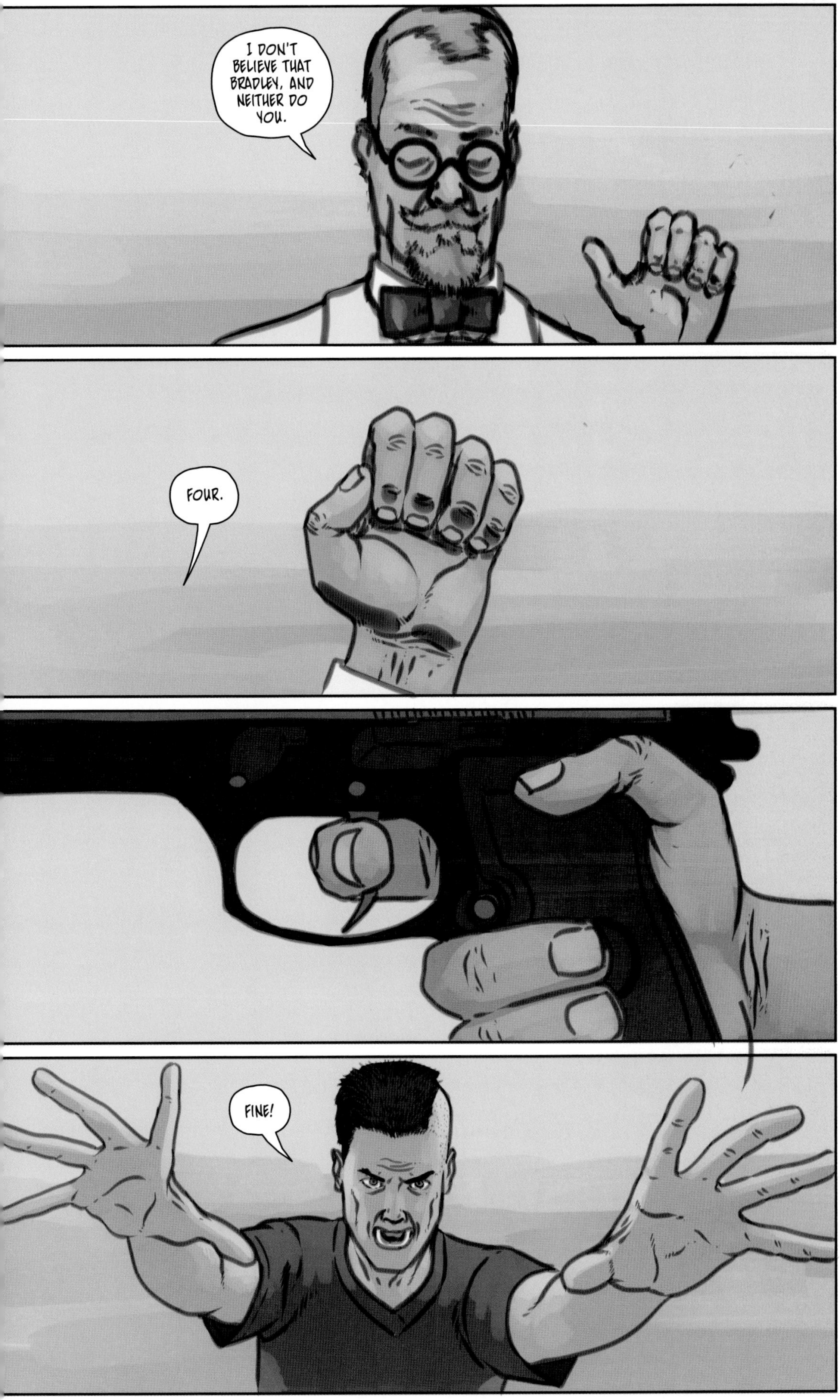
I DON'T BELIEVE THAT BRADLEY, AND NEITHER DO YOU.
FOUR.
FINE!

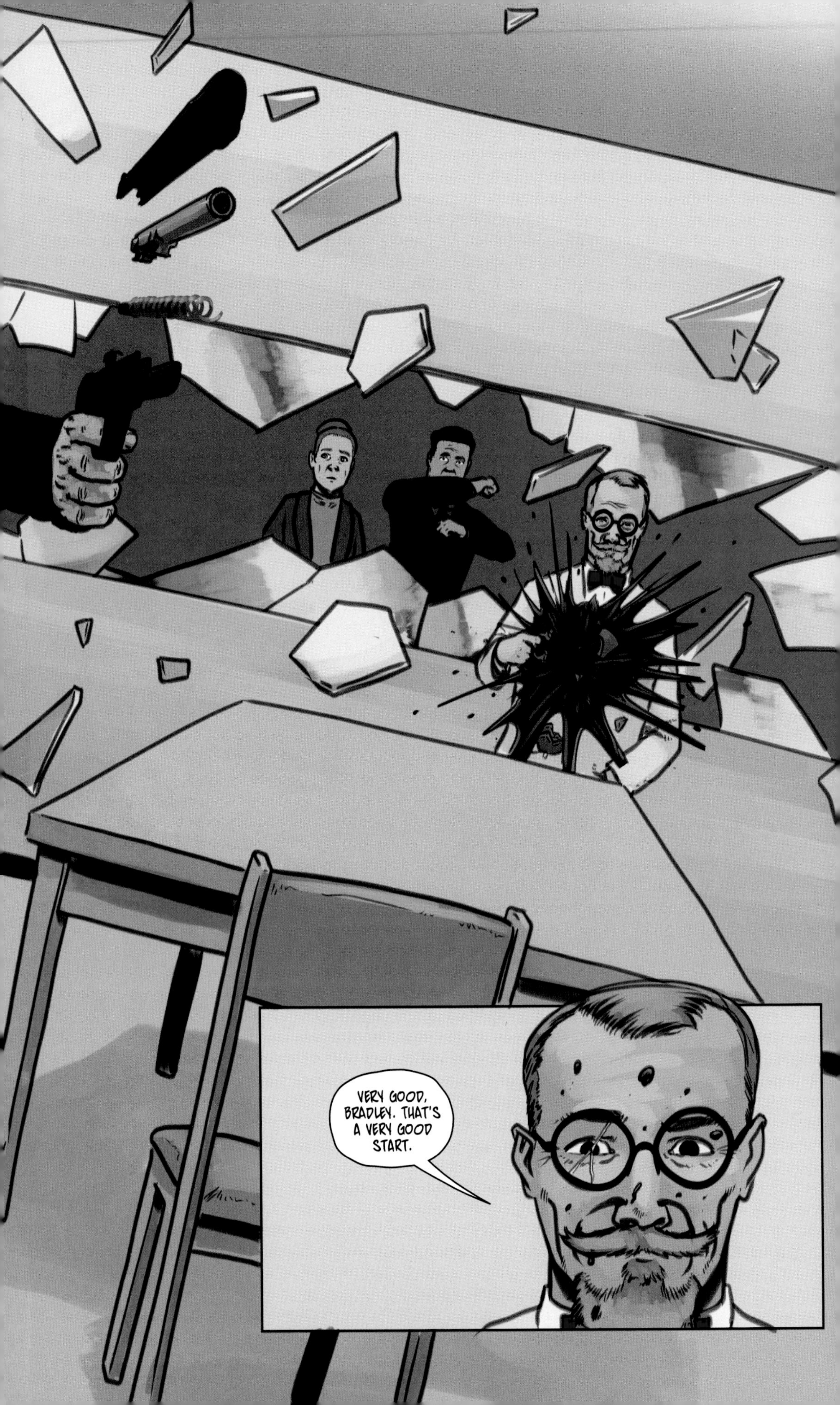
VERY GOOD, BRADLEY. THAT'S A VERY GOOD START.

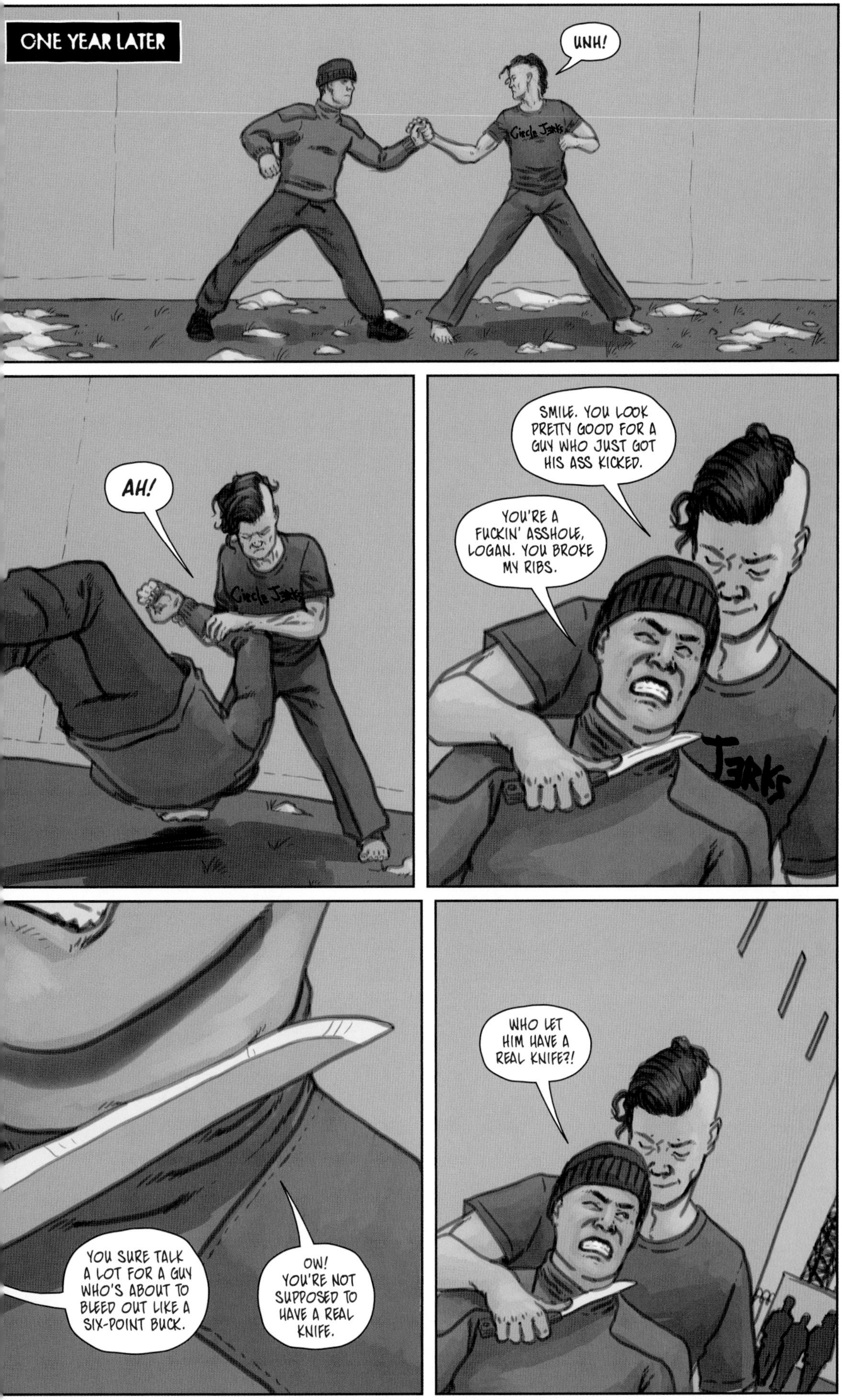

ONE YEAR LATER
UNH!
AH!
SMILE. YOU LOOK PRETTY GOOD FOR A GUY WHO JUST GOT HIS ASS KICKED.
YOU'RE A FUCKIN' ASSHOLE, LOGAN. YOU BROKE MY RIBS.
YOU SURE TALK A LOT FOR A GUY WHO'S ABOUT TO BLEED OUT LIKE A SIX-POINT BUCK.
OW! YOU'RE NOT SUPPOSED TO HAVE A REAL KNIFE.
WHO LET HIM HAVE A REAL KNIFE?!

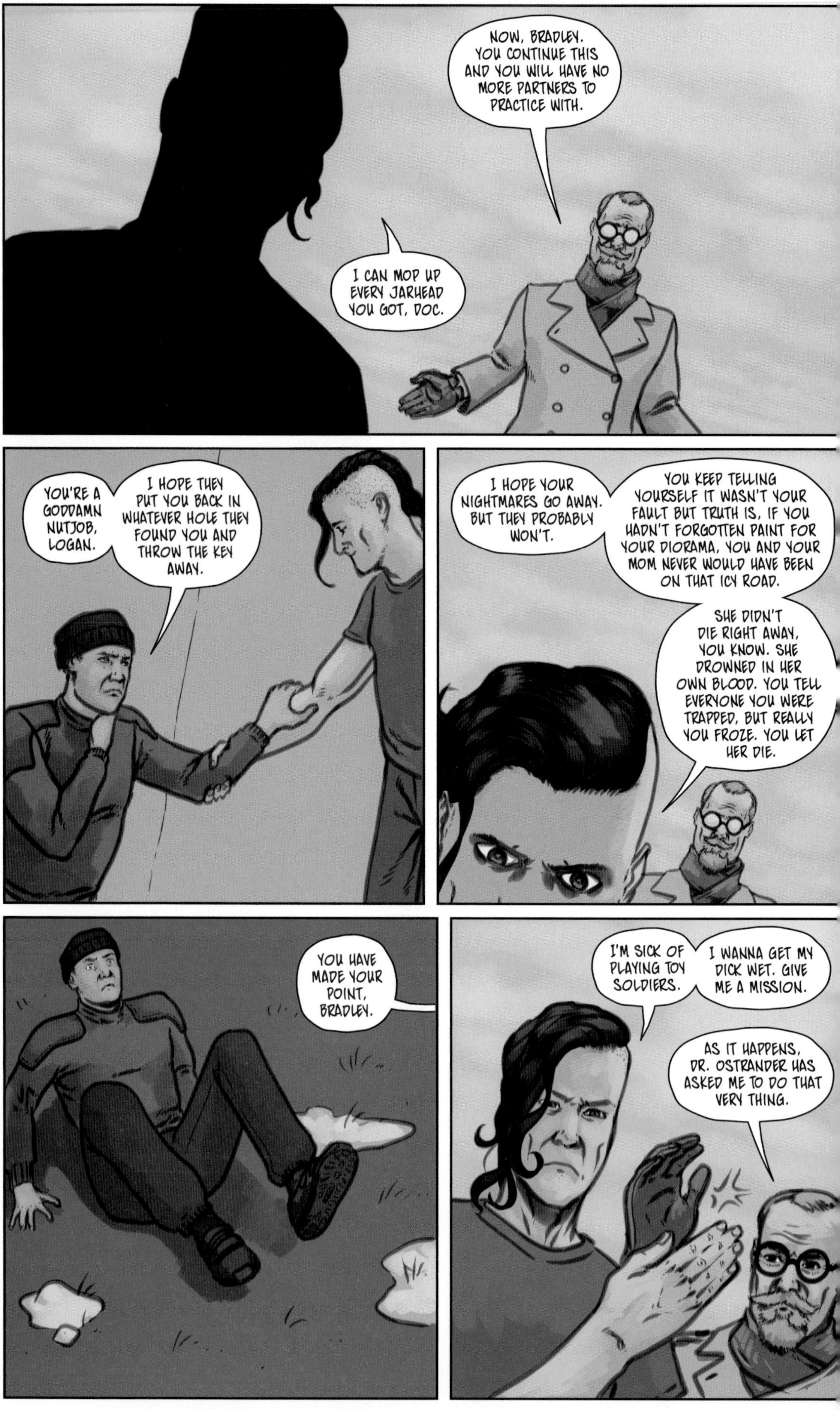
NOW, BRADLEY. YOU CONTINUE THIS AND YOU WILL HAVE NO MORE PARTNERS TO PRACTICE WITH.
I CAN MOP UP EVERY JARHEAD YOU GOT, DOC.
YOU'RE A GODDAMN NUTJOB, LOGAN.
I HOPE THEY PUT YOU BACK IN WHATEVER HOLE THEY FOUND YOU AND THROW THE KEY AWAY.
I HOPE YOUR NIGHTMARES GO AWAY. BUT THEY PROBABLY WON'T.
YOU KEEP TELLING YOURSELF IT WASN'T YOUR FAULT BUT TRUTH IS, IF YOU HADN'T FORGOTTEN PAINT FOR YOUR DIORAMA, YOU AND YOUR MOM NEVER WOULD HAVE BEEN ON THAT ICY ROAD.
SHE DIDN'T DIE RIGHT AWAY, YOU KNOW. SHE DROWNED IN HER OWN BLOOD. YOU TELL EVERYONE YOU WERE TRAPPED, BUT REALLY YOU FROZE. YOU LET HER DIE.
YOU HAVE MADE YOUR POINT, BRADLEY.
I'M SICK OF PLAYING TOY SOLDIERS.
I WANNA GET MY DICK WET. GIVE ME A MISSION.
AS IT HAPPENS, DR. OSTRANDER HAS ASKED ME TO DO THAT VERY THING.

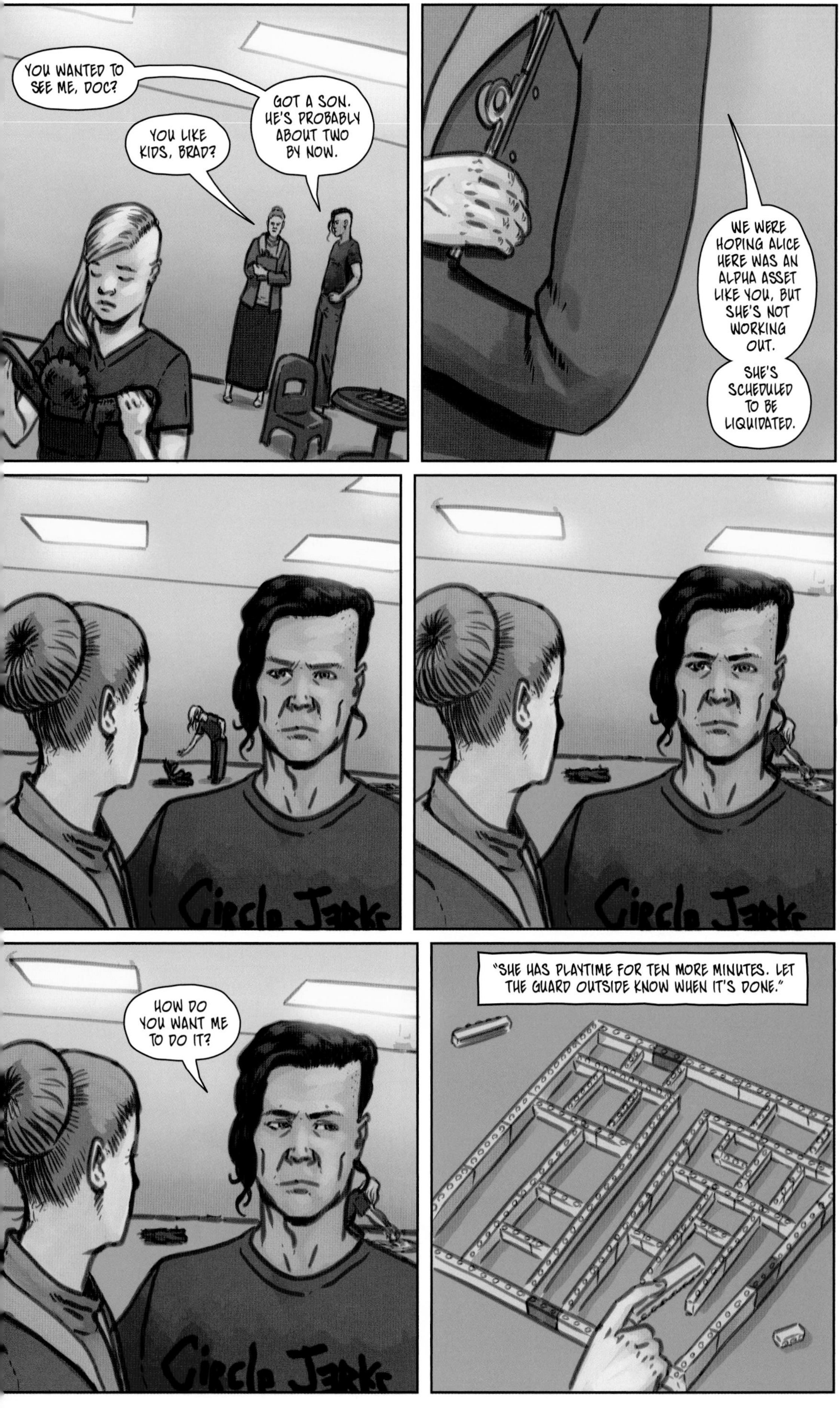

YOU WANTED TO SEE ME, DOC?
YOU LIKE KIDS, BRAD?
GOT A SON. HE'S PROBABLY ABOUT TWO BY NOW.
WE WERE HOPING ALICE HERE WAS AN ALPHA ASSET LIKE YOU, BUT SHE'S NOT WORKING OUT.
SHE'S SCHEDULED TO BE LIQUIDATED.
Circle Jerks
Circle Jerks
HOW DO YOU WANT ME TO DO IT?
Circle Jerks
"SHE HAS PLAYTIME FOR TEN MORE MINUTES. LET THE GUARD OUTSIDE KNOW WHEN IT'S DONE."

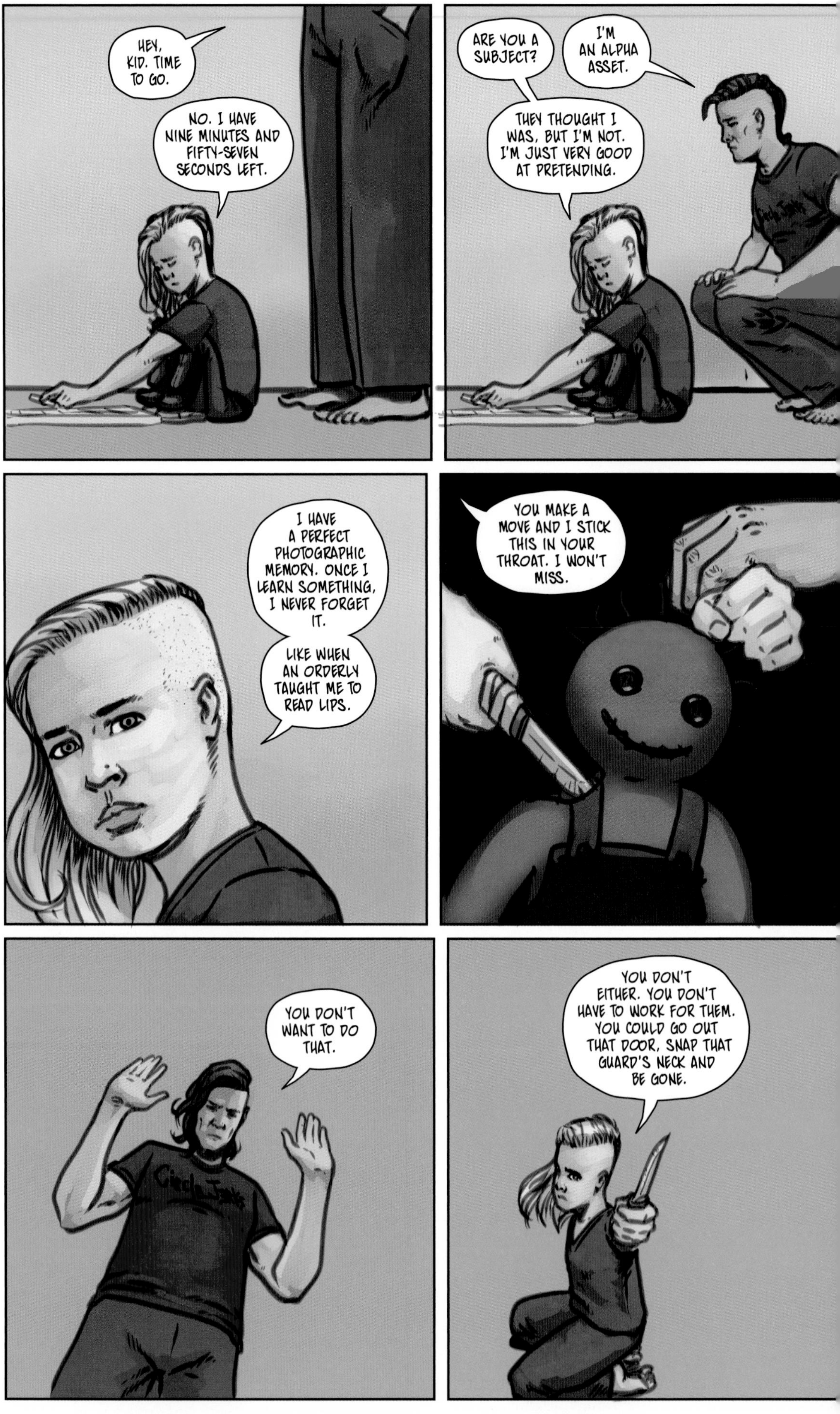
HEY, KID. TIME TO GO.
NO. I HAVE NINE MINUTES AND FIFTY-SEVEN SECONDS LEFT.
ARE YOU A SUBJECT?
I'M AN ALPHA ASSET.
THEY THOUGHT I WAS, BUT I'M NOT. I'M JUST VERY GOOD AT PRETENDING.
I HAVE A PERFECT PHOTOGRAPHIC MEMORY. ONCE I LEARN SOMETHING, I NEVER FORGET IT.
LIKE WHEN AN ORDERLY TAUGHT ME TO READ LIPS.
YOU MAKE A MOVE AND I STICK THIS IN YOUR THROAT. I WON'T MISS.
YOU DON'T WANT TO DO THAT.
YOU DON'T EITHER. YOU DON'T HAVE TO WORK FOR THEM. YOU COULD GO OUT THAT DOOR, SNAP THAT GUARD'S NECK AND BE GONE.

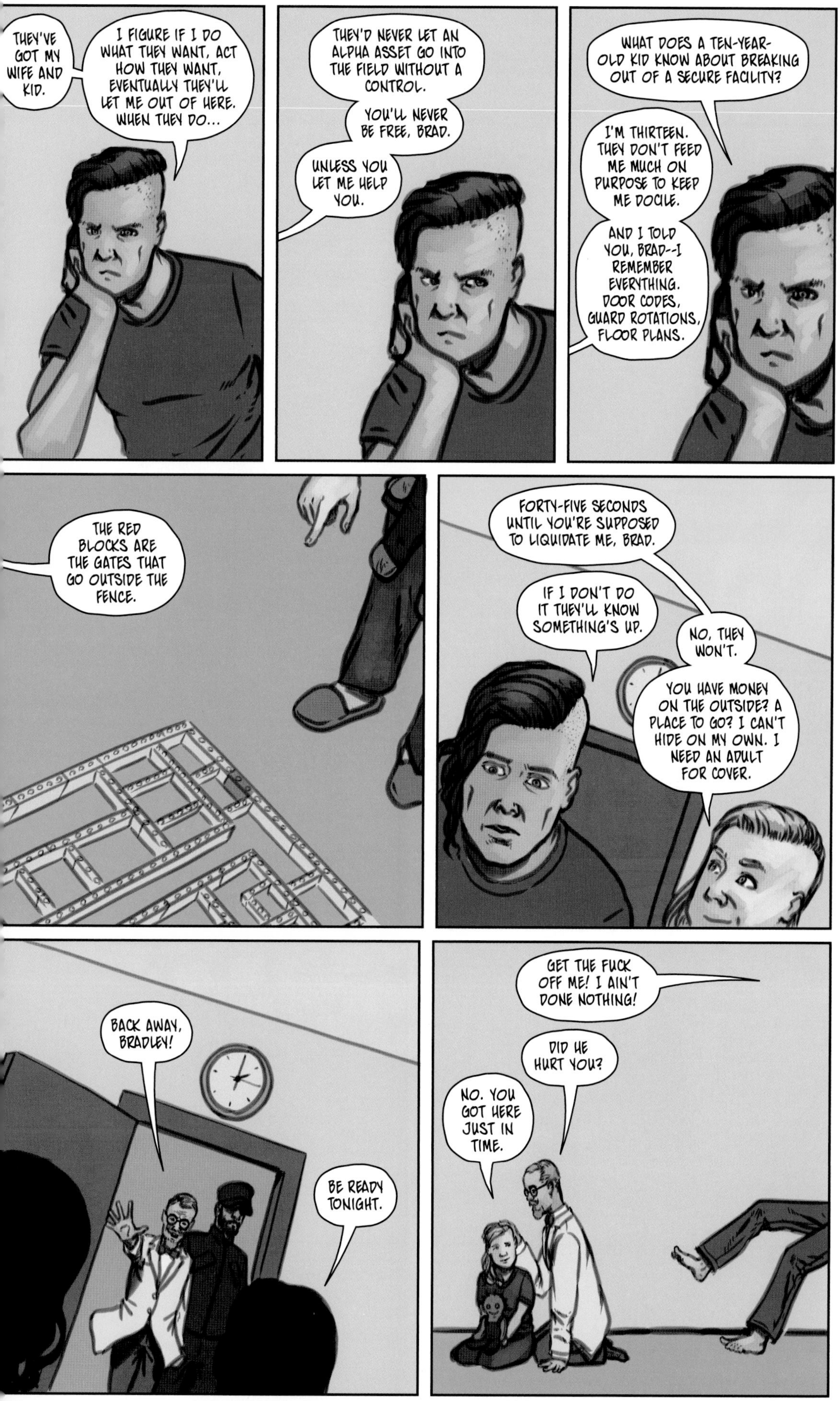
THEY'VE GOT MY WIFE AND KID.
I FIGURE IF I DO WHAT THEY WANT, ACT HOW THEY WANT, EVENTUALLY THEY'LL LET ME OUT OF HERE. WHEN THEY DO...
THEY'D NEVER LET AN ALPHA ASSET GO INTO THE FIELD WITHOUT A CONTROL.
YOU'LL NEVER BE FREE, BRAD.
UNLESS YOU LET ME HELP YOU.
WHAT DOES A TEN-YEAR-OLD KID KNOW ABOUT BREAKING OUT OF A SECURE FACILITY?
I'M THIRTEEN. THEY DON'T FEED ME MUCH ON PURPOSE TO KEEP ME DOCILE.
AND I TOLD YOU, BRAD--I REMEMBER EVERYTHING. DOOR CODES, GUARD ROTATIONS, FLOOR PLANS.
THE RED BLOCKS ARE THE GATES THAT GO OUTSIDE THE FENCE.
FORTY-FIVE SECONDS UNTIL YOU'RE SUPPOSED TO LIQUIDATE ME, BRAD.
IF I DON'T DO IT THEY'LL KNOW SOMETHING'S UP.
NO, THEY WON'T.
YOU HAVE MONEY ON THE OUTSIDE? A PLACE TO GO? I CAN'T HIDE ON MY OWN. I NEED AN ADULT FOR COVER.
BACK AWAY, BRADLEY!
BE READY TONIGHT.
GET THE FUCK OFF ME! I AIN'T DONE NOTHING!
DID HE HURT YOU?
NO. YOU GOT HERE JUST IN TIME.

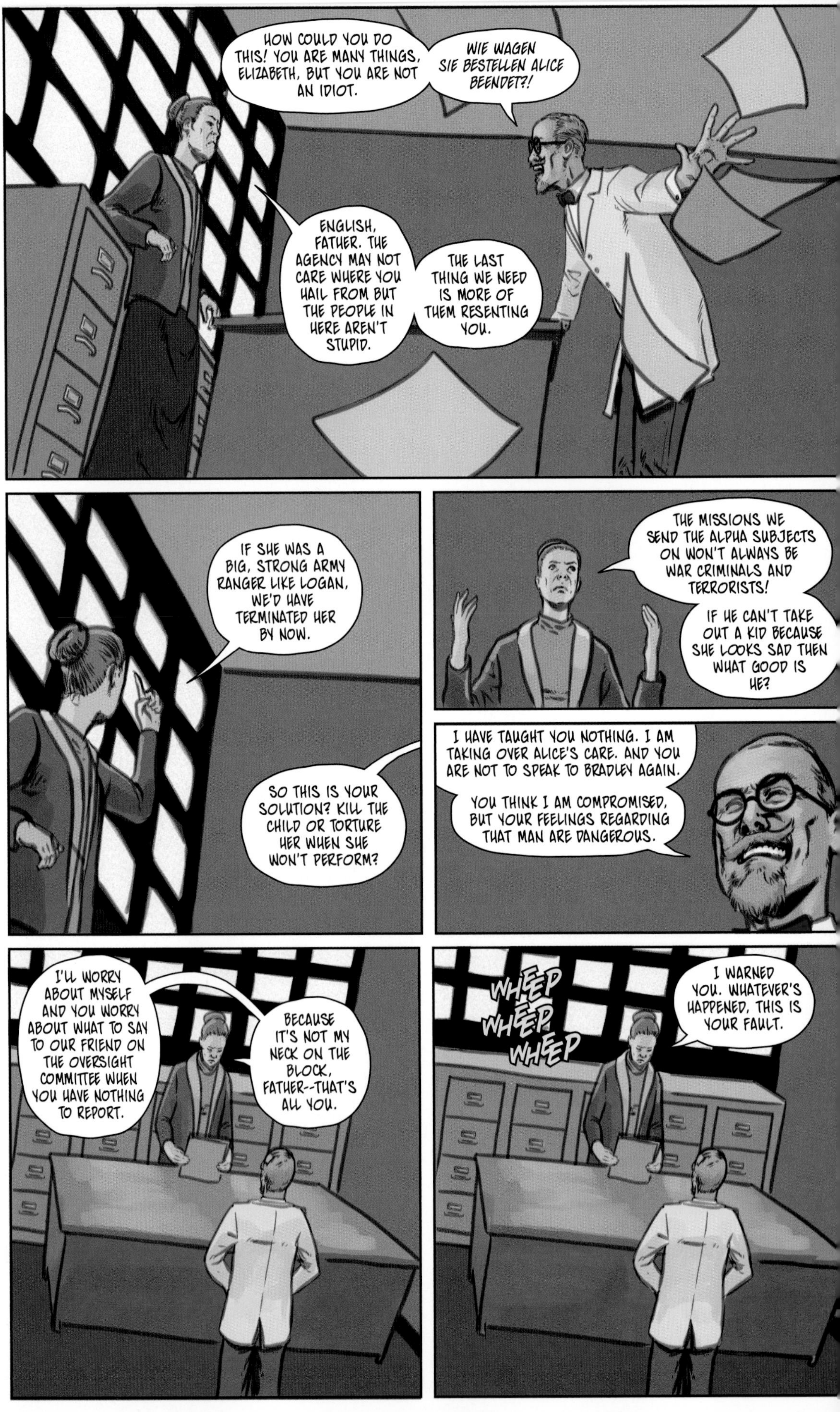
HOW COULD YOU DO THIS! YOU ARE MANY THINGS, ELIZABETH, BUT YOU ARE NOT AN IDIOT.
WIE WAGEN SIE BESTELLEN ALICE BEENDET?!
ENGLISH, FATHER. THE AGENCY MAY NOT CARE WHERE YOU HAIL FROM BUT THE PEOPLE IN HERE AREN'T STUPID.
THE LAST THING WE NEED IS MORE OF THEM RESENTING YOU.
IF SHE WAS A BIG, STRONG ARMY RANGER LIKE LOGAN, WE'D HAVE TERMINATED HER BY NOW.
SO THIS IS YOUR SOLUTION? KILL THE CHILD OR TORTURE HER WHEN SHE WON'T PERFORM?
THE MISSIONS WE SEND THE ALPHA SUBJECTS ON WON'T ALWAYS BE WAR CRIMINALS AND TERRORISTS!
IF HE CAN'T TAKE OUT A KID BECAUSE SHE LOOKS SAD THEN WHAT GOOD IS HE?
I HAVE TAUGHT YOU NOTHING. I AM TAKING OVER ALICE'S CARE. AND YOU ARE NOT TO SPEAK TO BRADLEY AGAIN.
YOU THINK I AM COMPROMISED, BUT YOUR FEELINGS REGARDING THAT MAN ARE DANGEROUS.
I'LL WORRY ABOUT MYSELF AND YOU WORRY ABOUT WHAT TO SAY TO OUR FRIEND ON THE OVERSIGHT COMMITTEE WHEN YOU HAVE NOTHING TO REPORT.
BECAUSE IT'S NOT MY NECK ON THE BLOCK, FATHER--THAT'S ALL YOU.
WHEEP WHEEP WHEEP
I WARNED YOU. WHATEVER'S HAPPENED, THIS IS YOUR FAULT.

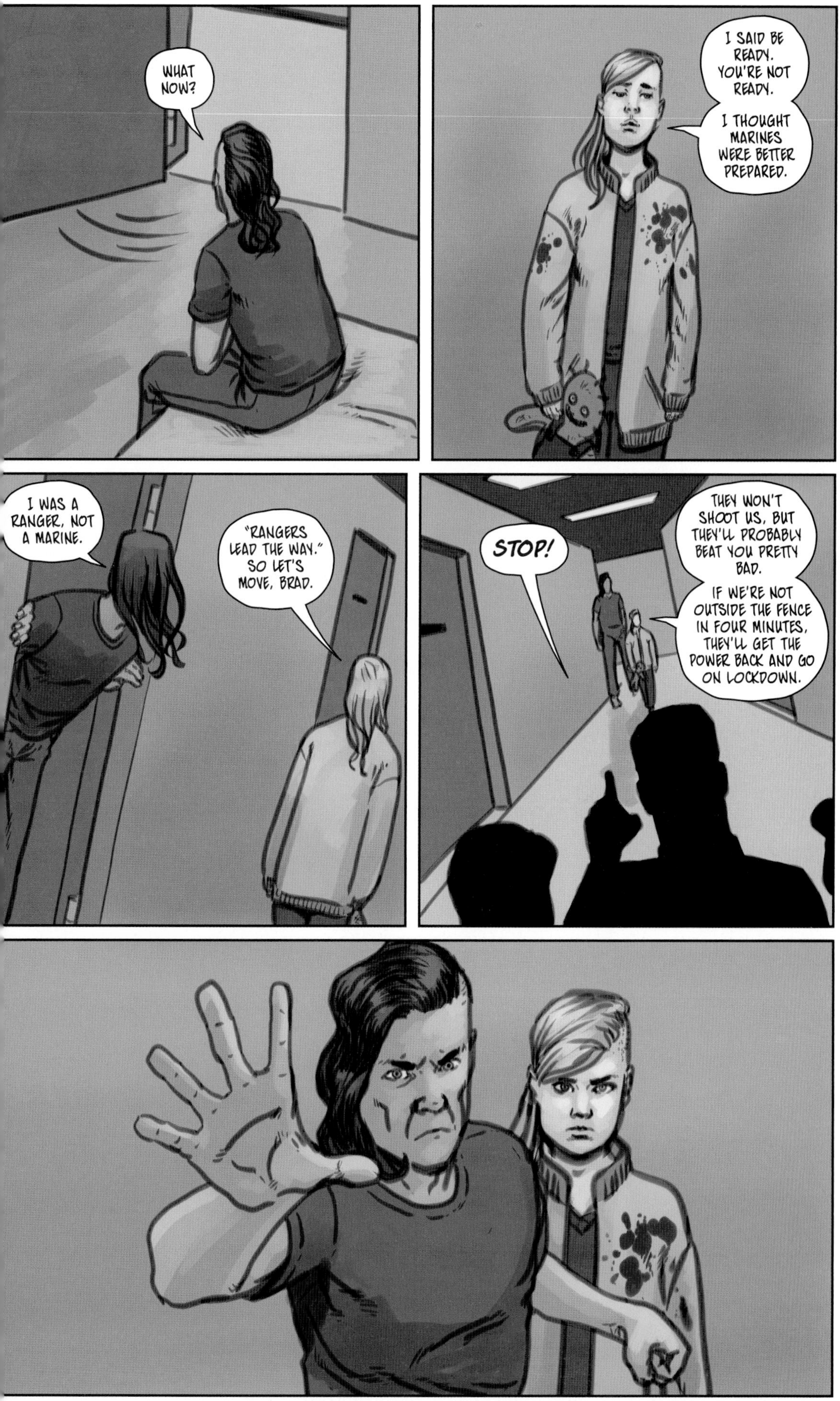

WHAT NOW?
I SAID BE READY. YOU'RE NOT READY.
I THOUGHT MARINES WERE BETTER PREPARED.
I WAS A RANGER, NOT A MARINE.
"RANGERS LEAD THE WAY." SO LET'S MOVE, BRAD.
STOP!
THEY WON'T SHOOT US, BUT THEY'LL PROBABLY BEAT YOU PRETTY BAD.
IF WE'RE NOT OUTSIDE THE FENCE IN FOUR MINUTES, THEY'LL GET THE POWER BACK AND GO ON LOCKDOWN.

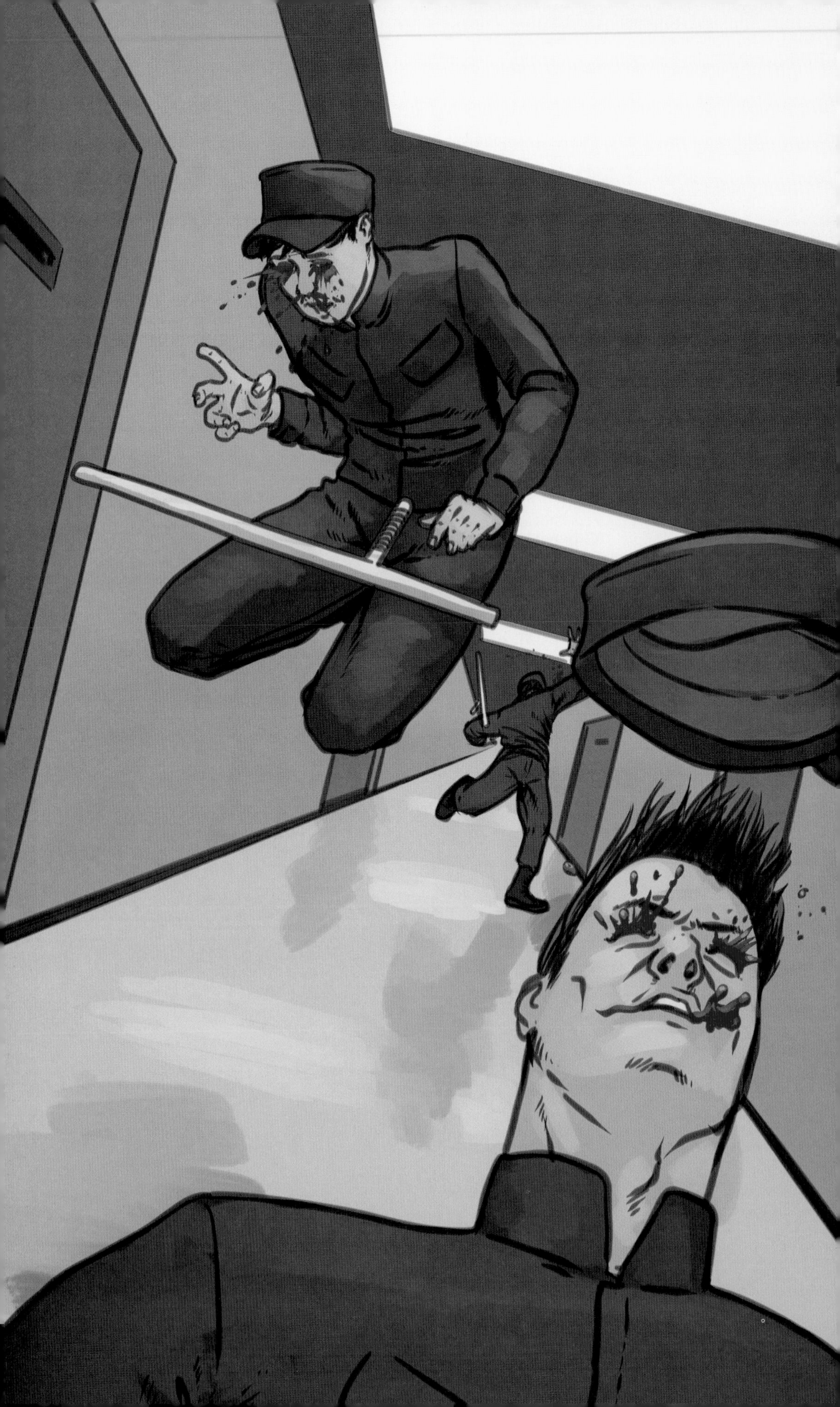

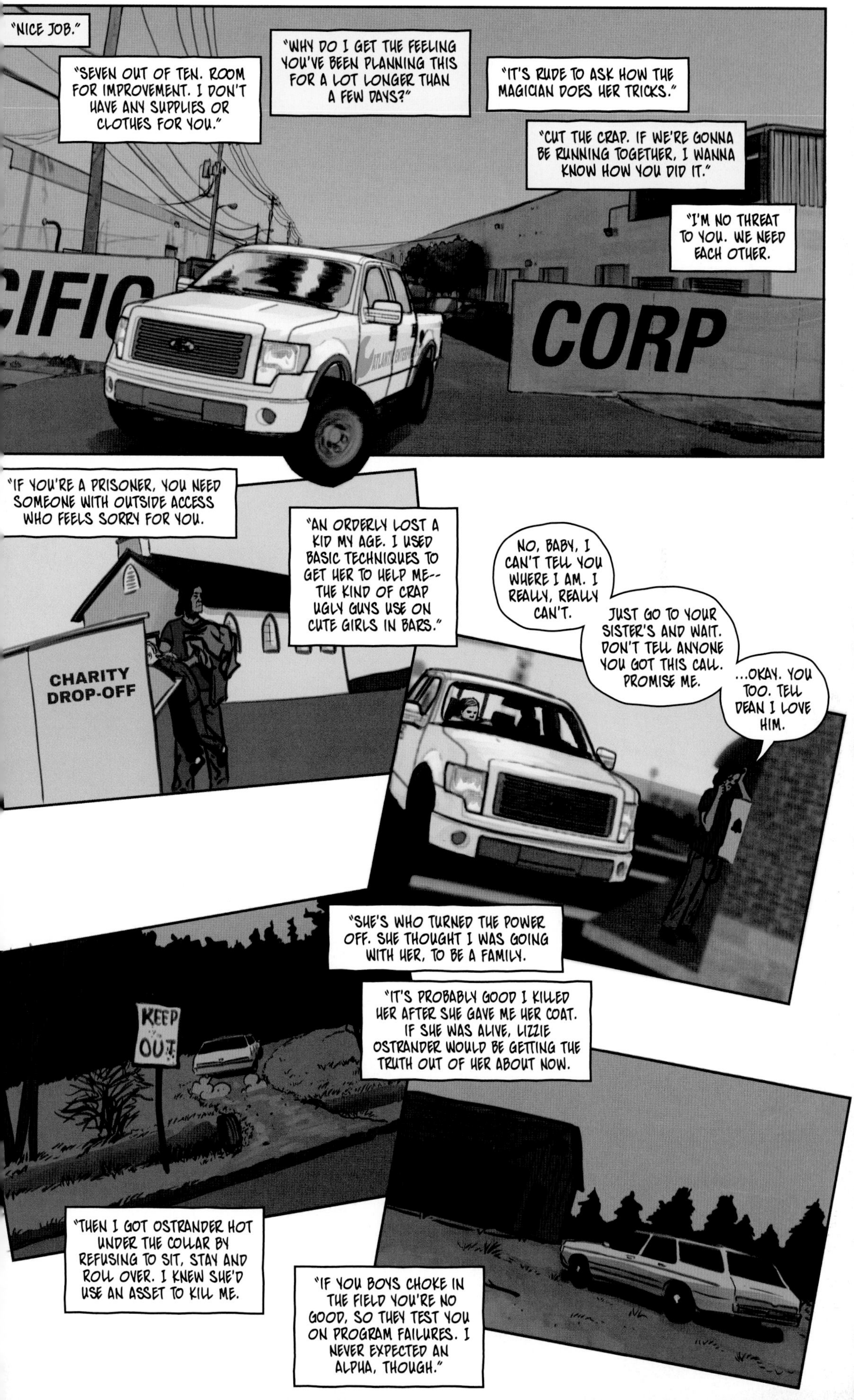
"NICE JOB."
"SEVEN OUT OF TEN. ROOM FOR IMPROVEMENT. I DON'T HAVE ANY SUPPLIES OR CLOTHES FOR YOU."
"WHY DO I GET THE FEELING YOU'VE BEEN PLANNING THIS FOR A LOT LONGER THAN A FEW DAYS?"
"IT'S RUDE TO ASK HOW THE MAGICIAN DOES HER TRICKS."
"CUT THE CRAP. IF WE'RE GONNA BE RUNNING TOGETHER, I WANNA KNOW HOW YOU DID IT."
"I'M NO THREAT TO YOU. WE NEED EACH OTHER.
CIFIC
CORP
"IF YOU'RE A PRISONER, YOU NEED SOMEONE WITH OUTSIDE ACCESS WHO FEELS SORRY FOR YOU.
"AN ORDERLY LOST A KID MY AGE. I USED BASIC TECHNIQUES TO GET HER TO HELP ME--THE KIND OF CRAP UGLY GUYS USE ON CUTE GIRLS IN BARS."
CHARITY DROP-OFF
NO, BABY, I CAN'T TELL YOU WHERE I AM. I REALLY, REALLY CAN'T.
JUST GO TO YOUR SISTER'S AND WAIT. DON'T TELL ANYONE YOU GOT THIS CALL. PROMISE ME.
...OKAY. YOU TOO. TELL DEAN I LOVE HIM.
"SHE'S WHO TURNED THE POWER OFF. SHE THOUGHT I WAS GOING WITH HER, TO BE A FAMILY.
"IT'S PROBABLY GOOD I KILLED HER AFTER SHE GAVE ME HER COAT. IF SHE WAS ALIVE, LIZZIE OSTRANDER WOULD BE GETTING THE TRUTH OUT OF HER ABOUT NOW.
KEEP OUT
"THEN I GOT OSTRANDER HOT UNDER THE COLLAR BY REFUSING TO SIT, STAY AND ROLL OVER. I KNEW SHE'D USE AN ASSET TO KILL ME.
"IF YOU BOYS CHOKE IN THE FIELD YOU'RE NO GOOD, SO THEY TEST YOU ON PROGRAM FAILURES. I NEVER EXPECTED AN ALPHA, THOUGH."

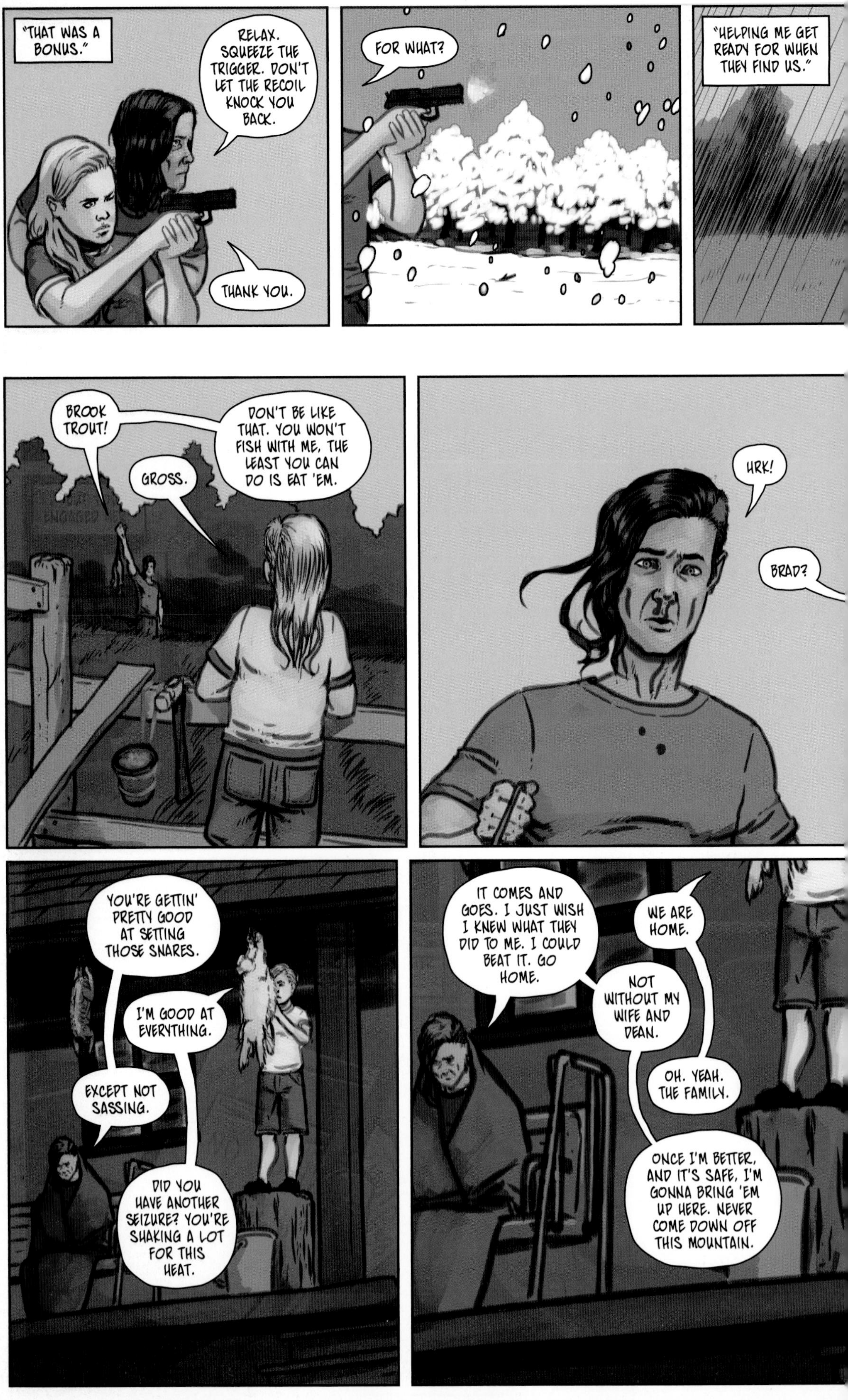
"THAT WAS A BONUS."
RELAX. SQUEEZE THE TRIGGER. DON'T LET THE RECOIL KNOCK YOU BACK.
THANK YOU.
FOR WHAT?
"HELPING ME GET READY FOR WHEN THEY FIND US."
BROOK TROUT!
DON'T BE LIKE THAT. YOU WON'T FISH WITH ME, THE LEAST YOU CAN DO IS EAT 'EM.
GROSS.
HRK!
BRAD?
YOU'RE GETTIN' PRETTY GOOD AT SETTING THOSE SNARES.
I'M GOOD AT EVERYTHING.
EXCEPT NOT SASSING.
DID YOU HAVE ANOTHER SEIZURE? YOU'RE SHAKING A LOT FOR THIS HEAT.
IT COMES AND GOES. I JUST WISH I KNEW WHAT THEY DID TO ME. I COULD BEAT IT. GO HOME.
WE ARE HOME.
NOT WITHOUT MY WIFE AND DEAN.
OH. YEAH. THE FAMILY.
ONCE I'M BETTER, AND IT'S SAFE, I'M GONNA BRING 'EM UP HERE. NEVER COME DOWN OFF THIS MOUNTAIN.

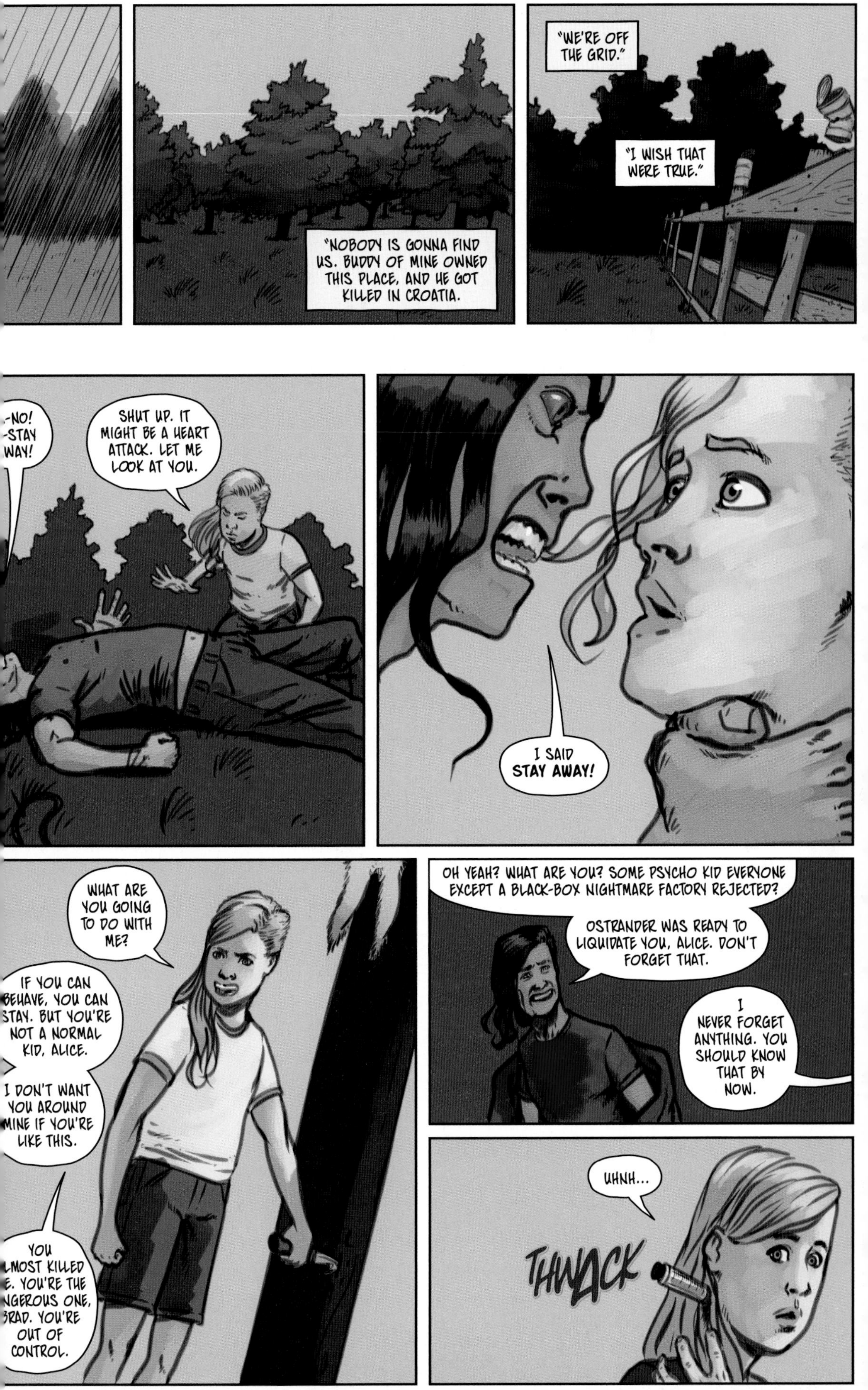

"NOBODY IS GONNA FIND US. BUDDY OF MINE OWNED THIS PLACE, AND HE GOT KILLED IN CROATIA.
"WE'RE OFF THE GRID."
"I WISH THAT WERE TRUE."
-NO! -STAY WAY!
SHUT UP. IT MIGHT BE A HEART ATTACK. LET ME LOOK AT YOU.
I SAID STAY AWAY!
WHAT ARE YOU GOING TO DO WITH ME?
IF YOU CAN BEHAVE, YOU CAN STAY. BUT YOU'RE NOT A NORMAL KID, ALICE.
I DON'T WANT YOU AROUND MINE IF YOU'RE LIKE THIS.
YOU LMOST KILLED E. YOU'RE THE NGEROUS ONE, 3RAD. YOU'RE OUT OF CONTROL.
OH YEAH? WHAT ARE YOU? SOME PSYCHO KID EVERYONE EXCEPT A BLACK-BOX NIGHTMARE FACTORY REJECTED?
OSTRANDER WAS READY TO LIQUIDATE YOU, ALICE. DON'T FORGET THAT.
I NEVER FORGET ANYTHING. YOU SHOULD KNOW THAT BY NOW.
UHNH...
THWACK

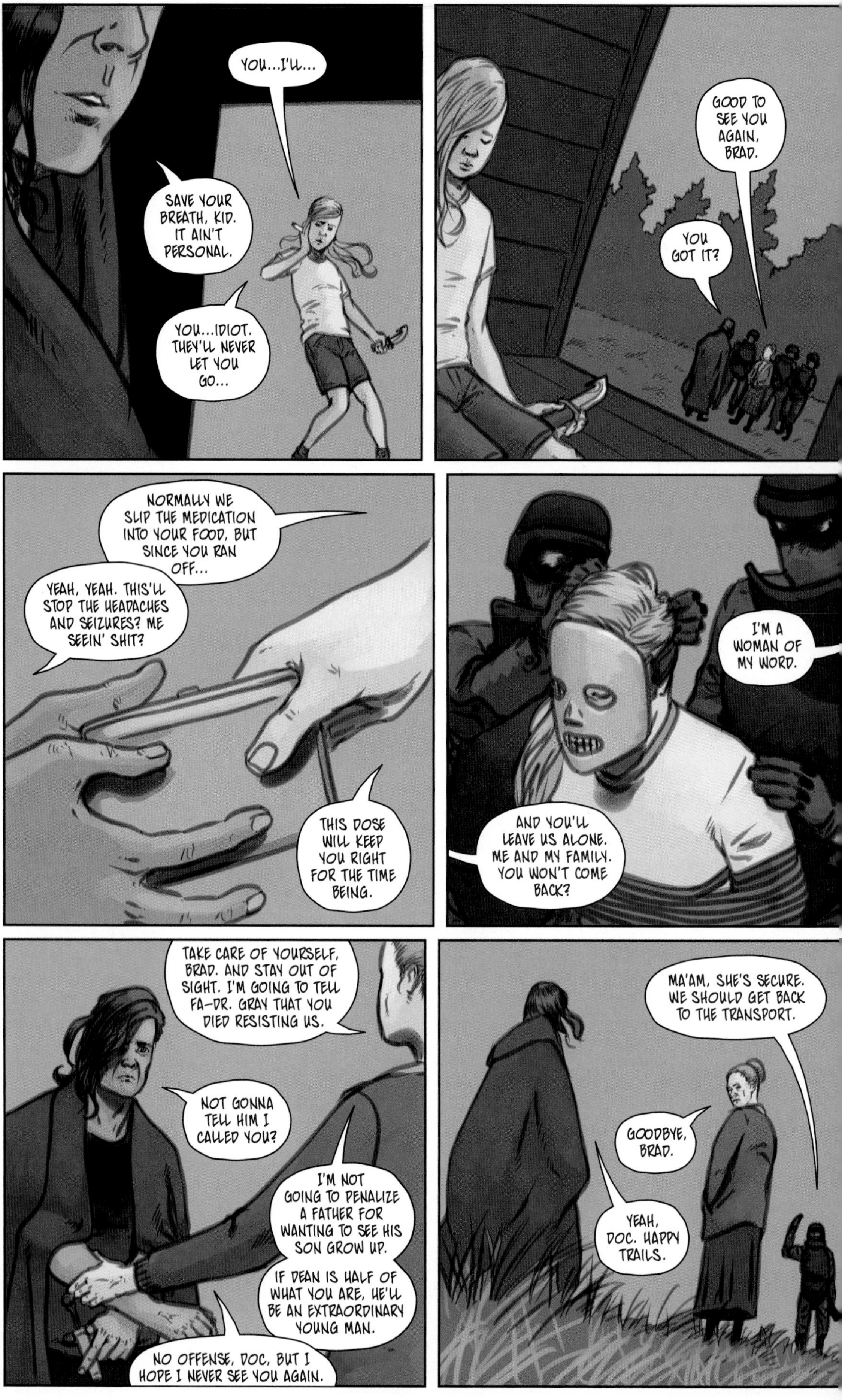
YOU...I'LL...
SAVE YOUR BREATH, KID. IT AIN'T PERSONAL.
YOU...IDIOT. THEY'LL NEVER LET YOU GO...
GOOD TO SEE YOU AGAIN, BRAD.
YOU GOT IT?
NORMALLY WE SLIP THE MEDICATION INTO YOUR FOOD, BUT SINCE YOU RAN OFF...
YEAH, YEAH. THIS'LL STOP THE HEADACHES AND SEIZURES? ME SEEIN' SHIT?
THIS DOSE WILL KEEP YOU RIGHT FOR THE TIME BEING.
I'M A WOMAN OF MY WORD.
AND YOU'LL LEAVE US ALONE. ME AND MY FAMILY. YOU WON'T COME BACK?
TAKE CARE OF YOURSELF, BRAD. AND STAY OUT OF SIGHT. I'M GOING TO TELL FA--DR. GRAY THAT YOU DIED RESISTING US.
NOT GONNA TELL HIM I CALLED YOU?
I'M NOT GOING TO PENALIZE A FATHER FOR WANTING TO SEE HIS SON GROW UP.
IF DEAN IS HALF OF WHAT YOU ARE, HE'LL BE AN EXTRAORDINARY YOUNG MAN.
NO OFFENSE, DOC, BUT I HOPE I NEVER SEE YOU AGAIN.
MA'AM, SHE'S SECURE. WE SHOULD GET BACK TO THE TRANSPORT.
GOODBYE, BRAD.
YEAH, DOC. HAPPY TRAILS.

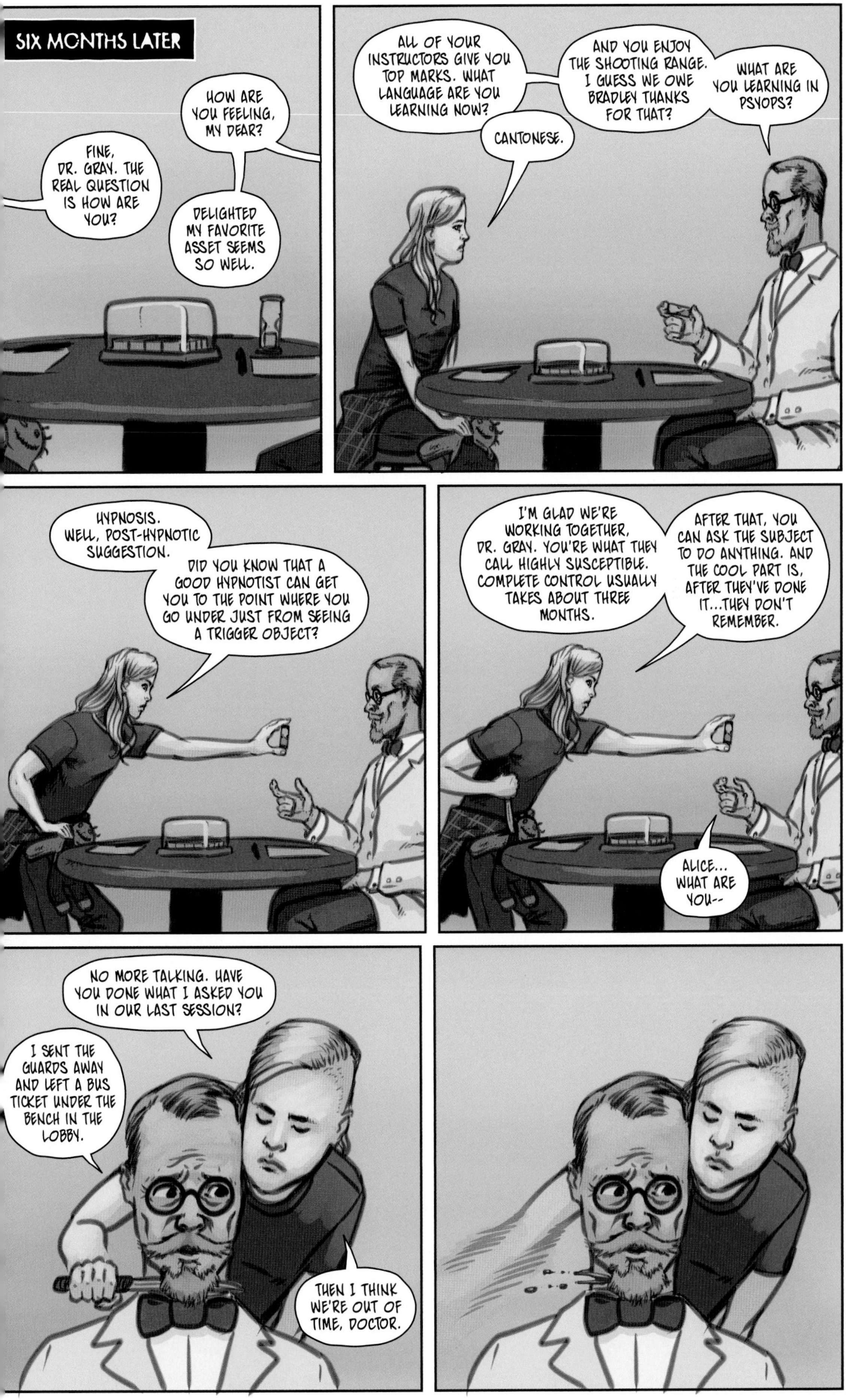
SIX MONTHS LATER
HOW ARE YOU FEELING, MY DEAR?
FINE, DR. GRAY. THE REAL QUESTION IS HOW ARE YOU?
DELIGHTED MY FAVORITE ASSET SEEMS SO WELL.
ALL OF YOUR INSTRUCTORS GIVE YOU TOP MARKS. WHAT LANGUAGE ARE YOU LEARNING NOW?
CANTONESE.
AND YOU ENJOY THE SHOOTING RANGE. I GUESS WE OWE BRADLEY THANKS FOR THAT?
WHAT ARE YOU LEARNING IN PSYOPS?
HYPNOSIS. WELL, POST-HYPNOTIC SUGGESTION.
DID YOU KNOW THAT A GOOD HYPNOTIST CAN GET YOU TO THE POINT WHERE YOU GO UNDER JUST FROM SEEING A TRIGGER OBJECT?
I'M GLAD WE'RE WORKING TOGETHER, DR. GRAY. YOU'RE WHAT THEY CALL HIGHLY SUSCEPTIBLE. COMPLETE CONTROL USUALLY TAKES ABOUT THREE MONTHS.
AFTER THAT, YOU CAN ASK THE SUBJECT TO DO ANYTHING. AND THE COOL PART IS, AFTER THEY'VE DONE IT...THEY DON'T REMEMBER.
ALICE... WHAT ARE YOU--
NO MORE TALKING. HAVE YOU DONE WHAT I ASKED YOU IN OUR LAST SESSION?
I SENT THE GUARDS AWAY AND LEFT A BUS TICKET UNDER THE BENCH IN THE LOBBY.
THEN I THINK WE'RE OUT OF TIME, DOCTOR.

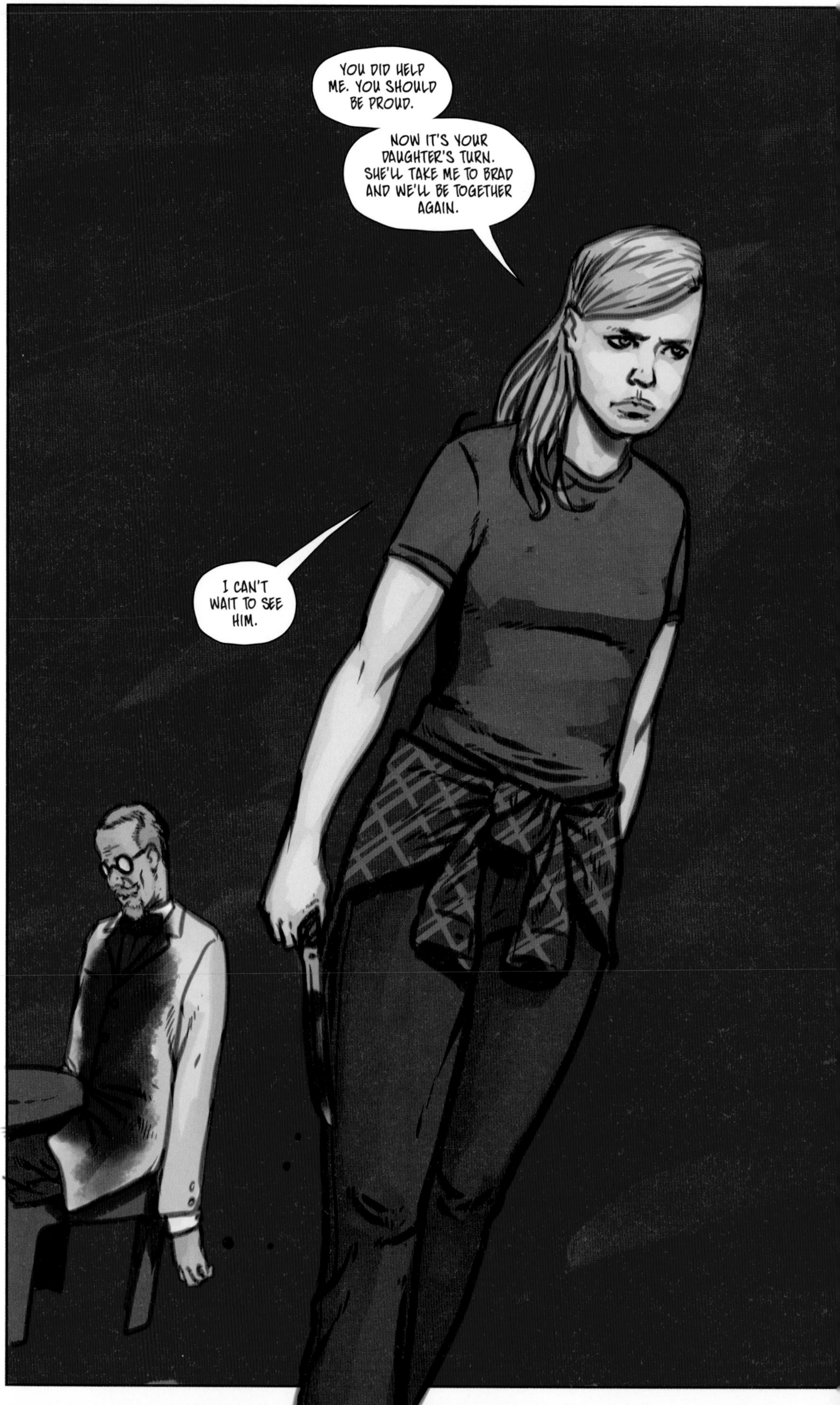
YOU DID HELP ME. YOU SHOULD BE PROUD.
NOW IT'S YOUR DAUGHTER'S TURN. SHE'LL TAKE ME TO BRAD AND WE'LL BE TOGETHER AGAIN.
I CAN'T WAIT TO SEE HIM.

CHAPTER EIGHT

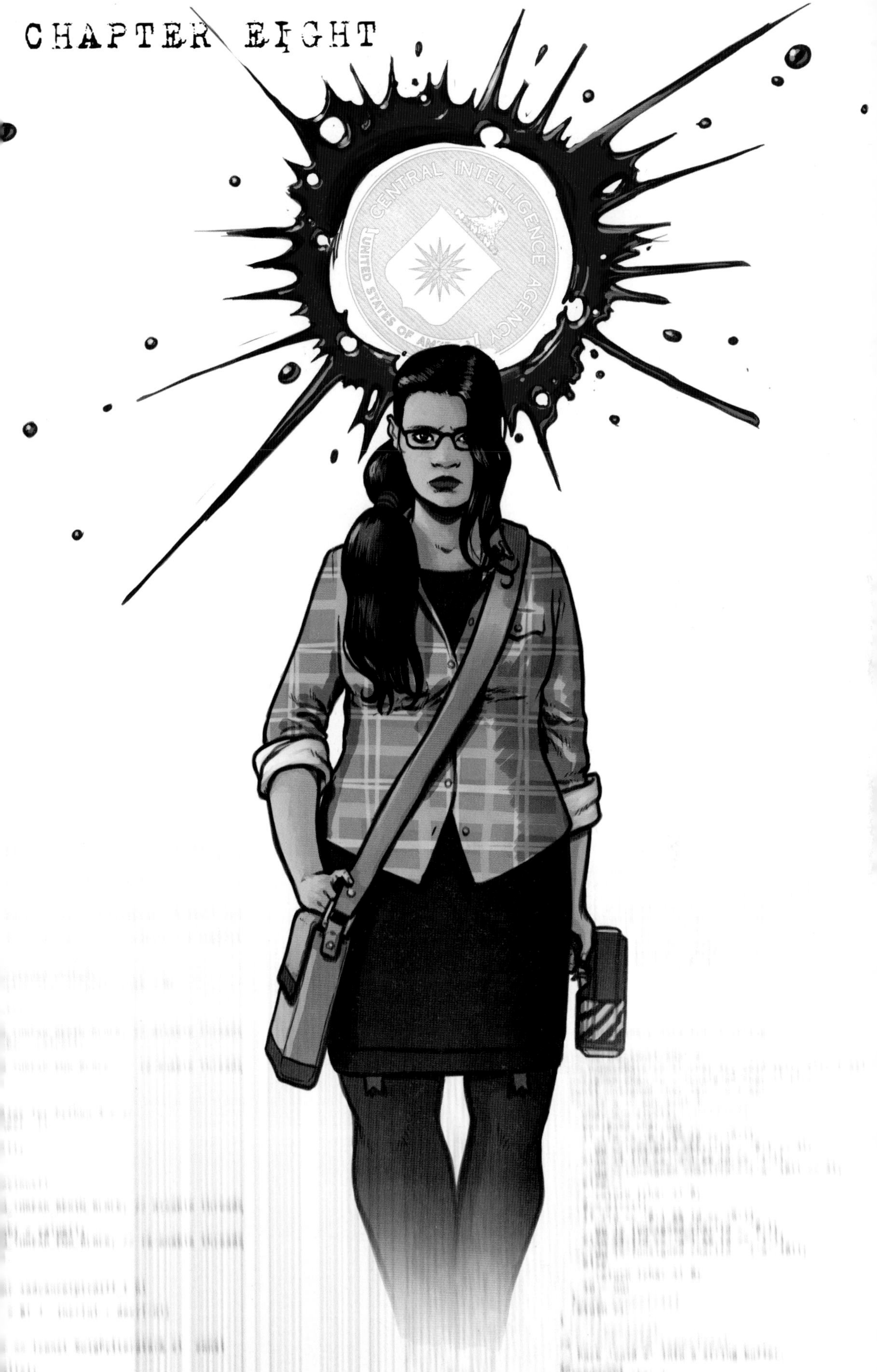
CENTRAL INTELLIGENCE AGENCY

Issue #8 Cover Art

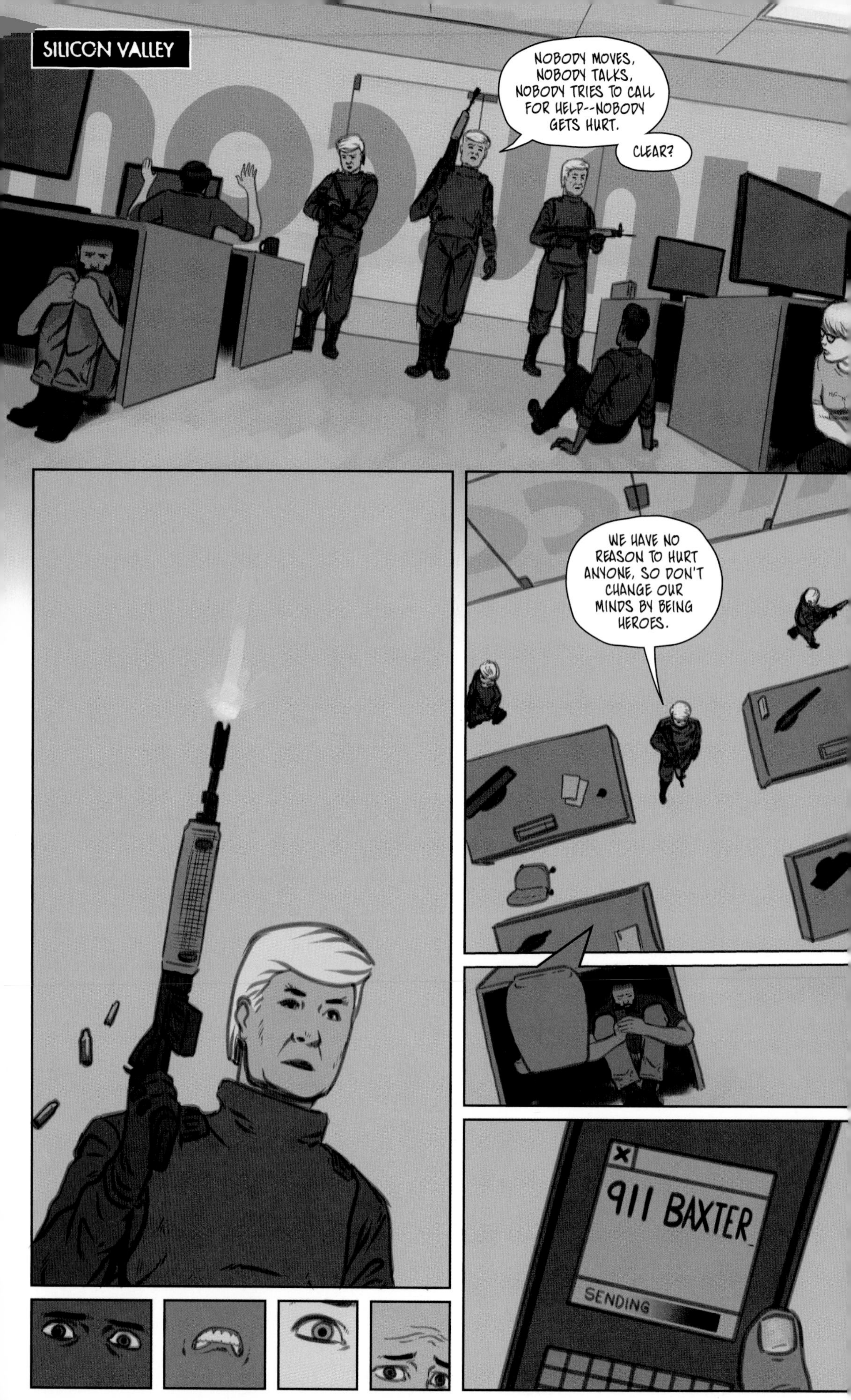
SILICON VALLEY
NOBODY MOVES, NOBODY TALKS, NOBODY TRIES TO CALL FOR HELP--NOBODY GETS HURT.
CLEAR?
WE HAVE NO REASON TO HURT ANYONE, SO DON'T CHANGE OUR MINDS BY BEING HEROES.
911 BAXTER_
SENDING

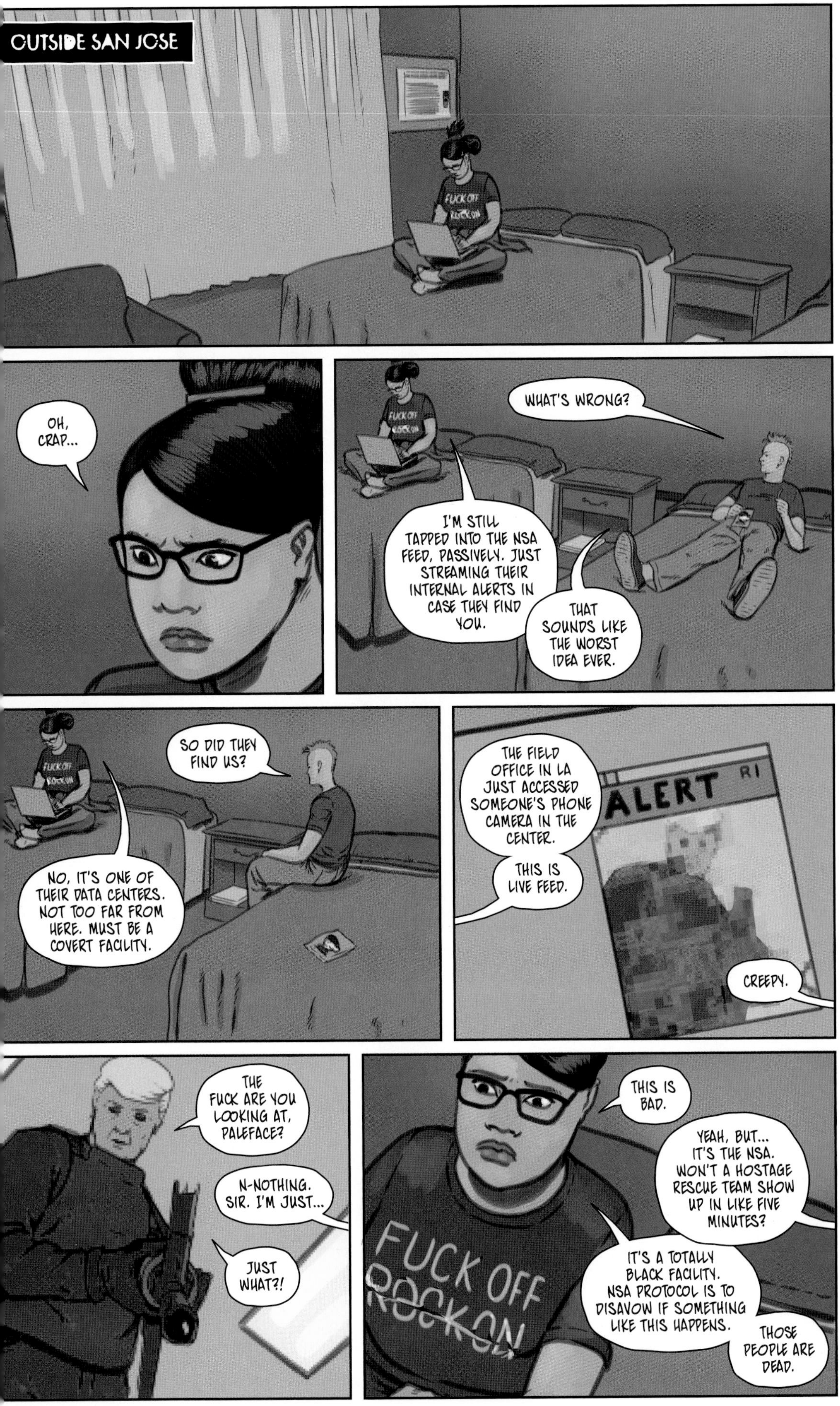
OUTSIDE SAN JOSE
FUCK OFF ROCK ON
OH, CRAP...
WHAT'S WRONG?
I'M STILL TAPPED INTO THE NSA FEED, PASSIVELY. JUST STREAMING THEIR INTERNAL ALERTS IN CASE THEY FIND YOU.
THAT SOUNDS LIKE THE WORST IDEA EVER.
SO DID THEY FIND US?
NO, IT'S ONE OF THEIR DATA CENTERS. NOT TOO FAR FROM HERE. MUST BE A COVERT FACILITY.
THE FIELD OFFICE IN LA JUST ACCESSED SOMEONE'S PHONE CAMERA IN THE CENTER.
ALERT
THIS IS LIVE FEED.
CREEPY.
THE FUCK ARE YOU LOOKING AT, PALEFACE?
N-NOTHING. SIR. I'M JUST...
JUST WHAT?!
THIS IS BAD.
YEAH, BUT... IT'S THE NSA. WON'T A HOSTAGE RESCUE TEAM SHOW UP IN LIKE FIVE MINUTES?
FUCK OFF ROCK ON
IT'S A TOTALLY BLACK FACILITY. NSA PROTOCOL IS TO DISAVOW IF SOMETHING LIKE THIS HAPPENS.
THOSE PEOPLE ARE DEAD.

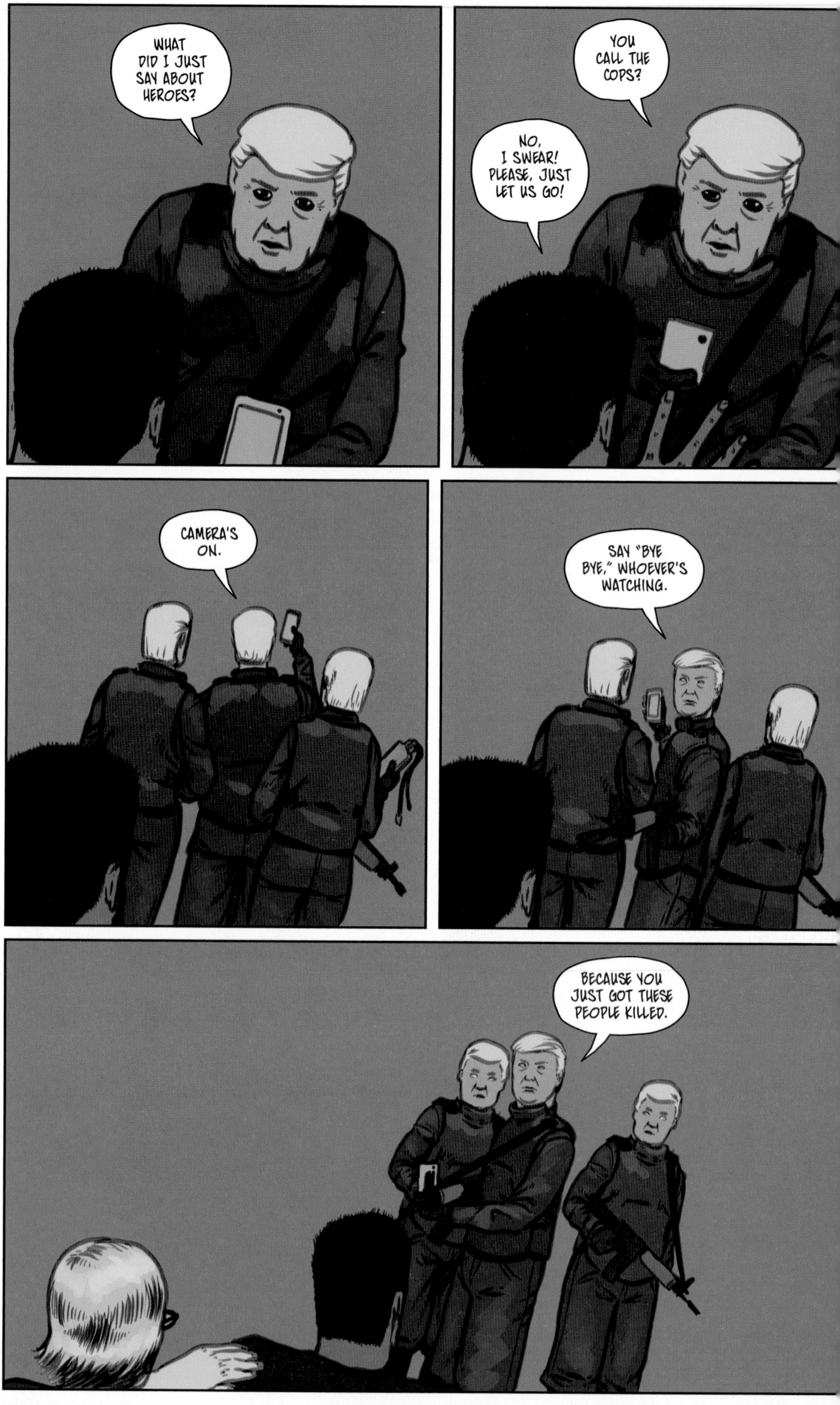
WHAT DID I JUST SAY ABOUT HEROES?
YOU CALL THE COPS?
NO, I SWEAR! PLEASE, JUST LET US GO!
CAMERA'S ON.
SAY "BYE BYE," WHOEVER'S WATCHING.
BECAUSE YOU JUST GOT THESE PEOPLE KILLED.

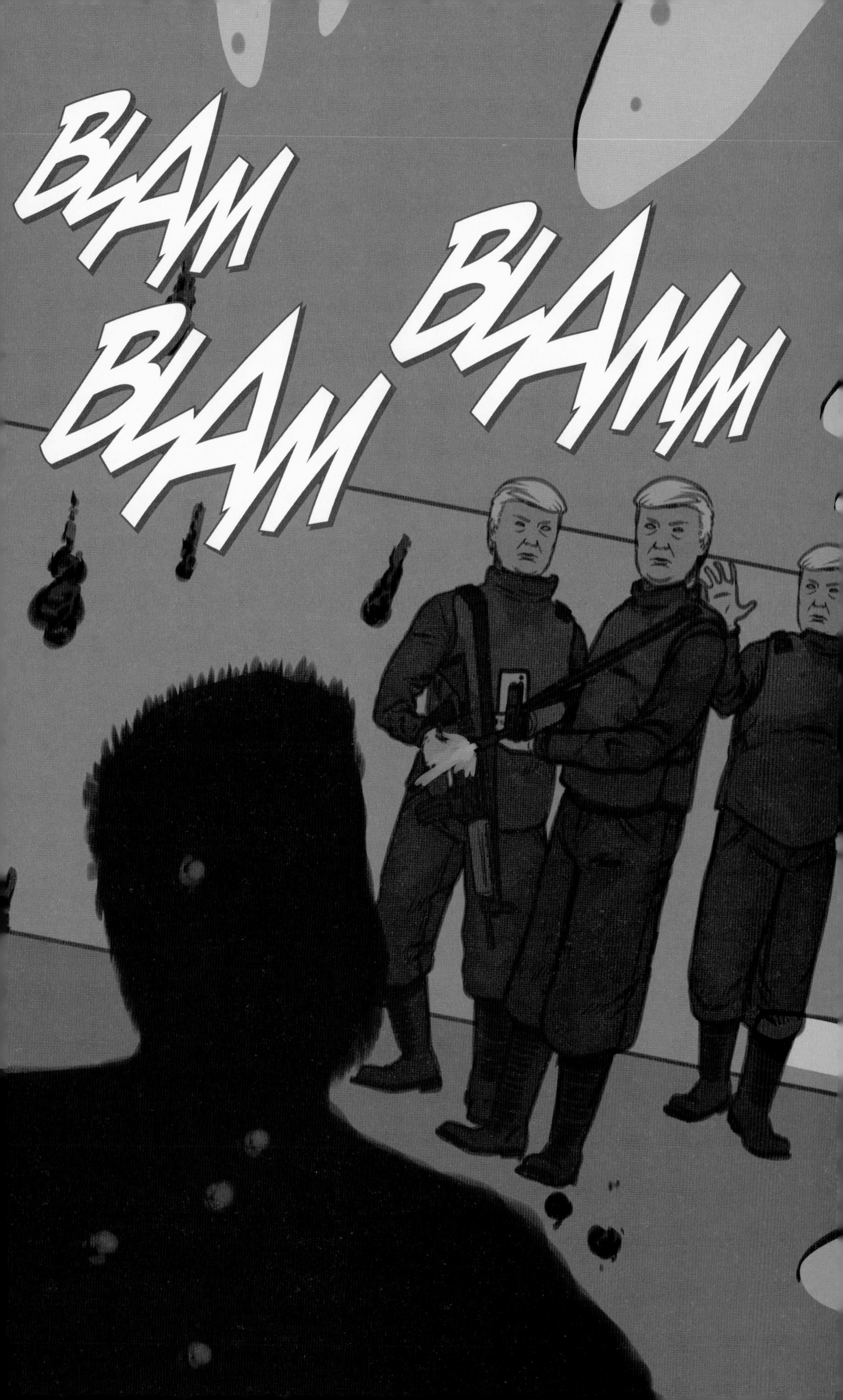
BLAM
BLAMM
BLAM

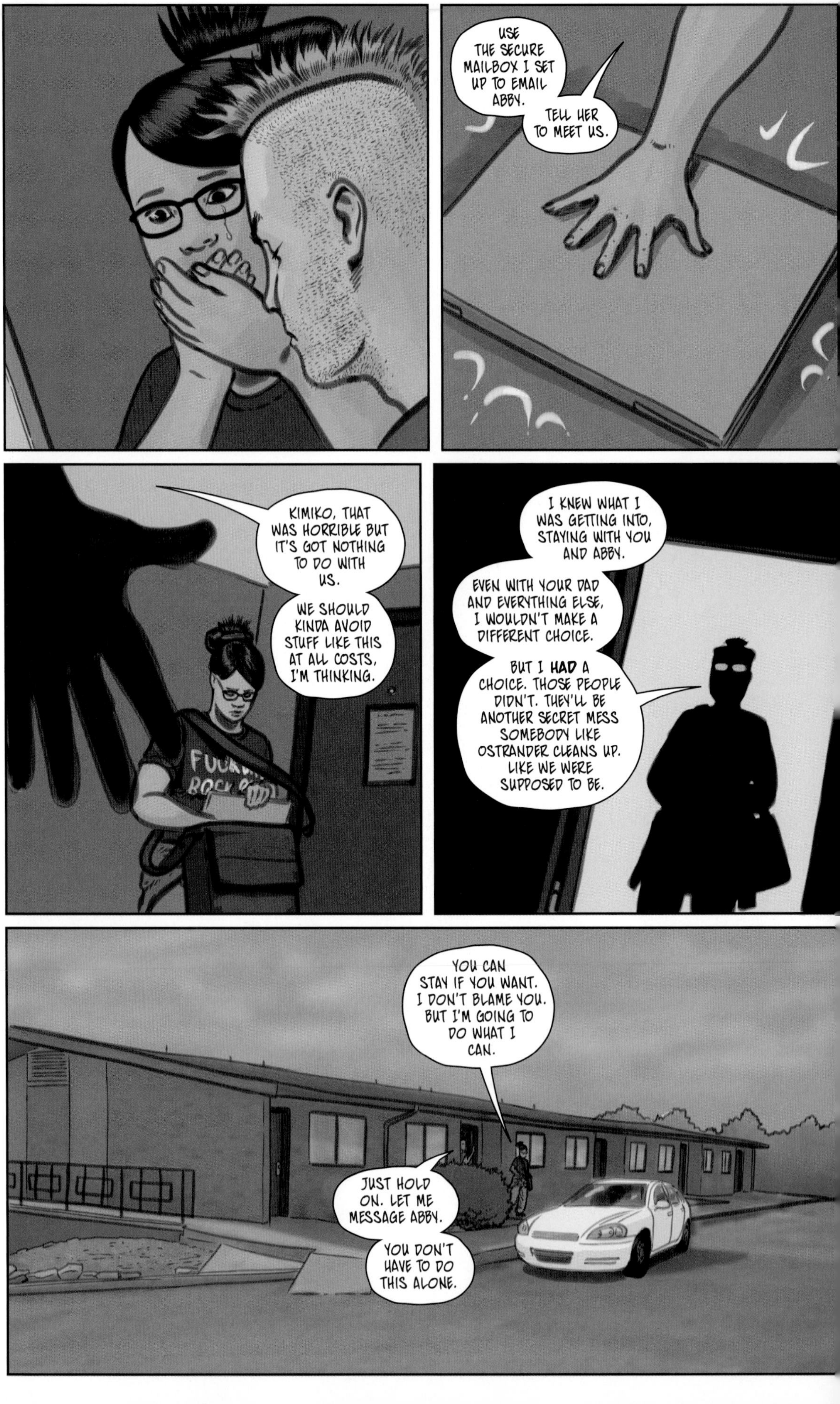
USE THE SECURE MAILBOX I SET UP TO EMAIL ABBY.
TELL HER TO MEET US.
KIMIKO, THAT WAS HORRIBLE BUT IT'S GOT NOTHING TO DO WITH US.
WE SHOULD KINDA AVOID STUFF LIKE THIS AT ALL COSTS, I'M THINKING.
I KNEW WHAT I WAS GETTING INTO, STAYING WITH YOU AND ABBY.
EVEN WITH YOUR DAD AND EVERYTHING ELSE, I WOULDN'T MAKE A DIFFERENT CHOICE.
BUT I **HAD** A CHOICE. THOSE PEOPLE DIDN'T. THEY'LL BE ANOTHER SECRET MESS SOMEBODY LIKE OSTRANDER CLEANS UP. LIKE WE WERE SUPPOSED TO BE.
YOU CAN STAY IF YOU WANT. I DON'T BLAME YOU. BUT I'M GOING TO DO WHAT I CAN.
JUST HOLD ON. LET ME MESSAGE ABBY.
YOU DON'T HAVE TO DO THIS ALONE.

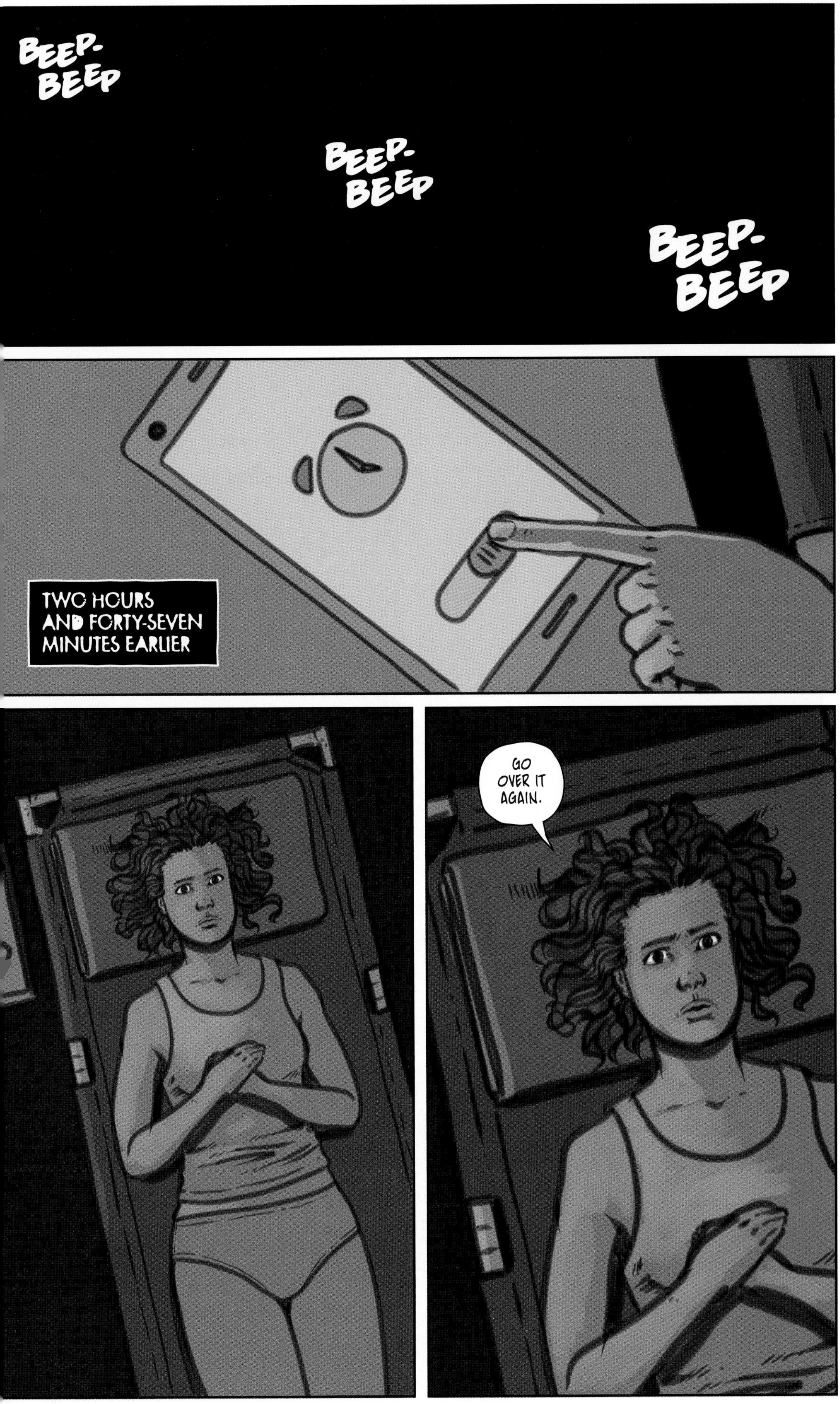
BEEP-BEEP
BEEP-BEEP
BEEP-BEEP
TWO HOURS AND FORTY-SEVEN MINUTES EARLIER
GO OVER IT AGAIN.

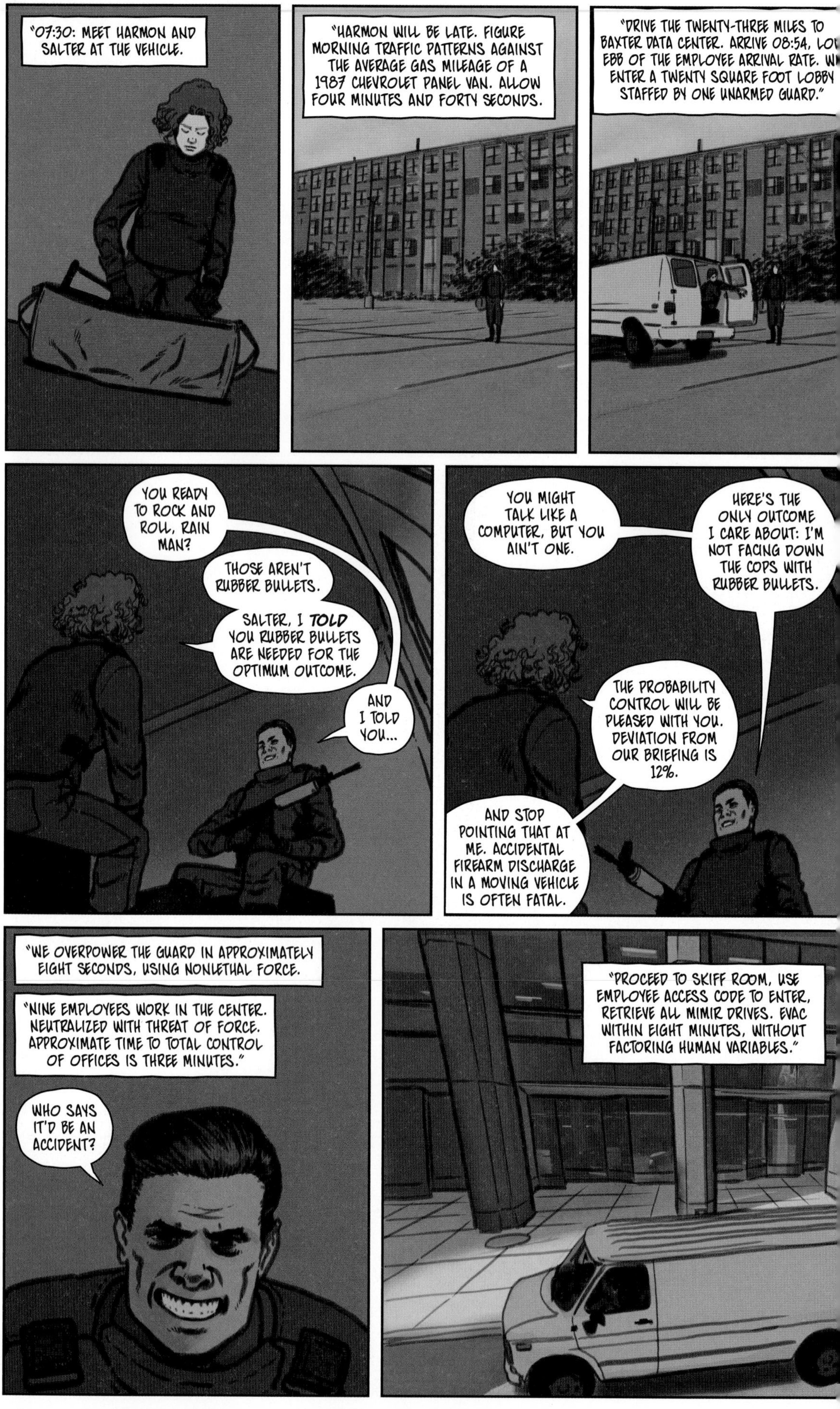
"07:30: MEET HARMON AND SALTER AT THE VEHICLE.
"HARMON WILL BE LATE. FIGURE MORNING TRAFFIC PATTERNS AGAINST THE AVERAGE GAS MILEAGE OF A 1987 CHEVROLET PANEL VAN. ALLOW FOUR MINUTES AND FORTY SECONDS.
"DRIVE THE TWENTY-THREE MILES TO BAXTER DATA CENTER. ARRIVE 08:54, LO EBB OF THE EMPLOYEE ARRIVAL RATE. W ENTER A TWENTY SQUARE FOOT LOBBY STAFFED BY ONE UNARMED GUARD."
YOU READY TO ROCK AND ROLL, RAIN MAN?
THOSE AREN'T RUBBER BULLETS.
SALTER, I ***TOLD*** YOU RUBBER BULLETS ARE NEEDED FOR THE OPTIMUM OUTCOME.
AND I TOLD YOU...
YOU MIGHT TALK LIKE A COMPUTER, BUT YOU AIN'T ONE.
HERE'S THE ONLY OUTCOME I CARE ABOUT: I'M NOT FACING DOWN THE COPS WITH RUBBER BULLETS.
THE PROBABILITY CONTROL WILL BE PLEASED WITH YOU. DEVIATION FROM OUR BRIEFING IS 12%.
AND STOP POINTING THAT AT ME. ACCIDENTAL FIREARM DISCHARGE IN A MOVING VEHICLE IS OFTEN FATAL.
"WE OVERPOWER THE GUARD IN APPROXIMATELY EIGHT SECONDS, USING NONLETHAL FORCE.
"NINE EMPLOYEES WORK IN THE CENTER. NEUTRALIZED WITH THREAT OF FORCE. APPROXIMATE TIME TO TOTAL CONTROL OF OFFICES IS THREE MINUTES."
WHO SAYS IT'D BE AN ACCIDENT?
"PROCEED TO SKIFF ROOM, USE EMPLOYEE ACCESS CODE TO ENTER, RETRIEVE ALL MIMIR DRIVES. EVAC WITHIN EIGHT MINUTES, WITHOUT FACTORING HUMAN VARIABLES."

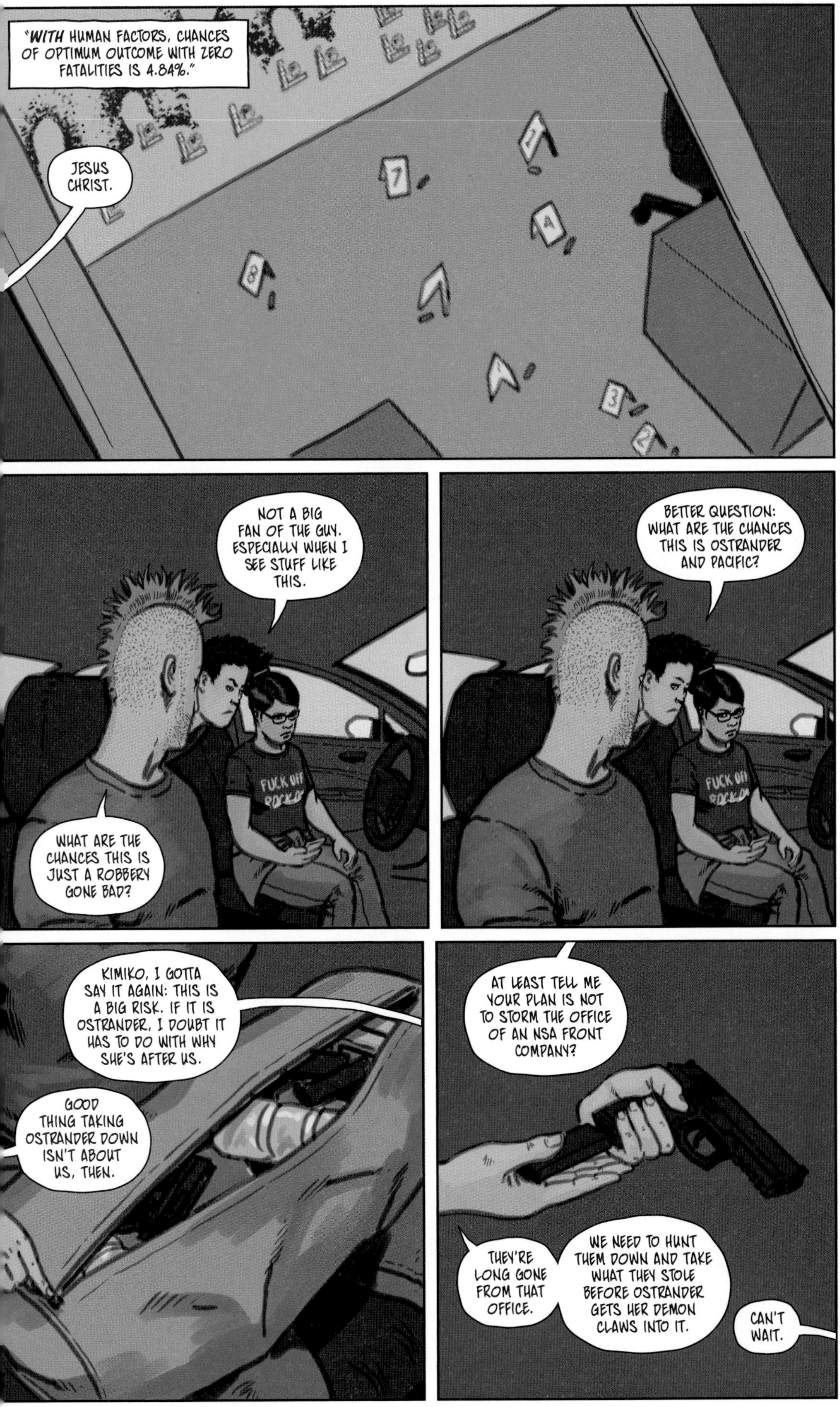
"WITH HUMAN FACTORS, CHANCES OF OPTIMUM OUTCOME WITH ZERO FATALITIES IS 4.84%."
JESUS CHRIST.
WHAT ARE THE CHANCES THIS IS JUST A ROBBERY GONE BAD?
NOT A BIG FAN OF THE GUY. ESPECIALLY WHEN I SEE STUFF LIKE THIS.
FUCK OFF
BETTER QUESTION: WHAT ARE THE CHANCES THIS IS OSTRANDER AND PACIFIC?
FUCK OFF
KIMIKO, I GOTTA SAY IT AGAIN: THIS IS A BIG RISK. IF IT IS OSTRANDER, I DOUBT IT HAS TO DO WITH WHY SHE'S AFTER US.
GOOD THING TAKING OSTRANDER DOWN ISN'T ABOUT US, THEN.
AT LEAST TELL ME YOUR PLAN IS NOT TO STORM THE OFFICE OF AN NSA FRONT COMPANY?
THEY'RE LONG GONE FROM THAT OFFICE.
WE NEED TO HUNT THEM DOWN AND TAKE WHAT THEY STOLE BEFORE OSTRANDER GETS HER DEMON CLAWS INTO IT.
CAN'T WAIT.

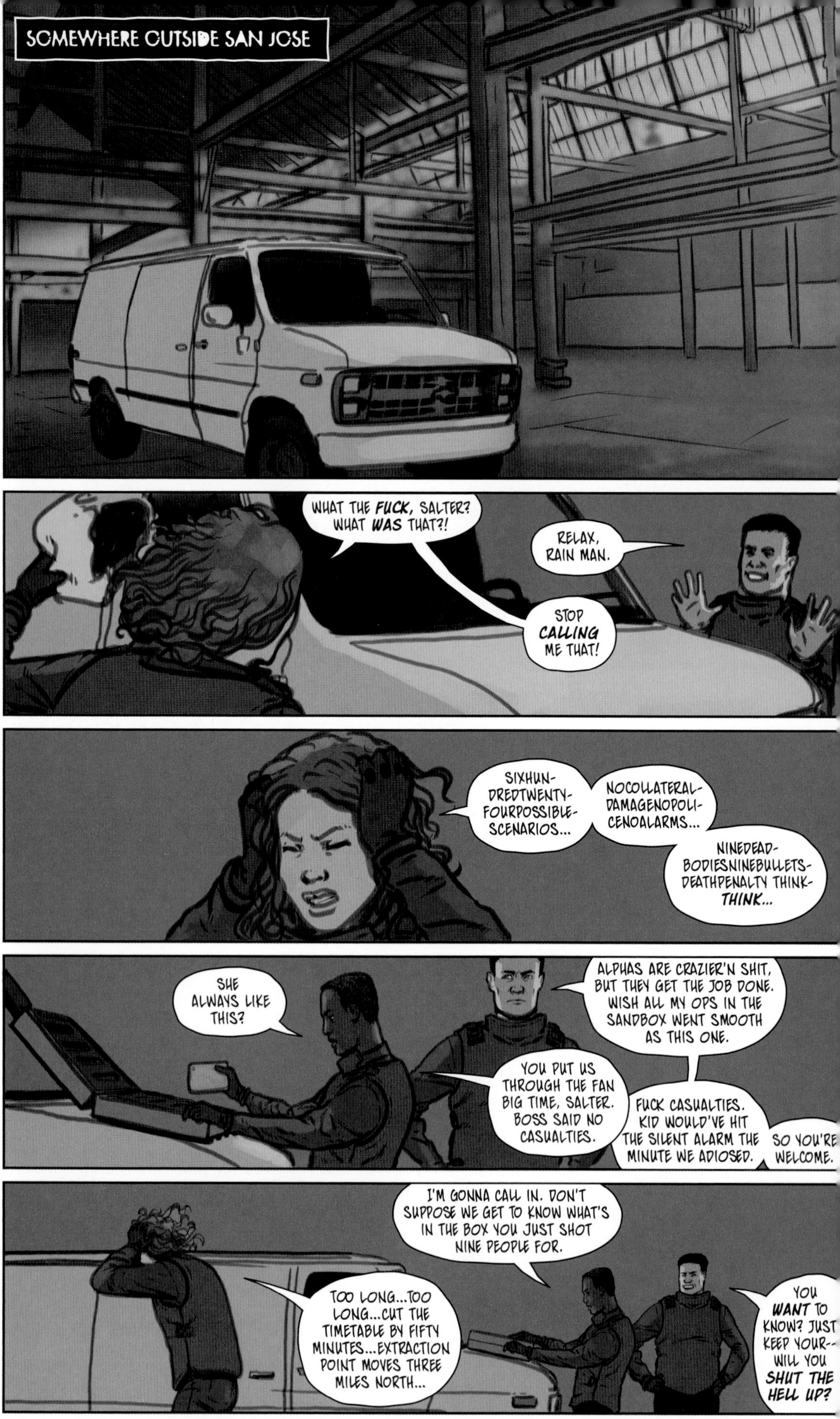
SOMEWHERE OUTSIDE SAN JOSE
WHAT THE *FUCK*, SALTER? WHAT *WAS* THAT?!
RELAX, RAIN MAN.
STOP *CALLING* ME THAT!
SIXHUN-DREDTWENTY-FOURPOSSIBLE-SCENARIOS...
NOCOLLATERAL-DAMAGENOPOLI-CENOALARMS...
NINEDEAD-BODIESNINEBULLETS-DEATHPENALTY THINK-*THINK*...
SHE ALWAYS LIKE THIS?
ALPHAS ARE CRAZIER'N SHIT, BUT THEY GET THE JOB DONE. WISH ALL MY OPS IN THE SANDBOX WENT SMOOTH AS THIS ONE.
YOU PUT US THROUGH THE FAN BIG TIME, SALTER. BOSS SAID NO CASUALTIES.
FUCK CASUALTIES. KID WOULD'VE HIT THE SILENT ALARM THE MINUTE WE ADIOSED.
SO YOU'RE WELCOME.
I'M GONNA CALL IN. DON'T SUPPOSE WE GET TO KNOW WHAT'S IN THE BOX YOU JUST SHOT NINE PEOPLE FOR.
TOO LONG...TOO LONG...CUT THE TIMETABLE BY FIFTY MINUTES...EXTRACTION POINT MOVES THREE MILES NORTH...
YOU *WANT* TO KNOW? JUST KEEP YOUR-- WILL YOU *SHUT THE HELL UP?*

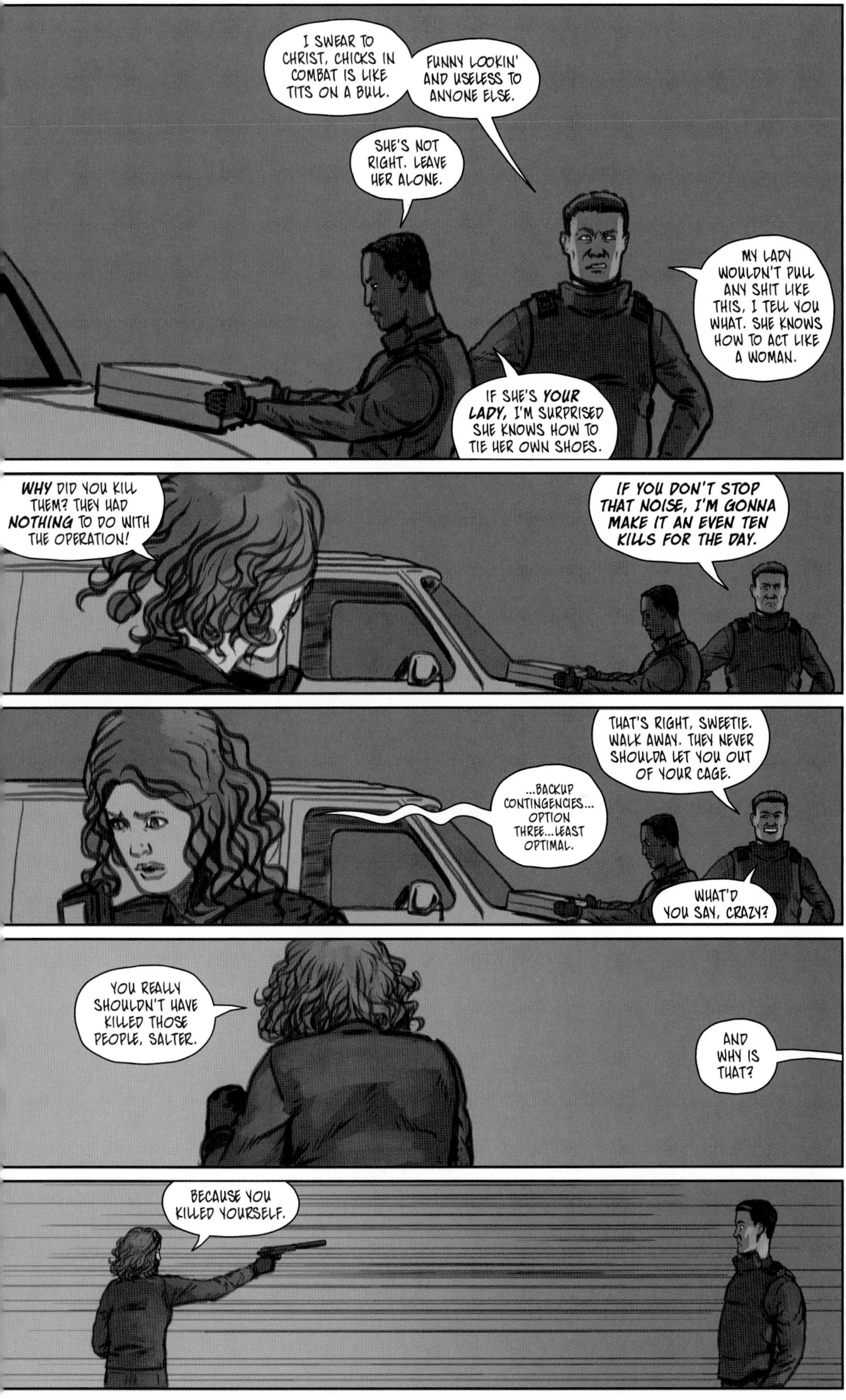
I SWEAR TO CHRIST, CHICKS IN COMBAT IS LIKE TITS ON A BULL.
FUNNY LOOKIN' AND USELESS TO ANYONE ELSE.
SHE'S NOT RIGHT. LEAVE HER ALONE.
MY LADY WOULDN'T PULL ANY SHIT LIKE THIS, I TELL YOU WHAT. SHE KNOWS HOW TO ACT LIKE A WOMAN.
IF SHE'S YOUR LADY, I'M SURPRISED SHE KNOWS HOW TO TIE HER OWN SHOES.
WHY DID YOU KILL THEM? THEY HAD NOTHING TO DO WITH THE OPERATION!
IF YOU DON'T STOP THAT NOISE, I'M GONNA MAKE IT AN EVEN TEN KILLS FOR THE DAY.
...BACKUP CONTINGENCIES... OPTION THREE...LEAST OPTIMAL.
THAT'S RIGHT, SWEETIE. WALK AWAY. THEY NEVER SHOULDA LET YOU OUT OF YOUR CAGE.
WHAT'D YOU SAY, CRAZY?
YOU REALLY SHOULDN'T HAVE KILLED THOSE PEOPLE, SALTER.
AND WHY IS THAT?
BECAUSE YOU KILLED YOURSELF.

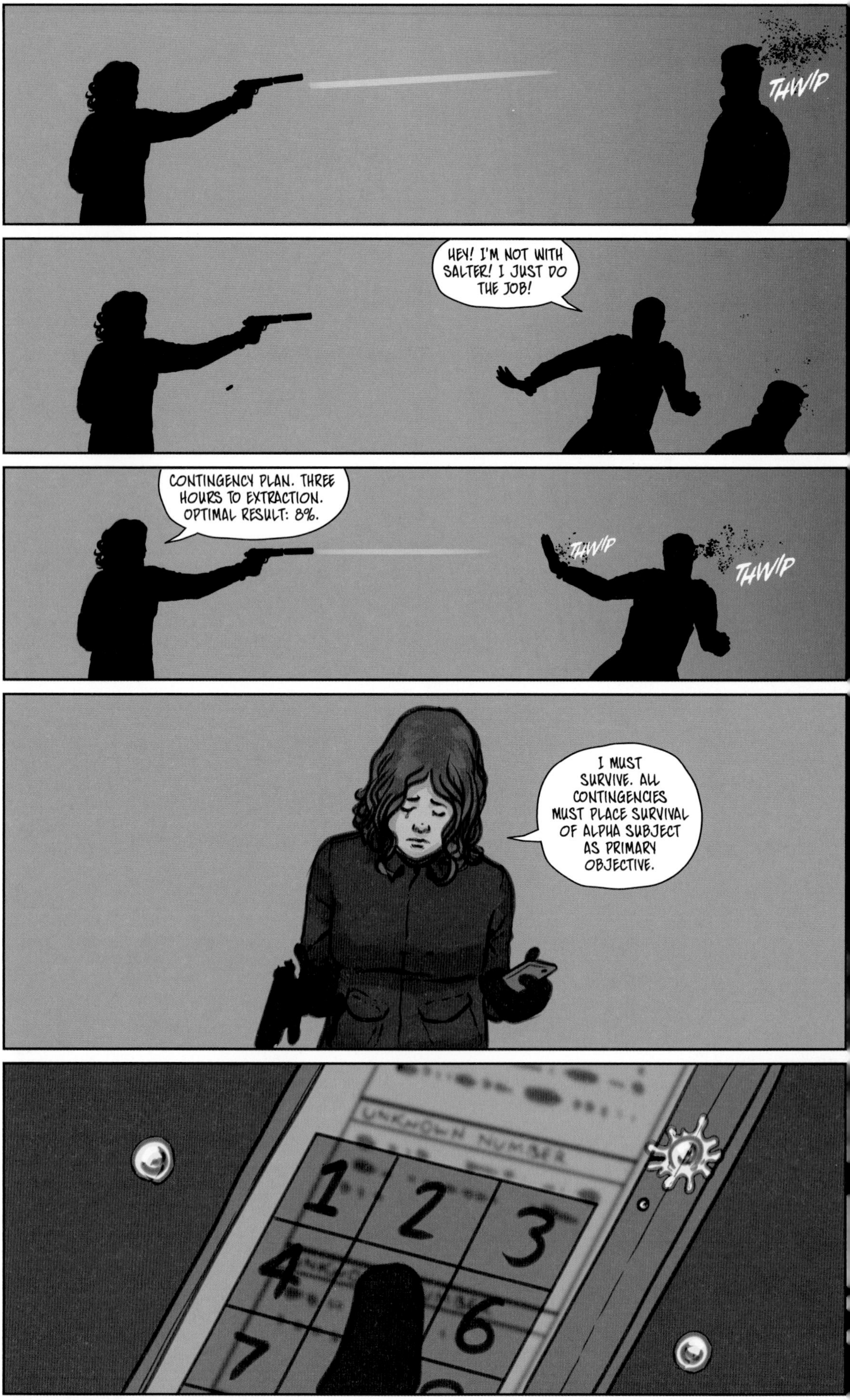
THWIP
HEY! I'M NOT WITH SALTER! I JUST DO THE JOB!
CONTINGENCY PLAN. THREE HOURS TO EXTRACTION. OPTIMAL RESULT: 8%.
THWIP
THWIP
I MUST SURVIVE. ALL CONTINGENCIES MUST PLACE SURVIVAL OF ALPHA SUBJECT AS PRIMARY OBJECTIVE.
UNKNOWN NUMBER
1
2
3
4
6
7

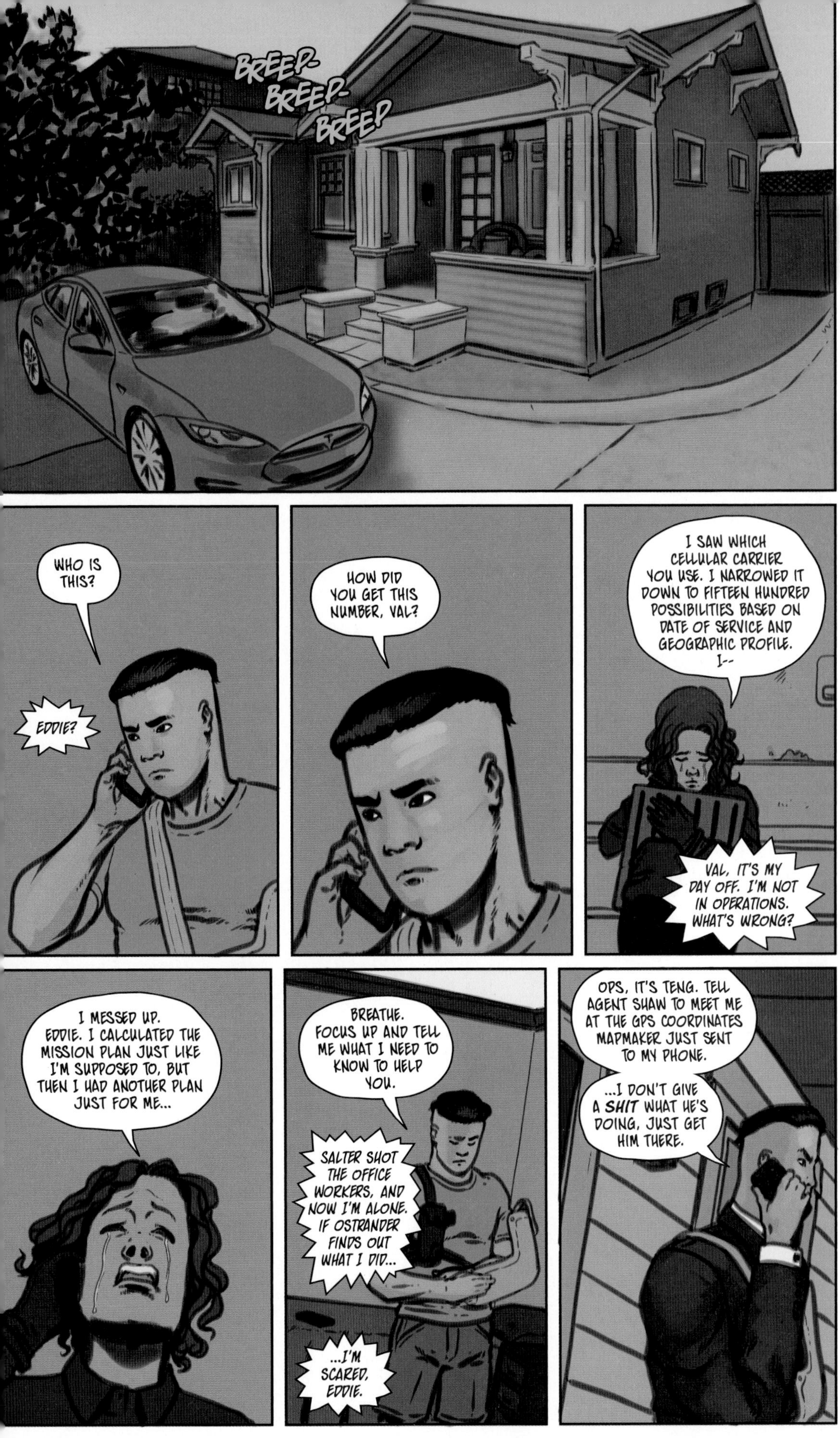
BREEP-
BREEP-
BREEP
WHO IS THIS?
EDDIE?
HOW DID YOU GET THIS NUMBER, VAL?
I SAW WHICH CELLULAR CARRIER YOU USE. I NARROWED IT DOWN TO FIFTEEN HUNDRED POSSIBILITIES BASED ON DATE OF SERVICE AND GEOGRAPHIC PROFILE. I--
VAL, IT'S MY DAY OFF. I'M NOT IN OPERATIONS. WHAT'S WRONG?
I MESSED UP. EDDIE. I CALCULATED THE MISSION PLAN JUST LIKE I'M SUPPOSED TO, BUT THEN I HAD ANOTHER PLAN JUST FOR ME...
BREATHE. FOCUS UP AND TELL ME WHAT I NEED TO KNOW TO HELP YOU.
SALTER SHOT THE OFFICE WORKERS, AND NOW I'M ALONE. IF OSTRANDER FINDS OUT WHAT I DID...
...I'M SCARED, EDDIE.
OPS, IT'S TENG. TELL AGENT SHAW TO MEET ME AT THE GPS COORDINATES MAPMAKER JUST SENT TO MY PHONE.
...I DON'T GIVE A SHIT WHAT HE'S DOING, JUST GET HIM THERE.

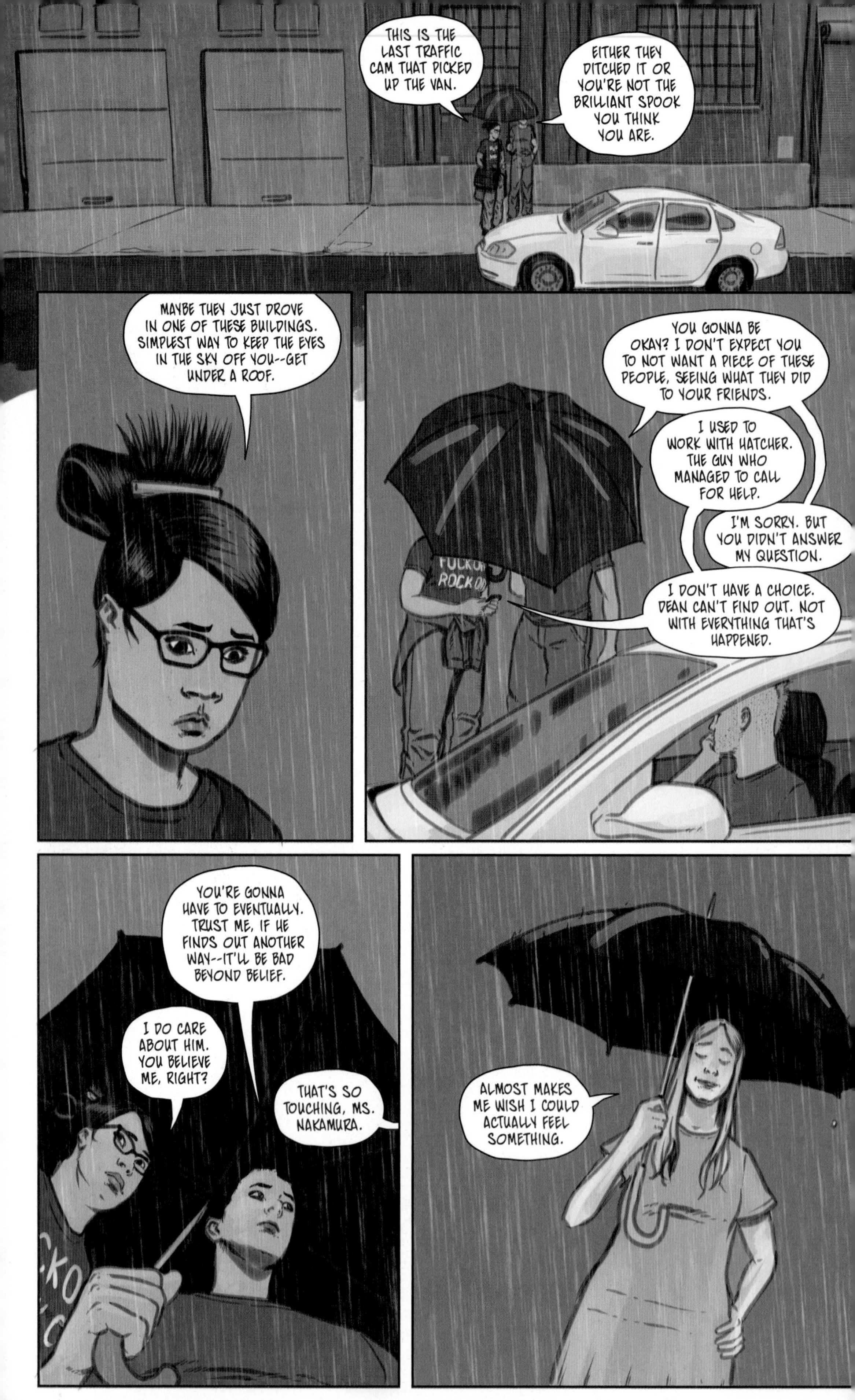
THIS IS THE LAST TRAFFIC CAM THAT PICKED UP THE VAN.
EITHER THEY DITCHED IT OR YOU'RE NOT THE BRILLIANT SPOOK YOU THINK YOU ARE.
MAYBE THEY JUST DROVE IN ONE OF THESE BUILDINGS. SIMPLEST WAY TO KEEP THE EYES IN THE SKY OFF YOU--GET UNDER A ROOF.
YOU GONNA BE OKAY? I DON'T EXPECT YOU TO NOT WANT A PIECE OF THESE PEOPLE, SEEING WHAT THEY DID TO YOUR FRIENDS.
I USED TO WORK WITH HATCHER. THE GUY WHO MANAGED TO CALL FOR HELP.
I'M SORRY. BUT YOU DIDN'T ANSWER MY QUESTION.
I DON'T HAVE A CHOICE. DEAN CAN'T FIND OUT. NOT WITH EVERYTHING THAT'S HAPPENED.
YOU'RE GONNA HAVE TO EVENTUALLY. TRUST ME, IF HE FINDS OUT ANOTHER WAY--IT'LL BE BAD BEYOND BELIEF.
I DO CARE ABOUT HIM. YOU BELIEVE ME, RIGHT?
THAT'S SO TOUCHING, MS. NAKAMURA.
ALMOST MAKES ME WISH I COULD ACTUALLY FEEL SOMETHING.

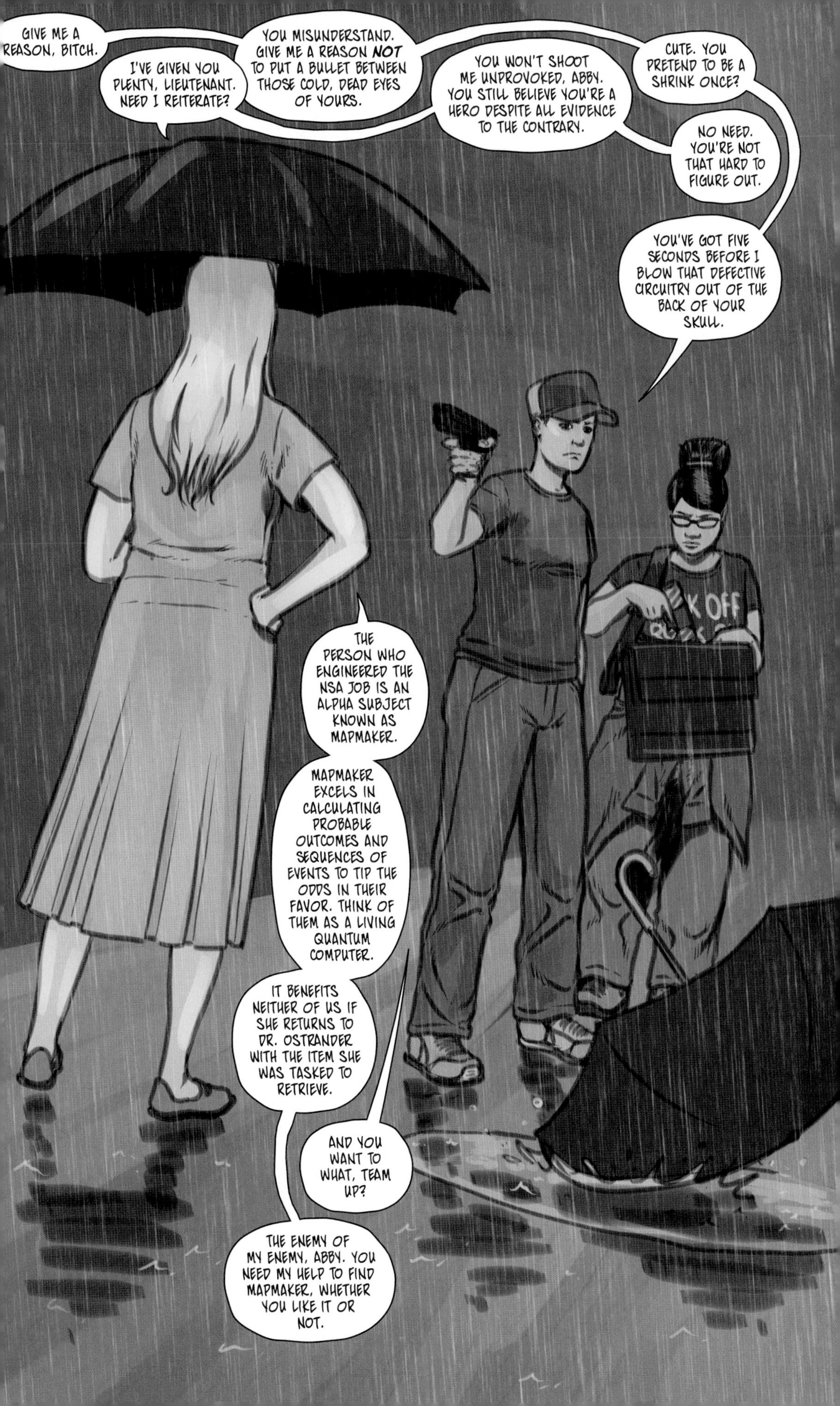
GIVE ME A REASON, BITCH.
I'VE GIVEN YOU PLENTY, LIEUTENANT. NEED I REITERATE?
YOU MISUNDERSTAND. GIVE ME A REASON NOT TO PUT A BULLET BETWEEN THOSE COLD, DEAD EYES OF YOURS.
YOU WON'T SHOOT ME UNPROVOKED, ABBY. YOU STILL BELIEVE YOU'RE A HERO DESPITE ALL EVIDENCE TO THE CONTRARY.
CUTE. YOU PRETEND TO BE A SHRINK ONCE?
NO NEED. YOU'RE NOT THAT HARD TO FIGURE OUT.
YOU'VE GOT FIVE SECONDS BEFORE I BLOW THAT DEFECTIVE CIRCUITRY OUT OF THE BACK OF YOUR SKULL.
THE PERSON WHO ENGINEERED THE NSA JOB IS AN ALPHA SUBJECT KNOWN AS MAPMAKER.
MAPMAKER EXCELS IN CALCULATING PROBABLE OUTCOMES AND SEQUENCES OF EVENTS TO TIP THE ODDS IN THEIR FAVOR. THINK OF THEM AS A LIVING QUANTUM COMPUTER.
IT BENEFITS NEITHER OF US IF SHE RETURNS TO DR. OSTRANDER WITH THE ITEM SHE WAS TASKED TO RETRIEVE.
AND YOU WANT TO WHAT, TEAM UP?
THE ENEMY OF MY ENEMY, ABBY. YOU NEED MY HELP TO FIND MAPMAKER, WHETHER YOU LIKE IT OR NOT.

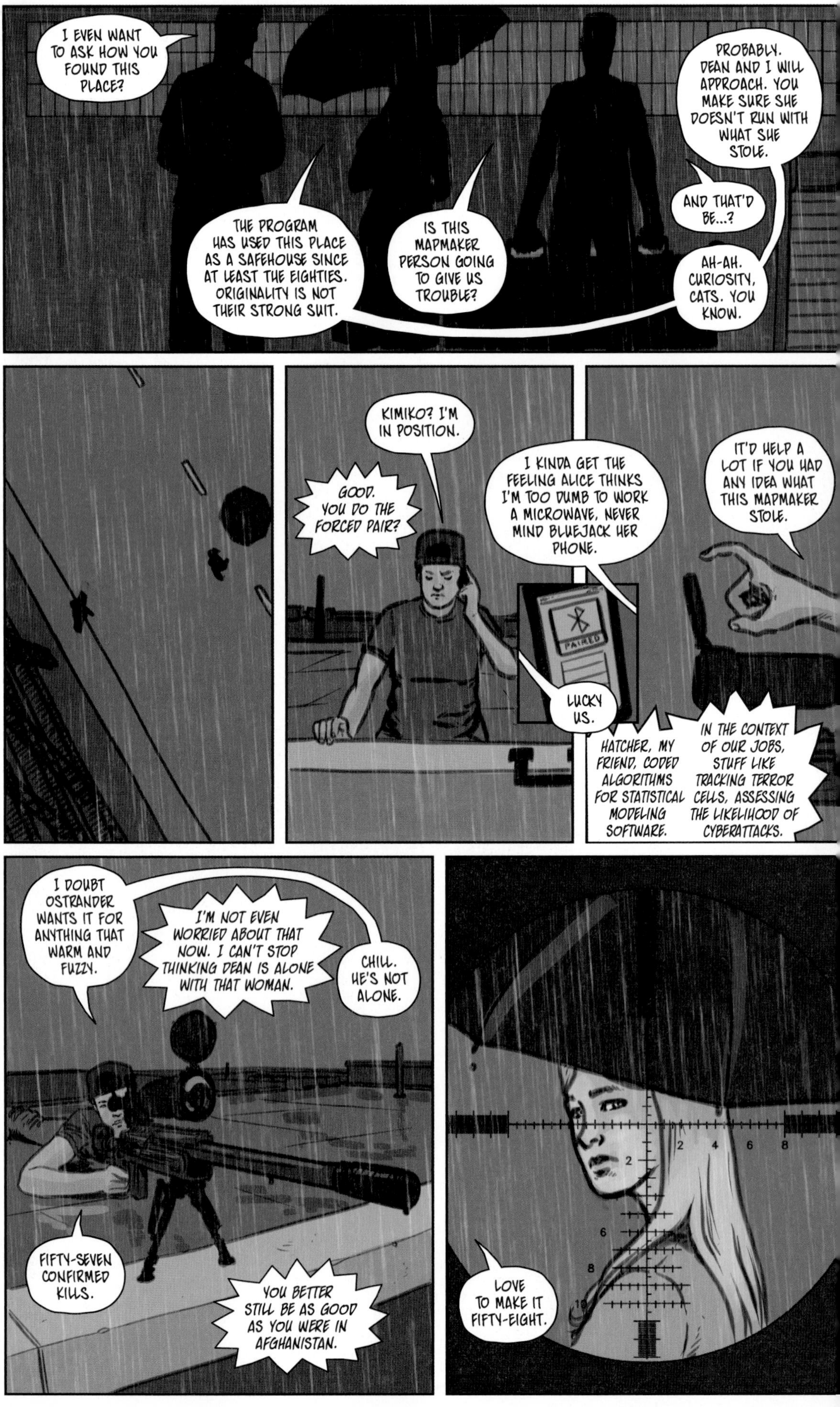
I EVEN WANT TO ASK HOW YOU FOUND THIS PLACE?
THE PROGRAM HAS USED THIS PLACE AS A SAFEHOUSE SINCE AT LEAST THE EIGHTIES. ORIGINALITY IS NOT THEIR STRONG SUIT.
IS THIS MAPMAKER PERSON GOING TO GIVE US TROUBLE?
PROBABLY. DEAN AND I WILL APPROACH. YOU MAKE SURE SHE DOESN'T RUN WITH WHAT SHE STOLE.
AND THAT'D BE...?
AH-AH. CURIOSITY, CATS. YOU KNOW.
KIMIKO? I'M IN POSITION.
GOOD. YOU DO THE FORCED PAIR?
I KINDA GET THE FEELING ALICE THINKS I'M TOO DUMB TO WORK A MICROWAVE, NEVER MIND BLUEJACK HER PHONE.
PAIRED
LUCKY US.
IT'D HELP A LOT IF YOU HAD ANY IDEA WHAT THIS MAPMAKER STOLE.
HATCHER, MY FRIEND, CODED ALGORITHMS FOR STATISTICAL MODELING SOFTWARE.
IN THE CONTEXT OF OUR JOBS, STUFF LIKE TRACKING TERROR CELLS, ASSESSING THE LIKELIHOOD OF CYBERATTACKS.
I DOUBT OSTRANDER WANTS IT FOR ANYTHING THAT WARM AND FUZZY.
I'M NOT EVEN WORRIED ABOUT THAT NOW. I CAN'T STOP THINKING DEAN IS ALONE WITH THAT WOMAN.
CHILL. HE'S NOT ALONE.
FIFTY-SEVEN CONFIRMED KILLS.
YOU BETTER STILL BE AS GOOD AS YOU WERE IN AFGHANISTAN.
LOVE TO MAKE IT FIFTY-EIGHT.

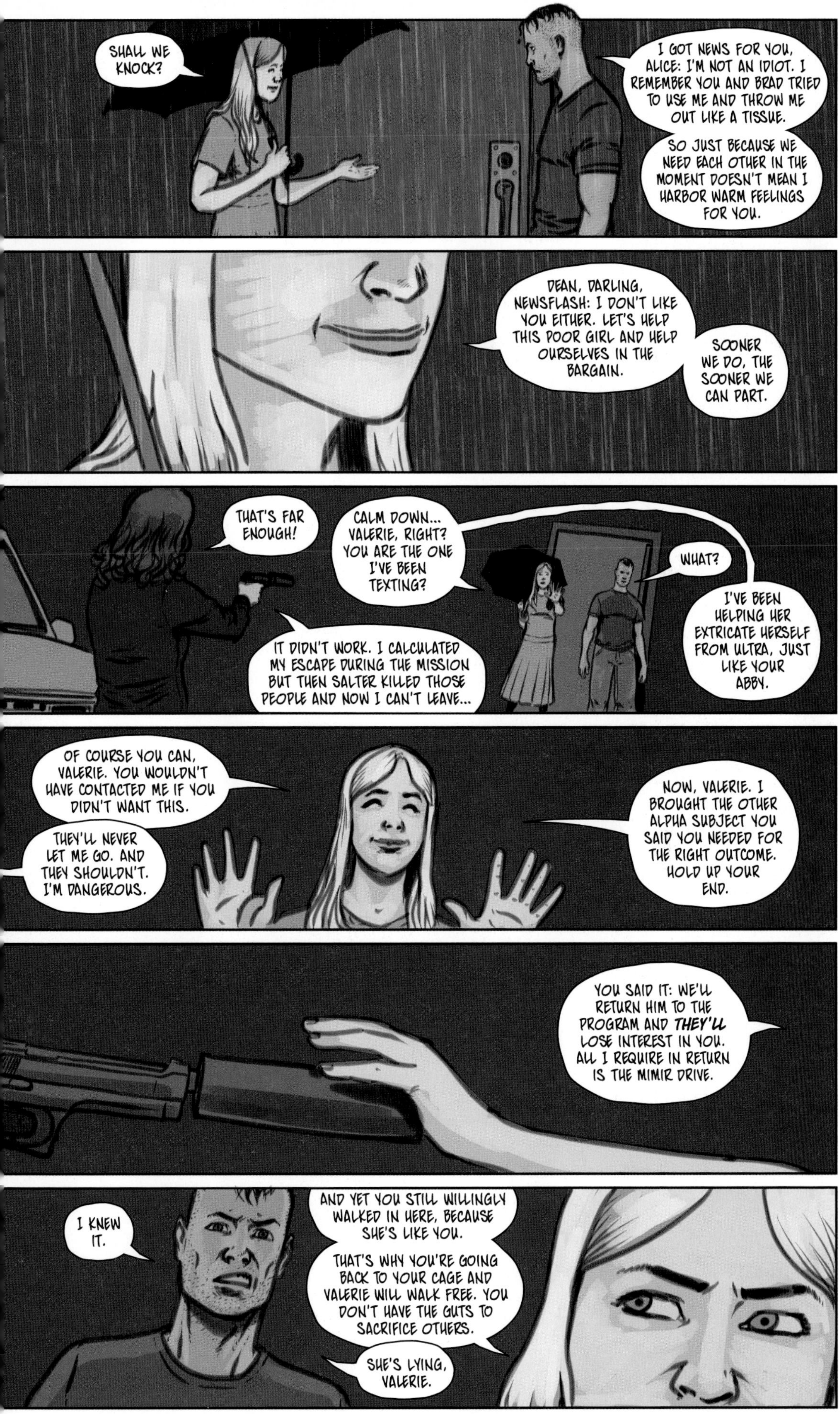

SHALL WE KNOCK?
I GOT NEWS FOR YOU, ALICE: I'M NOT AN IDIOT. I REMEMBER YOU AND BRAD TRIED TO USE ME AND THROW ME OUT LIKE A TISSUE.
SO JUST BECAUSE WE NEED EACH OTHER IN THE MOMENT DOESN'T MEAN I HARBOR WARM FEELINGS FOR YOU.
DEAN, DARLING, NEWSFLASH: I DON'T LIKE YOU EITHER. LET'S HELP THIS POOR GIRL AND HELP OURSELVES IN THE BARGAIN.
SOONER WE DO, THE SOONER WE CAN PART.
THAT'S FAR ENOUGH!
CALM DOWN... VALERIE, RIGHT? YOU ARE THE ONE I'VE BEEN TEXTING?
WHAT?
I'VE BEEN HELPING HER EXTRICATE HERSELF FROM ULTRA, JUST LIKE YOUR ABBY.
IT DIDN'T WORK. I CALCULATED MY ESCAPE DURING THE MISSION BUT THEN SALTER KILLED THOSE PEOPLE AND NOW I CAN'T LEAVE...
OF COURSE YOU CAN, VALERIE. YOU WOULDN'T HAVE CONTACTED ME IF YOU DIDN'T WANT THIS.
THEY'LL NEVER LET ME GO. AND THEY SHOULDN'T. I'M DANGEROUS.
NOW, VALERIE. I BROUGHT THE OTHER ALPHA SUBJECT YOU SAID YOU NEEDED FOR THE RIGHT OUTCOME. HOLD UP YOUR END.
YOU SAID IT: WE'LL RETURN HIM TO THE PROGRAM AND *THEY'LL* LOSE INTEREST IN YOU. ALL I REQUIRE IN RETURN IS THE MIMIR DRIVE.
I KNEW IT.
AND YET YOU STILL WILLINGLY WALKED IN HERE, BECAUSE SHE'S LIKE YOU.
THAT'S WHY YOU'RE GOING BACK TO YOUR CAGE AND VALERIE WILL WALK FREE. YOU DON'T HAVE THE GUTS TO SACRIFICE OTHERS.
SHE'S LYING, VALERIE.

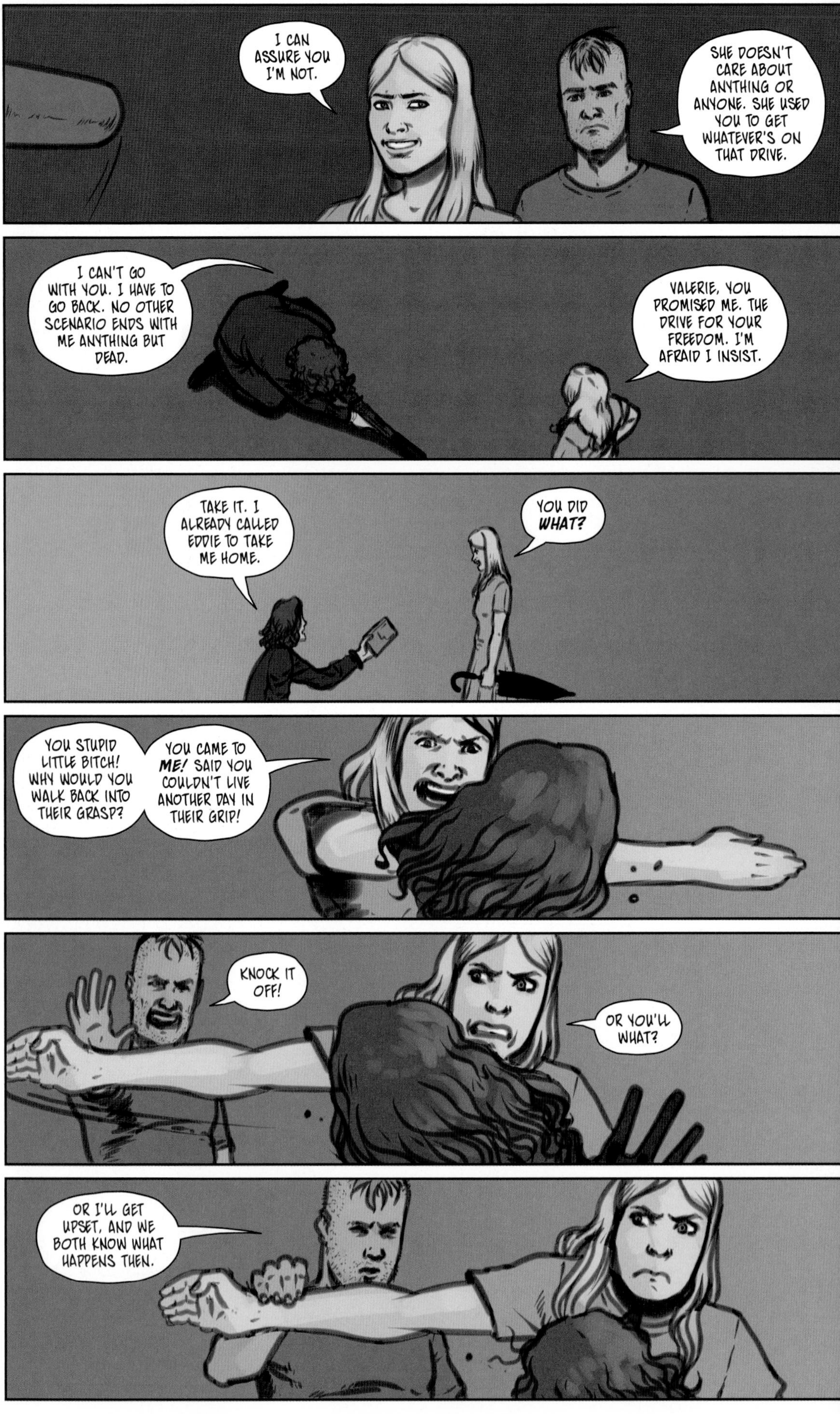

I CAN ASSURE YOU I'M NOT.
SHE DOESN'T CARE ABOUT ANYTHING OR ANYONE. SHE USED YOU TO GET WHATEVER'S ON THAT DRIVE.
I CAN'T GO WITH YOU. I HAVE TO GO BACK. NO OTHER SCENARIO ENDS WITH ME ANYTHING BUT DEAD.
VALERIE, YOU PROMISED ME. THE DRIVE FOR YOUR FREEDOM. I'M AFRAID I INSIST.
TAKE IT. I ALREADY CALLED EDDIE TO TAKE ME HOME.
YOU DID WHAT?
YOU STUPID LITTLE BITCH! WHY WOULD YOU WALK BACK INTO THEIR GRASP?
YOU CAME TO ME! SAID YOU COULDN'T LIVE ANOTHER DAY IN THEIR GRIP!
KNOCK IT OFF!
OR YOU'LL WHAT?
OR I'LL GET UPSET, AND WE BOTH KNOW WHAT HAPPENS THEN.

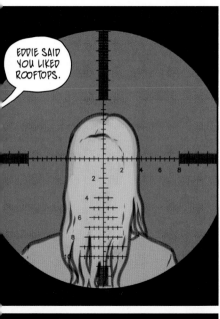

EDDIE SAID YOU LIKED ROOFTOPS.

FRESH AIR KEEPS ME AWAKE.

YOU'RE NOT GOING TO TAKE OUT MAPMAKER. STAND UP.

IF THAT GIRL IS MAPMAKER, YOU'RE GOING TO WANT ME RIGHT WHERE I AM.

REALLY. WHY IS THAT?

BECAUSE SHE'S NOT WHO I'M AIMING AT.

YOU THINK THERE'S ANYTHING BUT A CELL BACK THERE NOW THAT YOU TRIED TO RUN? YOU'RE JUST A BROKEN DOLL THEY WON'T HAVE ANY MORE USE FOR!

TAKE THE DRIVE AND GO! LEAVE ME ALONE!

I DON'T WANT THE DRIVE, VALERIE! I WANT TO HURT THEM, AND YOU'RE GETTING IN MY WAY. AND LITTLE GIRL, THAT IS NOT A PLACE YOU WANT TO BE.

STOP!

FINE. THE TRUTH? THERE'S NOTHING FOR HER HERE OR OUT THERE. HER BRAIN IS A PILE OF BROKEN GLASS. THEY USED HER UP.

SHE'S HOPELESS.

WHICH IS WHY I'M PUTTING HER OUT OF HER MISERY.

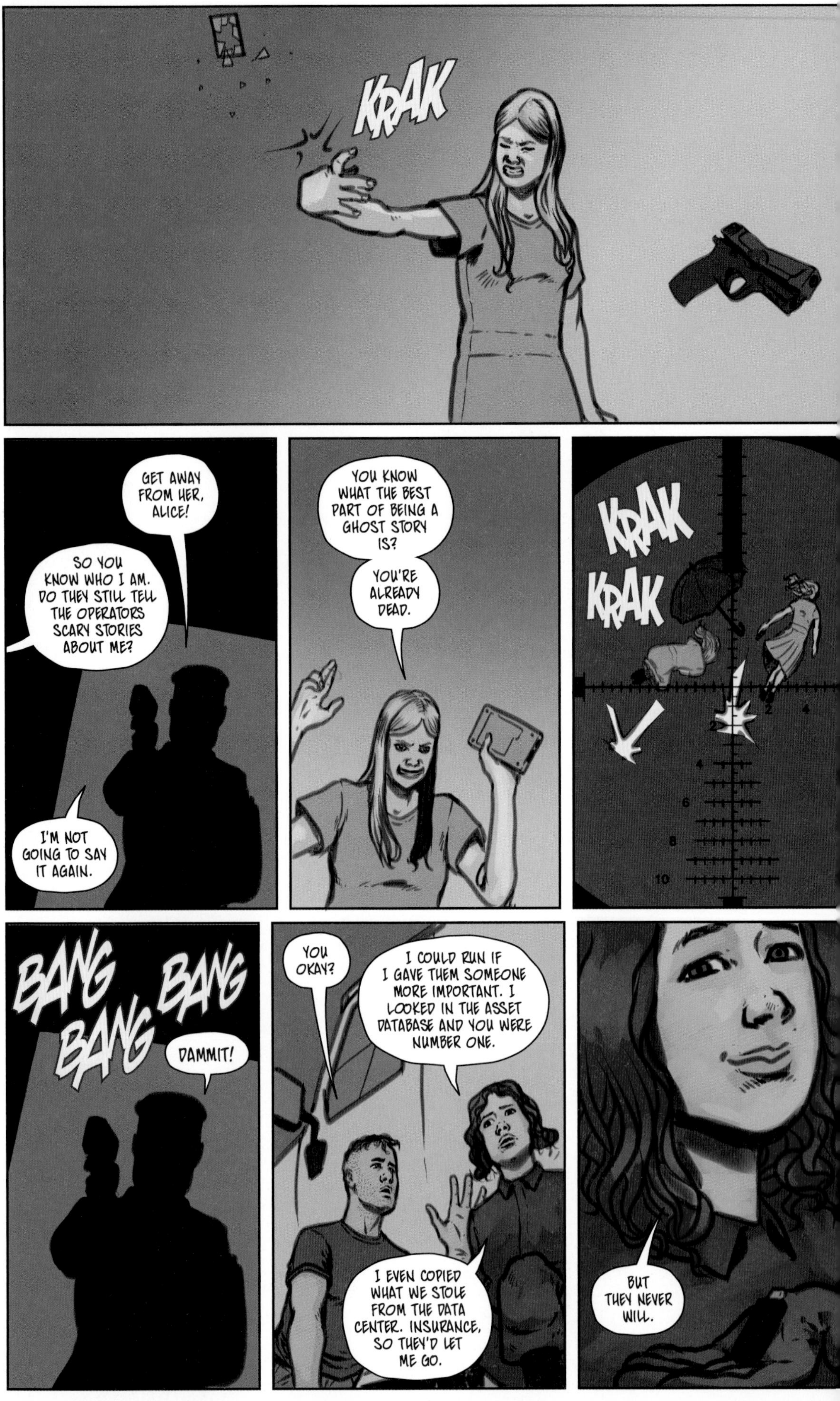
KRAK
GET AWAY FROM HER, ALICE!
SO YOU KNOW WHO I AM. DO THEY STILL TELL THE OPERATORS SCARY STORIES ABOUT ME?
I'M NOT GOING TO SAY IT AGAIN.
YOU KNOW WHAT THE BEST PART OF BEING A GHOST STORY IS?
YOU'RE ALREADY DEAD.
KRAK
KRAK
BANG
BANG
BANG
DAMMIT!
YOU OKAY?
I COULD RUN IF I GAVE THEM SOMEONE MORE IMPORTANT. I LOOKED IN THE ASSET DATABASE AND YOU WERE NUMBER ONE.
I EVEN COPIED WHAT WE STOLE FROM THE DATA CENTER. INSURANCE, SO THEY'D LET ME GO.
BUT THEY NEVER WILL.

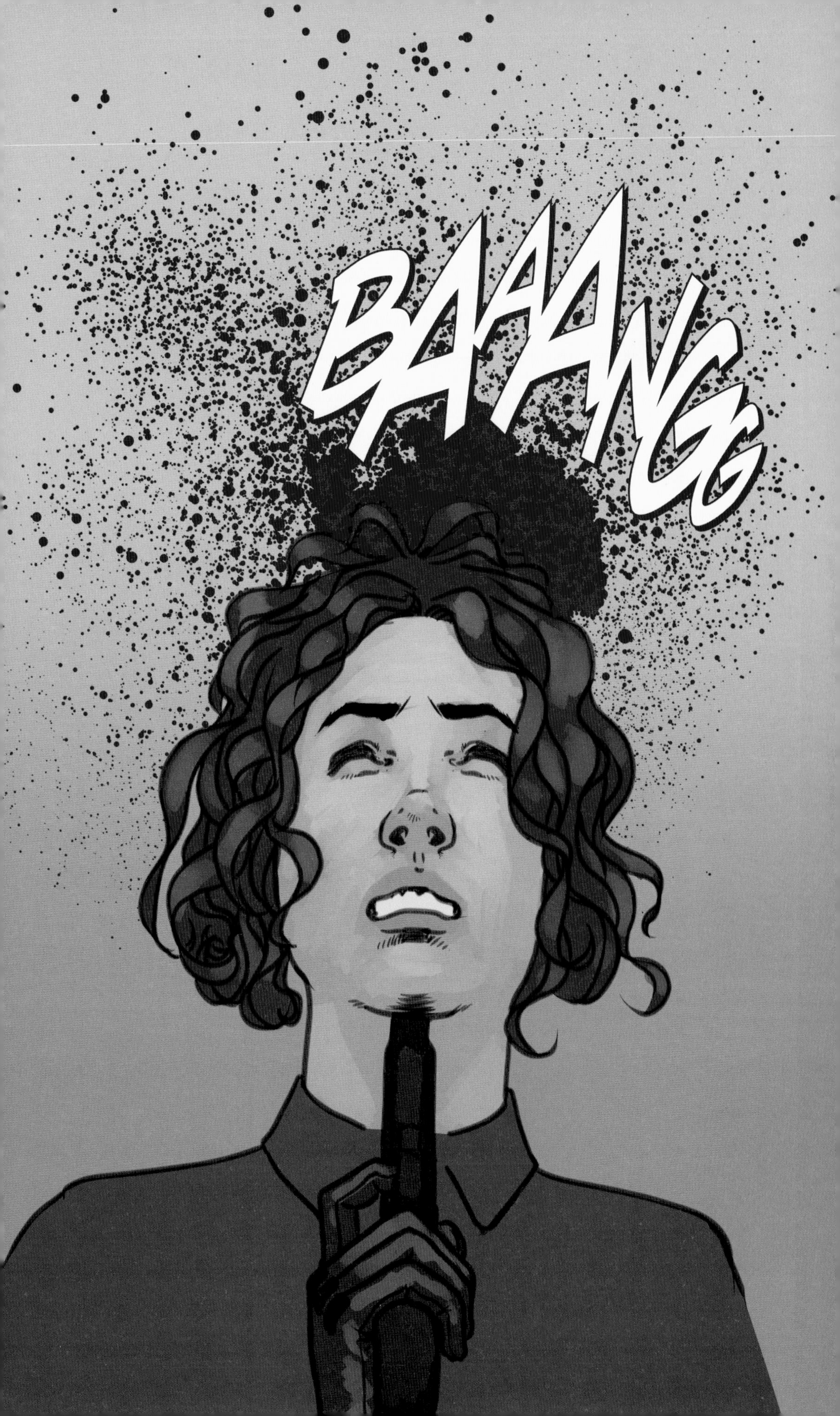
BAAANGG

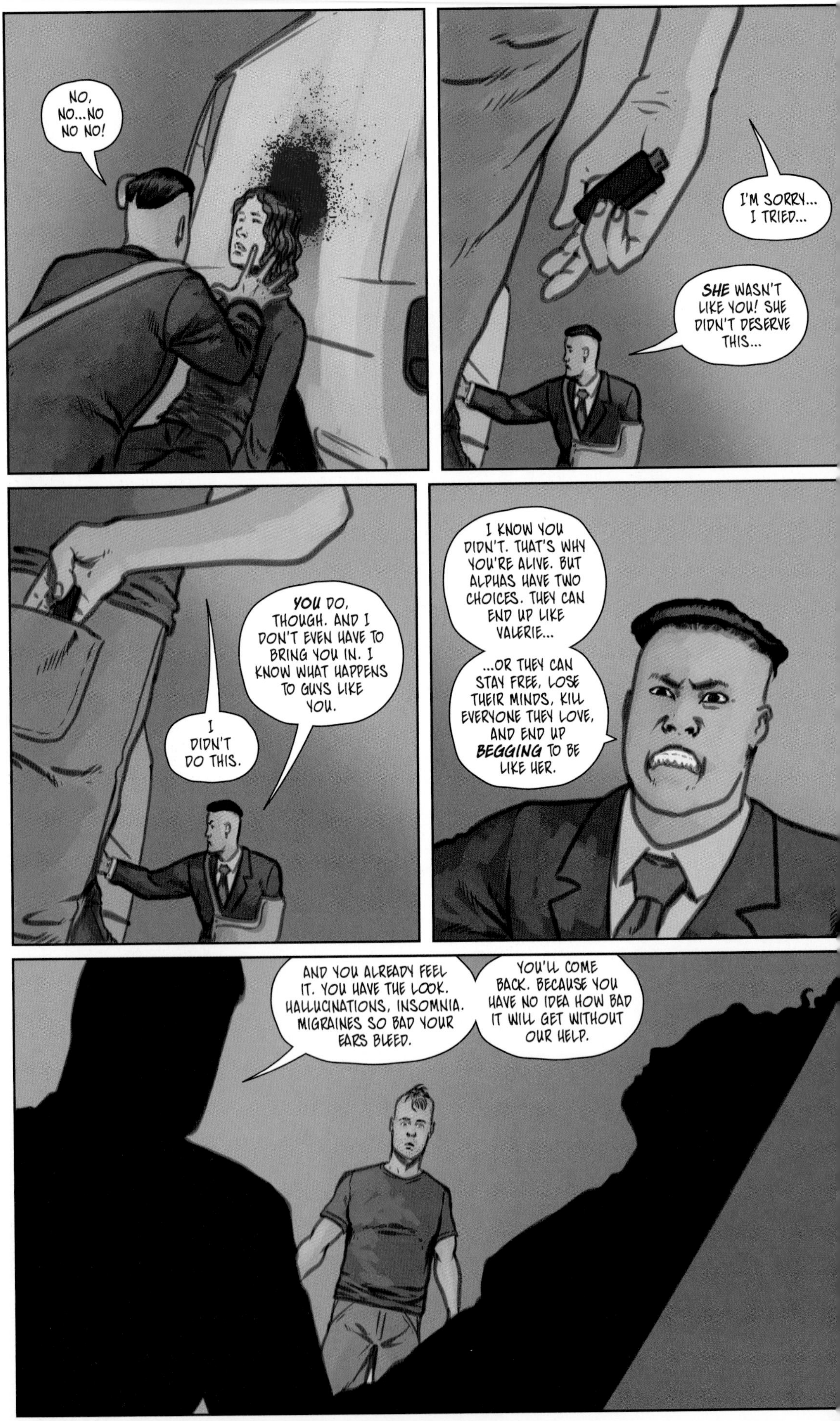
NO, NO...NO NO NO!
I'M SORRY... I TRIED...
SHE WASN'T LIKE YOU! SHE DIDN'T DESERVE THIS...
I DIDN'T DO THIS.
YOU DO, THOUGH. AND I DON'T EVEN HAVE TO BRING YOU IN. I KNOW WHAT HAPPENS TO GUYS LIKE YOU.
I KNOW YOU DIDN'T. THAT'S WHY YOU'RE ALIVE. BUT ALPHAS HAVE TWO CHOICES. THEY CAN END UP LIKE VALERIE...
...OR THEY CAN STAY FREE, LOSE THEIR MINDS, KILL EVERYONE THEY LOVE, AND END UP BEGGING TO BE LIKE HER.
AND YOU ALREADY FEEL IT. YOU HAVE THE LOOK. HALLUCINATIONS, INSOMNIA. MIGRAINES SO BAD YOUR EARS BLEED.
YOU'LL COME BACK. BECAUSE YOU HAVE NO IDEA HOW BAD IT WILL GET WITHOUT OUR HELP.

ALL THE FILES FOR THE MIMIR PROGRAM FROM THE NSA SKIFF ROOM.

EXCELLENT WORK, MR. TENG. YOU AND MR. SHAW BOTH.

SOMETHING ELSE?

I HOPE WHATEVER MIMIR IS WAS WORTH IT. VALERIE DIED FOR THAT BOX.

MIMIR WAS A NORSEMAN RENOWED FOR HIS WISDOM. ODIN HIMSELF CONSULTED MIMIR'S SEVERED HEAD.

YOU SHOULD BE GLAD IT'S WORTH SO VERY MUCH. BECAUSE MIMIR BEING MORE VALUABLE THAN BRINGING IN LOGAN AND PALMER IS THE REASON YOU AND SHAW ARE STILL BREATHING.

I TOLD YOU, ALICE WAS THERE. PALMER OVERPOWERED SHAW AND THEY ALL GOT AWAY.

DON'T LIE TO ME, EDWARD. IT DOESN'T SUIT YOU.

SENATOR STARK, PLEASE.

YES, I'LL HOLD.

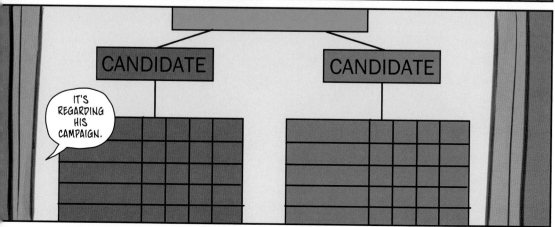

CANDIDATE

CANDIDATE

IT'S REGARDING HIS CAMPAIGN.

CHAPTER NINE

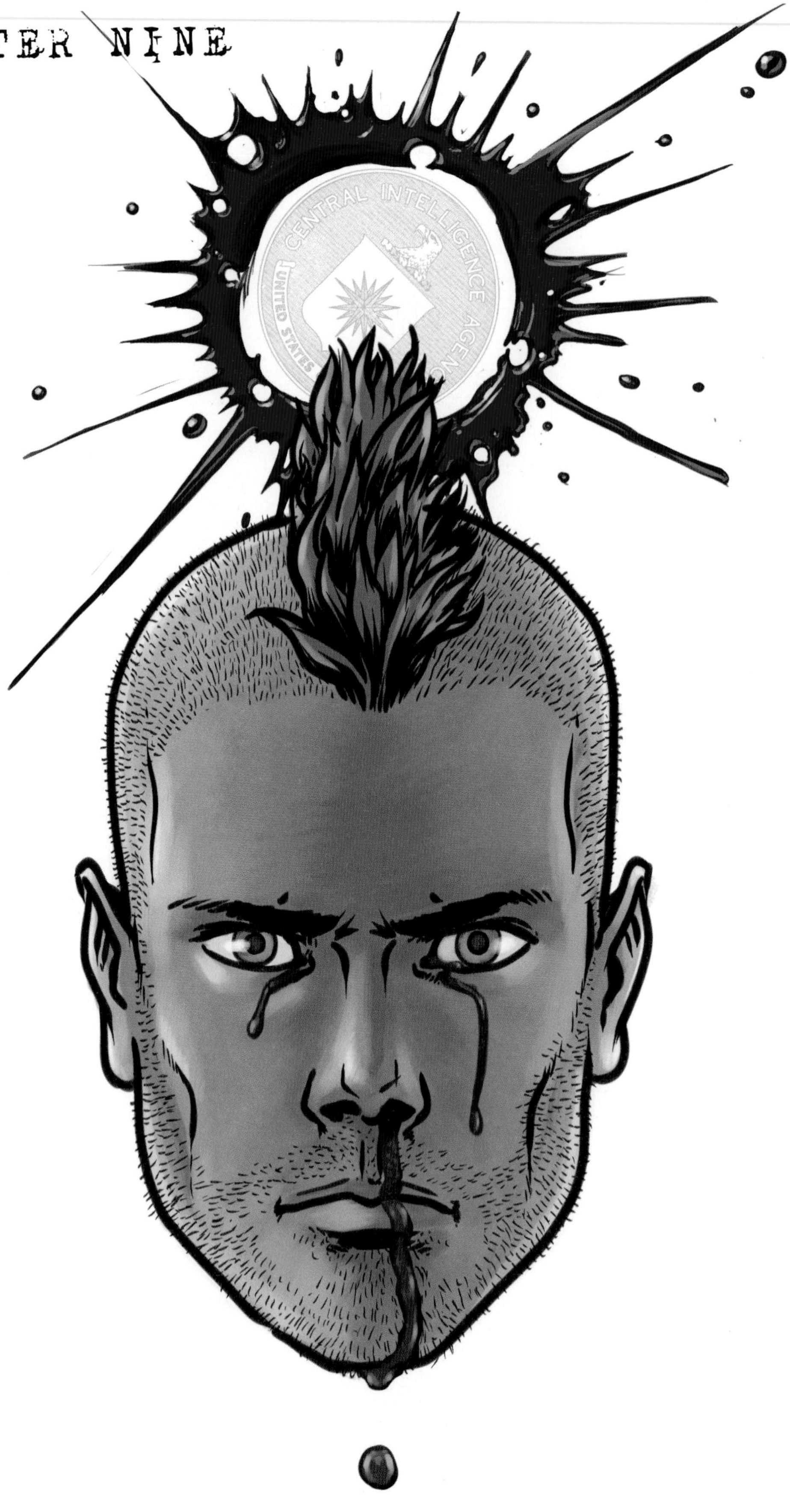
CENTRAL INTELLIGENCE AGENC
UNITED STATES

Issue #9 Cover Art

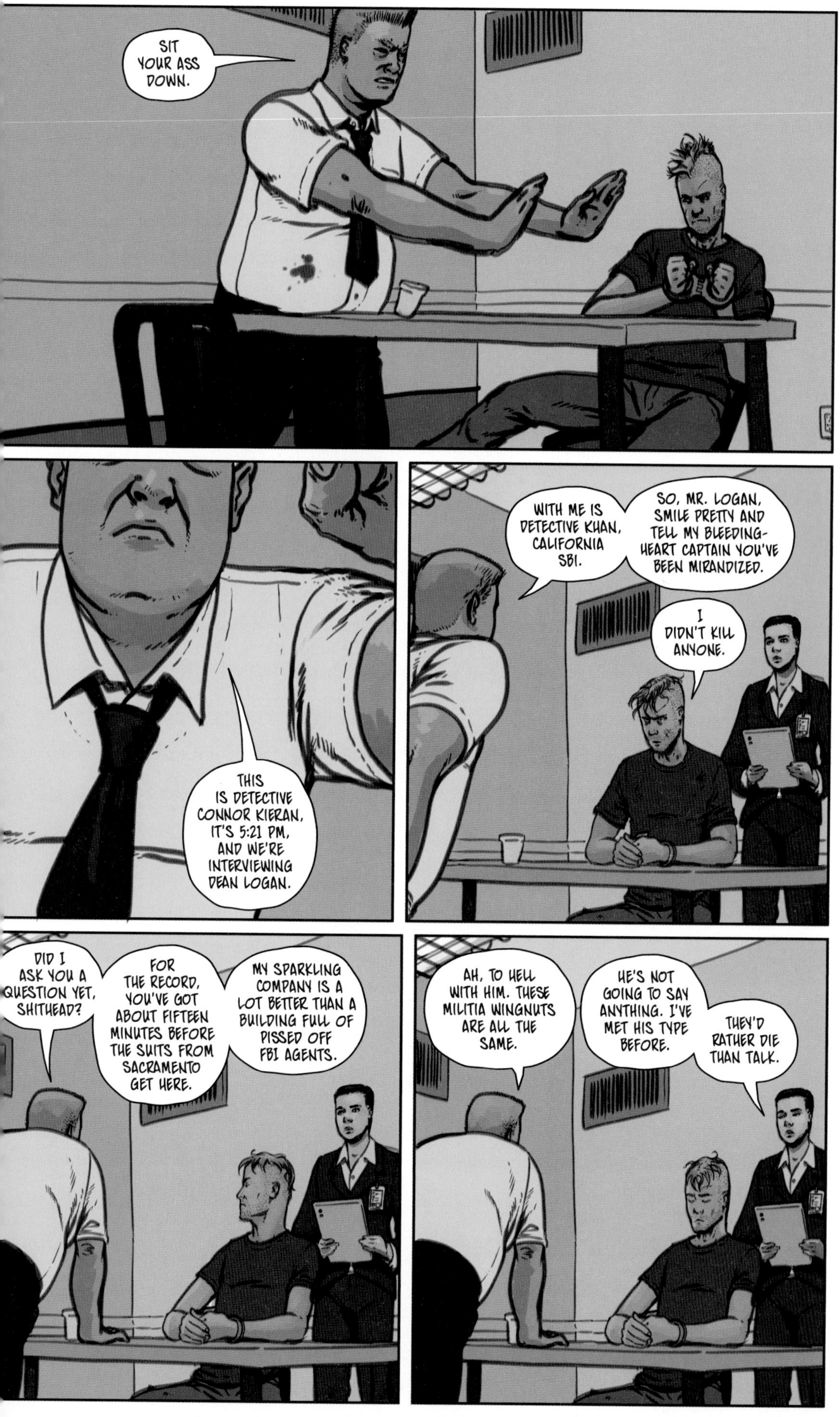
SIT YOUR ASS DOWN.
THIS IS DETECTIVE CONNOR KIERAN, IT'S 5:21 PM, AND WE'RE INTERVIEWING DEAN LOGAN.
WITH ME IS DETECTIVE KHAN, CALIFORNIA SBI.
SO, MR. LOGAN, SMILE PRETTY AND TELL MY BLEEDING-HEART CAPTAIN YOU'VE BEEN MIRANDIZED.
I DIDN'T KILL ANYONE.
DID I ASK YOU A QUESTION YET, SHITHEAD?
FOR THE RECORD, YOU'VE GOT ABOUT FIFTEEN MINUTES BEFORE THE SUITS FROM SACRAMENTO GET HERE.
MY SPARKLING COMPANY IS A LOT BETTER THAN A BUILDING FULL OF PISSED OFF FBI AGENTS.
AH, TO HELL WITH HIM. THESE MILITIA WINGNUTS ARE ALL THE SAME.
HE'S NOT GOING TO SAY ANYTHING. I'VE MET HIS TYPE BEFORE.
THEY'D RATHER DIE THAN TALK.

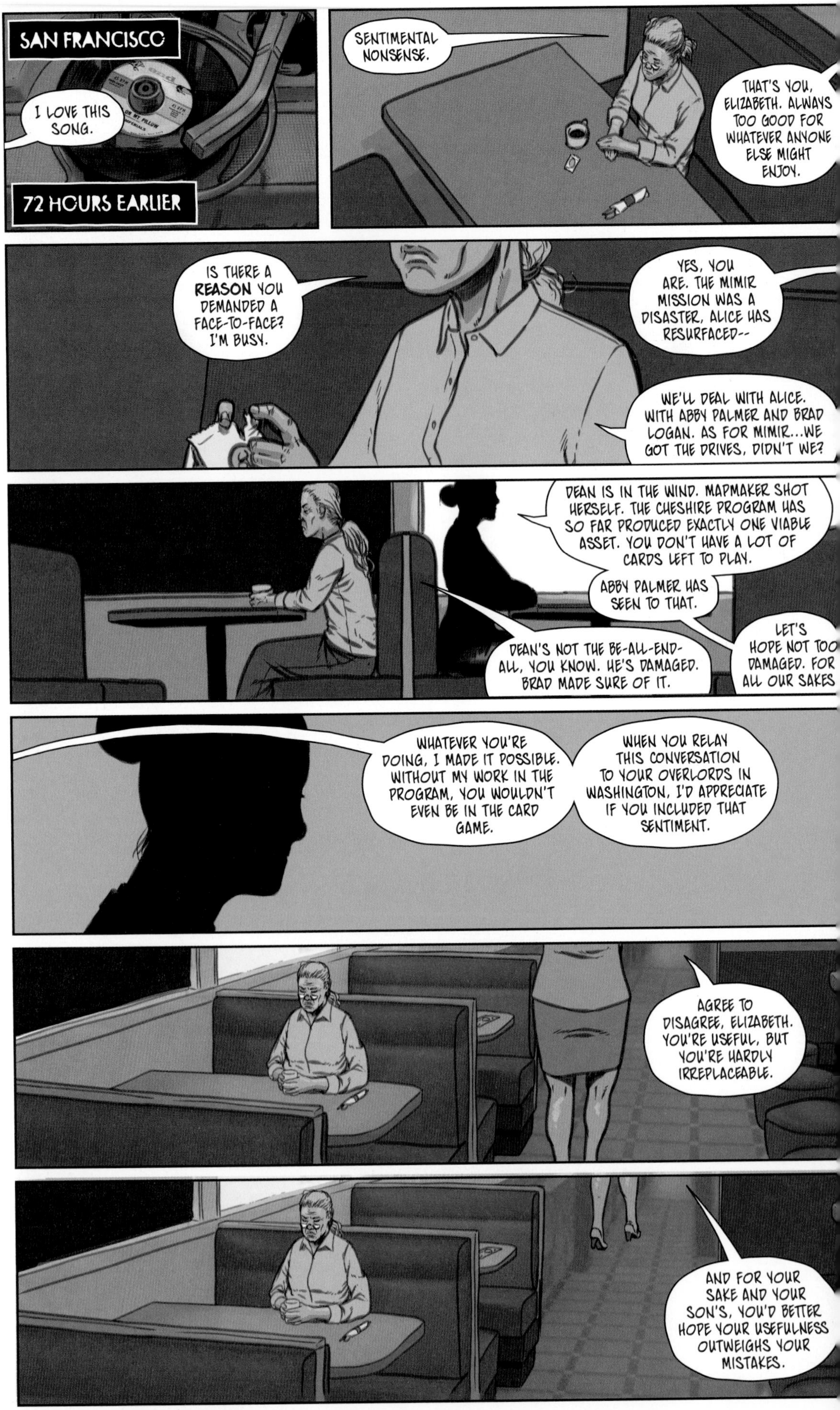
SAN FRANCISCO
I LOVE THIS SONG.
72 HOURS EARLIER
SENTIMENTAL NONSENSE.
THAT'S YOU, ELIZABETH. ALWAYS TOO GOOD FOR WHATEVER ANYONE ELSE MIGHT ENJOY.
IS THERE A **REASON** YOU DEMANDED A FACE-TO-FACE? I'M BUSY.
YES, YOU ARE. THE MIMIR MISSION WAS A DISASTER, ALICE HAS RESURFACED--
WE'LL DEAL WITH ALICE. WITH ABBY PALMER AND BRAD LOGAN. AS FOR MIMIR...WE GOT THE DRIVES, DIDN'T WE?
DEAN IS IN THE WIND. MAPMAKER SHOT HERSELF. THE CHESHIRE PROGRAM HAS SO FAR PRODUCED EXACTLY ONE VIABLE ASSET. YOU DON'T HAVE A LOT OF CARDS LEFT TO PLAY.
DEAN'S NOT THE BE-ALL-END-ALL, YOU KNOW. HE'S DAMAGED. BRAD MADE SURE OF IT.
ABBY PALMER HAS SEEN TO THAT.
LET'S HOPE NOT TOO DAMAGED. FOR ALL OUR SAKES
WHATEVER YOU'RE DOING, I MADE IT POSSIBLE. WITHOUT MY WORK IN THE PROGRAM, YOU WOULDN'T EVEN BE IN THE CARD GAME.
WHEN YOU RELAY THIS CONVERSATION TO YOUR OVERLORDS IN WASHINGTON, I'D APPRECIATE IF YOU INCLUDED THAT SENTIMENT.
AGREE TO DISAGREE, ELIZABETH. YOU'RE USEFUL, BUT YOU'RE HARDLY IRREPLACEABLE.
AND FOR YOUR SAKE AND YOUR SON'S, YOU'D BETTER HOPE YOUR USEFULNESS OUTWEIGHS YOUR MISTAKES.

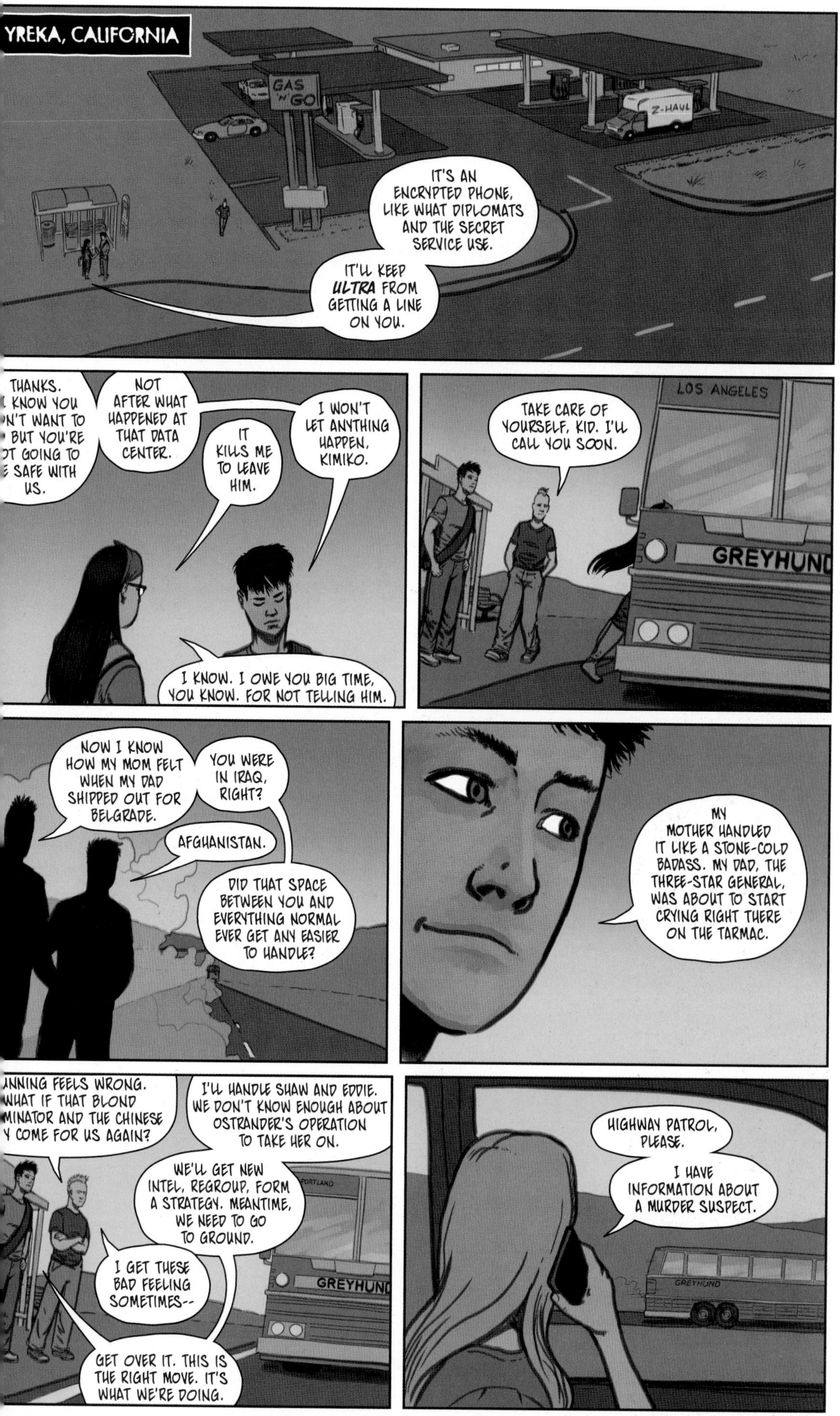

YREKA, CALIFORNIA
GAS 'N' GO
Z-HAUL
IT'S AN ENCRYPTED PHONE, LIKE WHAT DIPLOMATS AND THE SECRET SERVICE USE.
IT'LL KEEP ULTRA FROM GETTING A LINE ON YOU.
THANKS. I KNOW YOU DON'T WANT TO BUT YOU'RE NOT GOING TO BE SAFE WITH US.
NOT AFTER WHAT HAPPENED AT THAT DATA CENTER.
I WON'T LET ANYTHING HAPPEN, KIMIKO.
IT KILLS ME TO LEAVE HIM.
I KNOW. I OWE YOU BIG TIME, YOU KNOW. FOR NOT TELLING HIM.
LOS ANGELES
GREYHUND
TAKE CARE OF YOURSELF, KID. I'LL CALL YOU SOON.
NOW I KNOW HOW MY MOM FELT WHEN MY DAD SHIPPED OUT FOR BELGRADE.
YOU WERE IN IRAQ, RIGHT?
AFGHANISTAN.
DID THAT SPACE BETWEEN YOU AND EVERYTHING NORMAL EVER GET ANY EASIER TO HANDLE?
MY MOTHER HANDLED IT LIKE A STONE-COLD BADASS. MY DAD, THE THREE-STAR GENERAL, WAS ABOUT TO START CRYING RIGHT THERE ON THE TARMAC.
RUNNING FEELS WRONG. WHAT IF THAT BLOND TERMINATOR AND THE CHINESE GUY COME FOR US AGAIN?
I'LL HANDLE SHAW AND EDDIE. WE DON'T KNOW ENOUGH ABOUT OSTRANDER'S OPERATION TO TAKE HER ON.
WE'LL GET NEW INTEL, REGROUP, FORM A STRATEGY. MEANTIME, WE NEED TO GO TO GROUND.
PORTLAND
GREYHUND
I GET THESE BAD FEELING SOMETIMES--
GET OVER IT. THIS IS THE RIGHT MOVE. IT'S WHAT WE'RE DOING.
HIGHWAY PATROL, PLEASE.
I HAVE INFORMATION ABOUT A MURDER SUSPECT.
GREYHUND

NSA LISTENING POST, LOS ANGELES

YOU'RE TELLING ME THAT AFTER ALL THIS TIME, YOU STILL DON'T HAVE ANYTHING?

SIR, DEAN'S NOT INVOLVED IN WHATEVER PACIFIC IS PLANNING.

IF ANYTHING, THEY'RE PLANNING TO USE HIM AS A SCAPEGOAT.

WALK ME THROUGH IT AGAIN.

CAM 81 SF   ZOOM 1

"I MADE THE APPROACH IN SAN FRANCISCO SIX MONTHS AGO, AFTER DEAN'S NAME SHOWED UP IN THE DATA WE INTERCEPTED FROM PACIFIC'S DUMMY ACCOUNTS."

S:0115162 2205A88

81 SF   ZOOM 1X

WHAT KINDA ALGORITHM YOU USING?

JESUS, LADY! ANYONE EVER TELL YOU TO MIND YOUR OWN BUSINESS?

CONSTANTLY.

FUCK OFF, THEN.

BANK ATM

S:0115162 2205A88YL

CAM 81 SF   ZOOM 2

FOR THE RECORD, I DIDN'T SNEAK UP ON YOU. I FOLLOWED YOU.

OH, THAT MAKES IT ALL BETTER.

GO. AWAY.

SAW YOU LIFT THAT GUY'S WALLET ON THE BART. I PREFER TO CLONE CARDS, MYSELF.

GOT A RUSSIAN UP IN THE TENDERLOIN WHO BUYS THE NUMBERS ONCE I'VE GOTTEN THE CASH OUT.

BANK ATM

S:0115162 2205A88Y

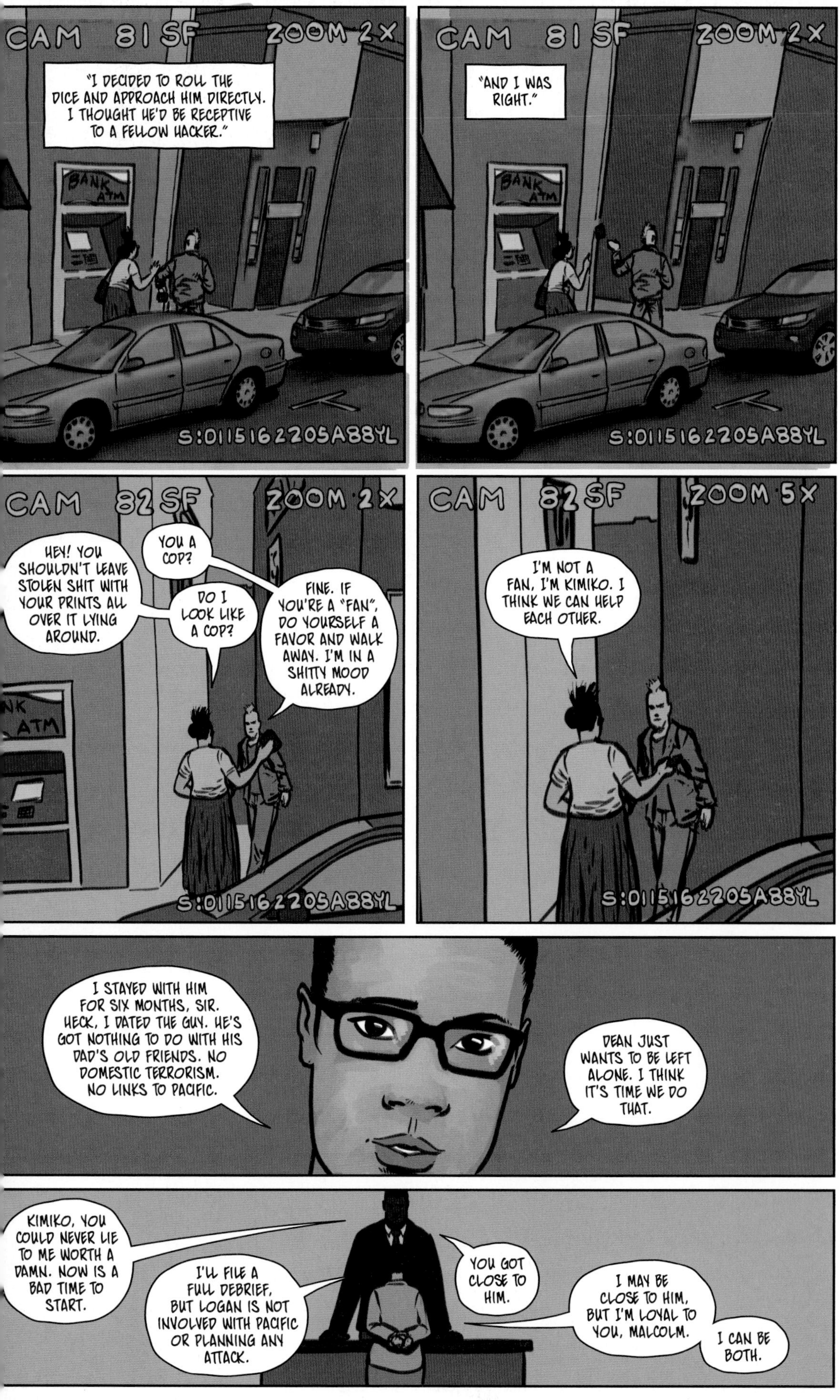
CAM 81 SF ZOOM 2X
"I DECIDED TO ROLL THE DICE AND APPROACH HIM DIRECTLY. I THOUGHT HE'D BE RECEPTIVE TO A FELLOW HACKER."
BANK ATM
S:0115162205A88YL
CAM 81 SF ZOOM 2X
"AND I WAS RIGHT."
BANK ATM
S:0115162205A88YL
CAM 82 SF ZOOM 2X
HEY! YOU SHOULDN'T LEAVE STOLEN SHIT WITH YOUR PRINTS ALL OVER IT LYING AROUND.
YOU A COP?
DO I LOOK LIKE A COP?
FINE. IF YOU'RE A "FAN", DO YOURSELF A FAVOR AND WALK AWAY. I'M IN A SHITTY MOOD ALREADY.
S:0115162205A88YL
CAM 82 SF ZOOM 5X
I'M NOT A FAN, I'M KIMIKO. I THINK WE CAN HELP EACH OTHER.
S:0115162205A88YL
I STAYED WITH HIM FOR SIX MONTHS, SIR. HECK, I DATED THE GUY. HE'S GOT NOTHING TO DO WITH HIS DAD'S OLD FRIENDS. NO DOMESTIC TERRORISM. NO LINKS TO PACIFIC.
DEAN JUST WANTS TO BE LEFT ALONE. I THINK IT'S TIME WE DO THAT.
KIMIKO, YOU COULD NEVER LIE TO ME WORTH A DAMN. NOW IS A BAD TIME TO START.
I'LL FILE A FULL DEBRIEF, BUT LOGAN IS NOT INVOLVED WITH PACIFIC OR PLANNING ANY ATTACK.
YOU GOT CLOSE TO HIM.
I MAY BE CLOSE TO HIM, BUT I'M LOYAL TO YOU, MALCOLM.
I CAN BE BOTH.

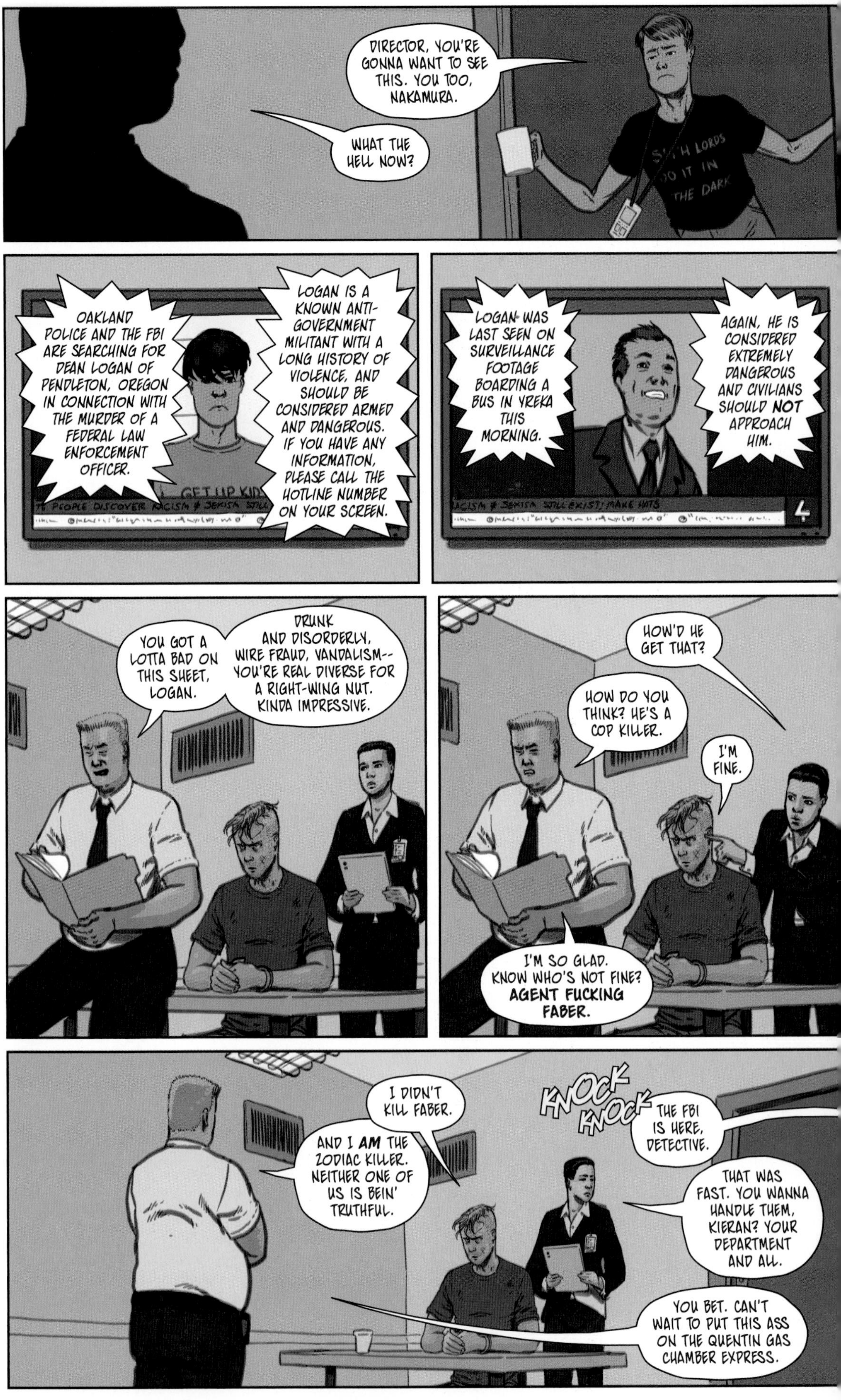

DIRECTOR, YOU'RE GONNA WANT TO SEE THIS. YOU TOO, NAKAMURA.
WHAT THE HELL NOW?
SITH LORDS DO IT IN THE DARK
OAKLAND POLICE AND THE FBI ARE SEARCHING FOR DEAN LOGAN OF PENDLETON, OREGON IN CONNECTION WITH THE MURDER OF A FEDERAL LAW ENFORCEMENT OFFICER.
LOGAN IS A KNOWN ANTI-GOVERNMENT MILITANT WITH A LONG HISTORY OF VIOLENCE, AND SHOULD BE CONSIDERED ARMED AND DANGEROUS. IF YOU HAVE ANY INFORMATION, PLEASE CALL THE HOTLINE NUMBER ON YOUR SCREEN.
LOGAN WAS LAST SEEN ON SURVEILLANCE FOOTAGE BOARDING A BUS IN YREKA THIS MORNING.
AGAIN, HE IS CONSIDERED EXTREMELY DANGEROUS AND CIVILIANS SHOULD **NOT** APPROACH HIM.
RACISM & SEXISM STILL EXIST; MAKE HATS
4
YOU GOT A LOTTA BAD ON THIS SHEET, LOGAN.
DRUNK AND DISORDERLY, WIRE FRAUD, VANDALISM--YOU'RE REAL DIVERSE FOR A RIGHT-WING NUT. KINDA IMPRESSIVE.
HOW'D HE GET THAT?
HOW DO YOU THINK? HE'S A COP KILLER.
I'M FINE.
I'M SO GLAD. KNOW WHO'S NOT FINE? **AGENT FUCKING FABER.**
I DIDN'T KILL FABER.
AND I **AM** THE ZODIAC KILLER. NEITHER ONE OF US IS BEIN' TRUTHFUL.
KNOCK KNOCK
THE FBI IS HERE, DETECTIVE.
THAT WAS FAST. YOU WANNA HANDLE THEM, KIERAN? YOUR DEPARTMENT AND ALL.
YOU BET. CAN'T WAIT TO PUT THIS ASS ON THE QUENTIN GAS CHAMBER EXPRESS.

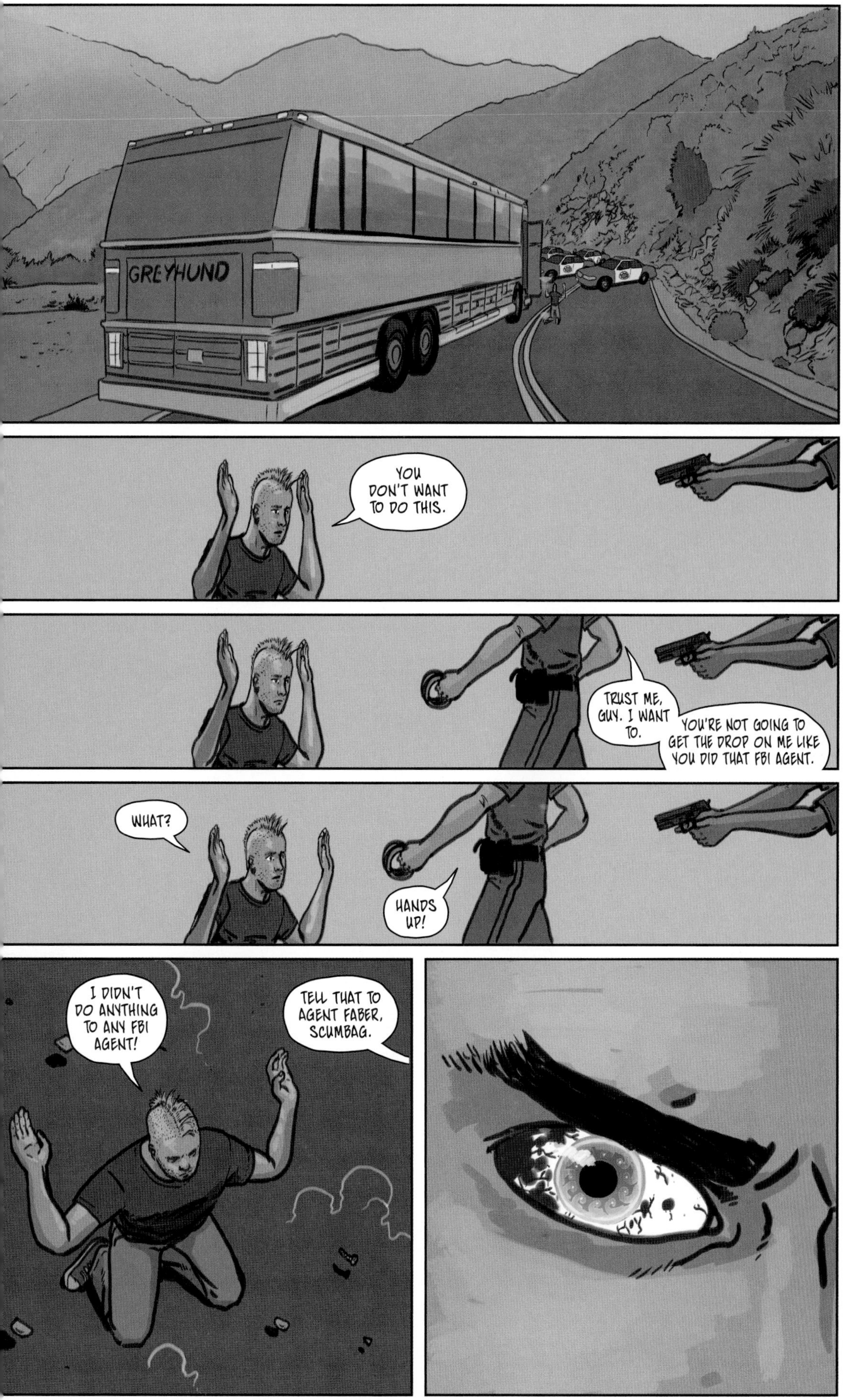
GREYHUND
YOU DON'T WANT TO DO THIS.
TRUST ME, GUY. I WANT TO.
YOU'RE NOT GOING TO GET THE DROP ON ME LIKE YOU DID THAT FBI AGENT.
WHAT?
HANDS UP!
I DIDN'T DO ANYTHING TO ANY FBI AGENT!
TELL THAT TO AGENT FABER, SCUMBAG.

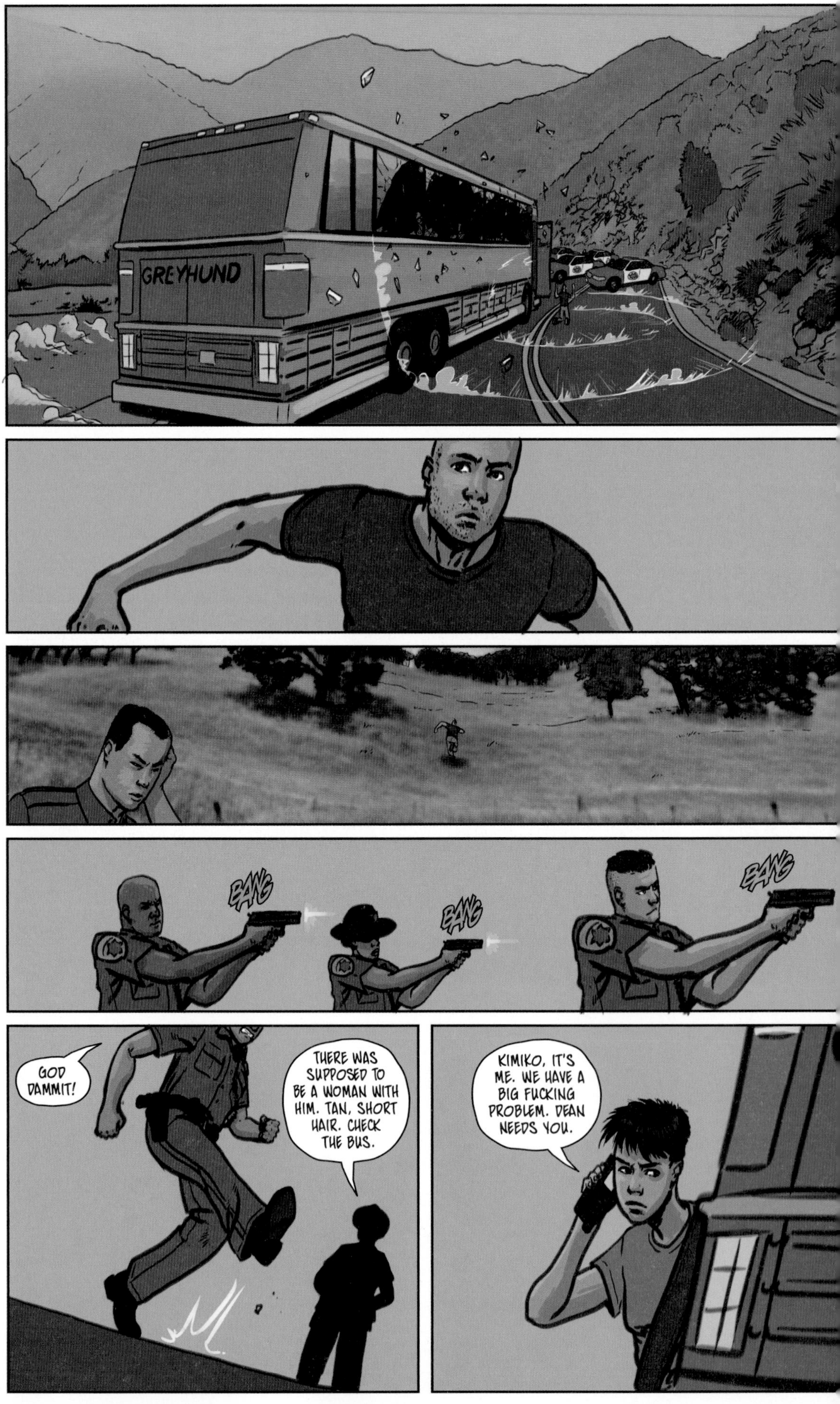
GREYHUND
BANG
BANG
BANG
GOD DAMMIT!
THERE WAS SUPPOSED TO BE A WOMAN WITH HIM. TAN, SHORT HAIR. CHECK THE BUS.
KIMIKO, IT'S ME. WE HAVE A BIG FUCKING PROBLEM. DEAN NEEDS YOU.

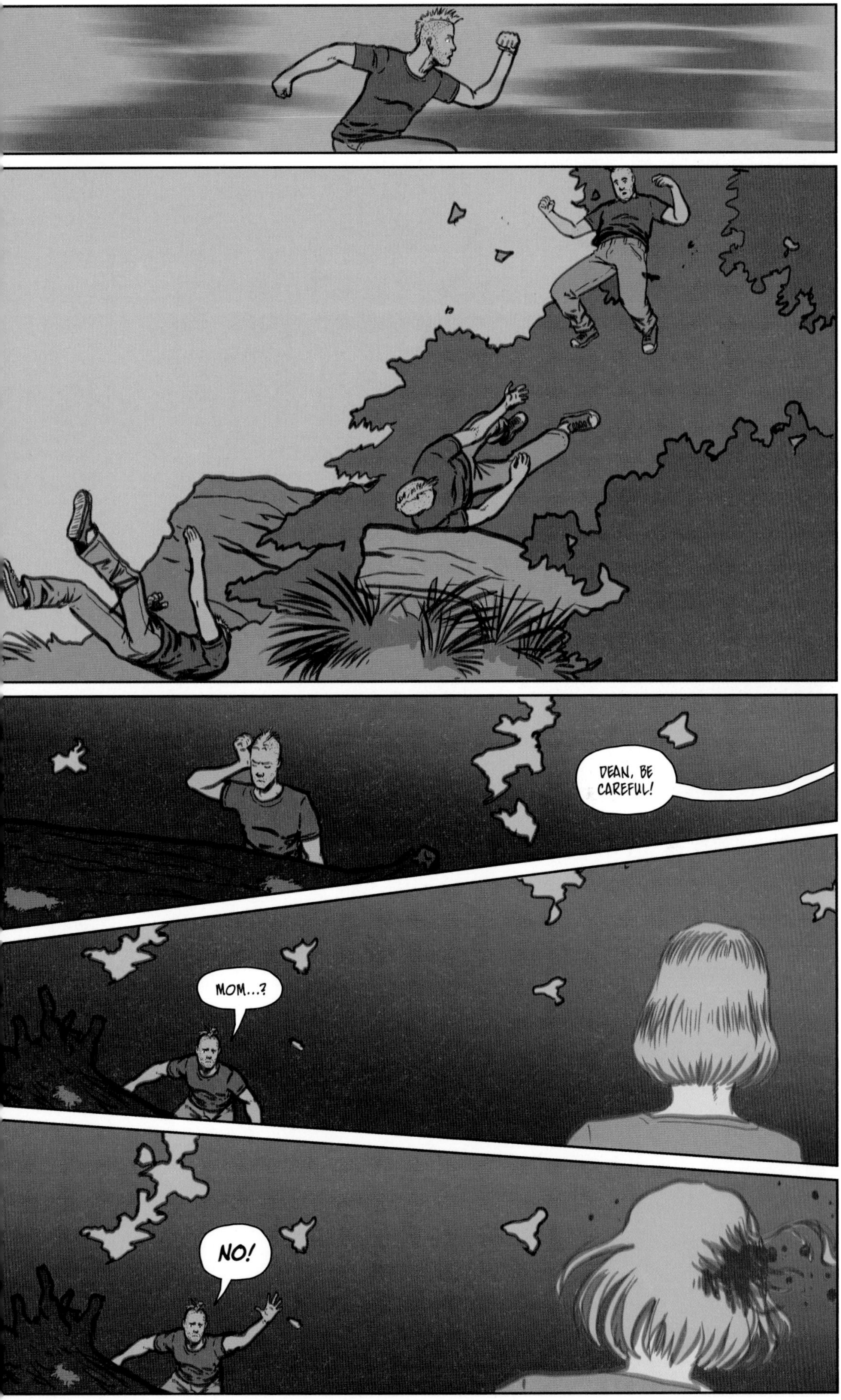
DEAN, BE CAREFUL!
MOM...?
NO!

NO WAY HE'D KILL FABER. THE GUY WAS AN ASS, BUT DEAN'S NOT CAPABLE OF THAT KIND OF VIOLENCE.

I KNOW. THIS HAS GOT TO BE OSTRANDER.

I CAN BE A FAKE COP LONG ENOUGH TO GET HIM OUT OF CUSTODY. WE CAN GO FROM THERE.

WHERE? A FEDERAL MANHUNT IS NOT GOING TO JUST STOP, ABBY. EVEN I CAN'T COVER TRACKS THAT WELL.

"ONE OF MY TRAINING OFFICERS IN RANGER SCHOOL HAD A STORY: RANGER IS IN A TRANSPORT OVER AFGHANISTAN.

"TALIBAN FIRES A SAM, PLANE CATCHES ON FIRE. PARACHUTES GO UP IN FLAMES. RANGER HAS A CHOICE: STAY AND DIE, OR JUMP.

"SO HE GOES TO THE CARGO DOOR AND HIS BUDDY SAYS, 'HEY MAN, YOU DON'T HAVE A CHUTE!'

"RANGER SAYS, 'ONE PROBLEM AT A TIME.'

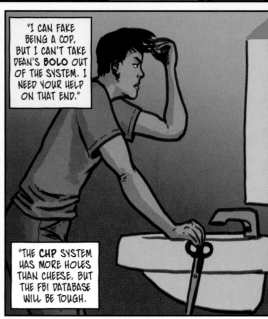

"I CAN FAKE BEING A COP, BUT I CAN'T TAKE DEAN'S BOLO OUT OF THE SYSTEM. I NEED YOUR HELP ON THAT END."

"THE CHP SYSTEM HAS MORE HOLES THAN CHEESE, BUT THE FBI DATABASE WILL BE TOUGH.

"I'LL TAKE A SICK DAY. COME UP WITH SOME EXCUSE. I'LL MEET YOU WHERE THEY'RE HOLDING DEAN AS SOON AS I CLEAR BEING GONE WITH MY DIRECTOR."

"NO. YOU STAY PUT. YOU'RE SAFE THERE, PLUS I NEED YOU TO BACKSTOP MY COVER ID TO THE FEDS WHEN THEY SHOW UP."

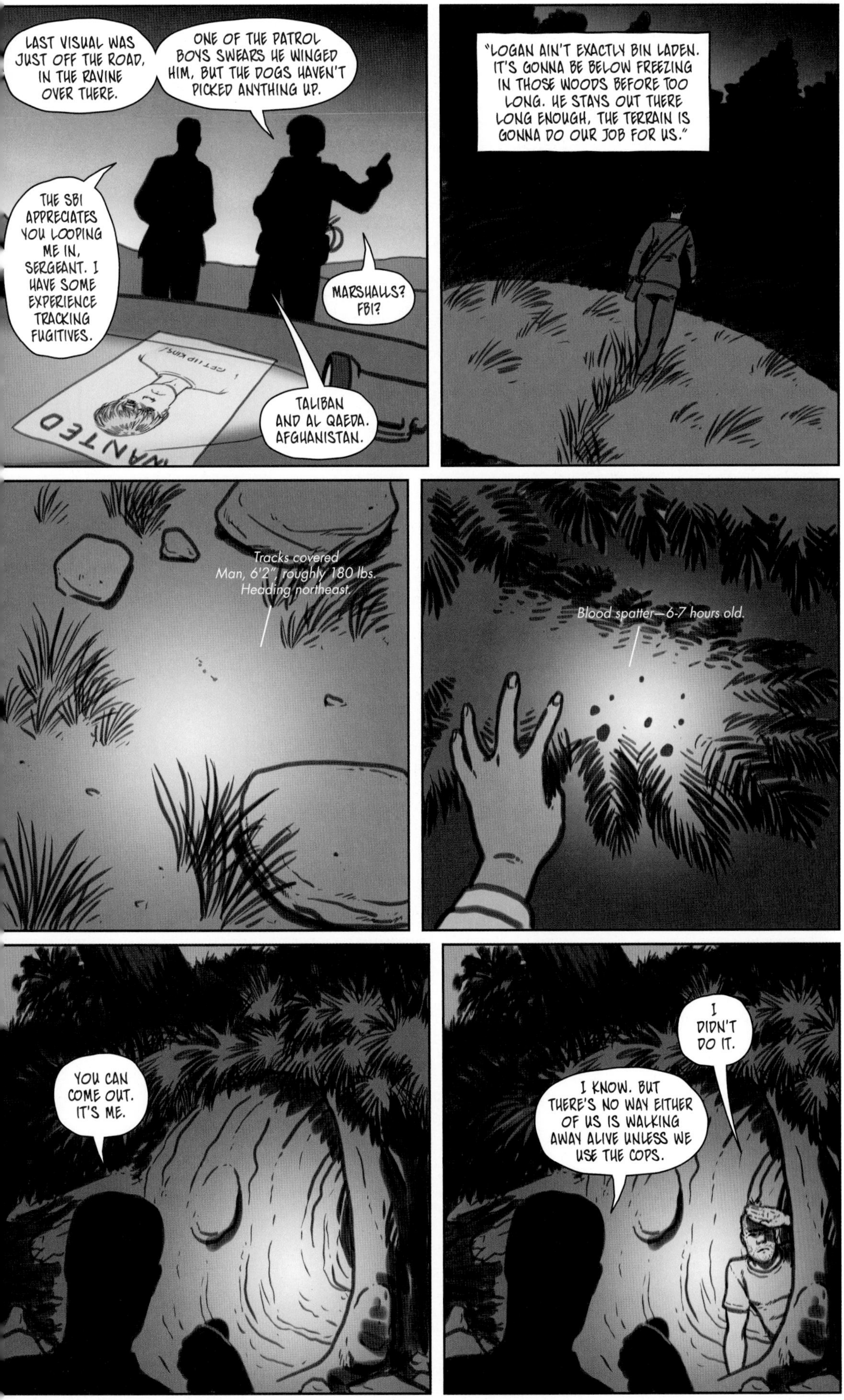
LAST VISUAL WAS JUST OFF THE ROAD, IN THE RAVINE OVER THERE.
ONE OF THE PATROL BOYS SWEARS HE WINGED HIM, BUT THE DOGS HAVEN'T PICKED ANYTHING UP.
THE SBI APPRECIATES YOU LOOPING ME IN, SERGEANT. I HAVE SOME EXPERIENCE TRACKING FUGITIVES.
MARSHALLS? FBI?
TALIBAN AND AL QAEDA. AFGHANISTAN.
"LOGAN AIN'T EXACTLY BIN LADEN. IT'S GONNA BE BELOW FREEZING IN THOSE WOODS BEFORE TOO LONG. HE STAYS OUT THERE LONG ENOUGH, THE TERRAIN IS GONNA DO OUR JOB FOR US."
Tracks covered
Man, 6'2", roughly 180 lbs.
Heading northeast.
Blood spatter—6-7 hours old.
YOU CAN COME OUT. IT'S ME.
I DIDN'T DO IT.
I KNOW. BUT THERE'S NO WAY EITHER OF US IS WALKING AWAY ALIVE UNLESS WE USE THE COPS.

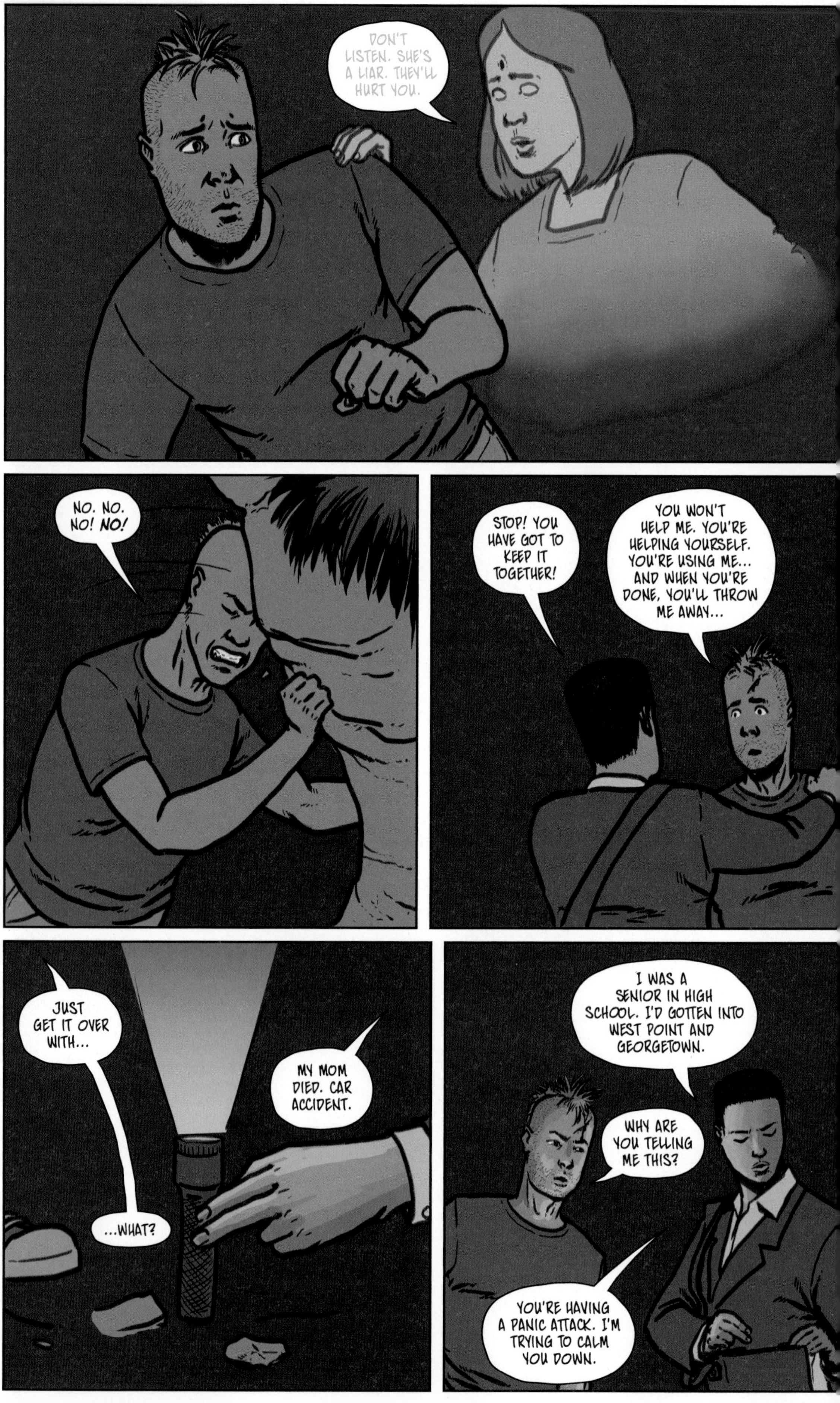
DON'T LISTEN. SHE'S A LIAR. THEY'LL HURT YOU.
NO. NO. NO! NO!
STOP! YOU HAVE GOT TO KEEP IT TOGETHER!
YOU WON'T HELP ME. YOU'RE HELPING YOURSELF. YOU'RE USING ME... AND WHEN YOU'RE DONE, YOU'LL THROW ME AWAY...
JUST GET IT OVER WITH...
MY MOM DIED. CAR ACCIDENT.
...WHAT?
I WAS A SENIOR IN HIGH SCHOOL. I'D GOTTEN INTO WEST POINT AND GEORGETOWN.
WHY ARE YOU TELLING ME THIS?
YOU'RE HAVING A PANIC ATTACK. I'M TRYING TO CALM YOU DOWN.

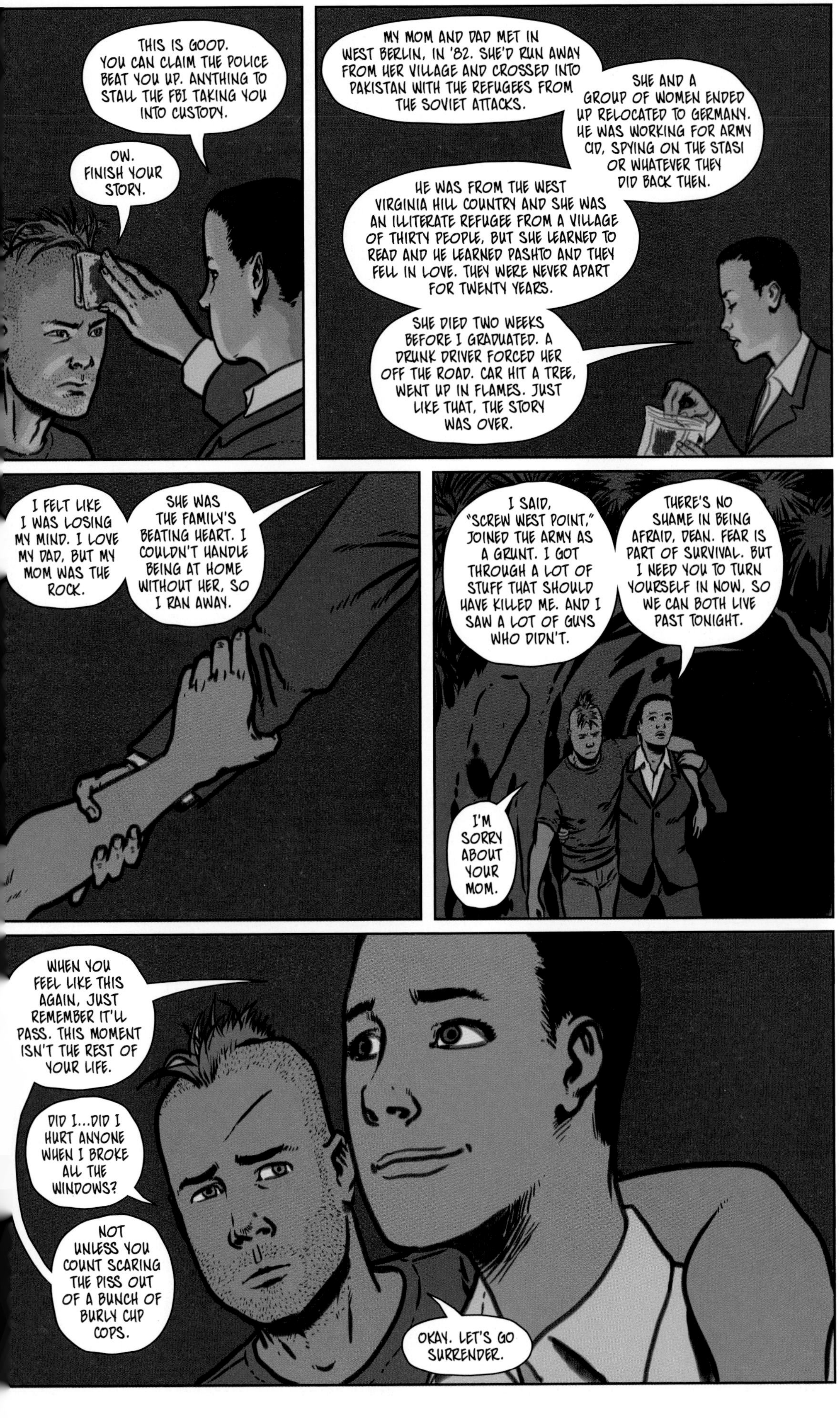
THIS IS GOOD. YOU CAN CLAIM THE POLICE BEAT YOU UP. ANYTHING TO STALL THE FBI TAKING YOU INTO CUSTODY.
OW. FINISH YOUR STORY.
MY MOM AND DAD MET IN WEST BERLIN, IN '82. SHE'D RUN AWAY FROM HER VILLAGE AND CROSSED INTO PAKISTAN WITH THE REFUGEES FROM THE SOVIET ATTACKS.
SHE AND A GROUP OF WOMEN ENDED UP RELOCATED TO GERMANY. HE WAS WORKING FOR ARMY CID, SPYING ON THE STASI OR WHATEVER THEY DID BACK THEN.
HE WAS FROM THE WEST VIRGINIA HILL COUNTRY AND SHE WAS AN ILLITERATE REFUGEE FROM A VILLAGE OF THIRTY PEOPLE, BUT SHE LEARNED TO READ AND HE LEARNED PASHTO AND THEY FELL IN LOVE. THEY WERE NEVER APART FOR TWENTY YEARS.
SHE DIED TWO WEEKS BEFORE I GRADUATED. A DRUNK DRIVER FORCED HER OFF THE ROAD. CAR HIT A TREE, WENT UP IN FLAMES. JUST LIKE THAT, THE STORY WAS OVER.
I FELT LIKE I WAS LOSING MY MIND. I LOVE MY DAD, BUT MY MOM WAS THE ROCK.
SHE WAS THE FAMILY'S BEATING HEART. I COULDN'T HANDLE BEING AT HOME WITHOUT HER, SO I RAN AWAY.
I SAID, "SCREW WEST POINT," JOINED THE ARMY AS A GRUNT. I GOT THROUGH A LOT OF STUFF THAT SHOULD HAVE KILLED ME. AND I SAW A LOT OF GUYS WHO DIDN'T.
THERE'S NO SHAME IN BEING AFRAID, DEAN. FEAR IS PART OF SURVIVAL. BUT I NEED YOU TO TURN YOURSELF IN NOW, SO WE CAN BOTH LIVE PAST TONIGHT.
I'M SORRY ABOUT YOUR MOM.
WHEN YOU FEEL LIKE THIS AGAIN, JUST REMEMBER IT'LL PASS. THIS MOMENT ISN'T THE REST OF YOUR LIFE.
DID I...DID I HURT ANYONE WHEN I BROKE ALL THE WINDOWS?
NOT UNLESS YOU COUNT SCARING THE PISS OUT OF A BUNCH OF BURLY CUP COPS.
OKAY. LET'S GO SURRENDER.

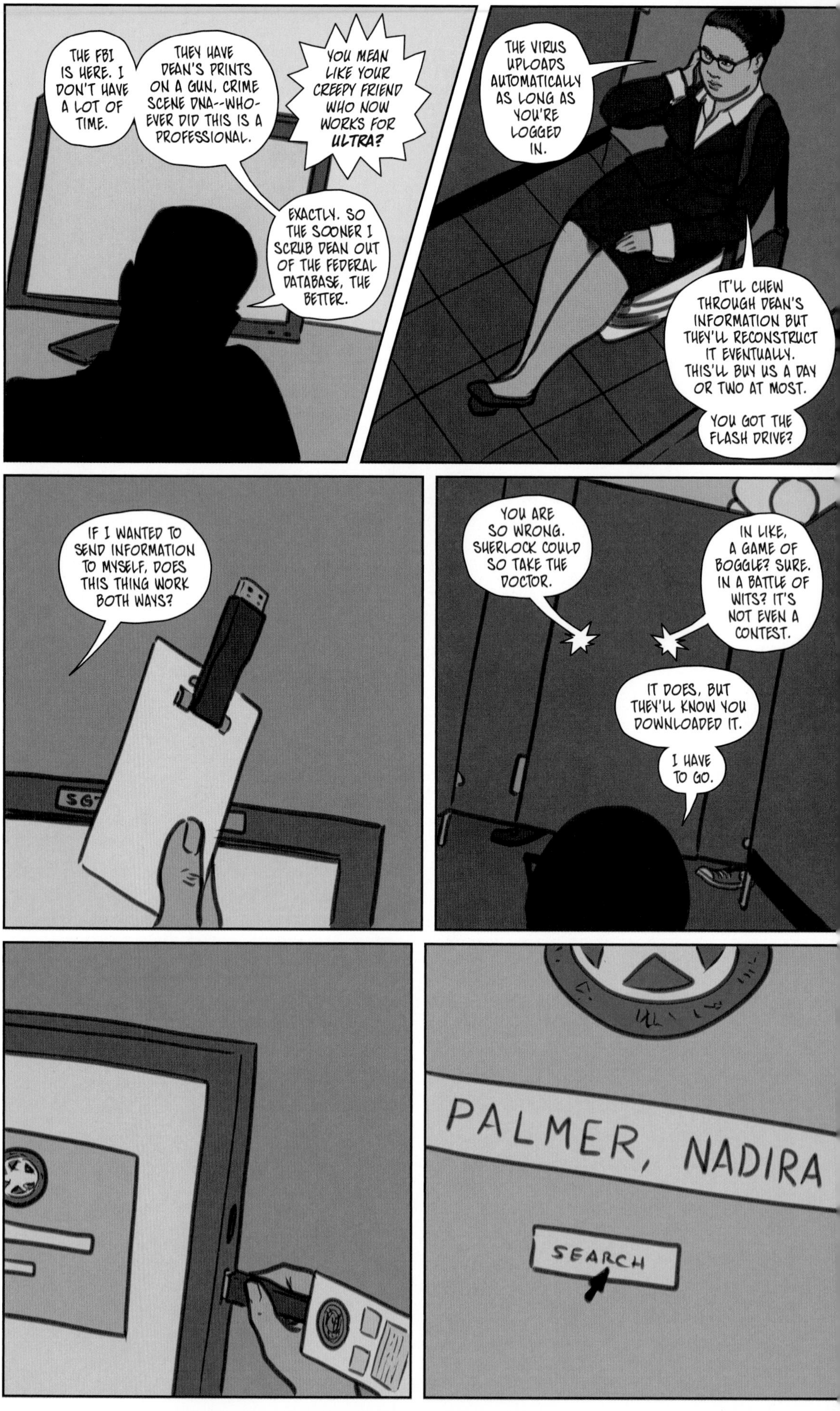
THE FBI IS HERE. I DON'T HAVE A LOT OF TIME.
THEY HAVE DEAN'S PRINTS ON A GUN, CRIME SCENE DNA--WHOEVER DID THIS IS A PROFESSIONAL.
YOU MEAN LIKE YOUR CREEPY FRIEND WHO NOW WORKS FOR ULTRA?
EXACTLY. SO THE SOONER I SCRUB DEAN OUT OF THE FEDERAL DATABASE, THE BETTER.
THE VIRUS UPLOADS AUTOMATICALLY AS LONG AS YOU'RE LOGGED IN.
IT'LL CHEW THROUGH DEAN'S INFORMATION BUT THEY'LL RECONSTRUCT IT EVENTUALLY. THIS'LL BUY US A DAY OR TWO AT MOST.
YOU GOT THE FLASH DRIVE?
IF I WANTED TO SEND INFORMATION TO MYSELF, DOES THIS THING WORK BOTH WAYS?
YOU ARE SO WRONG. SHERLOCK COULD SO TAKE THE DOCTOR.
IN LIKE, A GAME OF BOGGLE? SURE. IN A BATTLE OF WITS? IT'S NOT EVEN A CONTEST.
IT DOES, BUT THEY'LL KNOW YOU DOWNLOADED IT.
I HAVE TO GO.
PALMER, NADIRA
SEARCH

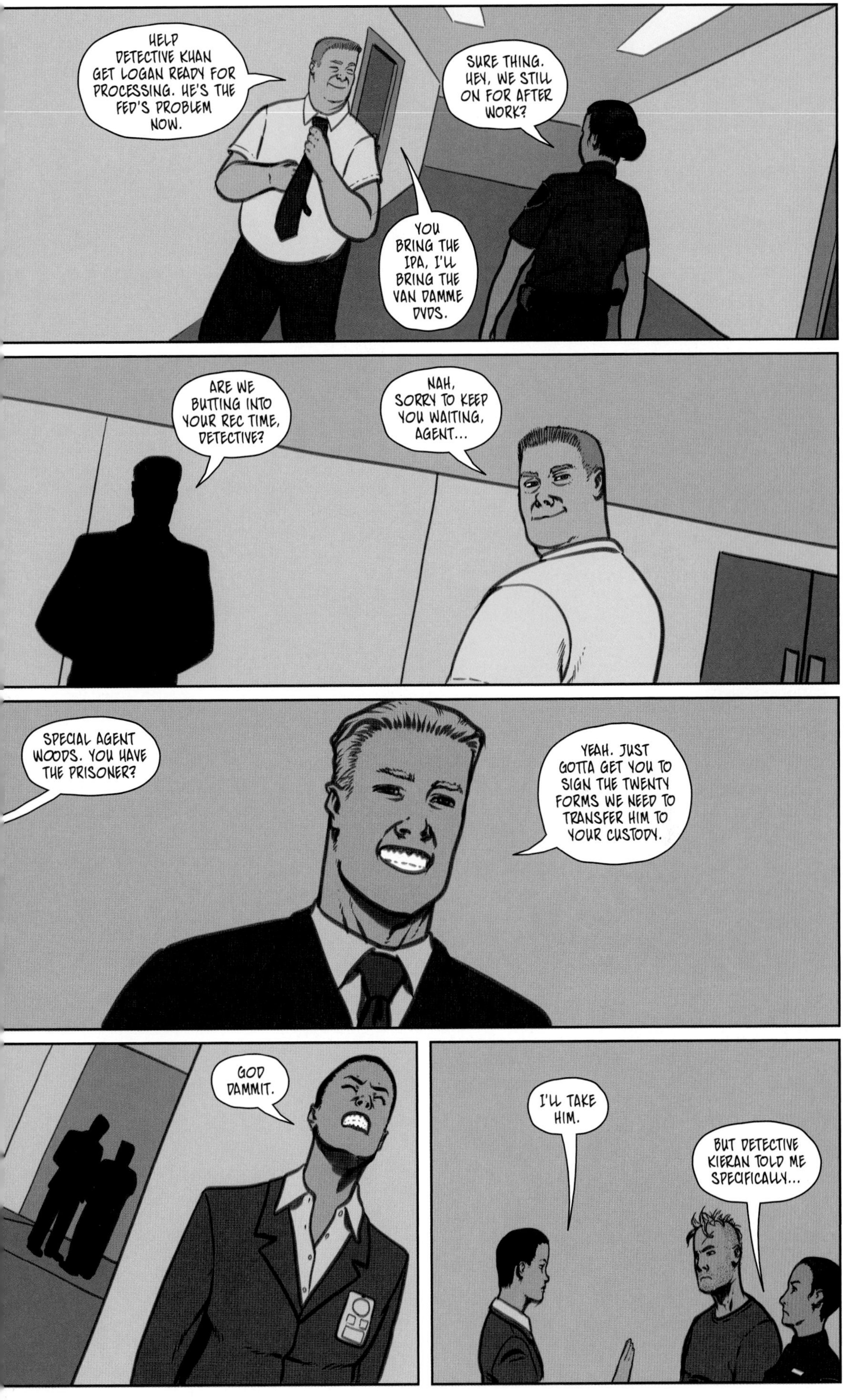
HELP DETECTIVE KHAN GET LOGAN READY FOR PROCESSING. HE'S THE FED'S PROBLEM NOW.
SURE THING. HEY, WE STILL ON FOR AFTER WORK?
YOU BRING THE IPA, I'LL BRING THE VAN DAMME DVDS.
ARE WE BUTTING INTO YOUR REC TIME, DETECTIVE?
NAH, SORRY TO KEEP YOU WAITING, AGENT...
SPECIAL AGENT WOODS. YOU HAVE THE PRISONER?
YEAH. JUST GOTTA GET YOU TO SIGN THE TWENTY FORMS WE NEED TO TRANSFER HIM TO YOUR CUSTODY.
GOD DAMMIT.
I'LL TAKE HIM.
BUT DETECTIVE KIERAN TOLD ME SPECIFICALLY...

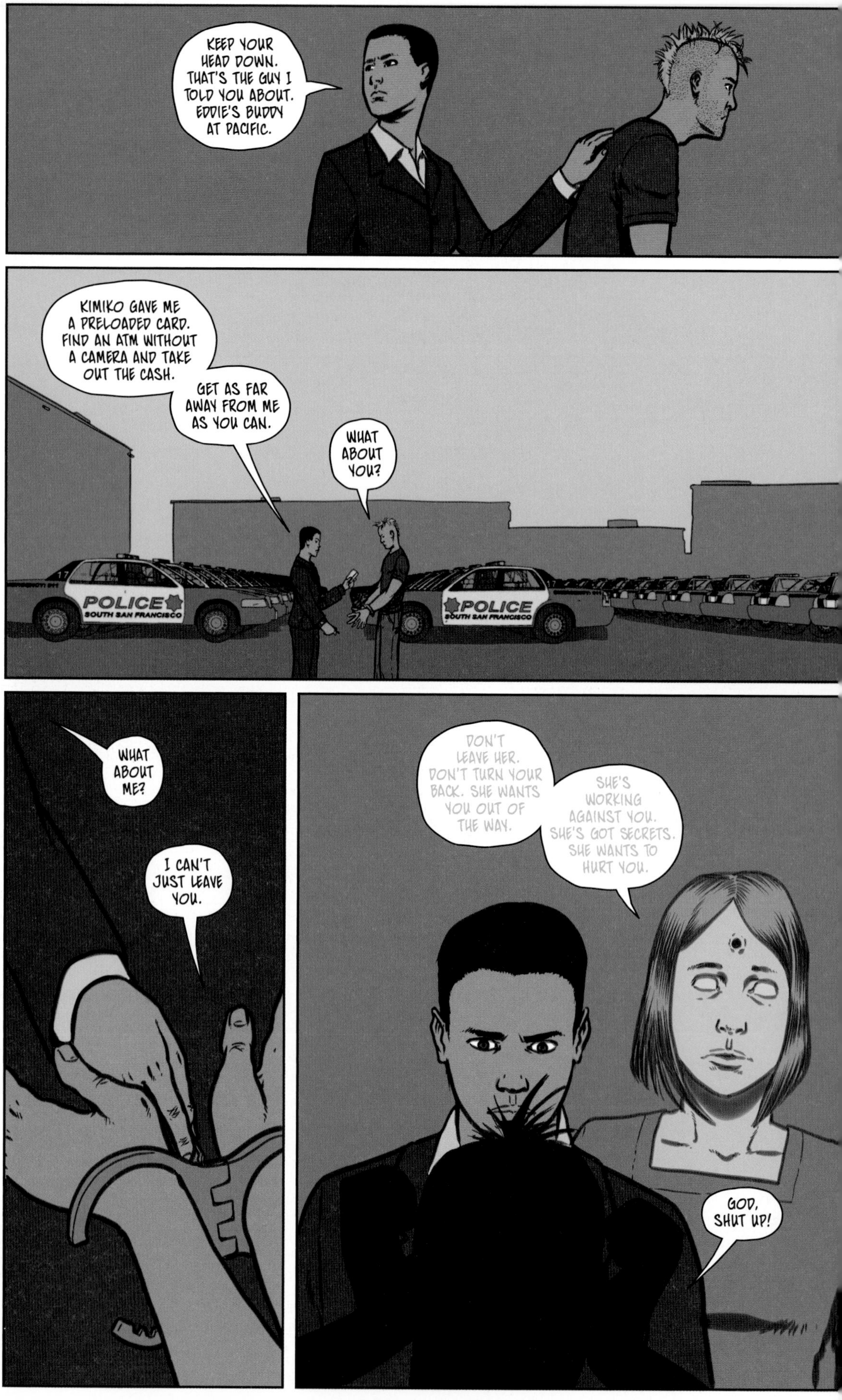

KEEP YOUR HEAD DOWN. THAT'S THE GUY I TOLD YOU ABOUT. EDDIE'S BUDDY AT PACIFIC.
KIMIKO GAVE ME A PRELOADED CARD. FIND AN ATM WITHOUT A CAMERA AND TAKE OUT THE CASH.
GET AS FAR AWAY FROM ME AS YOU CAN.
WHAT ABOUT YOU?
POLICE
SOUTH SAN FRANCISCO
POLICE
SOUTH SAN FRANCISCO
WHAT ABOUT ME?
I CAN'T JUST LEAVE YOU.
DON'T LEAVE HER. DON'T TURN YOUR BACK. SHE WANTS YOU OUT OF THE WAY.
SHE'S WORKING AGAINST YOU. SHE'S GOT SECRETS. SHE WANTS TO HURT YOU.
GOD, SHUT UP!

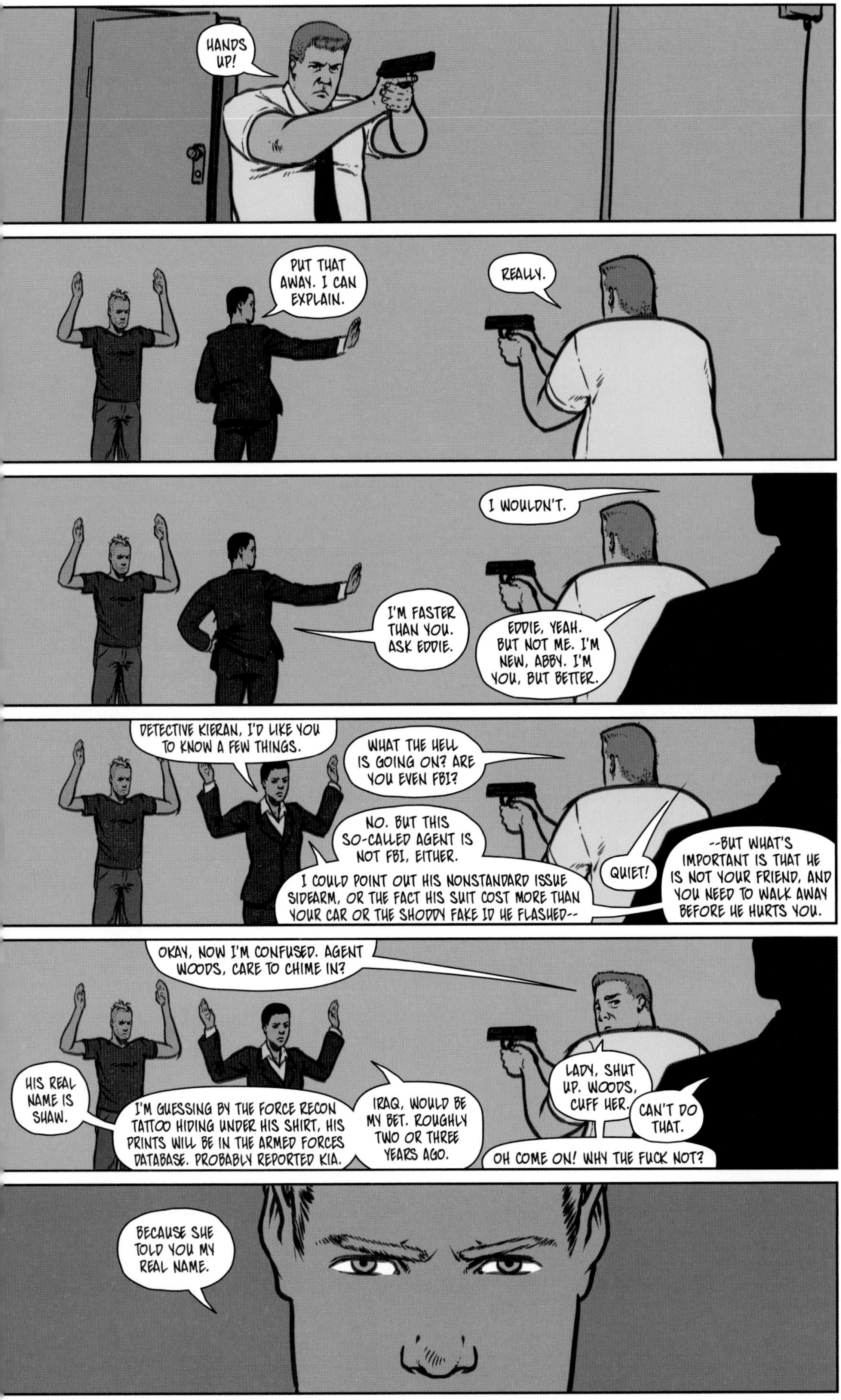
HANDS UP!
PUT THAT AWAY. I CAN EXPLAIN.
REALLY.
I WOULDN'T.
I'M FASTER THAN YOU. ASK EDDIE.
EDDIE, YEAH. BUT NOT ME. I'M NEW, ABBY. I'M YOU, BUT BETTER.
DETECTIVE KIERAN, I'D LIKE YOU TO KNOW A FEW THINGS.
WHAT THE HELL IS GOING ON? ARE YOU EVEN FBI?
NO. BUT THIS SO-CALLED AGENT IS NOT FBI, EITHER.
I COULD POINT OUT HIS NONSTANDARD ISSUE SIDEARM, OR THE FACT HIS SUIT COST MORE THAN YOUR CAR OR THE SHODDY FAKE ID HE FLASHED--
QUIET!
--BUT WHAT'S IMPORTANT IS THAT HE IS NOT YOUR FRIEND, AND YOU NEED TO WALK AWAY BEFORE HE HURTS YOU.
OKAY, NOW I'M CONFUSED. AGENT WOODS, CARE TO CHIME IN?
HIS REAL NAME IS SHAW.
I'M GUESSING BY THE FORCE RECON TATTOO HIDING UNDER HIS SHIRT, HIS PRINTS WILL BE IN THE ARMED FORCES DATABASE. PROBABLY REPORTED KIA.
IRAQ, WOULD BE MY BET. ROUGHLY TWO OR THREE YEARS AGO.
LADY, SHUT UP. WOODS, CUFF HER.
CAN'T DO THAT.
OH COME ON! WHY THE FUCK NOT?
BECAUSE SHE TOLD YOU MY REAL NAME.

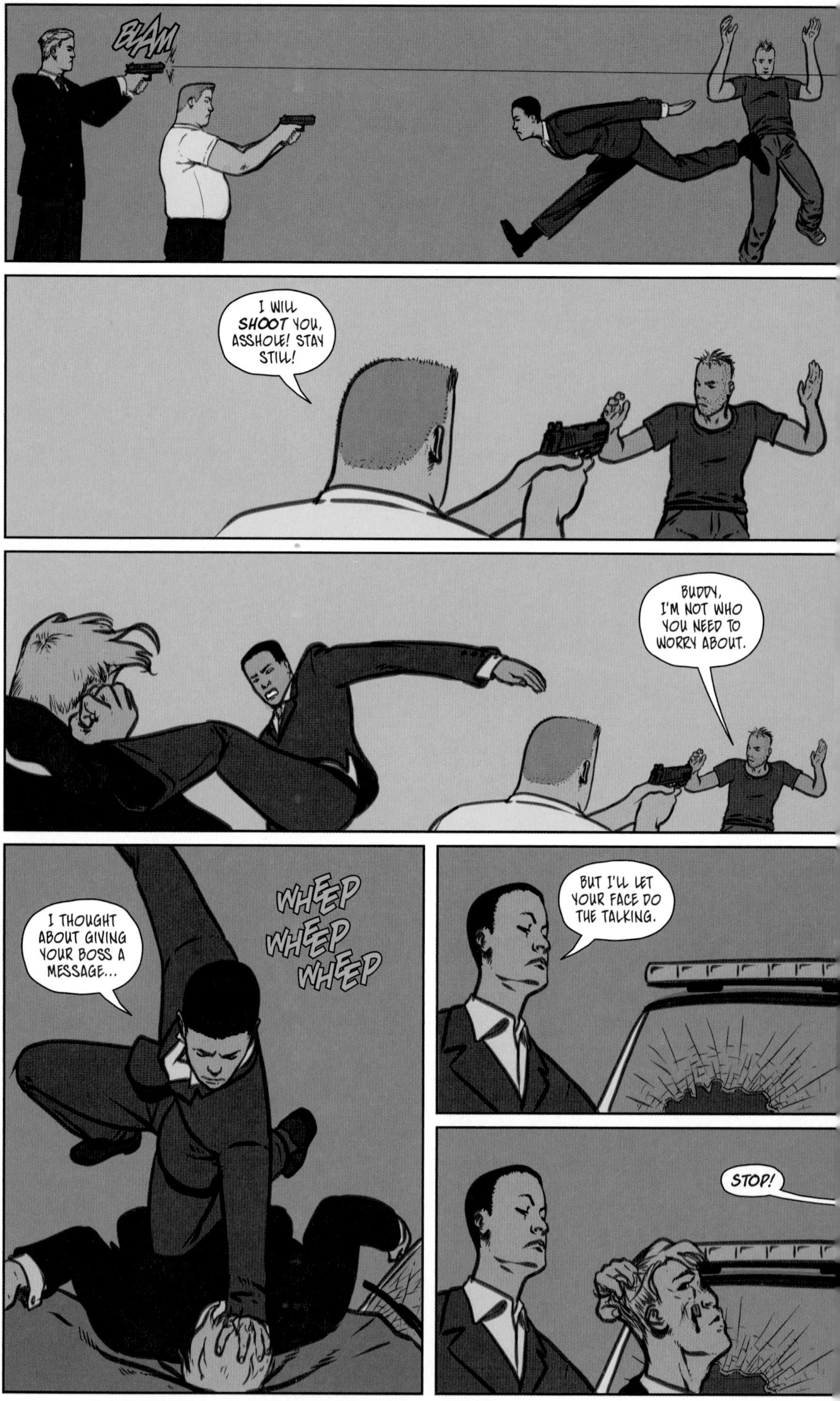
BLAM
I WILL SHOOT YOU, ASSHOLE! STAY STILL!
BUDDY, I'M NOT WHO YOU NEED TO WORRY ABOUT.
I THOUGHT ABOUT GIVING YOUR BOSS A MESSAGE...
WHEEP WHEEP WHEEP
BUT I'LL LET YOUR FACE DO THE TALKING.
STOP!

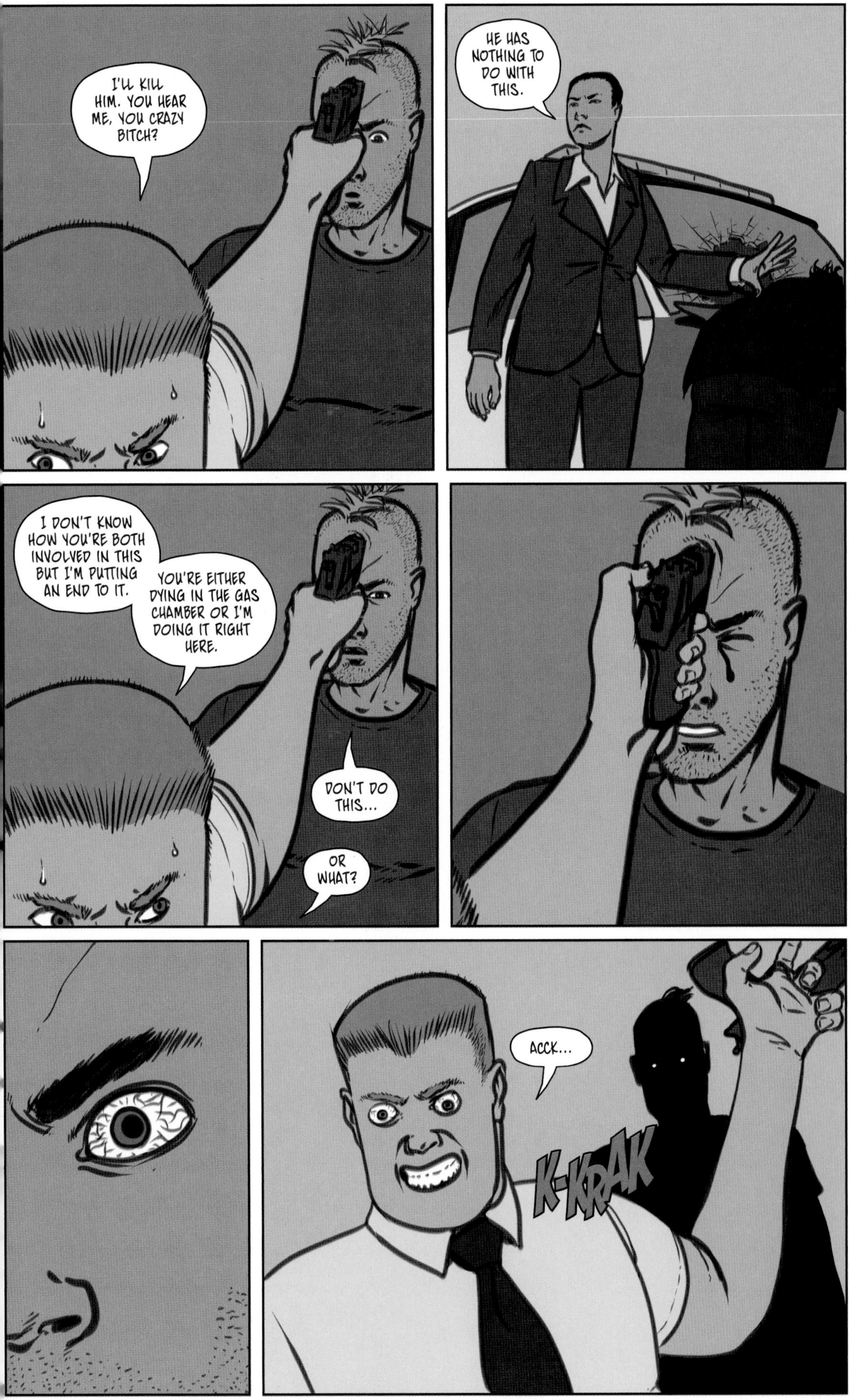
I'LL KILL HIM. YOU HEAR ME, YOU CRAZY BITCH?
HE HAS NOTHING TO DO WITH THIS.
I DON'T KNOW HOW YOU'RE BOTH INVOLVED IN THIS BUT I'M PUTTING AN END TO IT.
YOU'RE EITHER DYING IN THE GAS CHAMBER OR I'M DOING IT RIGHT HERE.
DON'T DO THIS...
OR WHAT?
ACCK...
K-KRAK

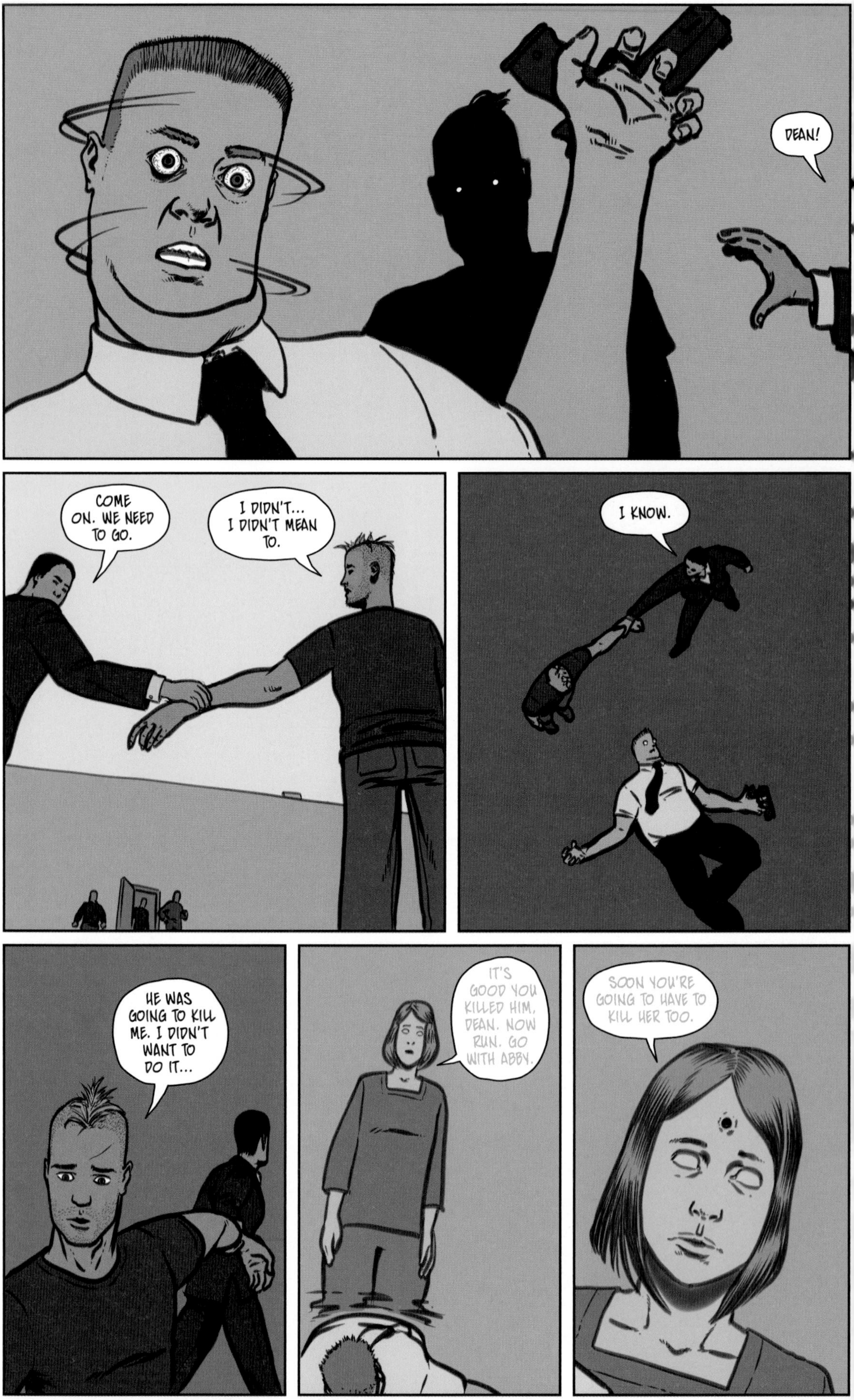
DEAN!
COME ON. WE NEED TO GO.
I DIDN'T... I DIDN'T MEAN TO.
I KNOW.
HE WAS GOING TO KILL ME. I DIDN'T WANT TO DO IT...
IT'S GOOD YOU KILLED HIM, DEAN. NOW RUN. GO WITH ABBY.
SOON YOU'RE GOING TO HAVE TO KILL HER TOO.

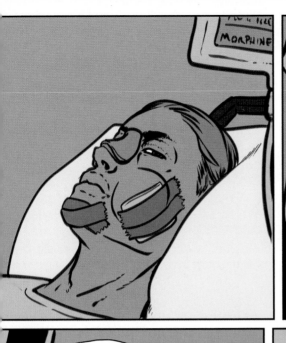

YOUR MRI WAS CLEAN--NO SUBDURAL BLEEDING. CONCUSSION WAS MINOR. YOU'LL BE ALL RIGHT, MR. SHAW. PHYSICALLY.

I'M SORRY, DR. OSTRANDER. I WASN'T PREPARED FOR THAT LEVEL OF AGGRESSION.

NO, YOU SURE WEREN'T.

TRANSPORT MR. SHAW BACK TO THE CHESHIRE COMPLEX FOR RETRAINING.

NO--

SORRY, MAN. I LIKED YOU, FOR WHAT IT'S WORTH.

EDDIE, COME ON. DON'T DO THIS TO ME. IT WAS ONE MISTAKE--

IF IT WAS UP TO ME, I'D GIVE YOU SOME PAINKILLERS AND LET YOU BACK IN THE FIELD. BUT IT ISN'T. DON'T MAKE ME CUFF YOU, GRANT.

FIRST VALERIE AND NOW ME? WHERE DOES IT STOP, EDDIE? WHERE?!

I WISH I KNEW.

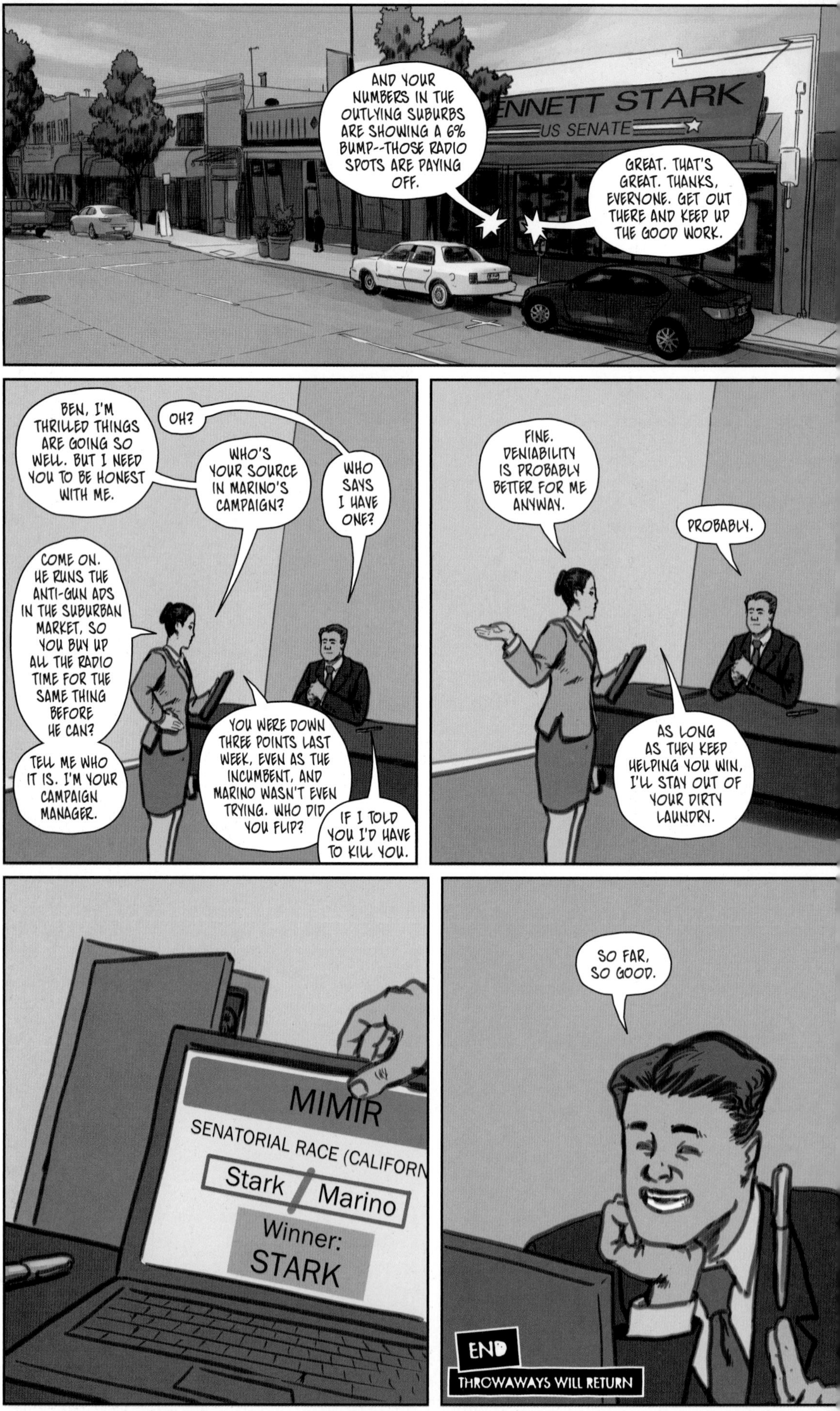
ENNETT STARK
US SENATE
AND YOUR NUMBERS IN THE OUTLYING SUBURBS ARE SHOWING A 6% BUMP--THOSE RADIO SPOTS ARE PAYING OFF.
GREAT. THAT'S GREAT. THANKS, EVERYONE. GET OUT THERE AND KEEP UP THE GOOD WORK.
BEN, I'M THRILLED THINGS ARE GOING SO WELL. BUT I NEED YOU TO BE HONEST WITH ME.
OH?
WHO'S YOUR SOURCE IN MARINO'S CAMPAIGN?
WHO SAYS I HAVE ONE?
COME ON. HE RUNS THE ANTI-GUN ADS IN THE SUBURBAN MARKET, SO YOU BUY UP ALL THE RADIO TIME FOR THE SAME THING BEFORE HE CAN?
TELL ME WHO IT IS. I'M YOUR CAMPAIGN MANAGER.
YOU WERE DOWN THREE POINTS LAST WEEK, EVEN AS THE INCUMBENT, AND MARINO WASN'T EVEN TRYING. WHO DID YOU FLIP?
IF I TOLD YOU I'D HAVE TO KILL YOU.
FINE. DENIABILITY IS PROBABLY BETTER FOR ME ANYWAY.
PROBABLY.
AS LONG AS THEY KEEP HELPING YOU WIN, I'LL STAY OUT OF YOUR DIRTY LAUNDRY.
MIMIR
SENATORIAL RACE (CALIFORN
Stark
Marino
Winner:
STARK
SO FAR, SO GOOD.
END
THROWAWAYS WILL RETURN

SCRIPT TO STORY

There's often a lot of changes that happen as part of the process of collaboration in comics. We thought you might find these pages to be an interesting behind-the-scenes peek.

Panel 1
We see Colin's feverish scribbles filling up the panel, Dean and Abby's faces emerging from the nightmare of twisted mouths and broken bodies that Colin's gift conjures up. Ostrander speaks in voiceover.

OSTRANDER (BOX)
It won't be long now.

Panel 2
Pull back to show Colin's room, floor now littered with nothing but sketches. It's clear he's been working nonstop since Ostrander put him on the case. Things are in disarray, his clothes and hair are dirty and mussed, and dark circles ride under his eyes.

COLIN
Can't see where. Hiding...

Panel 3
Ostrander crouches down behind Colin as we look at her from a low POV, Colin's pencil still working furiously as she squeezes his shoulders.

OSTRANDER
Keep trying, Colin. I know my boy would never let me down.

Panel 4
As Ostrander rises, a dribble of blood seeps from Colin's nose, splashing onto the drawing beneath his hand and obscuring Dean's face.

Panel 5
CU on Colin's feverish effort, more blood droplets spilling forth even as the pencil lead cuts through them.

COLIN
Never...

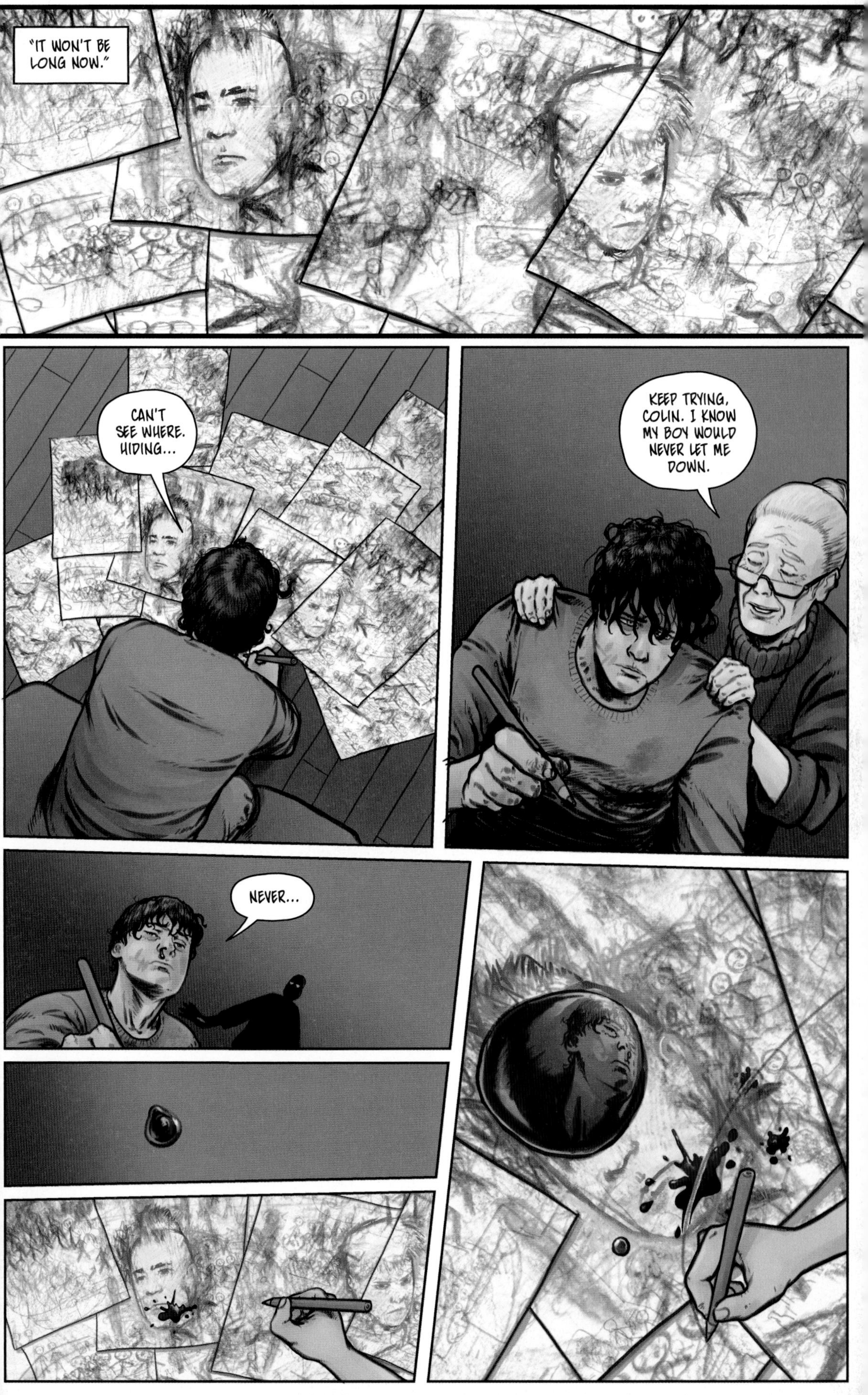
"IT WON'T BE LONG NOW."
CAN'T SEE WHERE. HIDING...
KEEP TRYING, COLIN. I KNOW MY BOY WOULD NEVER LET ME DOWN.
NEVER...

Panel 1
Cut to Abby lying prone on the bedroom floor where we left her. Her eyes are open and fixed, staring up without blinking.

CAPTION
MARIN COUNTY

ABBY (NAR.)
My name is Abby Palmer.

Panel 2-4
Three quick snapshots, going from Abby as a soldier with her crewcut to Abby as a street person to he bloody face from previous issues. Shouldn't take up more than 1 full-width panel would.

P2: ABBY (NAR.)
I was a soldier.

P3: ABBY (NAR.)
I was betrayed.

P4: ABBY (NAR.)
Now I don't know what I am.

Panel 5
Abby's POV, looking up from the ground. ***Steven we should discuss some kind of POV effect for her, now that she's been "activated" and has the programming Ultra gave her running full force.*** Something as simple as small text boxes popping up as information she "sees" beyond regular perception, such as whether someone is armed, small telling details—the same sort of effect we used i #1 for the fight scene in the church.

In this shot Kimiko bends over her, concern on her face.

KIMIKO
Abby? You're freaking me out, girl...

EFFECT TEXT:
Nakamura, Kimiko. Non-combatant. Threat: None.

ABBY (NAR.)
But I'm going to find out.

Panel 6
Abby sits up slowly, staring at her own hands. Kimiko retreats, holding her laptop. The screen is still visible.

ABBY
I'm okay. I wasn't ready for...that. But I'm okay.

Panel 7
Abby POV. She catches sight of the interface on Kimiko's computer.

EFFECT TEXT
1-terabyte encyption protocol. NSA proprietary software.

KIMIKO
You sure?

ABBY
...Yeah. I need some air.

ABBY (NAR.)
Maybe if I keep repeating that I'm okay, it'll eventually be true.

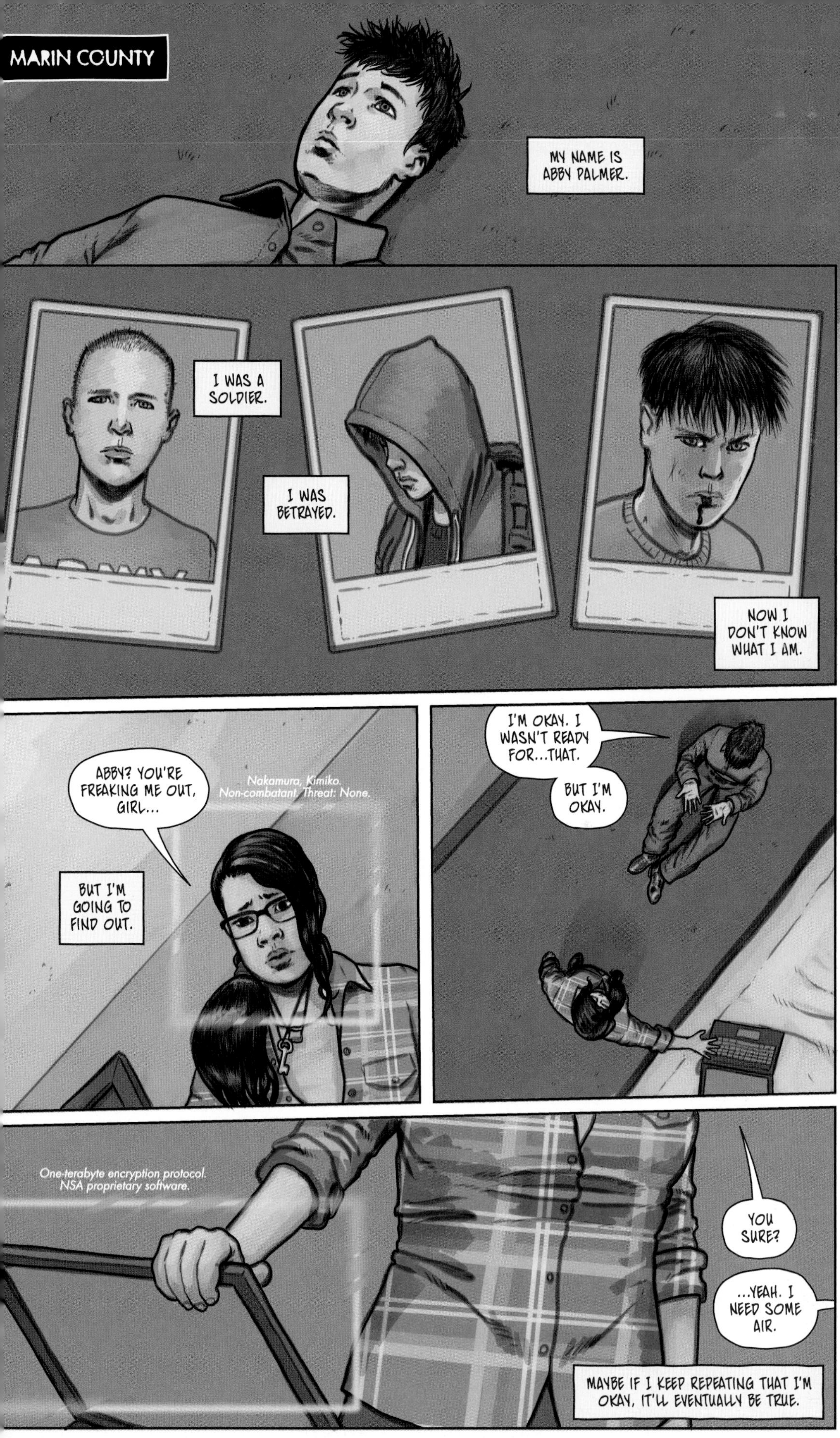

MARIN COUNTY
MY NAME IS ABBY PALMER.
I WAS A SOLDIER.
I WAS BETRAYED.
NOW I DON'T KNOW WHAT I AM.
ABBY? YOU'RE FREAKING ME OUT, GIRL...
Nakamura, Kimiko. Non-combatant. Threat: None.
BUT I'M GOING TO FIND OUT.
I'M OKAY. I WASN'T READY FOR...THAT.
BUT I'M OKAY.
One-terabyte encryption protocol. NSA proprietary software.
YOU SURE?
...YEAH. I NEED SOME AIR.
MAYBE IF I KEEP REPEATING THAT I'M OKAY, IT'LL EVENTUALLY BE TRUE.

PAGE 3

Time-lapse of Kimiko and Abby driving in a new stolen car far into the rolling farmland and forest of Northern California. Abby slowly recovers as the panels pass.

Panel 1
Abby leans her forehead against the window, still pale and shaky.

KIMIKO
So...where are you from?

ABBY
Spare the getting to know you. Where are we going?

KIMIKO
Dean and I set a meeting place if we ever get separated in a situation like this. ...Really, I'm curious. Where are you from?

Panel 2
Abby is eating a bunch of fast food while Kimiko sticks to french fries.

ABBY
Virginia Beach. Are you fasting or something?

KIMIKO
I'm a vegetarian. Or try to be. And I'm nervous.

ABBY
That I'll snap and take you out?

Panel 3
It's getting on to night, and they pair are stopped at an out of the way gas station. Abby leans against the ca Everything she's watching has the POV effect.

CAP1 (a truck)
1988 Dodge Ram

CAP2 (the driver, a man with rolled sleeves and faded Army tattoos)
Male, 180 lbs. Infantry veteran, two tours in Vietnam. THREAT ASSESSMENT: SAFE

CAP3 (Kimiko, pumping gas and not looking at Abby)
Kimiko Nakamura. STATUS: Unknown
THREAT LEVEL: HIGH
TERMINATE

Panel 4
Abby massages her temples as they drive on, the sun now coming up.

KIMIKO
You okay? We're almost there. Sorry it took so long, and for the lack of real bathrooms, but...

ABBY
Stick to back roads. Fewer cameras, fewer cops..

KIMIKO
Sometimes I forget for five seconds you're hot Arabic Jason Bourne.

ABBY
I'm Pashtun. Half.

Panel 5
Kimiko turns down a dirt road, barely visible as a turnoff.

KIMIKO
Your mom?

ABBY
Yeah. She's dead, before you ask.

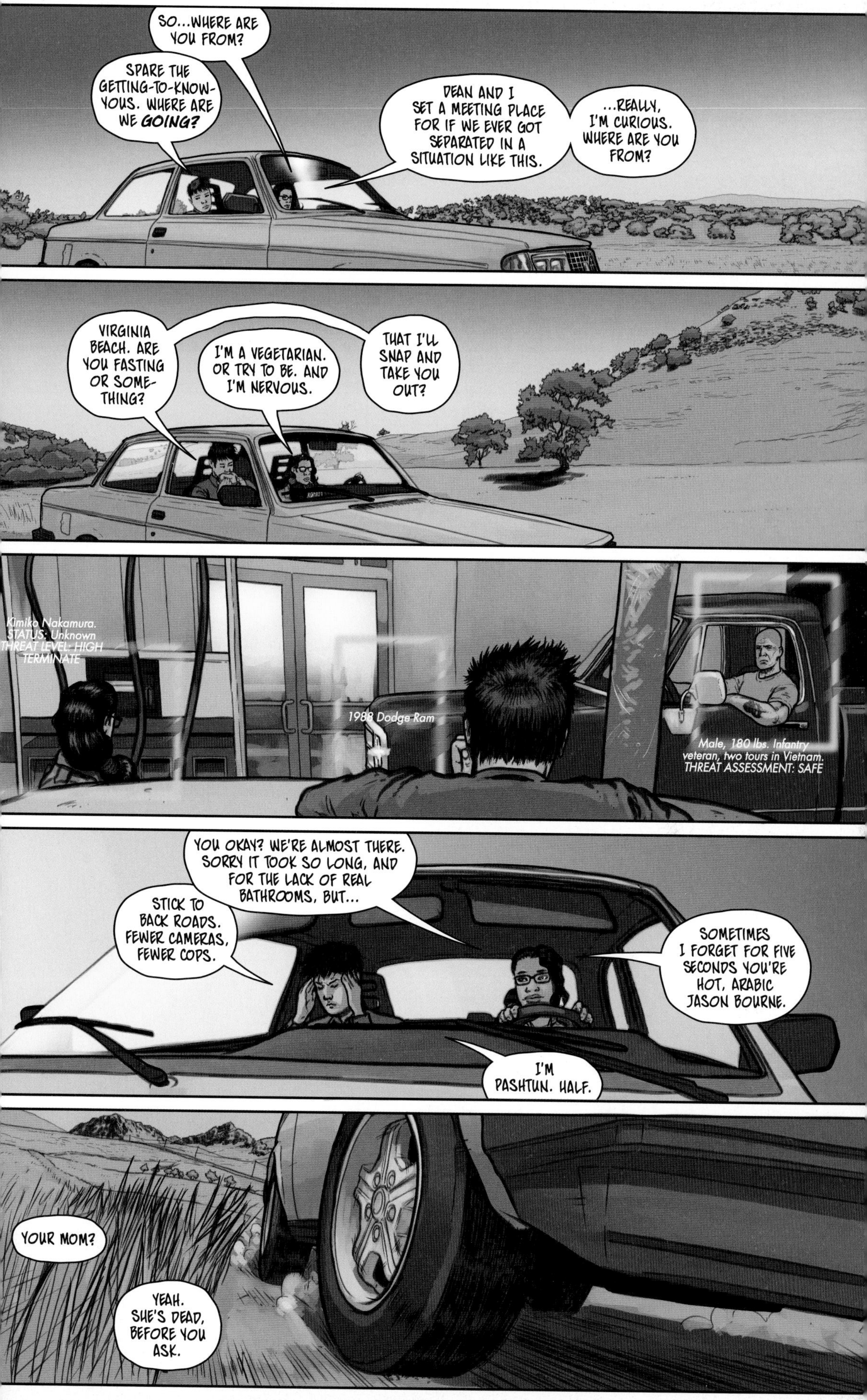
SO...WHERE ARE YOU FROM?
SPARE THE GETTING-TO-KNOW-YOUS. WHERE ARE WE *GOING?*
DEAN AND I SET A MEETING PLACE FOR IF WE EVER GOT SEPARATED IN A SITUATION LIKE THIS.
...REALLY, I'M CURIOUS. WHERE ARE YOU FROM?
VIRGINIA BEACH. ARE YOU FASTING OR SOME-THING?
I'M A VEGETARIAN. OR TRY TO BE. AND I'M NERVOUS.
THAT I'LL SNAP AND TAKE YOU OUT?
Kimiko Nakamura. STATUS: Unknown THREAT LEVEL: HIGH TERMINATE
1988 Dodge Ram
Male, 180 lbs. Infantry veteran, two tours in Vietnam. THREAT ASSESSMENT: SAFE
YOU OKAY? WE'RE ALMOST THERE. SORRY IT TOOK SO LONG, AND FOR THE LACK OF REAL BATHROOMS, BUT...
STICK TO BACK ROADS. FEWER CAMERAS, FEWER COPS.
SOMETIMES I FORGET FOR FIVE SECONDS YOU'RE HOT, ARABIC JASON BOURNE.
I'M PASHTUN. HALF.
YOUR MOM?
YEAH. SHE'S DEAD, BEFORE YOU ASK.

Panel 1
Establishing shot of a quiet street lined with Craftsmen homes and trees, in the rainy Pacific Northwest.

CAPTION
PORTLAND, OREGON

SHRINK (Box)
How are you sleeping, Brad?

Panel 2
Zoom in on a large, well-kept gem painted in muted greens, with a bronze placard reading DR. ADAM STANTON, PSY.D out front.

BRAD (Box)
Same as ever.

STANTON (Box)
Tell me about some of your nightmares.

Panel 3
We are inside now, and see from Stanton's POV, his pad covered in session chicken scratch.

BRAD
Nightmares aren't real, right? They're your brain making shit up to deal with trauma?

STANTON
Schools of thought differ. In vets with PTSD recurring dreams are almost universal.

Panel 4
Brad stares out the rain-streaked window. He's younger, still in a military haircut that's starting to grow out, eyes hollow and haggard just as Abby's were when we first met her.

BRAD
My old man was in 'Nam. He used to get drunk and think all his buddies that got fragged in the paddies were there with him.

STANTON
Mental illness was left untreated more often than not back then. Did your father ever hurt you?

BRAD
No. And I didn't see any buddies fragged. Everyone I saw was already dead.

Panel 5
Brad turns back to Stanton, slumping in his chair.

BRAD
The stuff I see in my sleep ain't nightmares. It's just memories. I gotta handle it.

STANTON
You saw mass graves, Brad. You saw the worst humanity has to offer.

STANTON
Just because Sarajevo is not the jungle doesn't make what happened any less traumatic.

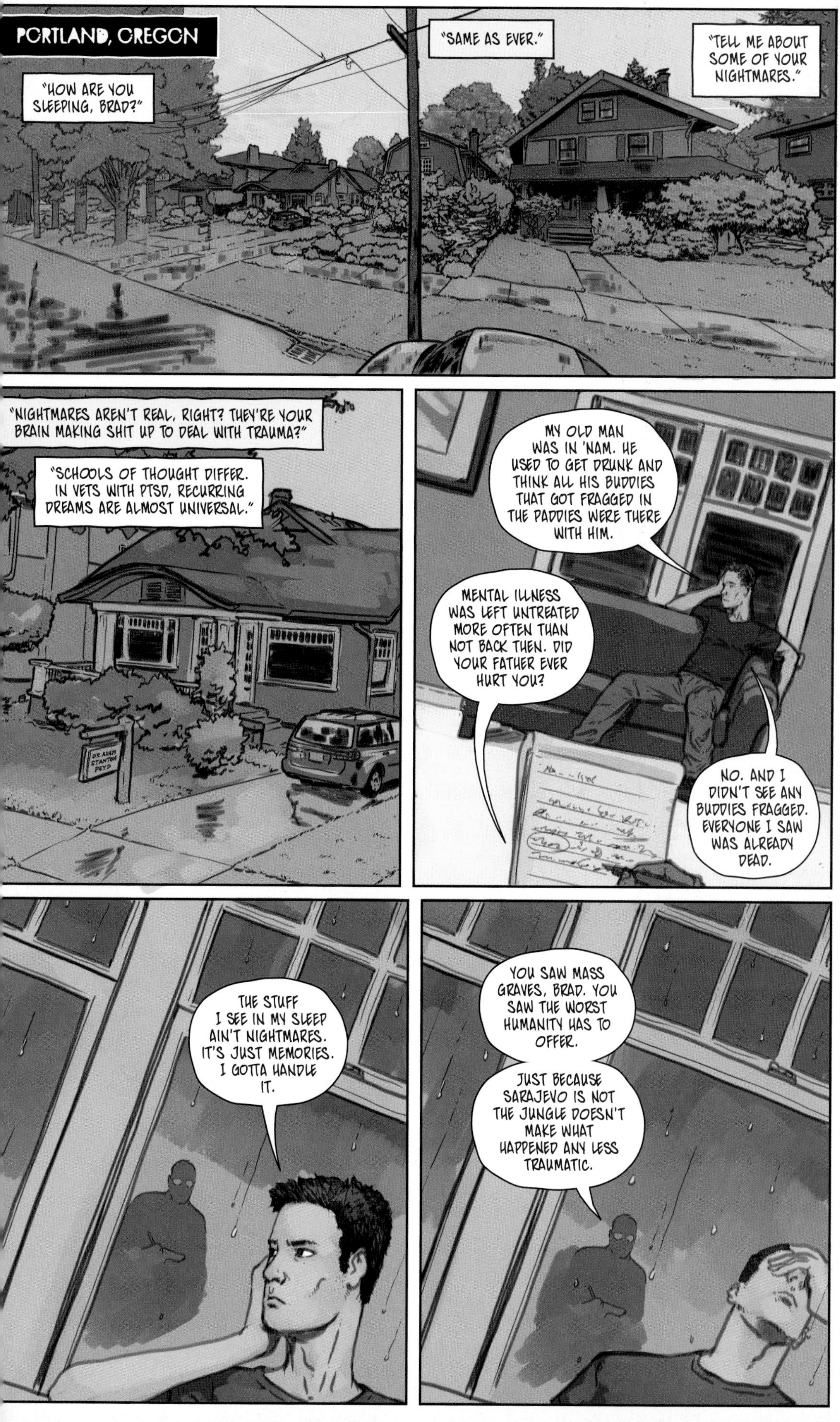
PORTLAND, OREGON
"HOW ARE YOU SLEEPING, BRAD?"
"SAME AS EVER."
"TELL ME ABOUT SOME OF YOUR NIGHTMARES."
"NIGHTMARES AREN'T REAL, RIGHT? THEY'RE YOUR BRAIN MAKING SHIT UP TO DEAL WITH TRAUMA?"
"SCHOOLS OF THOUGHT DIFFER. IN VETS WITH PTSD, RECURRING DREAMS ARE ALMOST UNIVERSAL."
DR ADAM STANTON PSYD
MY OLD MAN WAS IN 'NAM. HE USED TO GET DRUNK AND THINK ALL HIS BUDDIES THAT GOT FRAGGED IN THE PADDIES WERE THERE WITH HIM.
MENTAL ILLNESS WAS LEFT UNTREATED MORE OFTEN THAN NOT BACK THEN. DID YOUR FATHER EVER HURT YOU?
NO. AND I DIDN'T SEE ANY BUDDIES FRAGGED. EVERYONE I SAW WAS ALREADY DEAD.
THE STUFF I SEE IN MY SLEEP AIN'T NIGHTMARES. IT'S JUST MEMORIES. I GOTTA HANDLE IT.
YOU SAW MASS GRAVES, BRAD. YOU SAW THE WORST HUMANITY HAS TO OFFER.
JUST BECAUSE SARAJEVO IS NOT THE JUNGLE DOESN'T MAKE WHAT HAPPENED ANY LESS TRAUMATIC.

Panel 1
Brad stands, pressing his hand against the window glass.

BRAD
Seein' those holes full of dead people isn't what landed me in the padded room.

STANTON
No. You told the admitting doctor you were hearing voices.

Panel 2
Brad expands his fingers, the window glass cracking and shattering to become the blown out window of a Bosnia tenement, and instead of Portland we look down at Brad standing in the street, wearing a uniform with a blue NATO armband, rifle slung across his back, speaking to young Bosnian girl in a headscarf.

BRAD
Everything in the city was blown to hell when we got there. Bombing raids on the Serbs to cold-cock 'em before ground forces deployed.

Panel 3
Brad and the girl are tentatively making friends, he holding out a Hershey bar and she smilin shyly.

BRAD (Box)
We were just talking. She was a couple years older than my kid. I showed her a picture of him

BRAD
She said the Serbs shot her brother and raped her mother and sister. She and her grandmother were all that was left.

Panel 4
The stone wall just behind the girl's head shatters as a sniper's bullet erupts.

SFX
KRACK!

BRAD (Box)
The Serbian snipers were the real deal, guys who'd been picking off civilians for years alread just as practice.

BRAD (Box)
You could tell it was an old gun—thin high crack rather than a boom like the SR-25—Russian probably. Some grandpa's relic from the Red Army.

Panel 5
Brad dives for cover as the girl, screaming, covers her head, frozen in place. The bullets driv Brad away from her, exploding just behind him as he runs.

SFX
KRACK! KRACK! KRACK!

BRAD (Box)
Doesn't matter in the hands of an expert. He herded me out of the street like I was cattle.

BRAD (Box)
Like I was in the way.

Panel 1
From behind the cover of a pile of broken concrete and steel, Brad stretches out his hand.

BRAD
Kid! Run!

Panel 2
The frozen girl takes a tentative step, but the dirt in front of her erupts with the puff of a bullet.

SFX
KRACK!

GIRL
Ahh!

Panel 3
In a nightmarish centerpiece panel, we see the tracks of bullets all around the poor girl, hemming her in the spot while Brad watches helplessly.

BRAD (Box)
I was pinned down—I was forward recon and radios were for shit in all that wreckage. No backup.

BRAD (Box)
Every time she moved he took a shot at her. Made her stand like a little statue. We stayed there for hours

Panel 4
The sun is starting to set over the nightmarish scenario. The girl is sagging, clearly almost unable to star

BRAD (Box)
Twilight is when I felt him stir. Felt his mind pick up from that razor blade concentration it takes to be a shooter as good as he was.

BRAD (Box)
I heard him, but it was all gibberish. Thoughts is a language I didn't speak. Then he spoke out loud. The g translated.

SNIPER
<Language effect>

GIRL
He talks to you. He says: American! You can walk away for a small price.

BRAD
Oh yeah? Tell him to stick his ugly face out and I'll pay with two rounds in the brainpan.

Panel 5
Brad peers around the rubble at the poor girl, tears pouring down her face now as she speaks.

GIRL
"I will execute the whore. Then you may walk past her body in peace."

GIRL
"I see the top of your skull. It is her or a bullet that will come out of your eye."

GIRL
Let him do it. I'm dead. You have a child...

BRAD
Shut up! Let me think!

Panel 6
Close on the girl. A laser sight paints the center of her forehead.

GIRL
He says: "Time's up."

KID! RUN!

AHH!

KRACK

"I WAS PINNED DOWN--I WAS FORWARD RECON AND RADIOS WORKED FOR SHIT IN ALL THAT WRECKAGE. NO BACKUP.

"EVERY TIME SHE MOVED HE TOOK A SHOT AT HER. MADE HER STAND LIKE A LITTLE STATUE. WE STAYED THERE FOR HOURS.

"TWILIGHT IS WHEN I FELT HIM STIR. FELT HIS MIND PICK UP FROM THAT RAZOR BLADE CONCENTRATION IT TAKES TO BE A SHOOTER AS GOOD AS HE WAS.

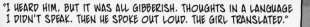

"I HEARD HIM, BUT IT WAS ALL GIBBERISH. THOUGHTS IN A LANGUAGE I DIDN'T SPEAK. THEN HE SPOKE OUT LOUD. THE GIRL TRANSLATED."

HE TALKS TO YOU. HE SAYS: AMERICAN! YOU CAN WALK AWAY FOR A SMALL PRICE.

OH YEAH? TELL HIM TO STICK HIS UGLY FACE OUT AND I'LL PAY WITH TWO ROUNDS IN THE BRAINPAN.

"I WILL EXECUTE THE WHORE. THEN YOU MAY WALK PAST HER BODY IN PEACE."

"I SEE THE TOP OF YOUR SKULL. IT IS HER OR A BULLET THAT WILL COME OUT OF YOUR EYE."

LET HIM DO IT. I'M DEAD. YOU HAVE A CHILD...

SHUT UP! LET ME THINK!

HE SAYS: "TIME'S UP."

AFTERWARD

So here we are. It's been a little over a year in readers' time, but for me, THROWAWAYS is creeping up on having encompassed three years of my life. I still have a hard time believing I get to put out a comic every month for a living—but I'm not complaining.

Comics are continuity, for me. As a kid not living in the most stable circumstances, I always had a box of random DC and Marvel back issues from the seventies to keep me company. Comics stretch over entire portions and chapters of your life—three years is a long time in the real world, and I've gone through some huge life changes while Steven and I have been bringing THROWAWAYS to you. But the books—writing and reading them—are a constant, and I find that incredibly comforting.

No matter where you are, who you're with, or what's happening in the world, if you read comics you can always come back to the story, sometimes years or even decades later. Many of those random single issues I kept in a box in my closet as a ten-year-old are part of a series that is still running. But for me, I always loved the trades the most—stories I could revisit over and over again, take myself from issue #1, page 1 all the way to the last panel of the last page.

THROWAWAYS is far from the last page—I have a wall (yes, a wall) in my house covered with cards and notes that map out the entire series—but it always makes me glad to think about sharing that common thread with everyone reading. Comics are magic that way—the only art form that keeps creators and readers together for sometimes their entire lives.

Looking forward to what comes next,
Caitlin Kittredge
August 2017